PRAISE FOR HELEN FIELDS

'Read it in two sittings. I literally had no choice. A fast and enthralling thriller'
Paul Finch

'Watch out Rebus, McRae and Perez, there's a new detective in the running to become Scotland's fictional top cop . . . a real cracker of a page-turner that is truly difficult to put down'
Scotland Correspondent

'Deliciously dark and gritty. Another winner from the hugely talented Helen Fields'
Caroline Mitchell

'Must read! With nail-biting twists at every turn, this will have readers gripped from start to finish'
Closer

'Compelling, breathtaking and a tense ride from that unbelievable opening scene right to the last word. Brilliant!'
Angela Marsons

'A tightly plotted tale of obsession and manipulation'
Woman

'An edge-of-the-seat thriller from this accomplished writer'
Isabel Ashdown

'Without a doubt, this is one of the best first detective series I have read'
Woman's Way

'Utterly compelling and dizzyingly twisted, with characters so real they could step off the page'
B P Walter

PRAISE FOR *THE SHADOW MAN*

'*The Shadow Man* is so chilling. With a dark, compelling plot and brilliantly drawn characters, you will be hooked from the first page'
Debbie Howells

'*The Shadow Man* is a terrifying police procedural, packed with suspense and a killer from your worst nightmares. A truly unique protagonist pitted against a chilling killer, it was hard to put this book down until the very end'
Vicki Bradley

'Atmospheric writing, breath-taking pace and fascinating characters. I loved it'
Suzy K Quinn

'A VERY dark read! Complex, intriguing characters, a compelling plot and good dynamics between partners make this a standout read of the year so far'
NetGalley Review, 5 stars

'From the first page to the last, this story grabs you and doesn't let you go. An absolute page-turner of a book and spine tinglingly brilliant! Set against the backdrop of Edinburgh, the characters and the city literally come alive on the page. You feel every emotion the characters go through'
NetGalley Review, 5 stars

'This is the best book I have read for quite a long time. It kept me hooked throughout and although I've enjoyed all of Helen's books, I think this surpasses her others – which takes some doing'
NetGalley Review, 5 stars

'Thoroughly enjoyed this book. Brilliant storytelling with a cracking pace'
NetGalley Review, 5 stars

'This is a standalone novel from Helen Fields – whose Perfect detective series I LOVE – and golly, it is clever. It is quick, and it is shocking in some areas – but the depth of research and quality of writing is exceptional'
NetGalley Review, 5 stars

'A five-star read! A brilliant new character in Dr Woolwine and also a very creepy villain. I like the way a character from the brilliant DI Callanach series is in the book also. Would love to see this as a new series'
NetGalley Review, 5 stars

THE SHADOW MAN

Helen Fields practised criminal and family law as a barrister. She prosecuted and defended in the Crown Court, as well as undertaking courts martial and Coroner's Court cases. Together with her husband David, she runs a media company. She is best known as the author of the DI Callanach series set in Scotland. She splits her time between Europe and the United States.

Helen can be found on Twitter at @Helen_Fields.

By the same author

Perfect Remains
Perfect Prey
Perfect Death
Perfect Silence
Perfect Crime
Perfect Kill

THE
Shadow
Man

HELEN FIELDS

Published by AVON
A division of HarperCollins*Publishers* Ltd
1 London Bridge Street
London SE1 9GF

www.harpercollins.co.uk

HarperCollins*Publishers*
1st Floor, Watermarque Building, Ringsend Road
Dublin 4, Ireland

HarperCollins*Publishers*
1st Floor, Watermarque Building, Ringsend Road
Dublin 4, Ireland

A Paperback Original 2021
2
First published in Great Britain by HarperCollins*Publishers* 2021

ISBN: 978-0-00-837930-8

Typeset in Bembo Std by Palimpsest Book Production Ltd, Falkirk, Stirlingshire
Printed and bound in UK by CPI Group (UK) Ltd, Croydon CR0 4YY

For Caroline Hardman

Funny, talented, kind and (thankfully) extremely patient

Prologue

From a distance, the grave appeared freshly dug and empty. To the birds overhead though, vision sharp enough to spot the briefest wiggle of worm or skitter of insect, an older coffin was visible in the depths of the hole. Time had rotted the wooden lid. Time, and the pressure of another coffin stacked on top of it. A family grave stores both more memories and more bodies than a single resting place.

This hole in the ground, if earth could tell tales, would be fit to burst with stories. Of bodies come and gone. Of hope and disappointment. Of dirt disturbed more often than any resting place should ever have to bear. Few visitors attended that sombre space, and those who did had not ventured to the far edge for many years. The cemetery was ancient and unused to new requests for burials. It stood beyond the outer limits of the city, in a circle of trees that kept prying eyes out and the spirits of the dead in.

One man came and went as needed. He visited a grave there – and sometimes brought others with him. He would sit in the grass and talk to a gravestone, listening intently, as if waiting for a response. Sometimes he would dig a coffin up, and sometimes he would bury it. Always the same one. Half the time, there was a soul to inter. Sometimes, more than one. Months later he would reappear. Then he would clear out the coffin. Place new flowers at the gravestone. Put away the remains in the boot of his car, after careful stripping and cleaning. Drag the coffin into the bushes and fill the hole in the earth.

The birds did not sing on the days he appeared there. No rodent ran through the grounds or hopped from tree branch to tree branch. The sun hid behind clouds. The world seemed to know more tears were to be shed. Now, the uppermost section of the family grave stood empty again. Merely a matter of waiting for the space to be occupied. Time stood still here, the same ritual repeated, until the grave was little more than a revolving door between one world and the next.

Chapter One

A sleeping woman watched over by the stranger who had hidden for hours in the shadowed bay of her bedroom curtains. That's all there was to the scene. He was a spider, patient and unmoving, poised to drop and stun his prey. There was no malice to it. Only need. The white sheet covering her body rose and fell with each breath in the oblivion of slumber. Three steps forwards and he could reach out and touch her, run his hands through her long dark hair, press the half moon of his fingernail into the dimple that punctuated her right cheek as she smiled. His arms would wrap around her frame perfectly.

In his mind, he'd measured every part of her. Twice, he'd passed by close enough to brush her body with his, once in the street, once in the school playground. The latter was a risk, but it had proved fruitful. In the beginning, he'd been concerned that the watching phase might be dull. How wrong he was. Familiarising himself with the lives of the ones he'd chosen had become his oxygen as the rest of his world had started to fade.

He ran appreciative fingers over the top of the dresser at his side. No dust. No sticky fingerprints from the children. Angela was all wife, mother, and homemaker. Her bedroom was the epitome of family. Photographs adorned the walls. A wedding, more than a decade ago, with a bride leaning into the arms of her groom, her dress demure, hair pinned up with just a few curls left hanging. A promise for later that night, Fergus thought.

It had taken months of patience to find a time when her husband would be away, then he'd struck gold. The man of the house had treated the children – a boy of seven and a girl of five – to a camping trip for a night, enjoying Edinburgh's idyllic August. The husband couldn't have realised it, but the experience would be good practice. After tonight, he would be a single parent unless he married again. Fergus couldn't imagine why anyone would try to replace Angela. She was everything.

Each morning she walked her children to school, the boy racing ahead, sometimes on a scooter, while the girl held fast to her mother's hand. He liked to watch them all together. Angela's face wore an indelible smile when she was with her offspring. He'd never seen her looking tired or cross. In all the hours, all the journeys he'd witnessed, she hadn't rolled her eyes, yawned or snapped at them. In the photos on the bedroom walls, she was not just a parent but utterly engaged in the act of parenting. He studied those pictures one last time, committing each to memory. There she was hugging her son as he clutched some sports trophy, and there she was laughing as she made cupcakes with her daughter, beaming with love. And there they were as a family on their bikes, pausing as a passerby took their photograph, defining togetherness.

Fergus had been in that bedroom before. He'd taken pieces of her home with him. A silky soft shirt from the laundry basket. A lipstick from her handbag. Nail clippings from her bathroom, still showing the colour of her toenail varnish. There was a whole section dedicated to her in his own bedroom, and a file. Paper, not digital. He was ill, not stupid. Computers could be hacked. The information he'd gathered was from the real

4

world. Her date of birth and marriage certificate had been obtained from official records. He knew where she shopped, which doctor's surgery she attended, who her friends were. A timeline constructed from his labours provided an accurate structure of her week.

Her kitchen bin was an endless source of intelligence. She rarely chose precooked meals or processed foods, preferring fresh fruits and vegetables. There were no magazines, but the odd newspaper was recycled. Angela liked hard soap bars rather than liquid soap dispensers. And she was on the pill. The discarded wrapper from the previous month was in his file, too. No more children planned, for now at least. She was content.

Edging closer to the bed, he breathed in her scent. She'd bathed before slipping between the sheets. He'd been in the house long before that. Easier to allow her the reassurance of checking each window and door, believing that anything that might do her harm was safely beyond the boundaries of her home. As she'd soaked in the steaming water, lavender bubbles caressing her skin, he'd made sure her curtains were drawn and taken the keys from the lock in the back door. No point taking chances. If she got spooked or surprised him and ran, he couldn't allow her to exit the property.

When all was secure, he'd sat outside her bathroom door and listened to her humming. He'd imagined her running the pale green flannel up and down her arms, her legs, between her breasts and around the back of her neck. He'd waited as she'd read the book he'd noticed on her bed, resting on a freshly laundered towel and her dressing gown. When he'd heard the cascade of water that signalled her standing, he'd shifted position into the window alcove, behind her curtains, focusing on breathing silently and remaining still. There were windows open in the upstairs bedroom to allow some of the cooler night air in, and he'd planned to close those once she was sleeping soundly. If she screamed, the noise would travel out into the crescent, and her neighbours would be alerted. Fergus couldn't allow that to happen.

Now, she was right in front of him. So much hard work had brought him to this moment, he almost couldn't bear for it to end. Until he looked in the mirror. Hung on the end wall of the bedroom, opposite the window, it reflected Angela's pretty head on her pillow, and the man looming over her. While her hair was gleaming and vibrant, his harshly shaven mat was greying prematurely, thinning more than anyone in their late thirties should have to tolerate. His eyes were pale in the scant light that entered from a streetlamp beyond the curtains, but he could still make out their watery blue, surrounded by creases of red on white. But it was his skin that told the real story. A greener shade of white. Waxy, sallow, wanting.

Fergus Ariss was dying.

However long he had left, there was insufficient time to achieve everything. He'd dreamed of travelling. In his twenties, he'd had a world map on his wall. The idea was to scratch off a section of chalky paint every time he took a trip. A school visit to France had offered one country beyond the United Kingdom's borders, then came a friend's stag weekend in Amsterdam. He'd always wanted to go to the USA. To explore Peru. The Great Wall of China was his ultimate goal. Now, he had to fulfil all of his dying wishes in Scotland. Even the borders were too far to cross at this stage.

His body had betrayed him. There was nothing the doctors could do, in spite of their protestations that he should let them assist. He could smell the rot of his own body. No herb or spice could mask the taste of death in his mouth. There was pain and grief, then there were moments of clarity when he understood that death would be a release. Months of hospital treatment weren't the answer. Prolonging life regardless of the quality of that time was nothing more than fading away. He didn't want to fade any more than he already had. He wanted to blaze a trail into the next life. But there was so little time, and so much left to do. Starting with Angela.

After creeping around the end of the bed and slipping off his shoes, he slid his body weight gently onto the mattress. A smile flitted across Angela's face as his body joined hers. He fitted behind her like a puzzle piece, and she murmured as he slid his arm over her waist, pushing his face gently into her neck and breathing the scent of her shampoo. She was so warm in his arms. So soft. Destined for him.

Then she woke, took a breath sharp enough to push Fergus' chest from her back, and every muscle in her body seized. She jolted, but he'd been ready for it. He squeezed his arm around her, dragging her backwards into him, snaking his free hand under her neck and over her mouth.

'It's all right,' he whispered. 'Angela, you have to trust me. I'm not here to hurt you.'

She tried kicking, going for his shins with her heels, but the sheet hampered the force of her movements, and Fergus shifted his right leg on top of both of hers. Her breath was hot and wet in his hand, and her head was a wild creature whipping left and right. He waited it out. There were no surprises. He'd played the scenario out in his head hundreds, maybe thousands, of times. In his pocket was a handkerchief, and on it was a carefully measured dose of chloroform. There were things he wanted to do with Angela, and those things required her not to fight him. Fergus wanted her pristine.

'Let it out,' he said. 'I know you're scared and confused, but I chose you.'

Angela heaved forwards, rolling her mouth hard onto his fingers and biting down. Fergus tried to keep his grip on her, but his hand betrayed him. His fingers shot out straight and his wrist flicked backwards, giving Angela the space to bend her head forwards then smack it backwards into Fergus' face, the rear of her skull a true weapon, splitting Fergus' nose from between his eyes to below the bridge. The pillow became a mess of bloodied hair. He couldn't see, and his face was a mask of agony. Only his right arm and leg remained steadfast, holding her in place. She spat, and a chunk of something warm and soft landed on his hand as he pinned her to the bed. The flesh was from his finger, he realised as he rolled her onto her back and slid his body on top of hers before she could attempt an escape.

''S all righ', lemme help you,' he muttered.

Blood droplets from his face burst juicily as they hit hers. Angela began to sob.

'I'm not cross. Don't cry,' Fergus said.

Fergus pulled the handkerchief from his pocket with his right hand, shifting his left forearm to rest solidly across her breastbone. She gushed air.

'Please don't . . .'

'Hurt you? Why would I? I'm your one true love, Angela.'

He pressed the handkerchief to her lips. A cotton kiss in the dark. Angela's hips bucked beneath him, and he imagined a different bed, her holding him, wanting him on top of her.

Her neck arched. She did her best to fight, but he wanted her compliance more than she wanted her freedom. Desperation had fine-tuned him into an extraordinary beast. He could smell her toothpaste, and it was a field of wild mint. The diamonds in her eyes were more riches than he had ever imagined he would own.

Then the bedside lamp was arcing through the air. Had it been switched on, he knew it would have left a rainbow of light in its wake. Even as he saw it coming, he recognised it was too late for avoidance. Shattering on contact with his

8

cheekbone, the pottery base turned gravel and took root in his flesh.

Angela fought harder as Fergus swayed, his head a wasp nest as he reeled from the injuries to his nose and cheek. The important thing was to keep the handkerchief over her mouth until she was asleep, but his hand was trembling and weak, and now he could see two Angelas, neither of them clearly. His hand needed help to maintain the pressure, so he pushed his forehead down on top of his own hand, doubling the force and allowing him to close his eyes for a moment. If he lost consciousness now, it was over. If she got out from under him, he was done. Everything he wanted, what pathetic time he had left, would be smoke.

She battered him with one fist. He had to take back control until she complied.

With one last monumental effort, Fergus raised his body a few inches then slammed his whole weight onto her ribcage. He grabbed her wrist with his free hand and her fingertips scratched weakly at his knuckles. The bed was wet, he realised. His knee rested in a damp, warm patch. That was fine. A success, in fact. She was relaxing. Surrendering. His whole head buzzed and burned, tidal nausea swept over him. Fergus let her hand slide from his grasp as the world pixelated then faded. His body covering hers like a blanket, the handkerchief then his hand and finally his head resting on her mouth, Fergus could resist unconsciousness no longer.

Was it possible that death was coming for him so much sooner than he'd anticipated? Fergus breathed deeply, trying to catch hold of the pain, yearning to stay in the moment with Angela, but there was a roundabout spinning mercilessly in his head, and he couldn't get off her, couldn't have lifted his head or moved his hand from her mouth if his life had depended on it.

Angela's body juddered beneath his.

He couldn't get off.

Angela inhaled ragged, raw breaths through her nose as the chemical held over her mouth worked its magic.

He couldn't get off.

The last breath he heard leave her body was an inhuman rattle. He longed to comfort her, to tell her he was sorry. There was so much he'd wanted to do with her, and it had all gone so dreadfully wrong. Now, he had to start over. And first he would have to find someone new.

Chapter Two

Night-time was her time. The day's colours had faded, and in the grey hues she was finally equal to those around her. Connie Woolwine exited the imposing Balmoral Hotel and crossed the road towards Leith Walk. It was midnight, and still the heat bounced up off Edinburgh's roads. The late-licence pubs were turning out. She could hear both singing and sobbing from the crowds of revellers, depending on the level of drunkenness. Carrying only her hotel key card in one pocket of her jeans and her mobile in the other, she walked past the crowds, enjoying the stretch in her legs after a long flight and the sense of liberation she knew would come from allowing herself to get lost in a foreign city.

It was her first trip to Scotland. Six hours and counting. The buildings were so steeped in history and architectural perfection that they might have been conjured rather than built. Lights from tall buildings scattered moving images on the bustling streets. It was humanity soup, reminding her a little of Boston, Massachusetts. Taking a left into Union Street, she marvelled at how safe the city felt. Every person who lived there a 24-hour witness to the comings and goings around them. So much connectivity. Edinburgh's city centre was a human body, each street a blood vessel, with so few areas that were exclusively business or commerce. It was a city you could live in, rather than simply exist.

A catcall interrupted her thoughts, and she turned her head towards the man who'd issued the unwelcome quasi-compliment. Other men surrounded her as she made eye contact with the one who'd expressed an interest. A cloud of alcohol fumes assaulted her nose, and she breathed in beer and cheap liquor freshly deposited into the stomachs of the twenty-somethings who were obviously suffering a high level of drunken delusions.

'You on your own then, love?' the catcaller asked.

The accent was English rather than Scots. She'd spent enough time in London to recognise the East End vowel sounds.

'I'm meeting someone. Excuse me,' she replied, keeping it light but icy as she tried to take a step forward.

'You're American. Should've known with an arse like that. Don't see many that tight where we're from.'

He moved clumsily forward and Connie sidestepped him, pushing her shoulder between two of his mates to exit the group.

'Don't be a bitch. We were just having a laugh,' one of his companions added.

She allowed herself a private eye-roll and kept walking.

'Stupid cow. Can't take a joke,' he insisted when she didn't retaliate.

Keeping her gaze forward, she neither rushed nor slowed down.

'Think you're better than us, do—'

His hand was on her right buttock for no more than a second before she'd grabbed it by the wrist, wheeled around, and dug her thumbnail hard and deep into the half-moon lunula at the base of his index fingernail. Connie released him as his scream hit the air, and he leapt backwards, clutching his hand.

'She bloody tasered me or something. Shit.' He clutched his hand to his stomach, eyes watering.

Connie turned and stood her ground.

'The pain's already gone,' she said. 'It only lasts while the pressure's on. You assaulted me and I'm entitled to defend myself. I'm going to walk up the road now, and none of you should follow me. I have a tendency to overreact when someone touches me. Next time, the injury won't be so transient.'

There was a group shuffling and some muffled swearing, but no one seemed keen to take her on. Connie nodded, turned and continued towards Gayfield Street. She was expected in the gardens at Gayfield Square imminently, and she didn't want to keep the man waiting.

She left at a regular pace. Running would have been a mistake. Showing any level of fear always was. Predatory men were no different than mountain lions – that was how it had been explained to her in the self-defence classes she'd attended religiously in her early twenties. A mountain lion could be fooled into thinking you weren't lunch if you stood your ground, made yourself look big and stared it down. Turn away, run, show weakness, and you were a walking entrée. Ordinary testosterone-fuelled men were rarely intimidating to her now, though. Drunk idiots threw punches. Icy-cold restraint was much harder to fight.

Connie turned a corner and realised that the word 'gardens' after the name Gayfield was something of an overstatement. The grass had withered in the exceptional heat. A couple of forlorn benches were available as seating, and there were trees around the edge of the flora that had been preserved in the midst of the rectangle of buildings, but that was it. Cars were parked all around the edge, and there wasn't a square yard that escaped being overlooked by some building or other. It wasn't somewhere she could feel relaxed as she read a book on a blanket, or picnicked with a friend. It was a walk-through more than a venue to stop and smell the roses.

'Are you waiting for someone?' a man asked.

He stood a short distance behind her, taller than her by a head at well over six feet.

'Did you know it was me, or do you randomly walk up to women at night and say that, because it's likely to get you in trouble?'

'God, yes, stupid of me. I should've simply introduced myself. I just assumed . . .'

'That's okay.' She held out a hand for him to shake. 'It's Detective Inspector Baarda, right?'

He was in his late forties, tall with curly brown hair, broad shoulders, and a physique that shouted former sportsman who'd recently begun to lose the will to exercise.

'Right.' He shook her hand enthusiastically. 'And you're Dr Woolwine.'

'Connie,' she said. 'Let's walk.' Dropping his hand, she led the way off the grass and into the road, looking up at the surrounding buildings as they went. 'Not much in the way of obvious CCTV, in spite of all the buildings. Do the police have anything at all?'

'Little if any that will help. Sunset was eight thirty-eight on 20 August. Elspeth Dunwoody disappeared at around nine thirty p.m. She was seen entering the gardens at five past nine from another road, and her car was caught on cameras two roads away at nine twenty-four p.m. After that, nothing. Most of the CCTV is focused on doorways and the pavement areas. There's a distant shot of her climbing into her car, but nothing close up.'

'You've seen the footage?' Connie asked, standing centrally on one particular parking spot and taking photos of the 360-degree view around it on her mobile.

'Not yet. I only arrived from London this afternoon. I checked in with the Major Investigation Team, looked through the file, then checked in at my hotel and came here. Apologies, I should have made it a priority to view the CCTV. Careless of me.'

'You don't have to apologise to me; I'm just the hired help. To be honest, I'm not even sure what I'm doing here at this stage. It's not my usual kind of case. Here, stand with me. I want to know which of these flats are residential and which are business.'

'Um, should we not perhaps wait until a more social hour for that sort of—'

'Nope,' she said. 'Now, look around and give me a percentage idea of the curtain-twitching response we get.'

'Sorry, what exactly are you about to—'

Her scream was an arrow through the midnight air, piercing the fiercest double glazing and the thickest of curtains.

'One, two, three, four . . . There we go,' Connie muttered as the first onlooker peered out, followed by the flicking on of lights and the opening of windows.

'Someone will phone the police,' Baarda said quietly.

'Good. I'd like to know precisely how long before there's a reaction to an incident around here.'

A door opened and a man walked out sporting a plaid dressing gown. Connie couldn't suppress the smile.

'Do you need assistance? Is that man bothering you?'

'Thanks for checking on me. And he's a police officer, so we're good.'

'Well, then you've woken up the entire square for no reason. Perhaps you'd like to explain yourself.'

He exuded the attitude that only the truly monied managed to develop and a loudness of voice that was designed to indicate superiority. Connie ran a distracted hand through her hair

15

and shoved her hands in her pockets as she stepped closer to the male.

'Were you at home between nine and nine thirty p.m. on August 20th?' Connie asked, ignoring the request for an explanation as if she simply hadn't heard.

'I suppose I must have been. I rarely go out in the evenings, but I don't see the relevance of the question.'

'Did you hear any screams that evening? Anything that made you look out of the window or feel concerned. Perhaps your neighbours mentioned a disturbance to you the next day.'

'No, nothing like that. It's a quiet square most of the time, but certainly when most of the traffic has left the city at the end of the day.' He pulled his dressing gown cord sharply and smoothed his hair. 'I should go in.' He looked up at the neighbouring windows, many of whose frames were now filled by curious faces.

'Of course,' Connie said. 'Appreciate the help.'

Baarda stared at her as the man walked, head held high, back into his home. Connie smiled as he disappeared. She couldn't get her head round dressing gowns.

'Do you have one of those?' she asked Baarda, a slight lift at one corner of her mouth.

'I, er, suppose I do. Could I just ask . . .'

'You can,' she said. 'But please feel free to stop asking if you can ask something before you actually ask it. Kind of a waste of time. It's not as if I'm ever going to say no.'

Baarda's phone rang.

'Ah, yes,' he said. 'No need to send units. We're in that exact location. No incident here. Righty-ho.'

'Righty-ho?' Connie laughed. 'Holy crap, it's like I joined the cast of *Downton Abbey*. Where did you go to school, Eton?'

Baarda's darkening cheeks were visible even in the poorly lit square.

'You did! Wow, I thought Eton was reserved for royalty.'

'Popular myth,' Baarda murmured. 'You do know we're still being watched. We should probably relocate somewhere more discreet.'

'Probably,' Connie said in her best British accent, standing her ground and staring back at the onlookers. 'Elspeth wasn't disappeared from here, though. She went willingly. This is a high-end residential area with people who respond to noise, so it's unusual. Scream in New York and people just turn up their TVs. Here, the residents actively object. There were what, twenty, maybe even thirty eyes on us? At nine thirty in the evening, someone would have taken a look, and Elspeth would have screamed a lot louder and longer than me if she were being abducted.'

'And yet she's gone,' Baarda said.

Connie folded her arms and leaned against a lamppost, face turned towards the stars.

'People disappear every day. They can't cope with the stress of their job or discover they've got a terrible illness. They suddenly see their face in the mirror and decide they hate themselves. I could give you a thousand reasons. I may not be able to tell you yet why Elspeth's gone, but I can tell you that no one forced her into a car here against her will.'

'Because she didn't scream?' Baarda asked. 'They might have been holding a knife to her throat or a gun to her back. Silence isn't necessarily indicative of acquiescence.'

'It's not,' Connie said, pointing at him. 'But modern media's done us a few favours that have changed our behaviour. Women in particular understand that once you climb into a car with an assailant, you've given away the power. You'll most likely be raped, probably killed after that. Most women would risk a bullet or a knife wound rather than get into a car, well aware that the journey would likely be their last.'

'And if her abductor had threatened her children? Not difficult to do – say their names, ages, the home address, perhaps their school. What mother wouldn't comply to protect her offspring?'

'Offspring?'

'Children,' Baarda said.

'I know what it means,' she said. 'It's just kind of clinical. But I agree, that's a much more effective way to manipulate a woman. Her abductor would have to have been stalking her for some time. If it were me, I'd have tried to leave a trail. Dropped my bag, slipped off my watch or a ring, tripped and left blood droplets on the ground. Anything to say I was here and now I'm gone. I'm in danger. I take it the area's been forensically searched?'

'Apparently so. Nothing found,' Baarda said. 'So what's your competing theory?'

'That you catch more flies with honey than with vinegar. Why threaten a woman and make her skittish when you can present yourself in a perfectly believable way? Fake IDs are easy to get hold of – pretend to be a police officer. Tell her that she's needed at the scene of an accident, for example. Get her out of the city into a dead-end road. From there, it's pretty simple.'

'Her car hasn't been found,' Baarda noted.

'Not yet,' she said. 'Tell me something, what are we doing here?'

Baarda gave a fleeting smile and shrugged his shoulders.

'Police work,' he said.

'I'm a forensic psychologist. I help work up profiles on serial killers. Yet here I am, paid for at the taxpayers' expense. You've even been drafted up here out of London.'

'Edinburgh's MIT are flooded. They have officers out of the jurisdiction working with Interpol and others missing owing

18

to ill health. They needed cover,' Baarda said. 'No mystery there.'

'Except this isn't a murder case. It's a disappearance with no sign of foul play or a struggle. Come on, you know more than you're telling. Share.'

'How do you know that?'

'You shrugged. A shrug is an affectation. It's rarely involuntary, like widening your eyes when you're shocked. You were trying to appear casual and deflect. It's a dead giveaway.'

Baarda sighed. 'I was given the heads–up that she's someone's daughter-in-law.'

'Businessman, celebrity or politician?' Connie asked.

'Does it matter?'

'Only if you want an accurate profile of her abductor. If she disappeared for political reasons, it'll be a different personality type to someone who'll kidnap for financial reasons. If it's someone prominent in lawmaking or enforcement, it could be a revenge scenario. I could list endlessly, but it'd be faster to summarise with yes, it matters.'

'Head of a global tech company, widely known for his philanthropy, more political contacts than I could name . . . and I take your point.'

'But somehow that's been kept quiet so far. Not even a hint of a media leak.'

'My guess is that everyone involved believes this is an extortion attempt and that a leak could mean a sudden and tragic end to Elspeth's life. I was as surprised as you that I was paired up with a profiler. As far as this being at the taxpayers' expense goes, I'm sure contributions will be made that far outweigh the actual cost to the country, but this way we have the entire police facilities and intelligence at our disposal.'

'I see,' Connie murmured, moving closer to him and lowering her voice. 'You know, I can't profile someone we're not sure exists. Sounds to me as if Elspeth was living a high-pressure life. The sort of life where you might just hop on a train then hitch a lift somewhere until you're well and truly lost.'

'Do you think that's what she did?' Baarda asked.

'I'm a forensic psychologist, not a psychic. I'll need to meet with the family tomorrow if I'm going to help. Can you set that up?'

'Sure, but not until morning.' He looked at his watch. 'It's too late to call anyone now. I hired a car. I can give you a lift back to your hotel if you like?'

'That'd be good,' Connie said. 'Thank you.'

'Not at all. There wasn't much choice of vehicle left, I'm afraid. I had no option but to take the bright yellow monstrosity over there.' He gestured to the far side of the square.

Connie stared blankly. 'No one warned you?' she asked.

Baarda frowned.

'I'm an achromat. A head injury when I was eighteen resulted in a bleed in my skull. When they operated to remove the haematoma from my brain, I was left able to see only in black and white, and shades thereof. I'm afraid you'll have to learn to do better with your descriptions where colour's concerned.'

'You literally can't see any colour at all?'

'I remember colours, but not as abstracts. I can place colour linked to an object, a place, sometimes even an emotion. You'll get used to it.'

'Have you?' he asked.

Connie paused. 'I find it easier to read facial expressions accurately, landscapes are somehow more beautiful, sunsets are disappointing, and I may appear in clothes that clash. That about covers it.'

'I doubt that,' Baarda said. 'I can't imagine a world without colour.'

'This isn't a world without colour,' she corrected softly. 'It's a world where I have to paint the colours in with my mind.

20

You'd be surprised how much more you notice when you have to work this hard at it.'

'Is that why you began to specialise in profiling, because of your perspective on the world?' Baarda pointed his keys at the line of cars, and lights flashed back at him.

'No,' Connie said, walking to the passenger side. 'I became a profiler as a matter of survival.'

Chapter Three

The cherry-red BMW sat in the sweeping driveway, abandoned. Connie had her back to it, hands on her hips, staring instead at the police officers who had arrived at the scene first.

'Retrace your steps in your mind,' she told them. 'Each one of you. From when you drove in and first saw Elspeth's vehicle, to getting out of your cars and walking towards it. Which window did you look through? Who touched which door? Think hard about what you saw.'

'Respect, ma'am, but I don't see how it's going to help even if we can remember . . .' one of the bolder Police Scotland officers attempted.

'Call me ma'am again, and see how much I like it,' Connie said.

'It's an expression recognising authority over here,' Baarda intervened.

'When an American police officer calls you ma'am, he's either about to arrest you, or he wants you to shut the fuck up and move away. I'm guessing this situation is the latter. So listen up and think. Were all the doors properly shut when you arrived?'

There was vague nodding.

'Because if they weren't, it suggests a hurried exit, or that she was surprised when she was exiting the vehicle.'

'Um, the driver's door might have been open a wee bit,' another officer stuttered. 'I grabbed the handle to open it and I can't be certain if it was properly secured.'

'Well done, that's the detail we're looking for.' Baarda's comment covered Connie's obvious sigh.

'And the keys?' Connie continued.

'Still in the lock, ma'am. I mean, miss. We haven't moved them.'

'The neighbours have been spoken to,' Baarda explained. 'Looks as if the car's been here a while, although there's no precise timeline.'

'Whose house is it anyway?' Connie asked.

'Elspeth Dunwoody's best friend. The family is currently away sailing in the Caribbean and has no idea why the car would have ended up here. No one had spoken to Elspeth for a couple of weeks before her disappearance.'

'Public or private best friend?' Connie asked.

'Is there a difference?' Baarda looked confused.

'Some best friends you only speak to occasionally, never get round to seeing in person because the bond is strong enough to withstand little contact. They're difficult to trace unless you're on the inside. If, however, she's an "out on the town" best friend, or an "always standing at the school gates together" best friend, then someone would have noticed. It would have been easy enough to find this address and to come up with an excuse to get Connie here.'

'Check that out straight away,' Baarda instructed the uniformed officers.

They scuttled off, looking relieved to be going.

'She's not inside the property; it's been thoroughly checked. Her mobile isn't in the car, but her handbag is,' Baarda said.

'No keys, no handbag. No clothes missing from her wardrobe, and a genuinely distraught husband and kids. It doesn't look good.'

'Best will in the world, it doesn't take a forensic psychologist to figure that one out.'

'Why do people say that?' Connie mused, working her way around the vehicle and looking it up and down. 'Best will in the world. It always precedes an insult. Not a big, in-your-face kind of insult. Just something slipped in sideways.'

'I'm so sorry, I didn't mean to insult you. It's just that it seemed obvious.'

'You are institutionally apologetic. Seriously, you've got to get past that.' She knelt down by the passenger side door and looked more closely at the paintwork. 'There's something on here. Tell me what you see.'

Baarda joined her, the two of them on their knees in the gravel staring at the door.

'It's red and has formed a droplet, but it hadn't dripped very far when it dried, so there isn't much of whatever liquid it is. But that's red on red. How did you see it when you can't make out colour?'

'It's easier for me, actually,' Connie said. 'Your brain fools you. It sees a patch of red against a mass of other red information and it's hard to differentiate. My brain only deals in shades. The additional liquid on top of the red paint made a denser shadow. The usefulness stops there when I have no clue what the liquid might be. Could have been engine oil or mustard for all I'd have known.' She took out her mobile and photographed the spot. 'We have scenes of crime incoming, right?'

'We do. I'm guessing if that's Elspeth's blood then we're either waiting for a ransom call, or looking for a corpse.'

'Not enough evidence to assume that, even if it is her blood,'

Connie said. 'Don't tell her husband yet, but get this rushed through the police labs – and I mean rushed like fast food, not rushed like passing new legislation.'

'Point taken. I'll chase it up personally. I should be able to get next-day DNA results if I make a couple of calls.'

'That's impressive. What squad were you with in London?'

'Met Operations. I have a few years' experience in what used to be called the kidnap unit. I suspect they were perfectly happy to pack me off up here. I don't think I quite fit the Met Ops' new cool, slightly unshaven, three hours a day in the gym, alpha-male type.'

'Are there no women in Met Ops?' Connie asked.

'They're also more alpha-male than me, I'm afraid,' he smiled. 'Actually, recent studies have proved that the alpha typing is often a handicap when it comes to higher-ranking promotions and long-term personal partnerships. Management wants quiet calm and diplomacy with an analytic brain, and relationships require longevity with warmth and humour.'

'Sir!' The shout came from near the driveway entrance in some bushes.

Connie and Baarda made their way towards the officer calling them, standing far enough back not to corrupt the scene.

'What is it?' Baarda asked.

'Shoe, just the left one. Definitely female, and it matches the description given by the missing person's husband.' The officer held up one gloved hand.

From her fingertips dangled a pale slip-on sports shoe with little scuffing or wear. It was fairly new, and it hadn't been in the dirt long, Connie concluded.

'Any blood spatters on it?' she asked Baarda, who stepped forward to inspect it.

'Nothing visible. Can you point to where exactly you found it?'

The officer pointed about a metre from her feet, approximately two metres into the undergrowth.

'So either it flew off her foot when she was kicking and resisting, or she was sufficiently aware of what was happening to make sure she left us a sign that she'd been taken against her will and threw it in there. Her assailant couldn't let her go and risk wasting time searching for it,' Connie said.

'So we set up camp in the husband's house and wait for the ransom call then,' Baarda said quietly.

'If she's lucky,' Connie said. 'That really depends on what her kidnapper wants from her, doesn't it? Drive me back to my hotel? I need to write up my notes.'

'Now? Shouldn't we be reporting back to the family and going into the police station for a briefing? I usually leave note-taking until the evenings.'

'You're a policeman, DI Baarda. You follow procedure, have meetings, share information, chase up leads. My job here is not the same.' She walked to the passenger door of his car and climbed inside, clicking her seat belt securely and double-checking its reactive lock mechanism by tugging on it firmly as Baarda got in next to her.

'I just assumed you'd want to be as involved as possible. You know, the more information the better, make sure no one's missed anything.'

'I'm here to paint a picture of the man or woman who currently has possession of Elspeth. I'm assuming it's a he, but there could be a she behind this if it's extortion, a revenge kidnapping or an attempt to distract from a different sort of offence. That could be anything from insurance fraud to corporate manoeuvring given her connections.

My task is usually much simpler. When you have a string of dead bodies there are patterns, victim similarities, situational similarities. Even then, I can't be distracted by processes, procedures and police politics. Here, I'm throwing darts at a profiling board almost blindfolded. So I need to go back to square one, and see if I can do justice to the fact that I'm being paid. I can't do that in the middle of probable chaos in a police station. You're my filter.'

Baarda pulled away, waving gratefully at the uniformed officers who cleared the road to let him pass.

'You worked extensively with the FBI, I've been told. Why did you never become an agent?'

'That was the dream.' Connie stared out of the window as they passed mottled heathered verges that disappeared into bushes. 'My achromatopsia prevented me from becoming an agent, so I chose a profession that would allow me to work with the in-house profilers.'

'What do you miss?' Baarda asked.

Connie looked at his face. The question was vague, but the tenderness of his features gave away his meaning. She softened her usual brusque tone, aware that her manner was professional bordering on stony. It was a persona she'd cultivated to counteract some institutional misogyny along the way, and not a little condescension when people learned that she was 'colour-vision impaired'. The person who'd coined that phrase had left the room soon after she'd responded to him, never to be seen on the same working squad as her again.

'Mainly clichés. Twinkling Christmas lights, the waves when the weather is just starting to change. I used to sit on my parents' back porch and watch the sea for hours. Now it's just more of the same.'

She paused for a moment, trying to do the question justice. Baarda kept his silence where most would have felt the need to fill the space. She respected the fact that he was able not to. In her opinion, men could be measured by such minuscule but enormous details.

'The sparkle of a ruby. The endless shades of green on a single tree. Seeing images of earth from space, and viewing our tiny place in the universe in all its breathtaking beauty. When I was a child, my parents took me to visit the Grand Canyon. I'd been given my first camera. I was maybe ten. Anyway, I was going through an artistic phase, so every photo I took was in black and white. My parents had my favourite shot blown up, framed, and I must have fallen asleep staring at that image through most of my puberty. And God, I wish I'd taken a colour photo. That's my only memory of the Canyon. That goddamned black-and-white photo. One of the most beautiful places in the world and I have no memory of it in colour. That's irony worthy of a poem, right?'

'I'd miss seeing the light shine off my red setter's coat,' Baarda said.

Connie laughed. 'That's a great image. What's its name?'

'His name's Tupperware. We made the mistake of letting my then four-year-old daughter name him, and that was her favourite word at that time. But a promise is a promise. The more we tried to persuade her to choose something more . . . well, doggy, the more intractable she became.'

'Oh my God, you have to chase a red setter around the park shouting Tupperware? That's the best thing I've ever heard.'

'I don't get home to see him – or the kids – as much as I'd like at the moment.' His voice dipped.

'Why not?'

'Oh, you know, life gets in the way.'

'That's bullshit. Life gets in the way of golf or visits to the in-laws or trips to the chiropractor, but home literally is a person's life. What could get in the way of that?'

He shrugged. 'My wife's currently having an affair. She's been perfectly honest about it. No attempt to cover it up, which I appreciate. I felt it was easier to give her some space while she figures out what she wants.'

Connie didn't miss a beat. 'Do you still love her?'

'I believe so,' he said.

'Do you know who she's having an affair with?'

'One of the other officers from Met Ops. Makes it all a bit awkward. Probably the reason everyone was so pleased when I got packed off up here.'

'Holy shit, Baarda,' Connie whistled. 'Do you think you might be suppressing some anger beneath that super-polished exterior?'

'Not at all. I obviously hadn't been meeting her needs, she'd made that pretty clear, so what was I to expect? I have to take my share of the blame.'

'Careful with that,' she said. 'Taking the blame for someone else's choices lets them justify their deviancy with no checks or balances. You want to let her off the hook that easily?'

'You don't know her, and you don't know me.'

Connie looked back at him. His neck was strained as he drove, his hands a vice around the steering wheel.

'I'm sorry, that was rude. I'm never rude. I hope you can . . .'

'Stop,' Connie said, her voice only a whisper above the engine's purr. 'The apology should be mine. Let's call it quits with the personal revelations for today, okay?'

Baarda's mobile rang. He put the call on speaker.

'Sir, we're being bombarded with requests to comment from the press. I don't know how it leaked, but they know about our missing person, including her identity and her connections.'

'Shit,' Connie muttered.

'And Elspeth's husband just received the call. There's a request for five million to be paid in fifties. We have forty-eight hours. Elspeth Dunwoody's voice could be heard in the background saying, "Please help." It's confirmed as her. Her father-in-law's been informed. We're working on tracing the call and the payment details.'

'Very good,' Baarda said, closing the line. 'Well, that's you off the hook. Looks as if we've got all we need.'

'Except Elspeth,' Connie muttered. 'What are the statistics on getting her back alive in these circumstances?'

'We work on an average of fifty to eighty live UK kidnappings per year. Most of them resolve successfully.'

'How many don't?'

'A handful,' Baarda said. 'Deaths usually occur while we're closing in and the kidnapper panics, then concludes it would be easier not to leave any witness who could identify them.'

'Poor Elspeth,' Connie said. 'I hope she doesn't know that.'

'We'll do all we can,' Baarda said. 'The contact is a positive sign. I'm hopeful that we'll get her back unharmed.'

'I'm glad you're feeling hopeful, but I very much doubt Elspeth is right now. Wherever she is.'

Chapter Four

'Marry me,' the man said.

Elspeth Dunwoody was doing her best not to gag. The food he was feeding her was stale and rank. Her body was still in the process of attempting to oust whatever chemicals he'd forced into her on her friend's driveway. Since then, she'd been going through phases, all of them extremes, each passing through her with the speed and force of an express train. Currently she was numb and sick. For some reason she was finding impossible to fathom, there was a stranger on one knee in front of her, presenting a ring in a box. She turned her head to one side and gagged, almost losing the flat square of cheese and the few dry crackers that had been her lunch. He didn't even seem to notice.

'Marry me,' he repeated.

Elspeth peered at the ring. The gold band had tarnished and worn thin, and the single stone had no lustre, sitting forlorn and grey in spindly golden claws. She lifted her own left hand and waggled her fingers, knuckle-side to his face, showing off the ring that was already lodged there.

'I can fix that,' he said, a bottle of liquid soap appearing from the floor at his side.

He squirted a generous amount onto his own palm then rubbed it onto her ring finger. Her wedding and engagement rings, those 24-carat traitors, slipped off without a moment's hesitation. A quick towelling dry, and he pushed on his ring of choice. She wished she still had enough bile in her stomach to be sick over her new accessory, but her body wasn't performing to command.

'Ceremony,' he mumbled.

She gazed at him through the soreness of dehydrated, tear-blanched eyes. Scrawny, with sallow skin that would reject sunlight and sunken eyes sat atop the twin brown half moons of insomnia and malnutrition, his hands shook as he wandered around, picking up one object and setting down another, murmuring to himself constantly.

'Didn't get shoes,' he said, slapping his own face hard.

The sound echoed against the windowless walls.

The floor was tatty old carpet, scratchy beneath her one bare foot. Her absent shoe was in a bush, waiting to be discovered, and in her mind it had become a living thing, lying quietly as it looked anxiously skywards, hoping for a face to peer down and notice it, rescuing it gently. That shoe was her message in a bottle. She'd bought the pair only two weeks earlier, loving the softness of them as she admired their bright yellow canvas and black elastic laces. They'd been an extravagance, but then she'd never had to worry about money. She'd never had to worry about anything before, she realised now. Wealth and privilege had shielded her from everything except illness and the more distressing news broadcasts. To combat those, she'd been an enthusiastic supporter of numerous charities. Over the years she'd helped raise millions for social issues such as homelessness and child poverty, and made sure the new teenage cancer wing on a nearby hospital was completed to the highest standards, fully equipped and as homely as could be.

'Put it on,' the man said, laying a greying, too large wedding dress over her lap. Elspeth stared at it.

'You want me to do *what*?'

'Going to get ready,' was his reply.

He shuffled through a doorway that led into a bedroom beyond. What the other rooms held, Elspeth hadn't yet discovered. Standing was painful. She'd spent the first twenty-four hours after her abduction bound and laid on her side, knees up, wrists roped behind her back. Her captor had carried her from driveway to vehicle, and from there into a house. When her bindings were finally cut, she'd remained in position, moving only inch by inch, tendons stiff and muscles seized. In spite of regular yoga classes and trips to the gym, it had taken only that brief time to weaken her.

Now, she was undoing the zip on a wedding dress that surely hadn't been worn for decades. The lace was ripped and the stale yellow of old pub wallpaper. Stepping into it, she shed silent tears for her own husband. Her parting words to him had been snappy and churlish. She'd been desperate to return home and make things right with him. Now she might never have the chance. She pulled the dress up over her chest and slipped her arms into the puffy sleeves. A cloud of dust burst upwards into her face, leaving her choking. The smell was of attic and rodent droppings.

'You look beautiful,' the man said.

He'd reappeared with ghostlike stealth around the door. Elspeth wrapped her arms around her waist.

'Here, I'll zip you up. My brother should have been here. He'd have been my best man. That's something I'll have to fix a bit later. Couldn't get to it in time for the wedding. Not the right time to feel sorry for ourselves though, is it? This is the first day of us spending the rest of our lives together.'

His clothing was a perfect match for her dress in terms of age and state. The sleeves of his jacket ended inches up his arms, but the rest was far too bulky for his frame. The blue-and-green kilt hung off him, no socks, and too high over the knee. It had been made for someone short and round, whereas he might not have eaten for months, every bone digging at his skin from the inside. He had to be dying. The thought warmed her.

Moving to face her, he took hold of both of her hands. Elspeth swayed slightly. On a different day, at a different venue, that sway had been taken as a sign of delirious happiness. She'd been a bride overcome by the emotion of the moment, the watching crowds and the promise of a lifetime of love and devotion. Her parents had clutched one another joyfully, so certain of her choice of partner. A string quartet had played classical music, and her bridesmaids were her sister's twin girls dressed in tea rose pink with daisies in their hair. Elspeth imagined her husband's face and wondered if she would ever touch it again.

The man opposite her now coughed into her face with no thought for whether or not he should cover his mouth. Elspeth looked sideways at the bizarre painting on the wall and sang a song in her head. The words were a jumble in her mind, and she couldn't remember all of them. Her mother had sung it to her as a girl, something about cambric shirts and a sickle of leather. There was a tune and she wanted to hum it, but now the man holding her hands was raising his head grandly and puffing out his chest, and oh sweet God, he began speaking as loudly as if they were in a cathedral with a thousand people watching their nuptials. Elspeth knew her mouth was hanging open as she stared, but there wasn't a threat he could issue that could wipe the horror and incredulity from her face.

'Is there any person here present who knows of any reason why this man and this woman should not be joined in holy matrimony?'

There was a pause. Elspeth had been alone with him in that room for what had seemed like forever, and still she felt the need to look around. There was no one. He was talking to absolutely no one. Still he paused, waiting the proper amount of time, in case of an interjection.

Stepping a few inches closer to her, lowering his head to look fiercely into her eyes, he began to recite his vows.

'I, Fergus, take thee, Elspeth Brenda, to be my wedded wife, to have and to hold, from this day forward, for better, for worse, for richer, for poorer . . .'

Fergus? Elspeth racked her brains. She'd never met anyone called Fergus, not even heard the name in the context of a friend. And yet he knew her middle name. Did he know it was her grandmother's name? Did he also know that her grandmother, Brenda, had been an unstoppable woman who'd never accepted what she'd been told was her place? Brenda would have done something. She'd have talked this man – this Fergus – into releasing her, or beaten him into submission. And what was she doing? Playing weddings with a maniac. Elspeth did her best to breathe but the air was poison. Now, he was smiling at her. Actually smiling. Waiting for her to say something. She couldn't understand what.

'I'll help you,' he said. 'Repeat after me . . . I, Elspeth, take thee, Fergus . . .'

'I, Elspeth . . .' she muttered, glancing around again.

Had she lost her mind? Were there people watching them who she simply couldn't see?

'Say the words. Say the words. Say them, say them, say them.'

He fist-hammered the wall to punctuate each syllable, throwing his head back and opening his mouth to its most extreme cavity before letting loose a feral scream from the depths of his throat.

Elspeth covered her mouth with one hand, tried not to scream in response. She shuffled backwards as he swayed on his feet, his whole head tipped back as if he could consume his rage whole. The purpling skin of his cheeks swelled, and he growled and howled, still thumping the wall, shifting from one foot to the other.

She took a deep breath and closed her eyes, willing herself to unsee the lashing tongue and ground-down back teeth. It was time to save herself.

'I, Elspeth, take thee, Fergus,' she said, the words a mush amid her sobs. Again. 'I, Elspeth, take thee, Fergus.' That was better. Louder, clearer.

He stopped howling and just stood, mouth still a gaping hole aimed towards the ceiling, swaying on his feet. But he was listening now.

'To be my wedded husband,' she said.

Fergus' mouth began to close and his chin dropped. His eyeballs were still playing pinball in their sockets, and his breathing was ragged and harsh, but – to quote a phrase Elspeth's husband loved – he was back in the room.

'To have and to hold, from this day forward, ' Elspeth said. She reached out her hand, hating herself for weakness, for complying, but knowing saving herself this way was probably all she could do. 'For better for worse; for richer, for poorer; in sickness and in health.'

At that he smiled. Too many teeth and too much gum, too wide and wild. It wasn't just his body that was sick, she realised. And he wasn't just some pervert. If she had to put a label on it, to really capture what she'd just seen of him, she would call him a demon.

'In sickness and in health. That's good,' he panted. 'Go on.'

'To, um, give me a moment.' Elspeth shook her head, desperate to find the words. She'd been doing so well. What came next?

'Love,' he said, smiling at her and stepping even closer so that their joined hands brushed against both of their stomachs. The foulness of his breath gave the air an acid bite.

'Of course,' she said. 'To love, cherish and obey, till death do us part.'

Fergus shuddered.

'Death.' His shoulders heaved. 'Won't part us. I won't let it.' He ran dirty fingers over his scalp, circling his palm around the top of his head clockwise, anticlockwise.

Elspeth tried not to stare at the bristles of hair that came away, leaving little oily stubs.

He reached for Elspeth's hands again. She gritted her teeth against the sensation of grease on his fingertips, knowing she would still be able to smell his touch on her later. Probably forever.

'Finish it.'

'According to God's holy ordinance; and thereto I give thee my troth,' she said.

He leaned into her body, letting his head drop onto her shoulder, nuzzling into her neck. The desire to gag again was a time bomb in her throat.

'Nearly forgot,' he muttered. 'Stupid me. Stupid boy.' He dipped his right hand into his trouser pocket, and drew out a gold band that he slid onto her finger, nestling it close to the engagement ring, before placing a larger gold band in Elspeth's left palm, extending his ring finger for her to continue the ceremony.

She stared at the symbol of eternity. Together forever. Always bound. Making herself one with a monster. With a shaking right hand, she took the precious metal band and pushed it, slowly, onto his ring finger. A saline droplet exploded on the rim of the jewellery, spattering the back of his hand. He must have considered it a joyful tear, wrapping an arm around her shoulders and pulling her close into his chest.

'I know,' he said. 'I know. It's a lot. I feel the same. I've waited so long for this day, and you look so beautiful. It's hard not to be overwhelmed.'

Fergus kissed her forehead then released her, pushing the ring more firmly onto his own finger and taking a half step back before raising his head once more.

'I now pronounce you husband and wife,' he told the roughly finished ceiling.

The words echoed around them.

A gavel fell in Elspeth's head.

Fergus punched the air. She leapt backwards.

'Yes!' he shouted. 'Fucking yes. I'm married. We did it!' He picked her up, arms around her hips, and hoisted her into the air, twirling her round and whoop-whooping.

He was stronger than he looked, but then she'd learned that the first time he'd picked her up and thrown her into the boot of his car. She made herself rigid rather than gripping his shoulders for balance, half hoping he wouldn't drop her and crack her head on the floor, half hoping he would. It would mean a quicker end to the insanity.

'It's our honeymoon, Mrs Ariss,' he said, staring up at her, eyes shining with a terrifying mixture of adoration and desperation.

It took Elspeth's breath away.

She'd been wrong. He wasn't just a monster. Monstrosity was singular and predictable. It was consistent and reliable. The man who honestly believed he'd just joined her in wedlock was also a child in an adult's body. He could kidnap her, then feed her and keep her warm. He could strip her of the wedding band she cherished then celebrate his own union with her.

Drug her then tell her he adored her. She wished he were just a monster. There were rules for those. Never look under your bed. Keep the closet door shut. Make sure your bedroom window was locked at night. But there were no rules that would keep you safe from this.

This was a credible, well-informed source of information that could tell you something awful had happened to her best friend, and that he'd been sent to ask her to go there immediately. This was a gentle voice with a concerned manner, who knew everything about her and her life. This was a planner and a stalker, super-fan and hater. She'd lost her life in a heartbeat to land in a fucked-up hellhole of a honeymoon with a psychopath.

'We should consummate it,' Fergus muttered, more to himself than to her.

Elspeth backed up against the wall.

'It's not legal unless we consummate the marriage. I read that once. In the old days there'd have been witnesses.' He laughed and looked away. 'We won't have any of those, but we'll know, won't we? That we did it all properly, I mean.'

Elspeth shook her head, raising her hands and making small fists in front of her mouth.

'Don't-want-to,' she stuttered, her breath hitching between each word.

'We'll have to at some stage, for it to be real.'

'We should . . .' She tried to get some air into her lungs. 'We should celebrate first. I mean, we just got married. Do you have any wine, beer even? Anything?'

He patted his body up and down as if he might find some hidden, long forgotten bottle secreted on his person.

'I think – and I may be wrong – but I think possibly I've some whisky in the cupboard downstairs. Would you like me to go and look? I can't let you come with me, obviously.' He frowned. 'Not that there's another woman here. I don't want you to get the wrong impression of me. God, would you listen to me? You make yourself comfortable and I'll find us something to toast with.' He hustled out.

Elspeth waited until she heard the key turning in the lock before ripping the wedding dress from her shoulders. Fergus Ariss was deluded about many things, but not about the need to keep her secured. She was his prisoner first, his wife second. He knew she would bolt given the opportunity.

The alcohol would help, one way or another. If she could persuade him to drink enough and minimise her own intake, perhaps she could disable him. It was clear from the state of his face that he'd been in other altercations, and recently. His nose was still scabbed in a long line from top to bottom, and his forehead bore yellow patches with a faint purple trim that highlighted the old bruising. One of his fingers was bandaged. If she could attack those still-vulnerable parts of him, perhaps she could cause him additional pain.

Smoothing her T-shirt and her hair, she sat back down on the ancient heavy sofa and tried to control her breathing. She did it in yoga every week. Surely all those hours of practice had to count for something. Breathe in, expand her chest fully from the bottom of her ribcage, breathe out slowly, making sure her shoulders and neck were relaxed.

Fergus Ariss was going to rape then kill her. She couldn't fool him. She could barely stop herself from shaking.

Breathe in. Imagine she was an empty well that she was filling with life-giving cool spring water, cleansing and refreshing her.

If she tried to attack him and it didn't work, what then? Presumably he'd beat her skull in with his bare hands, or drug her like he had when he'd kidnapped her, maybe wait until she came round again and then take his time torturing her. Maybe this time she'd wake up in a cage.

Breathe out. Let all her worries flow out on that used-up air, sending the toxins from her system into the atmosphere. Be aware of the strength and potential of her own body, of how alive she felt, how vital.

How terrified.

Yoga was bullshit, she decided. If she'd taken self-defence classes three times a week instead, she wouldn't be in the position she was. What a waste of time and Lycra.

The door opened, and for the first time she saw where Fergus kept his keys. A length of sturdy chain was wrapped around his waist beneath his clothes, the keys no more than a few inches from the junction of the chain. If she disabled him, she would have to drag him and lift him up to use the keys in the lock.

Fuck, she thought. Bastard son of all the fucks she had never given before.

Fergus grinned and raised the bottle in one hand, and a pair of plastic cups in the other.

'Found it!' he announced needlessly. 'You took your dress off. Why would you do that?' Fergus stared at the crumpled heap on the floor.

'I was just getting comfortable, like you said,' she smiled. Her efforts felt feeble and poorly acted. 'I wanted to hang it, but there's nowhere in here to do that. Perhaps you could look after the dress for me . . . afterwards.'

Turning her face slightly sideways, she gave him a look from beneath her eyelashes. It was grotesque, the faux flattery of a man to make him think she wanted him when she was preparing to get him drunk then smash a bottle over his skull. But somehow, he was oblivious to the fact that her smile was a snarl, and that her soft words were the worst lines of dialogue ever constructed.

'I'll do that,' he said, matching the soft tones of her voice with his own. 'Afterwards.'

Sitting down next to her on the bed, he filled one of the plastic cups with a generous measure of whisky, keeping the other empty. He passed her the full cup.

'Shall I pour yours, then?' she offered sweetly.

'Oh no, I don't drink at all. I just wanted to be able to hold a glass so we could toast one another. I take too much medication to be able to drink alcohol. I'm afraid to say your husband isn't in the best shape at the moment. I'm hoping you'll be able to help me with that, though. So much about our physical self is in being fulfilled and happy. You know that, right, with all the yoga and Pilates you do? I really admire that about you. Being in touch with your body. Perhaps you can show me some exercises. It might help me.'

'You don't drink at all,' Elspeth repeatedly slowly.

'No. Too many painkillers in my system. You enjoy that, though. Don't feel as if you shouldn't drink just because I can't.'

He kept the whisky bottle firmly in his hand and away from her reach. Elspeth stared into the depths of the full plastic cup. This was the decision, then. Fight him and maybe die. Or drink herself into a state of unconsciousness and live another day when he'd finished doing what he wanted to her. Her choice.

'Cheers,' she said, raising the glass to him and giving the slightest bow of her head. She didn't even grimace as the cheap liquor burned her throat.

'*Slainte*,' he replied, raising his own plastic cup and mimicking taking a drink. 'Now we can really get to know one another, body and soul. I shall cherish every moment of it.'

'Refill?' Elspeth asked, her voice a too-bright mask for the twilight of fading hope beneath.

'Of course,' he said. 'As many as you want.'

It wouldn't be enough, Elspeth thought. However much

alcohol was in that bottle, it couldn't prepare her for what was to come. She gave up trying to pretend to be cheerful and allowed herself to cry instead.

Chapter Five

'She's taken it,' the female undercover officer announced, her voice relayed into the earpieces of every officer posted around Waverley railway station waiting for the kidnapper to pick up the ransom payment. 'Red hair, twenty-five to thirty-five, Caucasian, approximately five foot six, slim build. Jeans, white trainers, grey hoodie. She's exited the ladies' toilets.'

'All eyes on,' Baarda said, Connie listening in at his side. 'Is the tracker on the bag working?'

'Yes, sir,' a male voice reported. 'She's heading onto a platform and boarding a train.'

'Follow her,' Baarda ordered.

'Got to show my badge to get through. If she looks back, she'll clock me,' the pursuing officer said.

'Let her get a few steps ahead then show your ID and get on that train. Do not lose visual.'

Baarda's laptop screen showed the woman disappearing onto a crowded commuter train, then the officer with the concealed headcam started jogging to catch up. He climbed on board and began walking rapidly through the carriages. The woman wasn't in sight.

'She's exited the train,' a woman's voice picked up the story, 'but she's not carrying the bag the cash was in. There are several supermarket bags in her hands instead. She's gone into a crowd. I'm following.'

'Confirm when you have a clear sighting,' Baarda said.

'She's out the other side. Can't see any bags, though. Her hands are free.'

'Where are the bags she was carrying?'

'Not sure, sir,' someone replied quietly.

Baarda sighed. 'All the other people in the crowd she went through need to be surveilled for those bags. Which supermarket were they from?'

'Multiple supermarkets, sir. There are hundreds being carried in the station right now. It's rush hour. We don't know who we're looking for.'

'The tracker was in the middle of the rolls of notes. Where is it?' Baarda demanded.

'Exiting via the Princes Street steps, but we don't know who's carrying it, sir.'

'Do you want me to pick the woman up?' the female officer asked.

'No. If she fails to report in to Elspeth's captor, they might panic and kill the hostage. Unit one, follow the tracker. Unit two, follow the female at a safe distance. The money's irrelevant. We just need to know where they're holding Elspeth.'

'What happens now?' Connie asked Baarda.

He stretched his neck. 'You tell me. Are these the actions of criminals likely to make good on their word and release the victim, or not?'

'They're well organised, skilled, and there are several people involved. They're less likely to respond emotionally to external stresses because they've thought consequentially and will have planned for all possible outcomes. One of those will be the need to kill the hostage. Deciding a course of action might be necessary isn't the same thing as being able to take a life though, unless they've done that before. Many murderers only find killing traumatic the first time they do it.'

'That's rather clinical.' Baarda regarded her solemnly.

'Sorry, did you want me to reassure you that it's all going to be okay?'

'I may not have known you very long, but bland reassurance isn't the first thing that comes to mind when I think of you.'

'DI Baarda?' a voice crackled down the line. 'You're wanted at the city mortuary.'

Edinburgh's mortuary wasn't far from Waverley station as the crow flew, but by car during rush hour, the journey seemed to take forever. Inside the mortuary, an assistant walked them through to a postmortem suite.

A woman with the build of a sparrow and the energy of a tornado was storming around the room, clicking files on a computer screen, holding a microscope slide on one hand and talking either to herself or to the corpse lying beneath a sheet on a gurney.

'Ah, you're here. Now I know you were busy, but there's something you should be aware of. You'll need to suit up before you step any closer.'

Baarda and Connie reached for the necessary overalls.

'My name's Ailsa Lambert, I'm the chief forensic examiner.' She bustled across to pick up a set of photos and open them, holding up the relevant shot. 'This drop of blood from your missing person's vehicle flagged as a match on our system. In the circumstances, I decided you should come straight in.'

'Where was she found?' Baarda asked.

'At home, in her bed.'

'That can't be right. We have officers there now waiting for

46

confirmation as to whether or not Mrs Dunwoody has been found.'

'Oh, this isn't Mrs Dunwoody. Apologies. I thought you'd have been told. This poor young woman is Angela Fernycroft.' She peeled back the sheet to reveal a darkly dappled face, its humanity long since disintegrated.

Baarda closed his eyes for a moment. Connie grabbed a nose and mouth mask from a dispenser, flipped the elastic over her head and stepped in to get a closer look at the face.

'Her lips are weird. Like, really badly chapped. Is this weathering? Had she just come back from a ski trip or a desert hike?'

Ailsa Lambert folded her arms and peered over the top of her glasses. Connie decided it was like being watched by a mistrustful bird. The pathologist was tiny and probably old enough to have been her grandmother, and yet her energy felt more like it was coming from a high-functioning twenty-something.

'Perceptive,' Ailsa said. 'You're the American psychologist. While you're very welcome, I was wondering how that came about.'

'Intersection between politics and money,' Connie said, picking up the stack of photos again. 'So the drop of blood on Elspeth Dunwoody's car was from this woman?'

'Oh no,' Ailsa said. 'The blood on the car, while we know it's from a male, has no identified source. Which you might think is unusual given how much of the same DNA was found at the scene of this woman's murder.'

There was a pause, just two or three seconds, but the atmosphere in the room dropped notably even in the necessary chill.

'I have to make some calls,' Baarda said. 'Excuse me.' He left the room.

'This is fascinating,' Connie continued. 'Cause of death? May I?' She indicated the sheet that still covered the remainder of the body.

Ailsa peeled it back for her. 'You've seen plenty of dead bodies, I take it. That's a rare level of enthusiasm.'

'God, I'm sorry, that's not how I wanted to come across. Truth is, I envy you this. It's where so much of the real work is done. I'd have loved your career. You guys make it possible to drag the beasts from their lairs.'

'I've never heard it put quite like that.' Ailsa gave a tiny wry smile as she held a magnifying glass over Angela's lips. 'What you identified as chapping is in fact burns. The skin is badly damaged, not just over the sensitive area of the lips, but also in the nasal passages, extending out as far as the chin and lower parts of the cheeks – I'm sure you can see the discoloration of the pigmentation that forms a rough circle.' She motioned at the edges with the end of her pen.

'Carry on,' Connie said.

'Cause of death was respiratory failure, although a cardiac event would have killed her anyway if her lungs hadn't ceased to work first.'

'Chloroform,' Connie said. 'So there's a high probability this is our kidnapper. If this was his first intended victim, perhaps he just got the dosage wrong. Makes sense. He'd have changed tactics when he took Elspeth Dunwoody. Hopefully that means she's still alive.'

'That's not all, I'm afraid. There was one other DNA match on the system. Still no name, and it dates back five years on an unsolved case.'

Connie put her hands on her hips. 'Now what are the goddamn chances of that?'

'I'd say really rather low, assuming that wasn't merely rhetorical,' Dr Lambert replied.

'Was it another murder?' Connie asked.

'That remains to be seen,' Dr Lambert said. 'The crime was neither confirmed nor solved. I pulled only cursory details from the online file. A young woman was apparently heard calling for help in Advocate's Close just off the High Street. It was around two a.m. and the witness, another young woman walking alone had, quite rightly, opted to fetch help rather than intervene. By the time police arrived, they found a bundle of possessions, an empty sleeping bag, signs of a struggle, with bags kicked over and contents strewn. Neither weapon nor blood. However, a twenty-pound note was left on the pavement next to the possessions. That was seized for forensic testing.'

'How many different sources of DNA are on any given banknote at one time?' Connie asked.

'A lot,' Dr Lambert conceded. 'But the forensic report said this DNA came from saliva. Recent, I would guess, as it hadn't been in a pocket or wallet long enough to have rubbed off or become so tainted that it was unreadable.'

'Who was the missing woman?'

'I don't have an answer for you there, either. No identification in the possessions. We have her DNA from the sleeping bag, but it never matched anything on the police national database. No physical description of her. No age. Just a mystery and a lot of assumptions. Not even any specific evidence that a crime had been committed.'

'And still, I don't like it.' Connie folded her arms. 'Do you have the crime scene photos here for Angela's death?'

'I do,' Ailsa said. 'Come into my office.'

She pulled the sheet back up and stripped off her gloves. Connie followed suit before sitting silently at a computer screen studying one photo after another.

'That's a lot of blood,' Connie said.

'It is,' Ailsa said. 'Some of it is definitely from his nose – he must have had a substantial bleed – and it contains a level of mucous material. It was pooled on her neck, upper chest and in her cleavage.'

'Pooled? So she was on her back, and he was just lying on top of her. Was she raped?'

'No. No sign of any sexual assault at all. No semen anywhere.'

Connie pushed her chair backwards, letting it glide a foot or so before it came to a natural halt. She crossed her arms and stretched out her legs, staring at the ceiling.

'So he just lay on top of her, bleeding? That can't be right. What other injuries did she suffer?'

'A severe blow to the back of her head. Not enough to fracture the skull, but it would have given her concussion. There's a substantial bump – you can feel it but not see it through her hair. Otherwise general bruises, scratches, defence wounds. We also have his DNA from skin scrapings beneath her fingernails. And his blood in her mouth.'

'Good girl,' Connie smiled.

'Good girl indeed. Sequence of events?'

'She's in bed, maybe asleep, maybe not yet, but he doesn't disturb her when he enters. Husband's off the hook, right?'

'Airtight alibi. He was away with the children for the weekend,' Ailsa explained.

'Figures. Chloroform deaths are almost inevitably unrelated assailant crimes. He goes for it, puts the chloroform over her mouth, she fights back. Reverse headbutt, injures his nose. Which part of him does she bite?'

'Now that I can help with. A section of inner finger, probably middle, just a few millimetres long and a few wide, was recovered from the carpet.'

'He passed out on top of her,' Connie said. 'He had the chloroform over her mouth and he just passed out. How long before she was found?'

'The next morning. One of her young children ran into her bedroom and found her.'

'Holy shit. That's thirty years of therapy, right there.'

Ailsa pursed her lips and Connie made a mental note to cut out the expletives.

'Just one DNA source at the crime scene?' Connie asked.

'Just one,' Ailsa confirmed.

'With Elspeth Dunwoody we have a complex set-up with ransom decoys and solid organisation. Angela's murderer made no attempt to conceal his forensic identity. He attacked her in bed knowing that if anything went wrong, he'd leave a trail. Oh, hell . . .'

Connie returned to the computer, found a search engine and typed frantically. She scrolled through clip after clip of Elspeth Dunwoody at various events, listening to her voice recordings wherever she found them. Finally, she replayed footage from a charity ball, twice, three times. Ailsa Lambert peered over her shoulder and they watched it together.

'So we join with the other foundations here tonight to fight malaria, to ensure safe systems for both avoiding the disease and treating it. I'd like to ask you all to please help. No contribution is too small . . .' Elspeth's voice lingered over the crucial words, her throat cracking with emotion.

Connie played the relevant words one last time.

'Please help.'

Baarda appeared in the doorway.

'The people who demanded the ransom don't have her,' Connie said. 'Elspeth's voice recording was taken from old footage and played back. It was clever.'

'Clever or not, if the ransomers don't have her, then who does?' he asked.

Chapter Six

Fergus lay on his bed, staring at the ceiling. He could feel his blood slowing to a crawl around his arteries and veins. His lungs seemed to be allergic to the air. Beneath him the sheets had moistened to a cotton swamp, filthy with toxins and reeking with body odour.

An oxygen tank sat next to his bed like some bizarre relative waiting for interaction, the plastic mask dangling from a clear tube offering little relief from his symptoms. Taking his own pulse, he noted its elevated beat, feeling the irregularity and wondering what his heart looked like internally right now. Grey and worn, struggling to pump effectively. He pictured it as a semi-deflated tyre, ready to burst next time too much pressure was applied.

Throwing a selection of pills into his mouth and washing them down with an energy drink, he wished for sleep. No amount of beta blockers seemed to kill his pain. High-strength sedatives would offer some assistance, but there was no guarantee he'd wake up from them. Suicide wasn't the end he wanted. His eyes filled with tears. It was so unfair. He wasn't a bad man, yet such bad things were happening to him. The sickness that had him in its grasp didn't care about its victims' track records. It didn't matter that he had never abused drugs or alcohol, that he'd never come to the attention of the police or the courts. He was going to pay the ultimate price, leaving behind a barely blotted copybook and so much wasted potential.

Elspeth was supposed to save him. Fergus wanted to impress his mother in the afterlife, to show her the man he'd become – a husband, a father, the perfect brother. Family was everything. Especially when you'd never really had one. He didn't want to die alone; nor did he want his mother to be disappointed in him again.

His wife was just the start of his plans. He'd worked so hard on making their home lovely. All Elspeth had to do was keep it clean and hygienic, particularly given how prone he was to sickness. His grandmother had reminded him of it regularly during his childhood. Back then he'd thought she was a fusspot. Now he knew better.

'It's cold out. You shouldn't be playing in the snow. You're not strong enough. As soon as you get wet, you'll be back in bed. You heard what the doctor said about your poor lungs.'

'Aw, Gran, that's stupid,' he'd declared.

It had been his phrase of choice from age eight to eleven. Everything had been stupid until his grandmother had ended up nursing him through illness after illness, homeschooling him, doing her best not to let him slip behind his peers. He'd attended school whenever he was well enough, and she didn't do a bad job except in French and the sciences – her weaker areas. With every illness, his immune system had eroded, slowly but surely, and Fergus had found himself lost in a sea of sadness. He'd been thirteen when the doctors first labelled it depression. Then there had been periods away from his grandmother's house, although they were vague and shadowy in his memory. Hospitals, only not exactly.

His grandmother had had few regrets when she finally passed. She'd wanted to see her grandson happy, naturally. She'd been a mother to him when his own had passed. No father. That was all anyone had told him, and he'd learned not to ask given the sulking it always caused.

Without her, he'd fallen into depression. If he'd had a surviving sibling, he often thought, it would have been different. Someone there to share the burden of grief. As it was, he'd stopped eating, shrunk into a reclusive home life, and found that without his grandmother's no-nonsense approach to vitamins, minerals and a strictly balanced diet, his body had begun to wage war on him.

At first his doctor had been falsely cheerful and given nothing other than common-sense advice. Try to get out more. It was amazing what the benefits of fresh air and exercise could do. Find someone to talk to, if not a friend then there were plenty of free groups around that provided support and counselling during periods of grief. He'd been asked about his personal relationships and stress. About his sex life and even, to his shame, about his masturbation habits. It had taken a whole year before anyone had taken him seriously, and by then there was the inevitable slow crawl towards blood tests and urine samples.

Two years in, and you could see every rib and every bony joint. He began missing increasingly lengthy periods from his work at the factory. Fergus' boss was making unpleasant noises about him becoming a liability. Eating had become a chore, often ending in a sudden, explosive vomiting session. As hard as he tried to replicate his grandmother's care routine, he was failing to thrive. Then came the news that his liver and stomach were suffering. The doctors had tried to tell him that it was nothing serious, but he'd seen and felt the truth. Finally, the tests had become more meaningful. There had been cameras inserted and scans taken. After that the doctors' voices had lowered in volume and softened in tone.

The horrible truth was that his organs had begun rotting inside his body. Perhaps exacerbated by his gran's passing, or perhaps it was just his time, a clock had begun to tick and the alarm was about to ring.

Sleep crept over him and he pinched the soft skin of his stomach fiercely. He didn't have time to nap. There was so much more to do. A new bed had been delivered that he needed to put together. The bedding was still in its plastic wrappers and needed to be washed before it could be put on the bed. If it still had the folds from the packaging, it wouldn't look nice at all. There were toys and games to put on shelves. The effort felt crushing. Swinging his legs off the bed, and bracing for the pain in his back as he rose, Fergus willed his shaking hands to comply with the need to grip screwdrivers and hammer nails. He took a photograph from the wall, and walked up the stairs to the upper apartment, checking the peepholes to make sure the hallway was clear before entering.

Inside, he took a moment to walk around and appreciate the place. The windows were bricked up, and each room was a fraction smaller than the original plans showed. A layer of soundproofing with plasterboard over the top had made a larger impact than he'd anticipated. But it was cosy. He'd painted the bedroom walls pink. The tiny kitchenette was summer morning blue, the lounge a sunny yellow. He peered into his and Elspeth's bedroom. The lazy woman was still asleep, or perhaps just hungover. Leaving her in silence, he entered the second bedroom.

Taping the photo on the wall first to motivate himself, he began unwrapping lengths of wood, cross slats, a bundle of screws and Allen keys.

A girl beamed at him from the photograph.

Not long now. This time it would all work out.

55

Chapter Seven

'So to summarise, you have five people in custody, and in spite of that you have thus far been completely unable to ascertain where Elspeth Dunwoody actually is,' Detective Chief Inspector O'Neill said, the sneer in her voice evidenced by her extended vowel pronunciation.

Connie looked across the desk at Baarda, who was cradling a steaming cup of coffee and maintaining a remarkable air of calm in spite of the hostility coming from the conference call speaker phone.

'As I explained, ma'am, the people we arrested are, in our opinion, no more than profiteers from the media release of the detail of Mrs Dunwoody's kidnapping. They manipulated an existing audio file to ensure they had a voice clip of her saying words that related to being held prisoner. Then they added background noise which we identified as St Mary's Episcopal Cathedral bells to make us think she was being held in central Edinburgh. Given her social prominence the amount of money they'd asked for was in keeping with our expectations. We had no choice but to follow the lead.

'We traced the five of them through text messages they'd

exchanged regarding the money pickup. They've been charged with extortion, and in the circumstances they can all expect to receive substantial custodial sentences.' Baarda kept his voice low and polite, while Connie wanted to disconnect and stop wasting time.

Edinburgh's Major Investigation Team had provided them with a briefing room, a phone, access to a kitchen that needed an introduction to basic hygiene levels, and a glass board. The latter had been covered with a rough tessellation of photographs, maps, forensic reports and statements. Blue lines with arrows indicated information flow. Red lines were reserved for evidential links and random white question marks were plastered wherever there were obvious gaps in the storyline.

'So what decent new leads do you have, now that your first line of investigation has collapsed?' O'Neill snapped.

'We have a DNA match with a male who murdered a woman in her bed. The same DNA was in a blood droplet on Elspeth Dunwoody's car, and our time would be better spent figuring out who that male is rather than relaying information to you. There's another DNA match in a cold case relating to the disappearance of a homeless woman. Is that not enough for you?' Connie asked.

Baarda stared at her open-mouthed.

'That would be Dr Woolwine, I suppose,' O'Neill drawled.

'Yes, ma'am, we're—'

'Don't interrupt, Baarda. I was told you'd been given access at all levels of the case, Dr Woolwine. Your insights, please.'

'My insights? We have three different categories of crime scene. Right now, I can't provide an outline of your suspect either physically, psychologically or in socio-economic terms.'

'Ma'am, it was Dr Woolwine who first realised that they did not actually have our kidnap victim,' Baarda explained.

'So I gather, about five minutes before everyone else figured it out, which no doubt was a huge help, except to contextualise just how incompetently the police investigation is being handled. I'm not seeing much progress from either of you with regard to Mrs Dunwoody's whereabouts, though. Best guess, Dr Woolwine, is Mrs Dunwoody alive or dead?'

'Alive,' Connie replied.

'Because?' O'Neill asked.

'Because we haven't found her body yet,' Connie said. 'Everyone's alive until we know for sure they're dead.'

Baarda scribbled a note on a piece of paper and held it up for Connie to read: 'Don't aggravate her.'

Connie shrugged.

A dramatic sigh issued from the phone speaker. 'I'll need an update tomorrow. One with information I can pass on that suggests we are moving forward. Witnesses, forensics, a sighting, intelligence. Just get me something. I'll be handing over daily supervision to Detective Superintendent Overbeck at MIT. You'll be answering to her on the ground there. Baarda, I saw Anoushka last night. She was asking me how long you'd be in Scotland. I told her hopefully only a couple more days. Don't make me a liar.' The line was dead before Baarda could respond.

'Who's Anoushka?' Connie asked him.

'My wife. She and DCI O'Neill are members of the same supper club.'

'You're fucking with me. A supper club? You know, I do my best to avoid forming stereotypes based on nationalities, but really . . .'

'Am I allowed to stereotype you based on your overuse of expletives?' Baarda asked.

'Yeah, if you want. I can even help. I'm a coarse American. I chew gum, watch endless sport on TV, and I'm as loud as possible as often as possible. Feel better?'

'Are you always so extreme?' he asked, adjusting his cuffs.

'I guess I am,' Connie said, standing up to peer at the photograph of Elspeth Dunwoody's car. 'Which is exactly the problem I'm having with our killer-cum-kidnapper. The crime scenes have zero in common. Angela Fernycroft died chaotically. Nothing about it made sense. If he intended to kill her, then why do it in a way that left him so vulnerable to injury? There was blood everywhere. She even managed to bite a chunk out of his finger, for Christ's sake.'

'He got in unnoticed, though. We still don't have evidence of a break-in. If she was asleep when he approached her, he also managed to secrete himself successfully for some time.'

'Good call,' Connie smiled at him. 'So he has a high level of impulse control when necessary, but poor final execution.'

'How can you be so sure he didn't mean to kill her in exactly the manner he did?' Baarda asked, joining Connie in front of the photos.

'The chloroform suggests he either wanted to move her, or to do something more specific that required a lengthy set-up. And the statistical analysis is all wrong for this type of crime. There was no sexual assault, but also nothing stolen. The drawers weren't turned out. So no robbery, no sexual assault in situ. What's the motive?'

'Would I be stating the obvious if I said murder?'

'Only to the extent that the murder of an adult female following a home invasion rarely goes down like this, unless he was known to her. That could explain why he didn't have to break into the house,' Connie mused.

'But none of his DNA has been found in any other room in the house. Why would she go to bed with a visitor on the premises, even someone she knew? If he was staying overnight, if he was her lover or an old family friend, we'd expect to find his DNA elsewhere.'

'It's going to remain a mystery until we catch this bastard, but if the entry was opportunistic, the invader would have been expecting other occupants. The fact that no one else was there means that he was likely armed with that information in advance.'

'You think he stalked her,' Baarda said.

'The evidence suggests that he stalked her.'

'So while the crime scene is chaotic, the offender himself may not be,' Baarda noted.

'Which makes Elspeth's abduction a big leap forward. He made contact with her, convinced her to move her vehicle somewhere familiar to her but that was also unoccupied at the time. He must also have had a vehicle available. The spot of blood on the car door was close to being pure bad luck.'

'So did he just plan the scenario with Elspeth better?' Baarda asked.

Connie shrugged. 'Criminals evolve. They adapt, hone their skills and perfect methodology, but this sort of leap is like humans skipping from tree-dwelling to building skyscrapers in a single generation.'

'You don't think that's possible?' Baarda asked.

'I think it's unlikely,' Connie said. 'A rapist will have flashed a woman first. A man who kills his partner will have been abusive over a period of time. But this' – Connie pointed at the photo of Angela Fernycroft's bedroom – 'feels clumsy and amateurish. It's a disaster that resembles a first offence by a psychotic teenager. And yet Elspeth Dunwoody disappeared into thin air. How did he get from A to Z so fast? Something changed for him between Angela and Elspeth, more than just trial and error.' She crossed her arms and shook her head at the photos. 'Then there's the twenty-pound note. Did you read the file?'

'I did. There's not a lot of content, given there's no evidence a crime was committed. The disturbance the witness thought she heard could have been an episode in a mental health break-down, drug-fuelled psychosis, an argument over territory or possessions between two homeless people. The fact that possessions were abandoned isn't unusual. There's no solid storyline, let alone a proper police complaint.'

'And yet the same DNA is on file.'

'You have a theory?' Baarda asked.

'The male we're looking for has been in the Edinburgh area for years. He was old enough to be walking the streets at night five years ago, so we can narrow the age range down to starting in the mid-twenties. He knows the city well. Advocate's Close is a back alley that runs beneath the structure of other buildings. Unless you knew it, you might assume that you couldn't exit at the other end. I'd say something about him gave her the creeps. Women who live on city streets develop good instincts for danger real fast.'

'Playing devil's advocate for a moment, what's to say he wasn't simply in the wrong place at the wrong time?'

Connie leaned forward, beaming. 'I like you, Brodie Baarda,' she said. 'You ask the questions that make me look good. Why wasn't he in the wrong place at the wrong time? If I was in Vegas and taking a bet, I'd call it like this. The saliva on the note is the killer detail. We pass DNA every time our skin cells touch something. We leave invisible smears when we don't wash our hands after using the restroom.'

'Oh, God,' Baarda said faintly.

'No, no, go with it, there's a point. Blood DNA has more innocent explanations than you'd think. But the loss of saliva is often specific to emotion and trauma. On cutlery, it's a no-brainer. On the end of a pen, I'd expect it. In a bathroom, loads of it after transference from a toothbrush or the sink. On a banknote? Disgusting, dirty things. No adult in their right mind puts their mouth on it. So the note caught some of his spittle.'

'He was upset . . .' Baarda said.

'Damn right he was upset. You can add angry, accusatory, and overwrought to that list of emotions. People rarely lose saliva when they're talking normally. The only other time is when people are fist-fighting or kissing. Do you know that if I kiss you right now, I'll transfer around eighty million germs from my mouth to yours?'

'Please don't,' Baarda said.

'Killjoy. Anyway, those are my thoughts, but I do have one question.'

'Is it about saliva?'

'No. However, I have many more exciting facts and statistics on the subject of bodily fluids if we're ever stuck on overnight surveillance together. My question is this. There's no assault, no body. So how come the twenty-pound note was DNA tested at all? You're not telling me Police Scotland has such limitless resources that it checks every homeless person's abandoned belongings based only on a call saying there's been a disturbance?'

'Five years ago, the then Detective Chief Inspector of MIT had a niece who'd developed a drug habit, become homeless, and disappeared off the radar. Police were under instruction to check any homeless woman they came across in her twenties. All the possessions in this case were checked to see if the girl who appears to have gone missing was the chief inspector's niece. It's an abuse of position, but an understandable one. Obviously it wasn't the Chief's niece, as we have no name to put to the belongings, but the file remained open and the DNA sample was kept on the database.'

Connie put her feet up on a desk and leaned her head back, closing her eyes.

'Did the DCI ever find his niece?' Connie asked.

'I couldn't ask him,' Baarda said. 'He died a couple of years ago.'

'Fucksticks,' Connie said. 'You're telling me that as the police were trying to find one missing girl, another went missing? Now here we are, five years later, with one dead woman and one missing. So are they all linked or not? I mean, is this your standard incredibly bad situation, or is it a really, truly fucking grand-scale disaster waiting to be uncovered?'

'It doesn't matter. We can only rescue the victim he has right now. Scale is irrelevant when you're the captive,' Baarda said.

'Did you just out-perspective me?'

'I did, and honestly, it was easier than I'd anticipated.' Baarda undid his top button and ran a tired hand through his hair. 'So what's our next move?'

'I have more questions. Lots of them. One of them can only be answered by the forensic pathologist. Want to swing by the morgue with me?' She picked up her bag and jacket.

'We call it a mortuary,' he murmured, pulling his car keys from his pocket.

'You can call it whatever you like, but let's go figure out if Elspeth Dunwoody is alive or dead.'

Chapter Eight

It wasn't much of a park, but it was better than being at home. Meggy Russell sat on the roundabout and watched the world spin. The metallic squeal from beneath her enhanced rather than diminished the ride. The screech-on-repeat reflected her own state of mind. Meggy had a bullying problem in the form of her step-mother, Carmen. If she'd had siblings to act as allies it might have been bearable, but until her father got home from work Monday to Friday it was just her and the awful Carmen in the house after school.

The park at the end of her road offered sanctuary whenever it wasn't freezing cold. There were swings that were comfortable enough to sit on and read for an hour, and a wooden playhouse designed for the smaller kids but that offered shelter from the rain as necessary. At the park she couldn't be yelled at or belittled, didn't have to listen to Carmen on the phone telling all of her friends what a drag it was being a step-mother.

Meggy, it had turned out, was an unnecessary pain in her step-mother's arse. Given that her father worked excessively long hours, Carmen dropped her at school and picked her up, supervised homework, and was supposed to cook nutritious meals and keep the house tidy. This was the quid pro quo for the fact that an underqualified thirty-year-old with no kids had no job, and no interest in getting one. The reality was that Meggy prepared her own food when she got home, did a hefty chunk of the housework, and had made the mistake of arriving home early from school one half-day when Carmen had forgotten to pick her up, to find her panting heavily, naked on the sofa while on her mobile to a person she referred to only as 'big man'.

Meggy had just gambled with that particular nugget of information, and lost. Her father (she'd recently learned a new phrase and was repeating it to herself at every given moment) was well and truly pussy-whipped. Her step-mother could do no wrong in Meggy's father's eyes. Blonde (from a bottle) and skinny (from using so many calories by being a total bitch), Carmen had only to lean over the kitchen sink sticking her butt out more than was strictly necessary, and her father would do literally anything she wanted.

As Meggy had imparted the story of Carmen's naked writhings and accompanying sex talk to her father, Carmen had appeared in tears from the master bedroom, phone records wiped, holding the shreds of one of her favourite dresses, and claimed that her step-daughter was acting up out of childish jealousy. Her freshly pussy-whipped dad had done what all men finally getting to fuck someone new and vastly younger than themselves might have done, and believed the step-mother. He bought Carmen a new dress to make up for the one 'Meggy' had destroyed, and grounded his daughter – like that made a difference in her life – punishing her by allocating all the household chores to her for the following month. Also big whoop, but her father had proved he needed a much more dramatic wake-up call. So Meggy was going to run away.

Not just down to the local shopping centre to hide in the

dressing room of some crappy store for a few hours until she was caught. Also not to her mother, current whereabouts unknown. When Meggy was four, her mother had decided a man named Garvin was a much more exciting prospect than reading bedtime stories, and disappeared off to live in a caravan in Bolton. She hadn't bothered to keep in touch with her husband or her daughter. It still hurt, but Meggy had learned that anger was a more effective way to handle rejection than sadness.

No, if there was running away to be done, it had to be properly planned. She needed money, a safe place to go, and travel plans. She might be twelve, but she was up to the challenge. Her teachers had for years described her as bright, organised, thoughtful, and mature. It was time to put those compliments to the test. A lone twelve-year-old would necessitate a call to the police from any decent-minded citizen. If she could pass as fourteen with makeup stolen from her stepmother and some borrowed clothes, it became a grey area. Old enough to go out alone at night. Mature enough to make some legal decisions herself. Able to go to a doctor alone. She'd done plenty of research. Enough that she could write a running-away blog even. Or start a hostel for kids run by kids. That would be the best. It would have beanbags and unlimited snacks, while requiring everyone to continue with their education, of course. And to eat some fresh fruit and vegetables. There was rebellion then there was self-destruction, the two things not to be confused. Reminded of the need for vitamins and fibre, Meggy took an apple from her pocket that she'd saved from the school canteen at lunch, and bit into it hard.

A man walked into the playground, sat down on a bench and opened a newspaper. Meggy lifted her head from the roundabout and checked the area for his kids. She liked meeting new people at the park. Sometimes she could have conversations with people who had no idea she was regarded as the school geek or the teacher's pet. That was nice. Sometimes those kids turned up with nice mothers, too, who would smile at Meggy and talk softly to her, ask about her school and her family.

Those days she would lie on the roundabout after the family had left and imagine being a part of it. A big sister to some wide-eyed kid who would want to sit with her and watch TV, or ask Meggy to play a game. Even better was the thought of being the little sister to someone cool, good-looking and street-wise. Someone who would sort out the bullies for her so she didn't have to. They were good imagination sessions. Today gave her nothing. Just one lone weirdo, reading some story with more pictures than text.

He wasn't looking at her and that was good. She knew better than to hang around a park with a man who was giving her the eye. The newspaper he was holding was quivering in the breeze, its corners whispering gently. Only it wasn't windy. Not at all. It was curious enough that Scotland was having such a hot summer, but the lack of wind was remarkable.

Meggy sat up and looked more closely. Sure enough, the hands clasping the outer edges of the tabloid were shaking. Not hard enough to make the headlines difficult to read, but with enough movement to remind her of one of the residents of a care home the school had made them sing carols at the previous Christmas. She'd been fascinated by how the human body could sustain life even as it destroyed itself. She had peered into the eyes of one of the elderly men and could see a trapped animal within, still conscious but terrified, looking for a way out. Bugger 'Hark the Herald' and 'Silent Night'. The reality for most of their audience was watching the clock as they waited to die.

The man changed seating positions and flexed his hands one after the other before returning to his reading. He glanced up at Meggy momentarily then looked away again. A brief spasm of his face signalled pain, and she considered going to ask if he was all right. But children weren't supposed to do that to adults. For some reason she couldn't fathom, it was regarded as disrespectful. Maybe if he'd been really old, but actually he looked younger than her dad, probably more like the step-bitch's age. That made her smile. She liked swearing in her head. It was a simple act of rebellion, but Meggy didn't care.

'Step-bitch, step-bitch, step-bitch,' she sang silently to herself.

The man's violent coughing stopped her. Perhaps he really did need help. Now, he'd put the newspaper down and was doubling over with the force of the coughs. Meggy stood up on the roundabout and checked the distant reaches of the park for dog walkers or joggers, anyone who might offer assistance if the man didn't stop hacking his guts up soon. She really wasn't sure what to do. She didn't have a mobile in her pocket. Her father had talked about buying her one last Christmas, but Carmen had said it was more of a teenager present – and Meggy didn't really need one anyway, as she got dropped off and picked up every day with her own personal taxi service. Her father had, of course, agreed with her step-mother.

It was only when he actually dropped his newspaper on the floor that Meggy jumped off the roundabout and took a tentative step towards him. Not that he was paying her any attention. He had one hand pressed to his mouth and the other clutching the wooden slats of the bench as if to stop himself from collapsing.

'Excuse me,' Meggy tried.

The coughing only became louder, drowning out any hope of being heard from that distance. She walked closer still.

'Are you okay?'

The man nodded – at least she thought he nodded – at her. But the coughing continued.

'Shall I pick up your paper for you?' she offered.

It was a pathetic thing to say, she knew that. He couldn't possibly finish reading anything in that state, but still, it felt like the polite thing to offer.

He pulled a handkerchief from his pocket and put it to his lips, wiping sideways when the hacking abated for a moment. That was Meggy's chance. She constructed a smile on her face, determined to give the appearance of being reassuring, and moved forward towards the paper just as the man deposited his handkerchief on the bench next to him.

Blood.

Tiny splatters, but blood nonetheless.

Meggy froze.

She didn't do blood. Not her own and certainly not anyone else's. The man paused his noise and stared at her, where she had frozen, mid-step, one leg raised slightly off the floor, looking at the handkerchief.

'Don't be scared,' he said. 'It looks worse than it is. Why don't you sit with me for a minute? That would make me feel better.'

He reached out for the bloodied cotton and pulled it back into his pocket.

Meggy shook her head. His eyes were bloodshot too, and she couldn't stop staring at them.

'Come on,' he said softly. 'I don't bite.'

He smiled and she saw gaps where there should have been teeth.

'My dad'll be waiting,' she said.

'Then why don't I drive you home?' He stood up, dropping the paper to the floor. 'I can get you there quicker than you can walk.'

She stared at the newspaper. He made no effort to pick it up. Meggy got the impression he'd never really been interested in it at all. She suddenly felt as if she needed to pee urgently, and she was cold. He reached a hand for her shoulder, only it wasn't shaking now. It was sure of its target, and those long fingers and yellowed nails looked perfectly strong to her. Strong and wrong.

Meggy bolted. She ran until she reached the gate to the park, and only then did she look over her shoulder, convinced he would be right behind her. Only there was no one there. The man was back on his bench. He'd picked up his newspaper after all and was reading it again. Forcing herself to come to a complete halt, Meggy stared at him. He was no threat to her now. Perhaps he never had been. She'd had no reason to run. He must have thought her crazy. Not that she was going back to the park today. Or tomorrow. Perhaps she'd give it a break for the week. He hadn't done anything wrong at all, now that she thought about it. Offered her a lift home, which was stupid. Who did that these days? There were so many warnings about the perils of accepting lifts from strangers. That was why she'd freaked out. And she was hungry. That wasn't helping.

She began the short walk home, then decided she would jog it instead. Jogging didn't mean she was still scared. It was good to get the exercise. With her hand on the back door handle, she already knew she wouldn't tell her step-mother about the coughing guy in the park. It would be put down to more attention-seeking behaviour and an overactive imagination. And what was there to tell anyway? Meggy Russell could look after herself. She was tough and smart, that's what defined her. She did her homework, had a shower, ate dinner and went to bed.

That night, Meggy Russell was still safe.

Chapter Nine

Connie stood in the postmortem suite, suited, hair net on, gloves ensuring she did nothing to disturb the evidence, and tried to imagine exactly what had passed between Angela Fernycroft and her killer, whose DNA had told them he was male and Caucasian but nothing else. Angela lay naked on a metal gurney, unable to help. Baarda was in another room taking one of the endless phone calls that plagued him. It was evening and quiet. Darkness had fallen as they'd driven over.

It was all too different. Her view wasn't the same as Angela's would have been. The brightness, the whole situation. Connie glanced into the corridor, checked no one was around, and pulled an empty cadaver trolley into the suite. She turned off the main lights quietly, leaving only that which seeped in from the small upper windows. Lying down on the empty trolley next to Angela, she turned on her side and stared at the dead mother of two.

'What woke you up?' Connie whispered, brushing a strand of hair back from Angela's face. 'Was it a noise?' She closed her eyes, imagining the crash of a leg into the chest of drawers in a house that was supposed to have been otherwise unoccupied.

'No. A noise like that would have had you moving immediately. He was right behind you when you woke. That's how your head got injured.'

Sitting up, she took hold of Angela's left leg and rolled it over the right, following with the left arm until Angela was on her side. Careful not to part the two gurneys and end up crashing to the floor, Connie moved herself behind Angela's body until her nose was within smacking distance of the back of Angela's skull, had there been life enough left in it to do so.

Sliding one arm over Angela's waist, she joined the scene.

'He spoke to you,' Connie said. 'He was holding you like a lover, but it was his voice that roused you. This man wanted you. He watched you and found something about you appealing. What was it? Did you remind him of someone? Maybe the two of you met previously, and you paid him attention.'

Connie lay quietly for a while, stroking Angela's hair as she considered how the corpse and her murderer might have crossed paths.

'The first thing he did when he had the opportunity was hold you. He'd longed to be where I am now, memorialising the moment you knew he existed. I don't think it was someone you knew. You'd have talked to them first, tried to reason with them.'

'I'm going to put the lights on now,' Ailsa Lambert's reedy voice informed her.

Connie stayed where she was and waited until Ailsa had brightened the room and come to stand over her where she lay.

'I thought I'd seen everything,' Ailsa said.

'I need to figure out if Elspeth Dunwoody is alive or dead. To do that I need to know what he whispered to Angela as he held her.'

'All right, I'll accept that as an explanation on a preliminary basis. I'd prefer it if we could continue the discussion with you in less close contact with this poor lady.'

'Sure,' Connie said, shifting off the table and rolling the sheet back over Angela's body.

'Unusual methodology. If I saw one of our Police Scotland officers trying something like that, I'd have reported them by now.'

'Are you after an apology, or for me to plead with you not to report me?' Connie asked, stripping off her gloves and throwing them into the disposables bin by the door.

'I'm not interested in either, as a matter of fact,' Ailsa said. 'I was told you had a question for me. While I have a few questions about your behaviour, let's start with what I can do for you.'

Connie nodded and leaned against a wall, arms folded.

'Is there any injury to Angela that suggests her assailant wanted to do her real harm, or that looks gratuitous or torturous?'

Ailsa mirrored Connie's stance, folding her arms, then raised her eyebrows as she thought about it.

'Only if you consider the use of the chloroform as a precursor to a rape. In terms of an actual injury, then no. Every mark on her body suggests an attempt at restraint rather than a violent assault.'

'Even though she bit him and broke his nose?'

'Even so,' Ailsa agreed. 'My turn. Why didn't you tell me you can't see colour?'

'Relevance,' Connie replied quickly. 'Did Baarda spill it?'

'No. A couple of times when we last spoke, I referenced coloured aspects of bruises and your eyes didn't go to the correct places. You have achromatopsia. If you'd told me, I could have described the injuries more appropriately for you.'

'There was me thinking your area of expertise was the dead.'

'I may be a pathologist rather than a psychologist, but if I had to hazard a guess, I'd say the reason I found you recreating a crime scene using the actual corpse involved is because you feel that your limited visual sense creates a barrier between you and the victim that you need to make up for in other ways. I want no apology, nor did I demand an explanation. You could, however, try to reduce the sarcasm when you're in my company.'

Connie took a breath, made a noise in the back of her throat, thought better of continuing the banter and uncrossed her arms instead.

'I'm sorry.'

'Accepted,' Ailsa said. 'So what caused it?'

'My sarcasm? It's been a lifelong condition.'

'I was asking about the achromatopsia, as you were aware. And I thought we'd reached an agreement.'

'Shit, sorry, Europe brings out the American in me in unfortunate ways. As far as the lack of colour vision goes, I suffered a head trauma during a game of lacrosse when I was eighteen. The injury wasn't diagnosed at the time, and I ended up hospitalised a month later. They performed surgery to deal with the bleed, which solved the neurological symptoms, but there was damage to my optical nerve. Could have been worse.'

'Indeed it could, but it was a life-changing event for you nonetheless. Walk with me,' Ailsa said, opening the postmortem suite door and turning into the corridor.

Connie followed.

'What made you choose forensic psychology as a profession?' Ailsa asked.

Ailsa took a side corridor and opened another door that led out into the warm night. Ahead was a solitary tree and some iron railings. She took a moment to breathe in the night, listening to the occasional social roar from the city's closest public houses and the intermittent traffic along Cowgate before looking to Connie for an answer.

'Personal experience,' Connie said. 'Did we swap professions without me realising?'

'Touché, but you don't just look at a crime scene and assess whether or not an offender is high or low IQ, you try to get inside their head. What I just witnessed steps beyond the border of being clinical. When you touch a corpse, interact with it, you create a bond. Flesh does not need to be living for us to feel a sense of responsibility towards it, or a desire to act kindly. Do you not find it puts something of a dent in your objectivity to get so intimate?'

'Everything I do is about figuring out motive. In this case, the motive will tell us whether or not he plans to kill again. My role is nothing like as intimate as yours. You take bodies apart, look within the most secret places. You move your hands around inside guts, literally touch brains. Nothing is hidden. I find it reassuring that if I die in unforeseen circumstances, someone like you will be here, following every pathway, inspecting every cell until you know what happened. A reckoning is important, even if it's after you're dead,' Connie said.

'Reckoning is an emotive term,' Ailsa noted. 'What conclusions have you drawn in this case so far?'

'I don't think he planned to kill the first time, so it doesn't seem as if that's his agenda. I'm more concerned that he's so ill-prepared for his victim's reaction that killing is something he'll do again by accident. Perhaps that's why he was more careful when he took Elspeth Dunwoody. I believe she's still alive, I'm just not sure why. There was a psychosexual force at play with Angela. She intrigued him. He didn't want just any woman – he wanted her. Not to dominate and hurt her but, God, I guess, to cuddle her. I don't know why I'm more grossed out by that than the thought of cold, hard violence.'

'Violence is primeval. This is the sort of blurred-line killing that makes us all feel stalked. He's a monster wearing mittens,' Ailsa said.

'You just coined the phrase "a monster wearing mittens"? And you were worried about me lying next to a corpse.'

Baarda walked out into the darkness behind them.

'Sorry to interrupt. Bad news, I'm afraid. A twelve-year-old girl has gone missing, believed abducted. MIT are calling their officers back to that as a priority. Did you get the answers you were looking for?'

'I did. Elspeth Dunwoody is alive. More than just alive. She's fulfilling a need her abductor has. He went to a lot of trouble not to harm her when he took her. He's already lost one target. It's unlikely he'll risk losing Elspeth as well. Dr Lambert, thank you, and apologies for the . . . oddness.'

'Not at all, although next time I'd prefer a warning. One last thing, how long was it from the lacrosse injury to when you first saw in black and white? I'm intrigued by injuries and their resolution. It helps my knowledge base.'

Connie looked at the tiny woman, inches shorter than her, years older, yet as on point and forceful as a missile. She considered lying, and decided Ailsa would know immediately if she did.

'A little over a year,' she replied. 'We should be going. Baarda's a kidnapping specialist, and Police Scotland sound like they could use all hands on deck.'

'Indeed,' Ailsa said. 'Call if you need me, day or night.'

They left the chief pathologist standing out under the stars.

'What was all that about?' Baarda asked.

'Nothing. She reminds me of my grandmother. The nice one. We should get back to the station.'

'You had a not-so-nice grandmother?' Baarda asked as they made their way to the car park.

'Misguided is probably the word. Impressed by titles and

professions. Too convinced by her own judgement to really see what was going on around her. You know the type.'

'I believe I do,' Baarda said, opening the car door for her.

She smiled gently at the old-fashioned gesture.

'So, tell me about this missing girl,' Connie said.

'Someone thinks they saw her being forcibly pulled into a car and raised the alarm.'

'Jesus, Baarda, how many people get abducted each year in the UK anyway? It's starting to feel like 1920s New York.'

'Around 5,000 per year. When it's a child, chances are it's a family member or friend. Unconnected child abductions are still extraordinarily rare.'

'Did the witness get a licence plate?'

'No. Unfortunately, it was another minor. Less observant and more chaotic in recollection.'

'Where was this?' Connie asked.

'School car park. Plenty of people currently at the scene. We've been asked to remain available at the station in case it turns out to be anything sinister, given my area of expertise.'

'Go to the school anyway,' Connie said. 'What's the point of sitting at the police station waiting to be asked questions by phone?'

'I thought you'd want to get on with the Dunwoody case while we're waiting. There might be nothing for us to do in any event.'

'My brain works best on one set of facts while it's occupied with something completely different. Also, that police station is cold, and it smells like takeout and armpits. I'd prefer to be outside, thank you.'

'If that's what you want. Likely to be a waste of time, though. Girl's probably had a fall-out with a parent and been dragged into a vehicle to take her home. The vast majority of these turn out to be false alarms.'

'You see, that's the problem with statistics. We rely on them to convince ourselves that we don't need to rush, that everything will turn out fine. Which in my experience is exactly when things turn out more fucked than you could ever have imagined.'

'Positive motivational talks not your thing, then,' Baarda muttered.

'Positive motivation is overrated.' Connie reclined her seat and closed her eyes. 'The only trigger human beings really respond to is abject frigging fear.'

Chapter Ten

Another of his teeth had fallen out that morning. Fergus had inspected it at length. It was a lower left molar, now in an egg cup on top of the microwave. He'd tried to recall when he'd last visited the dentist and couldn't. There had been so many medical appointments over such a protracted period that at some point he'd simply switched off from it all, attending those he could in a blur of travel – wait – answer questions – look away from the needle – wait – travel. The timeline of it all was meaningless. He wondered if he'd had toothache before the offending pearl had seen fit to desert him, but there was pain so often that he'd probably just beta-blocked it out. No doubt he was calcium deficient along with everything else. His gums bled all the time. He wasn't retaining iron. There was nothing he could do to stop the rot.

The disease was consuming him exponentially. He'd thought he had months, recently reviewed that time estimate and had concluded he should make that weeks instead. Now, he knew, he had just days left. If that was all, he had to move fast. No more watching, no more waiting, just forward momentum.

Which was why Meggy Russell was currently in the boot of his car and kicking up a storm.

She wasn't what he'd expected. At twelve, she was supposed to have been unprepared for him. Scared, and easy to threaten. Pliable. In fact, sweet little Meggy, who liked to go to the park alone and sit watching the clouds go by, often with a book in hand, apparently immune from the addiction offered by a mobile phone, had turned out to be a hellcat.

He'd waited for her outside the school library. She spent an hour there each day after lessons finished, presumably doing her homework before her mother picked her up. The mother hadn't been the normal type, either. Several years younger than he'd anticipated and a bit showy – that's what his grandmother would have called her. All tight leggings and false eyelashes. Her car had been easy to doctor that afternoon. Left out on the road a few doors down from their house, he'd sprung the bonnet and loosened the spark plugs. The mother never set off in good time to pick Meggy up, and the girl was regularly left stranded in the car park waiting for her ride.

He'd first seen Meggy back in May, during one of Angela's regular trips to Inch Park. The girl had watched Angela play with her children then shyly gone over to say hello. That was when he'd begun the process of watching Meggy as well – she was to be his gift to his new wife – before the whole Angela disaster. By then he'd done too much work. He couldn't waste months of studying Meggy's every move.

He'd been careful to keep himself hidden at her school. Parents were horribly suspicious and 'stranger aware', so he'd had to avoid the playground itself and kept to the tree-lined area across the road, turning up when the bulk of parents and buses had left, to establish the identity of the kids who stayed late. Meggy always went to the library first and got picked up late. He'd just had to follow the car home one day to figure out where she lived and what the home set-up was. The rest had been uncomplicated. Until he'd approached Meggy in the car park.

These days, he was having to take fewer precautions. When he'd begun his regime of stalking his future family, he'd had to be careful not to stand out. Now, though, with death's hand around his throat, all that mattered was taking what he wanted as quickly as possible. What did an arrest matter when he was looking at a much more permanent fate?

'Hi!' He'd waved happily to her as she'd exited the small grey-bricked block and walked to where her mum usually pulled up. 'It's Meggy, right? Sorry about this, but your mum's car broke down. She asked me to come and get you.'

Meggy had stared at him, not in a friendly way.

'My mum?' Meggy had asked.

'Aye, pretty lady, sporty-looking, goes by the name of Carmen Russell. You remember her?' he'd joked.

'My mum?' Meggy said again.

The look she was giving him could have lanced boils.

'Yes,' Fergus said, his voice losing its former jollity.

Meggy had her backpack clutched in her arms like a shield.

'How do you know her then?' she'd asked.

This question he'd anticipated.

'I live on your street, Durward Grove, just a few doors down. I saw your mum having problems with her car and offered to help. She explained that you'd be stuck at school with no one to fetch you.'

A new emotion had flickered across Meggy's face then, a ripple of self-doubt, he'd thought. 'We met in our local park, remember?'

'You were ill,' Meggy said.

'That's nothing to worry about; it was just a cough. Sorry if I scared you. I went to the doctor and got some medicine.

All better now.' He gave another grin to show her just how fine he felt.

She flinched and he put away his yellowing teeth with their recent addition of a raw section of empty gum.

'How long have you lived near us then?' Meggy asked.

'Couple of years. I see your mum at the local shops sometimes and we chat. She's very proud of you. Always talking about how well you're doing at school.'

A shutter came down. Whatever he'd said, Meggy was not just unconvinced, she was looking thunderous.

'Liar,' she said quietly. 'You'd better go. I'm going to tell a teacher.'

There was a fraction of a second where he didn't know what to do, but a lack of preparation was how Angela had ended up dead. It was the moment in which she'd whipped back her head and broken his nose. It was the stupidity of putting his hand over her mouth with nothing to protect his fingers from her teeth. Not this time. It couldn't go wrong again.

Fergus leapt forward, punching as he went. His fist hit Meggy's face full on in the nose. He knew from bitter personal experience how painful and debilitating that was. It did the trick perfectly. The girl went flat out backwards like a toppling domino. Her head hit grass rather than pavement. He was grateful for that. One unforeseen death was acceptable. More than that would be totally incompetent.

Slinging her backpack over his shoulder then sliding both arms beneath her, Fergus picked her up. The boot flipped open when he hit the switch on his key fob, and he deposited her flopping body inside. There wasn't time to secure her, that was his only problem. In his head, she was going to be utterly convinced by him knowing her mother and her address. She was going to climb into the back seat of the car and sit there patiently as he drove her home. He'd engaged the child safety on the rear doors, locked the windows mechanism, and had the back windows tinted for privacy months earlier. But there was something he hadn't anticipated – a wrong word. She'd known he was lying. He just had no idea how.

Now, he was halfway home and she was hammering at the boot of the car. It was upsetting. Almost as bad as Elspeth doing nothing but sobbing all day. He'd taken to slipping sedatives into her food to get some peace. He was going to need a new prescription from his doctor if he had to quieten both his wife and his daughter from now on.

Quarter of an hour later, he arrived home and readied himself for a fight.

Meggy was equally ready. The screaming started when the first rays of light hit the inside of the boot. He smashed an ungentle hand down on her mouth, leaned forward and growled at her.

'Keep screaming like that and you'll leave me no choice but to throttle you. You think I want that? I'm a nice man, Meggy, but you're not being a nice girl, and that's not fair. Now shut up, or I'll hurt you.'

That did stop her screaming, to his amazement. She glared at him, an unmistakably furious stare, more adult than childlike, as if he'd just crashed a wedding and vomited down the bride's dress.

Fergus looked away from her, pulling her arms upwards so he could throw her over his shoulder, and carried her into the house, setting her down only when they were inside the kitchen and he'd locked the door securely. The internal door through to the lounge was open. Meggy took a look at it, turned back to Fergus and ran at him full pelt, punching his groin as she charged.

'Fuck you,' she shouted. 'I'm going to kill you!'

Fergus held her by the shoulders, keeping her at arm's length.

'Does your mother let you speak to her with that filthy mouth?' he yelled.

'Carmen's not my mother. She's a bitch! You lied about everything. Help,' she yelled. 'Help me. I've been kidnapped!'

Fergus wished he could just hit her again, but Meggy's eyes were already blackening from the earlier blow he'd dealt her, and she had a dry trail of blood snaking from nose to chin. Carmen wasn't the girl's mother at all. His research had been flawed. That was what came of rushing. His head ached. He wanted her to be quiet now.

'I won't hurt you,' he told her. 'I mean, I will if you don't stop. I'll have to. I can't just let you carry on. But if you'll just quit it, everything'll be fine.'

'You're going to rape me. And kill me. I'm not stupid. I watch the news. They teach us about men like you at school.'

'Don't be disgusting. I've no intention of raping anyone. What would my wife think of me if I did that?'

Meggy took a step back, stared at him.

'Are you simple?' she asked.

Fergus gritted his teeth. He wanted to lie down. By now, Meggy should have been introduced to Elspeth, the two of them getting to know one another in their little flat. He was overdue his painkillers, and there was a sensation in his left arm that had started off no more than a pinching and was now circling around, vice-like, making it hard to breathe.

'I'm not simple. You shouldn't say that. It's rude.'

'You abducted me. You think your wife's going to care about anything else? Where is she, anyway? Is she here?'

Meggy turned and ran. Finally, Fergus thought. It would be easier to control her deeper inside the house than in the kitchen.

Reaching for a carving knife, long ago hidden on a high shelf, Fergus followed her in as she threw open doors, shouting at the top of her voice, screaming at him to stay away from her as she retreated to the stairs, taking them two at a time. At last, in the upper corridor, Meggy stopped, her entire concentration aimed at the silverware dangling from his right hand.

'Wait there,' he ordered, pointing the knife in her direction.

There was a single door off the landing. Fergus walked to it, checking an upper eyehole that was situated in the usual place, then kneeling down, knife still extended in her direction, to take a quick look through a second peephole that had been inserted at thigh height in the door. All clear. He detached a set of keys from his belt and threw them at her feet.

'Largest silver key,' he said. 'Open it up.'

Sluggish tears plopped onto the frayed carpet at her feet. She was all fought out. Between the pulsatile waves of pain in his temples and the rapidly worsening ice-pick sensation in his chest, Fergus could only be grateful. Snatching up the keys, Meggy expended her ebbing energy attempting to hurl a last insult before opening the door. All that arrived was a pitiful mewing sound.

'Tired,' Fergus murmured. 'Leave the keys in the lock and go in. I'll see you tomorrow.'

'What's in there?' Meggy whispered, peering inside, along the darkened corridor to where a single lamp cast light in a bedroom.

'New mother. Maybe you'll like this one better.'

He pushed Meggy forwards, locked the door behind her and stood at the top of the stairs. The steps beneath were a tide wavering towards him then away. Fergus extended quivering fingers, hoping to find the handrail in the same place he'd left it, but distance was stretching.

'Can't get back down,' he muttered. 'Light's gone off. Where's switch?'

He reached out blindly in his own personal dark, the

movement catching his brain unawares and turning him side-ways. One foot stumbled over the other.

Fergus went sideways into the void of the staircase, leading with his left shoulder, wondering how he could be falling when a second earlier he'd been standing completely still in his own home. He'd never been on a roller coaster, but he imagined it would feel like this. On the swings as a small child, he'd always imagined his mother smiling before him, arms outstretched. She wouldn't desert him now, not when he needed her most. As he began his cartwheel down the narrow staircase, he smiled, seeing her appear at the bottom, knowing no harm could come to him with her ready to keep him safe.

The side of his head hit first, five steps from the top. His neck followed with a crunch normally reserved for abattoirs, and the breath was crushed from his lungs as the left side of his ribcage connected thereafter. Still Fergus smiled.

He'd known it was coming. There was no tunnel, no bright light, no angelic choir welcoming him in, but no pain either. Better even than that, no fear. He could die knowing he finally had a wife and child who would miss him. No brother, he hadn't had time to organise that, but that wasn't going to stop him from passing over this time. Fergus Ariss was dying, and he was glad.

Chapter Eleven

The school grounds were awash with blue flashing lights. Connie and Baarda parked outside on the road and remained pavement-bound, watching. One side of the car park, just outside the entrance to the clearly marked library, was cluttered with officers talking over the head of a visibly upset Asian girl to an irate adult who might have been her mother. At the far end of the car park near the entrance to the road, other police officers were busy with crime scene tape, sticking markers on the ground and taking photographs. A high-pitched wailing echoed from an area largely hidden by a hedge. Connie could just make out another cluster of heads, some going to and fro, others leaning inwards.

'Guess they've figured out the missing girl's identity,' Connie said quietly.

Baarda was already looking up and down the road.

'What's up?' she asked.

'Cameras. The school should have some in the playground, but I'm not seeing any. No traffic lights on this road, and no industry or retail, either. If you were going to take a girl from a school in this area, given the lack of security, this would be a good target.'

'You think he found the school first, then identified a student who suited him?' Connie asked. 'That's clever.'

'That's what I'd have done. Minimise the risk of getting caught, then work a kidnapping backwards from that. Reverse-engineered crime. The issue is not the criminal. It's the efficacy of the police response. We should already be canvassing the neighbourhood for suspicious vehicles, or people seen hanging around. Always amazes me that the first reaction of so many officers is to group together and repeat information-gathering when the best course is to spread out and obtain diverse context.'

'You should get in there and tell them that.' Connie leaned back against Baarda's car, studying the body language of the schoolgirl as she looked from the police to her presumptive mother, appearing increasingly exasperated.

'I'm only on backup at request. I have no authority in there. Nothing worse than one officer treading on another's toes.'

'I think the scene requires less Eton manners and more leadership, don't you? No one's listening to that girl. If you can ignore your ridiculously frustrating tendency towards Victorian etiquette – no offence intended—'

'I doubt that,' Baarda muttered.

'Then I might be able to help with your witness before she's either fed information that organically changes her story, or she becomes exhausted and gives inaccurate information just to get everyone off her back.'

'How did you figure that out from here?'

'She's hugging herself, making fists with her hands, refusing to look at the woman who's either a relative or a guardian next to her. Shoulders getting higher by the minute. She's stressed and self-protecting. Do you need me to write a textbook, or do you want to assert yourself and maybe achieve something?'

'Keep up,' Baarda said, walking towards a small pedestrian gate near the library. 'And I resent the suggestion that I'm somehow so polite that it's a failing in my duty,' he remarked over his shoulder.

'That's not what I said,' Connie told him, jogging slightly to catch up. 'It's more that being with you is like being an extra in a Jane Austen movie.'

Baarda glared at her before flashing his badge at the officer guarding the gate. 'Kidnap unit,' he said. 'Superintendent Overbeck from MIT asked me to consult. Who's in charge?'

The officer pointed in the direction of the furthest congregation of bodies, and Baarda strode off in that direction. Connie turned her attention to the girl, who was now openly crying as too many people asked her questions at once.

'Okay, that's enough,' Connie announced as she forced her way into the circle of adults surrounding the child.

'Who're you? This is a crime scene, love. You're not allowed to be here.'

An enormous officer decided to insert himself in front of her, straining his shoulders outwards to increase his size.

'Dr Woolwine. I'm assisting DI Baarda, who's on secondment to MIT from the specialist kidnap unit. You should go and check with him. What I'm going to do now is take this young woman inside where it's quieter, sit her down and let her speak. Is that her mother?'

He deferred to the officer at his side, who nodded and stepped away for Connie to get closer.

'The girl's name is Melanie Chao. And yes, this is her mother. The lady was shouting the place down before she even got through the gate.'

The more senior officer whispered the last part, but it was unnecessary. The mother was still mid-rant in what Connie guessed was Mandarin.

'Mrs Chao, I need to take Melanie inside now,' Connie said, slipping her right shoulder into the small gap between mother and daughter, shielding Melanie's face a little from her parent. 'You can come with us; in fact, I'd encourage you to. This police officer here . . .' She waved a hand at the officer who'd provided the names.

'DC Champion,' he said.

'DC Champion will be coming with us to take notes. Melanie is in no trouble at all, but we need to get relevant information out of her fast without any distractions, so I'll be asking you to remain calm and quiet. Can you do that?'

Melanie stared at Connie, who pointed towards the library steps and set off before Mrs Chao could formulate an answer.

'Why do you need to question her again? She told the police everything she saw. My daughter should be at home studying. I want to know why she was outside at all. She was supposed to stay inside the library until five o'clock. Do the staff here not monitor students at all?' Mrs Chao continued the diatribe as she hurried along behind them.

Connie spotted a small room, directed Melanie to go ahead, then looked pointedly at Mrs Chao.

'A girl is apparently missing. I don't know much about the circumstances, and I understand this is very upsetting, but it's going to get much more upsetting very quickly if any harm comes to Melanie's schoolmate. I need your daughter relaxed before she tries to recall what she saw. I'm pretty sure Melanie is going to get special dispensation tomorrow regarding home-work, but now I need absolute quiet. You can come in, but you don't speak.'

'I don't see what more Melanie can—'

'Then you remain outside,' Connie said. 'Take a seat, Mrs Chao. I'm going to be as long as it takes to make your daughter feel safe and comfortable talking to me. You'll just have to wait.'

'I'll be silent,' Mrs Chao murmured, following Connie in.

Melanie was sipping from a bottle of water as they entered.

Connie sat Mrs Chao behind her daughter to keep the girl focused.

'Melanie, I'm not a police officer, and you don't have to speak to me, but I'm hoping you will. I'm a forensic psychologist, and at the moment I'm working with a policeman who's helping on this case. I want to help you clarify what you saw. DC Champion, can you give me a rundown of what you know so far?'

'Sure.' He flipped back a couple of pages in his notebook. 'At approximately half past four, Melanie ran into the library looking flustered. She tried to speak to the librarian, but the lady was on the phone, so Melanie was told to wait and remain quiet. She became increasingly upset, so the librarian finally hung up the call, at which point Melanie explained what she'd seen. The librarian spent some time trying to ascertain if it was accurate, but after some minutes, she did decide to call 999. She said that Melanie had seen what she thought might have been a girl being pulled into a car.'

Melanie began shaking her head furiously.

'No,' she said. 'That's not right. She wouldn't listen to me, and then everything she said to the police was wrong. I've been trying to explain.'

'Okay, we're going to do it slowly and just once,' Connie told her. 'I'm going to ask you questions, then you can take it from there. As much detail as possible. No pressure. No one's recollection is perfect. It's actually not possible. What I need is for you to close your eyes, put your hands loosely in your lap, and relax your shoulders.'

Melanie did as she was told. 'Are you going to hypnotise me?'

'No, we don't do parlour tricks. This is memory heightening. Like a visualisation technique. You ready?'

'Um, yeah.'

'Okay. What did you have for lunch?'

Mrs Chao butted in predictably and on cue. 'I don't see—'

'In or out, Mrs Chao, you decide. Last chance.'

Mrs Chao huffed. 'In,' she said quietly.

Connie watched Melanie give a tiny satisfied smile. Nothing won a child's trust like getting one over on an irritating parent.

'I had a ham sandwich and a smoothie,' Melanie said. 'It was all a bit over-chilled, like they had the fridges turned up too high.'

'Great. Did you eat it anyway?' Connie asked.

'Sure. I'd had PE in the morning, so I was hungry.'

'What classes did you have after lunch?' Connie continued.

'Chemistry and English.'

'Did anything annoy you in either of those classes?'

'No, nothing. Why is that . . .' Melanie paused. 'Wait. The boy in front of me in chemistry was chewing gum. I could hear him. English was fine, but the teacher set more homework than usual, and that's not fair when we have a maths test tomorrow.'

'Do you remember the look on your English teacher's face when she was setting the homework?' Connie asked.

Another pause.

'I can! She was screwing up her eyes and looking slightly away from us at the board, like she knew she was being mean,' Melanie said. 'Is that weird? Why can I remember that?'

'Because you were feeling cross at the time. Whenever you experience raised levels of emotion, your senses work overtime to assess a situation. You were cross, your body's natural reaction was to figure out what was going wrong in order to rectify the situation. All that increased brain function made you more observant, which means you have an accurate memory of the moment.'

'Oh,' Melanie said. 'I get it now.'

'That's good, but I don't want you trying too hard to remember anything. When we do that, we fill in blanks of information using common sense or deduction. But that's not true memory. At first you thought there was nothing annoying that had happened today, then it hit you. That's reliable memory because you weren't searching for it.'

'Got it. What do you want to know?'

'What time did you get to the library?' Connie asked.

'Three thirty, as soon as school finished. I came straight here. I put my coat on the back of my chair, took my books out of my bag and sat in the furthest corner from the front door because that's the quietest place.'

'What were you studying?'

'Well, maths, because like I said, we have—'

'A test tomorrow, but what exactly, Melanie? Were you using a textbook, did you have your calculator out?'

'No, I was revising from a worksheet. It's algebraic equations, so the calculator is irrelevant. I'd done one whole sheet – you have to write every step of each equation out and show your working – and I was moving on to the back of the sheet. Then I decided I wanted some fresh air and went outside for a minute and that's when I saw—'

'You're rushing now,' Connie said. 'Stop a minute. You're still inside the library, at the desk, working. Something inside you felt a need. What senses were triggered? Were you too hot, too cold, suddenly hungry, did your neck ache?'

Melanie's cheeks darkened in tone.

'What is it? There's nothing you can't tell us,' Connie said.

'It's stupid. Kind of embarrassing.'

'Were you embarrassed, then?'

Melanie nodded.

'Good. Find that feeling again. Were you still in your seat when you first felt that?'

'Yeah,' Melanie said quietly.

'Okay, in your own time, try to explain what was happening.'

'Well, I needed, you know . . .' She gave a sideways glance back at her mother, then rolled her eyes. 'I needed to fart, and there's no bogs in the library. I couldn't do that inside, so I went out.'

Mrs Chao was unable to resist the tut but managed to refrain from commenting.

'That's fine, Melanie. These are helpful memories. Nothing to be embarrassed about with us. This is in the past. I'm only asking you to concentrate on how you were feeling. Carry on.'

'Okay, so I just left everything where it was, and I suppose I kind of rushed out through the front door and down the steps, and then there's some hedges at the bottom closer to the road. I didn't want anyone walking past and hearing, you know?'

'I get it,' Connie said softly.

'My stomach was hurting a bit, and I sort of stood pretending to check my watch and look out at the road as if I was waiting for my mum. I didn't want anyone asking me what I was doing, and I realised there'd been some noise in the car park, but even now I'm not sure what it was. Voices, I think, but I only decided that afterwards. I don't remember any words. It's just like there was definitely something going on. I came back out from behind the bushes, and I was kind of just wanting to get back inside. I felt a bit daft, to be honest, rushing out like that. There was this guy putting something in the boot of a car. I wasn't really even looking at it, but there was something that made me keep on watching.'

'So he didn't pull the girl into the main bit of the car?' Connie checked.

'No. That was just what the librarian told the police on the phone. She wasn't really listening to me. I think at first she thought I was making it up. I tried to tell her she was getting it wrong while she was on the phone, but she told me if I wasn't quiet, I'd get a detention.'

'Let's go back,' Connie said. 'You're coming back up the steps, you're aware that something is going on but not concerned about it yet. Something to do with the man and the boot.'

'I just can't figure out what made me think it was a girl . . . I'm scared I just made it up in my head, and now there are parents here freaking out, and what if I was wrong?'

'Melanie, none of that's your problem, or your responsibility. That's what the police are for. You have a picture inside your head, and I need to see it. No rush, no pressure. Like I said, don't try to fill in the blanks. Relax again.'

The girl breathed in, out, depositing her shaking hands back in her lap.

'Is this a co-ed school?' Connie asked.

'It is,' DC Champion confirmed, taking a break from his note-taking.

'So there are boys here too, but you got the impression that it was a girl in trouble?'

Melanie's head flicked up.

'That was 'cos of the voices. They'd been arguing, and I knew there was a deep voice and a girl's voice.' She gave Connie a firmer smile.

'When you think back to what you heard, can you hear any of the words at all, maybe a name or a phrase? Any specific accents?'

'Didn't notice any unusual accents, so I guess they were from round here. I know I thought they were angry at each other. Speaking fast – and the words were all at the same time, like they were talking over each other.'

'That's really good, Melanie. Now, I want you to think about what you saw. Imagine where you were standing near the bushes.

Remember which way you turned to go back inside. To your left or your right?'

'My right,' the girl said softly.

'Good, now close your eyes again. It's all still there in your memory. You're outside, the ground is hard beneath your feet, because it hasn't rained for a while. There's some traffic noise from the road outside the school. You can hear the argument at a distance, and you know something unusual is going on. You need to get back inside and carry on working, because you haven't finished your algebra yet. So you turn to your right to go back towards the library steps. Just hold it there. Don't take a step yet. There's a tree out there, right? Between the edge of the library and the car park exit. So you didn't have a clear view to start with. When you begin to walk, which direction do you look in?'

'I was already looking towards the voices, but the tree was in the way then. It's leafy at the moment. As I reached the bottom of the library steps, it had all gone quiet. I took a couple of steps up, and by then I had a view past the edge of the tree. I could see the back of a man . . .' She paused.

Connie held a hand up to DC Champion and Mrs Chao to keep them quiet.

'Only at first I thought I wasn't looking at the people whose voices I'd been hearing. I wasn't sure it was a man.' Melanie banged a hand on the desk. 'I wasn't sure it was a man because he was so thin, like really crazy thin, and he was wearing all denim. These super-skinny jeans and this jacket with a tight waist, and I remember thinking I'd seen clothes like that in the retro store and that I'd never seen a man that thin.'

'His hair?' Connie asked.

'Don't know. I think he had some sort of hat or cap, but I'm not sure. I remember just staring at his legs and thinking I'd never seen a grown-up with legs like that.'

'Was he tall or short?'

She shrugged. 'Kind of tall. I wasn't close enough to compare him to me, but not, like, short or anything.'

'Skin colour?'

'White. Something happened when he closed the boot.'

Connie sat back in her chair. This time she didn't need to persuade anyone else to keep the silence. Melanie was breathing hard, her face a knot of concentration, head tilted to one side. Mrs Chao had one hand over her mouth, and DC Champion was leaning in, pen at the ready.

'No, it's no good. I can't remember anything else.'

There was an almost inaudible sigh. Champion sat back in his seat.

'No problem,' Connie said. 'What I'm really curious about is that at some point you looked away. Even though by then you were worried about the fact that there might be a girl in that car. I don't think I'd have looked away in those circumstances.'

Mrs Chao changed tack in a heartbeat.

'My daughter can't help any more. Now you're pressuring her. She's told you everything . . .'

Melanie reached a hand back to her mother, who met it with her own.

'It's all right, Mum,' she said. 'The lady's just helping. The man started to turn. I thought he was about to look at me. It was the first time I'd felt scared. Before that I was sort of curious. I wasn't sure what I was seeing.' Melanie put her head back and looked at the ceiling. 'When I came past the tree, he was still shutting the boot, but he had one hand in there until the last second, like he was pushing something down. It made me feel sick, because I remember thinking if he was pushing down, was something trying to push back up? I don't mean I was thinking that at the time, but now that feels right. Then I noticed how skinny he was, like – what's the word – gaggly?'

'Gangly?' Connie asked.

'Yes!' Melanie gave a light slap to the table. 'Have you seen that film, the one with Santa Claus and the Easter bunny and the Oogie Boogie man?'

It was Connie's turn to smile. '*The Nightmare Before Christmas*? I love that movie.'

'That's it. The man stood at the boot of the car was like Jack Skellington, like all bones so that his head looked too big for his body, but dressed in really crappy denim. It looked a bit dirty, too, kind of yellow.'

'Good,' Connie said.

'When he slammed the boot shut, he looked to his right, then to his left, and his head was turning in my direction and I didn't want him to see me looking, so I looked away as quick as I could and walked into the library.'

'Did you see much of his face?'

'No, I'm sorry. The car was dark, though — either blue or grey — and shite.'

'We're going to show Melanie some photos of different cars, to see what we can figure out about the make and model,' DC Champion said. 'She didn't notice the number plate.'

'Young people usually don't,' Connie said. 'Adult witnesses often miss vital information about an offender or the mechanics of a crime because we're all so conditioned by TV to get the licence plate. Often, that's been tampered with or stolen and doesn't help at all. I think the details Melanie's been able to recall by not focusing on the licence plate will prove much more useful.'

Melanie gave her a shy smile of thanks. 'Actually,' she added, 'about the number plate . . . the reason I didn't get it was because it was covered with mud. Like really covered, all over.'

'Clever girl,' Connie said. 'One last thing. Did you hear anything in particular when he drove away? Anything about the car and how it was moving?'

'Um, no, and I was listening carefully, because I wanted him to leave and not come into the library. I was still worried he might have noticed me.'

'So no squealing tyres or revving engine? Nothing like that?'

'Nope,' Melanie said. 'Nothing like that.'

Connie gave her a nod. She was pleased to see the mother still holding her daughter's hand. Parents reacted oddly to children when they were forced to interact with any type of official, whether that was the police, or doctors, or a school administrator. Melanie would be scared for a while, and she was going to need her mother to reassure her. Someone had kidnapped a kid, and when the media broke the story, every parent within a hundred miles was going to be freaked out.

'You did great. I'm going to leave DC Champion to look at those car pictures with you then hopefully you can go home. If you feel stressed or scared, it's important to ask for help. It's normal. Don't you keep that bottled up, okay?'

Tears appeared suddenly in Melanie's eyes.

'I'd better go have a chat with DI Baarda. The information you've given will definitely help,' Connie said. She exited the library to cross the car park and join a group of officers stood around a crying woman and a man with a face that encapsulated all the tension of an unexploded bomb.

'Are you normally late collecting her, Carmen?' the man demanded.

Older than Carmen by several years and by multiple style generations, they made an odd couple.

'Because if you're always this late, then someone could have figured out that she's always kept waiting out here,' he finished.

'Don't you dare do that. You're not going to make me feel guilty about this. Maybe Meggy's mother finally turned up and decided to try her hand at a bit of parenting,' the woman screeched.

'Meggy's mother left years ago. We've moved house twice since then, and she's not the least bit interested in Meggy. If she really did want to see her, she could have just asked. She knows I wouldn't ever stop her from seeing her daughter.'

Baarda stepped forward, hands at his side. Connie was impressed. Too many police officers intervened in heated situations with their arms up, palms forward, which without fail made people feel even more aggressive.

'We'll obviously do our best to trace Meggy's mother if you'll give us her details, Mr Russell, but we have to consider wider options.'

'None of this is helping. Do you have cars out around the city looking for my daughter? You should be closing all the roads within the city and checking every vehicle. Why are we standing around talking?' Meggy's father was ashen and shaking.

'The first thing we need to establish is that Meggy hasn't simply gone elsewhere, become bored of waiting or decided to go to a friend's house. There's no firm evidence yet that an abduction did actually take . . .' Connie caught his eye and raised her hand flat, fingers outstretched, dipping it left and right – maybe, maybe not. '. . . place.' His voice trailed off. 'Just give me a moment.'

Connie began walking away from the group, leaving Baarda to catch up with her, where they couldn't be overheard.

'What did the witness say?' Baarda asked.

'She heard raised voices, a man and a girl. Sounded like an argument, but she couldn't make out the details. Then everything went silent. He didn't drag the girl into the body of the car, though. That was the librarian summarising during the 999 call. Your witness says the man dumped something in the boot, and she got the impression he was having to put pressure down before he could shut the boot. We have a good description of him, less so of the vehicle. Muddy number plate, dark paint, blue or grey. The man looked around before driving off, presumably to see if anyone had witnessed the event. Drove off slowly, though, no obvious signs of panic, which if you've just stashed a girl in the boot of your car is unusually controlled.'

'How credible is the information?'

'Teenage girls are too often passed off as hysterical or attention-seeking. Something sounded wrong, so she checked it out, and she saw behaviour that made her feel scared. She didn't embellish or dramatise. I believe her.'

'Doesn't mean it's Meggy Russell. There could still be other explanations.'

'Any of which would require a coincidence at this moment. One girl thinks another has been kidnapped. Independently, parents turn up to collect a child who isn't where she should be.'

Baarda sighed. 'Okay. We'll put out a general alert, distribute Meggy's details. I'll get officers checking out Meggy's known friends in case she was reporting any concerns. We'll also need to access her social media, see if she'd made contact with anyone suspicious online.'

'I've done all I can. I'm going to Angela's house. I need to go back into the first crime scene, immerse myself in it, figure out what it was about Angela that attracted her killer. You coming?'

'I think they need my help here,' Baarda said.

'I think they do, too,' Connie said. 'Watch the woman – Carmen. The father's expressing distress and upset through anger. Carmen's just pissed off at getting the blame. Not sure I'm seeing much real emotion there.'

'You think she might be involved?' Baarda asked.

'It's not that, but she doesn't genuinely seem to care enough about Meggy, so maybe she was regularly late to pick her up. If that was the case, you'll need to check for suspicious activity in the area going back a while. I'd guess that someone was watching the family home as well as the school.'

'We'll start canvassing the area now,' he said. 'Thank you, Connie. I appreciate the assistance.'

'That's okay. Sorry I called you an extra from a Jane Austen movie.'

'No you're not,' Baarda said, already walking away. 'Detective Sergeant,' Connie heard him shout. 'I want a helicopter in the sky straight away looking for a dark blue-grey car leaving this area or parked up with mud-obscured plates. I want this man left in no doubt that we're looking for him.'

Chapter Twelve

Meggy stared at the inside of the door. The peepholes worked from the outside inwards. That was horrible. Being locked in was bad enough, but the thought of being locked in and spied on was extra disgusting.

As soon as he'd closed the door behind her, there'd been thumping and crashing on the staircase, and Meggy thought she'd heard him cry out. Slowly, she'd tried turning the doorknob, holding her breath with hopeful anticipation. She tried not to let her disappointment turn to tears, shifting her attention instead to the darkened flat. A bloom of light came from a crack in a doorway at the end of the corridor. Meggy wasn't a fan of darkness. She didn't dislike it as much as she hated the sight of blood, but still. She wanted to go to the light, to find a safe place.

Already she was imagining fashioning a weapon, searching for a phone, climbing out of a window. But the man was a creep, not an idiot. He'd known enough about Carmen to fool Meggy briefly and get her talking. He'd watched her, known Carmen was often late. And he'd been in the park that day.

She wondered how he'd found her. Not online. Meggy

couldn't be bothered with all that social media rubbish. YouTube videos sometimes for science projects, and there were some really funny ones on there. But it wasn't like she'd been fooled by some old git trying to make out he was fourteen years old and looking for a girlfriend. She knew better than to give out her details over the internet.

A faint cough came from the end room as Meggy contemplated what her next step should be. She backed up against the door, her breath a hot lump in her throat. There were two options. Either the man had delivered her to someone for purposes best not considered in detail, or there was someone else here, like her, trapped and scared. If she were a delivery – Deliveroo! her brain screamed with inappropriate jollity – then she would be expected, and avoidance would be temporary at best.

Taking a shaky step forward, one arm reached out to the wall to keep her steady, Meggy walked towards the light. Beneath her fingertips, the sensation was of damp and crumbling paint. Her feet, lifting slowly as she went, registered the stickiness of old carpet. But the worst of it was the smell. In the near dark, with so little else to think about, that smell was everything, and it was getting worse the closer she moved to the room at the end.

Unmistakably, nauseatingly, she knew it was human shit. There was a proper word for that, a non-swear word, but her advanced vocabulary had gone on strike. Her imagination hadn't. She had a vision of a genetically challenged half man, half beast, chained loosely to the floor, ready to pounce when she pushed the door fully open. A beast that needed freeing. Or that needed to kill. Or that needed to torture her first, then kill her, then eat her. Slow was worse, she told herself. Whatever was going to happen was going to happen. But she wasn't going to creep towards it like some stupid slug sliding inevitably towards the salt.

The battle cry she released was half Amazonian, half William Wallace. Raising her arm ready to strike, determined to go down fighting, she charged. Kicking the door, she flew into the room, eyes scrunched, teeth bared as she prepared for the horror within.

It took her a moment to find the creature. Shivering beneath an iron-frame bed, face shoved beneath a pillow, naked and stinking with the matter covering her legs and the floor, was a woman. Meggy didn't want to admit to herself that in spite of her terror, there had been a seed of hope that she might find an adult in there. Someone not evil, who would actually take care of her. This wasn't that.

'Is there anyone here who can help me?' Meggy asked. 'Please? I don't know where I am.'

There was more than one room in the flat. Perhaps there was a real grown-up in here somewhere.

The woman looked up at the sound of her voice. That was progress. At least she could still hear and understand. She looked at Meggy, glanced away, frowned, looked again.

Meggy took a small step towards her, and the woman did her best to slither into the far corner beneath the bed.

'I won't hurt you,' Meggy said, the words, those adult words, sounding entirely foreign coming from her mouth.

The woman was staring at the open doorway.

'That man's not here. He locked me in and left. It's just us then, is it?'

The woman stared at her then looked down at her own legs. She began to cry. Meggy considered doing the same. Half an hour earlier she'd been standing in the school car park and wondering what was for dinner. Now she was trapped in a mostly dark, unknown place with a woman who'd completely lost control of herself.

'My name's Meggy,' she said. 'What's yours?'

The response was louder sobbing.

She bent down and held her hand out to the woman peering from below the pillow. As she reached in, the mess on the floor gave off not just a stench, but palpable warmth. The realisation dawned that the woman had lost control of herself when she'd heard the door open. Presumably she'd thought the man was coming in. The full meaning of that sank in as Meggy stared at the physical and metaphorical pile of shit she'd landed in. If this grown-up couldn't fight him, couldn't bear the thought of what he might do to her, then how was Meggy supposed to survive it?

Weapon, she thought again. This is no good. Sitting here is doing no good. I have to find something to fight him with. She looked around. There were five plastic hooks on the wall, each with the same pale pink dress hanging from it, a darker pink ribbon at its waist, tiny white buttons down the front shaped like daisies. Who the hell needed five dresses exactly the same? Meggy wondered.

The light source was a small plastic child's lamp with a peeled-paint Disney figure at its base. Hitting him over the head with that would be like smashing someone over the head with a paper plate, but she did need it to look around with and that meant unplugging the short lead and finding other power points.

'I'm going to have a look round and I need the light. Will you be okay if I take it out of here?'

Then the woman met Meggy's eyes, shaking her head in tiny small jerks at first, then whipping it to and fro, her matted hair flying.

'No,' she moaned. 'No, don't take the light, don't, don't take it.'

'All right, but we have to do something, because I can't stay here. I'm going to have to move the lamp to look around, but you're coming with me, and we're going to find something to clean you. You'll have to do it, I'm not . . .' Meggy tried not to let too much disgust show on her face. 'But I won't leave you. What's your name?'

'Elspeth,' she whispered. 'How old are you?'

'Twelve,' Meggy said, delighted that the woman – Elspeth – was finally forming words. Less pleased when the woman began to laugh, then cackle, then to cry again.

'Twelve?' Elspeth cried. 'How can you help? We're going to die here. He's insane!'

'Stop,' Meggy ordered. 'Don't do that. If I don't cry then you're not allowed to, either. Grown-ups aren't supposed to be stupider than kids. It's not fair.' She marched across to the doorway, identified the nearest electrical socket then marched back to the lamp. 'I'm unplugging this now, but it won't be for long, so you need to get up and follow me. And you can't cry any more. It's crappy of you.' She pulled the plug and waited for the hysterics.

What she got was the noise of dragging then shuffling. A hand hit her shoulder first, then trailed down her arm to grasp her hand, hard. It was all Meggy could do not to pull away. Finding a weapon was important, but running water was coming a close second.

'Is there a bathroom? We have to deal with' – she waved a hand generally in the vicinity of Elspeth's body – 'all this.'

Elspeth managed a nod.

'Show me.'

They went out into the hallway. The bathroom was on the left.

In the ceiling was a small inset light. Meggy tried the switch on the wall.

'Won't work,' Elspeth said. 'He controls the electricity from outside for the light and the heating. If I'm good, he turns the lights on.'

'You should have a shower,' Meggy said. 'Tell me afterwards.'

The shower unit was nothing more than a head set into the wall and a circular base. No glass surround, or even a curtain that could have been pulled down.

As Elspeth showered, Meggy put her hand in the water to test the temperature. It was warm enough to be comfortable but not really hot. She looked around. A plastic sink sat in a vanity unit. He'd removed the doors of the cabinet the same way he'd taken the mirror from the wall. She didn't like it. The man was much cleverer than she'd wanted him to be. He'd thought about everything. Really thought about it, not just like some stupid TV show where you could see fifty different ways you could get yourself out of trouble.

It took a few minutes for the stench to subside, but eventually Elspeth stepped out of the shower and took a small towel from the radiator.

'I'm sorry,' she said quietly as she rubbed herself dry.

'That's okay,' Meggy told her. 'Do you have any clean clothes anywhere?'

'Pyjamas, in the bedroom. I'll wrap the towel around for now. His name's Fergus.'

'Fergus,' Meggy repeated. 'Did he tell you that? Only it might not be his real name. He wouldn't tell you his real name in case you escaped. Then you'd be able to identify him to the police straight away and they'd find his address . . .'

'I don't know if it's real,' Elspeth murmured. 'But we got married. He said it all had to be legal and binding.'

'You're married?'

'Not in a church. We did it here. He made me put on a dress and . . .' Her words got swallowed between a breath and a cry, the noise a seagull might have made.

There were too many questions in her head. About Fergus. About the wedding. What he'd done to Elspeth. If he'd hurt

Elspeth. If Elspeth thought he was going to hurt Meggy, too. But she didn't want to hear the answers. She knew that sooner or later, she'd end up asking anyway. But not yet. Not while she could barely stand and her whole world had become comic book quicksand.

'Show me everything,' Meggy said. Lamp, hands joined, onwards.

She tolerated playing mum and pulled Elspeth along behind her, lamp tucked under one arm as she used her free hand to follow the path of the wall through the door, across the hallway, bend down, find the socket. Plug in the lamp. It flickered then lit up the room. Meggy made a mental note to be careful with it. Break the bulb and they were in for a long, dark night.

Disentangling herself from Elspeth, Meggy waited for her eyes to understand the room. It was a painting. All of it. A rectangular room, much like a sitting room in any other flat, but the windows . . .

Meggy stepped forward to run her hand across the wall, reassuring her eyes that they hadn't disconnected from her brain.

'They're painted. Badly. He just painted windows onto the walls. Why would he do that? There won't be any light. I don't understand.' She looked at Elspeth, who shrugged uselessly.

Crude squares with the outlines of waving curtains at each side attempted to give the illusion of a blue sky and green fields beyond their glass. The cruel cartoon was badly rendered. The paint had run, as if the windows themselves were crying at the sickness of the world they hid.

There was a scruffy, grubby sofa, with stuffing appearing from the seams of its cushions, and a mismatched armchair, the sort with no legs, just one huge cubic base and a soft back. On the far wall, a bookcase had been painted with coloured tomes, no titles, filling the mock shelves. Worse even than that, on the other wall, he had painted a picture of a picture. Meggy closed her eyes for a moment then did another take.

A brown frame surrounded a childlike attempt at setting three sunflowers in a blue vase. It was hideous. There was no other furniture. No coffee table. That would be too easy to hit him with, she decided. There were no loose cushions or throws that could be dumped over a head or pushed in a mouth. She walked to the sofa and gave it a push. The weight made it immovable. Likewise the chair. Swallowing her disappointment, Meggy determined not to give up so easily.

The next room was another bedroom with a single bed. Meggy could see it was bolted to the wall and didn't bother attempting to pull it. The mattress was bare save for a pile of bedding on the end. No chest of drawers, just another illustrated window, and a magazine on the floor. Meggy picked it up to get a better look. The cover of *Cars, Guys, Gadgets* showed a shiny red sports car of an unknown make. She flicked through the pages, but there was no hidden letter, no clue as to their destiny. Nothing like the clues she'd have found if she'd been inside a children's TV drama. She threw it back on the floor.

'Is this his bedroom when he comes here?' she asked.

Elspeth shook her head miserably.

'Oh,' Meggy said, remembering the double bed in the room where she'd found Elspeth. She stopped asking questions about Fergus. 'Is there a kitchen?'

This time Elspeth unplugged the lamp, picked it up and held out her hand. They walked together in the dark. Meggy hadn't held anyone's hand for years, not even her own mother's and especially not her step-mother's. It was strange how you could go from being uncomfortable at a stranger's touch, to accepting, then grateful for it within the space of just minutes.

'Kitchen,' Elspeth announced. 'Plastic cutlery only. Paper plates. Not even any bin bags. Three plastic bowls for heating up food. A microwave bolted into the cabinet – I've already tried and failed to get it out. No oven. No kettle.'

'What do you eat?'

'He usually makes food downstairs and brings it up. Sometimes it's takeaway or stuff like beans or scrambled egg. We eat in the lounge.'

'What else do you do? I mean, there's no TV or anything.'

'He tells me about his day,' Elspeth said, clutching the towel harder around herself.

'There's one more room,' Meggy realised. 'What's in there?'

'That's your room. He made the bed up for you a couple of days ago. Do you want to see it?'

'Not really,' Meggy said. 'But I guess I'll have to.'

They shifted rooms again. Here was another single bed. A poor excuse for a pillow, one sheet on the mattress, another to sleep under, then two blankets on top.

'It doesn't get too cold at night. You'll be all right,' Elspeth said. 'Look in the wardrobe.'

Again, no doors on the huge wardrobe, but metal plates on the wall ensuring it couldn't be pulled over. There was a pile of soft toys, another of board games, and finally girls' clothes, some obviously too small or too big, but all pink. Every shade of it. Even a pink hat, scarf and mittens set ready for winter.

'Winter's, like, three months off. I can't still be here then. What can he do with us for that long? Shit.' She kicked the wardrobe. 'Shit, shit, shit!'

'We can play a game if you like.' Elspeth's smile was a wobbling crack in her face.

'Why would we play a game?' Meggy shouted. 'He's going to come back. Sooner or later he'll come back, and we have to be ready for him. I'm not staying here. This isn't where I live. Those aren't my clothes. And those stupid dresses on the wall in your room are just as freaky.' She kicked the wardrobe door one more time. 'Why aren't you fighting him? I'm a kid, and I know you have to fight. You can't just let people hurt you, or they just keep on doing it.'

'I know,' Elspeth whispered. 'I know I should fight, but he scares me. It's easier if I don't react and he doesn't get mad at me. Sometimes I think maybe he'll let me go if I do everything he wants. Perhaps he'll get bored, or I'll make him better. He's sick. Really ill.' She checked the doorway for signs of imminent entry before leaning close into Meggy's ear. 'He told me he's dying. If he dies, we can escape. We just have to be patient.'

Meggy slapped her. The sound was a footstep too far on a frozen pond.

'If he dies and we're not found quickly enough, we die, too,' Meggy hissed, ripping the plug from the socket and walking away, not caring if she collided with the wall or anything else, leaving Elspeth trailing after her in the dark.

Meggy stopped after a few steps. She didn't know where she was going. She wasn't prepared to stay in her 'own' bedroom. She wouldn't do as she was told. Why make it easy for him? Elspeth's bedroom still smelled of the accident she'd had earlier in the evening, and the sight of that double bed . . . Meggy couldn't bear to go in there. Twelve years old or not, she knew enough about life to know what Fergus – or Fuckface, as she was now thinking of him – was doing to Elspeth in that bed.

The thought made her sick. She swung round and grabbed Elspeth with both arms, pushing her face into the woman's shoulder.

'I'm sorry I hit you,' Meggy said. 'Please don't hate me. I don't know what to do now.'

Elspeth closed her arms slowly around Meggy's back, alternately patting and rubbing, holding her until the girl pulled away again.

'It's okay, you didn't hurt me,' she said. 'I know how this

must look. I tried to fight at first. I did all the things you've just done. Hunted for weapons, ways to escape, anything he hadn't thought of. Furniture to bar the door, a blocked-up window to call for help. I found the weird pink dresses he wants me to wear. He left me several of them in my room, but they're all exactly the same. It's freaky.

'There's nothing that'll help us, Meggy. He's our only contact to the outside world. If you want him to bring food, you have to be nice. If you want the lights on, you have to pretend that you've had a wonderful day and that you missed him. When he gets angry, there's this look on his face, like there's another version of him inside that's trying to burst out.'

'Does he hurt you?' Meggy asked quietly.

'Sometimes. Not all the time. Less if I'm careful.'

'Will he hurt me?'

'I think that depends how he finds you. It's like role play. Did you do that at school?'

Meggy nodded.

'I think it's the same. He likes it when I call him my husband. Puts him in a good mood, or a better mood, for a while.'

'I'm not calling him dad.' Meggy gave the carpet a stamp. 'No bloody way.'

'Listen to me. I know he looks like a reed in a storm, but he's strong. He carried me up here. I play his game because that keeps me safer until I can figure something else out. I think you should do the same. I know I'm an adult, and I know I should have better answers for you than these, but I just don't. Because he's not right, Meggy. He's not. I can't even explain it to you. I promise I'll try to protect you, but you have to help me. You can't wind him up and get into a fight with him.'

'If he touches me, I'll kill him.'

'I understand that,' Elspeth said. 'Maybe we'll get an idea for a plan really soon.'

113

'We have to keep trying,' Meggy said. 'You can't just give in. I'll be good if we can work out a way to escape.'

'Deal,' Elspeth said, opening her arms.

Meggy stepped into them, and they held each other as they cried, while beyond the door, at the bottom of the staircase, Fergus Ariss lay close to death.

Chapter Thirteen

Since regaining consciousness, Fergus had managed to crawl to his bedroom, but getting himself into bed had proved too much. The upper half of his body was flopped face down on the bed, knees remaining stubbornly on the floor. Neither arms nor legs were broken, in spite of the felled tree noises as he'd tumbled down step after excruciating step. His head was a different matter. The first four blows were memorable, but after that he'd lost count. There were broken fingers on his right hand, and the seat of his trousers was bloody. He could feel the cold damp starting to stiffen in the seat of his underwear. The origins of that didn't bear thinking about.

With no clear idea of how long he'd been unconscious, he had only the darkness to guide him. He'd been intending to fix some food for the woman and girl upstairs while they got acquainted. All they had in the flat was bread and snacks. Fergus tried to raise his head from the duvet and the cotton lifted up with his face. It took all his strength to use two unbroken fingers to peel himself free of the material. The world turned red.

He gazed at the rose-blossoming wall, fascinated by the

swirling mural, shades of dark cherry and poppy coming together then apart as he moved his eyes. Holding up his swelling hands, he watched as the patterns covered his sore flesh and aching bones. At last he could taste it. If red had a flavour, it should have been strawberry sweet and syrupy. This was a savoury dish, one left in the pan too long. Somehow still hot, but he could taste the saucepan, as if the metal had permeated the food. It stuck to his tongue, immune to his attempts to swallow it away. A waterfall tumbled through his ears, the crashing of an unstoppable liquid force. He had become a river of blood. It fell from his eyes and ears, trickled from his mouth, leaked from his lower opening. The sickness within his body had been released into the world. That was all right. He was ready to go now.

All he wanted was to leave in comfort, wrapped in the bed cover that had once belonged to his mother, her final embrace from beyond the grave. Breathing was difficult. Invisible hands squeezed his chest, and there was a tentacle around his throat. Grasping the bed cover, he put every ounce of everything he could muster into climbing up, pulling with his arms, pushing with the one leg that was still mobile – he couldn't feel the left any more, if it was even still there. Parts of him were becoming detached. His stomach was free-falling, leaving him floating in a pool of pain that had little effect. Pain was the engine light flashing in your car, nothing more. Once you conquered it, climbed inside it, you could see it for what it was. His body was sending him a message, and he got it.

The futility of trying to clamber onto the bed fully realised, he opted to bring the mountain to him instead. Little by little as he pulled, the bed cover shifted from the bed to the floor. He didn't look at the mess he was making on it, didn't want to see those bloody flowers taking root on the precious fabric.

As the last material slid to the ground with a hushed thud, Fergus' legs gave way entirely. Falling into the soft padding, he breathed as deeply as his lungs would allow, smelling soap and hand cream, freshly baked biscuits and mowed grass. All of home, of what it meant to him, in one sensory hit.

Pushing himself away from the bed, he managed to force his body to roll, still holding the cover. It went with him, cocooning around his torso so that only his face was still visible. He rolled another 180 degrees, leaving him facing a wall on which hundreds of images were displayed.

A woman with a baby on her lap. Pushing him in a pram. In the hospital minutes after he was born. Standing at the bottom of a slide, arms outstretched and ready to catch him. Looking admiringly the day he'd started school, his hair brushed and shining, smart new shoes that she'd saved up for all summer. Splashing in the freezing cold waves at the beach, oblivious to the cold as she played. In her best clothes at a family dinner.

There were other images not on the wall. Ones he tried to push away. What was the point in recalling pain? The day he'd realised he'd lost her. When he was told that his mother and brother were dead. Sometimes he forgot what she looked like and would have to reinvent her image in his mind.

Now, both legs were numb and he could smell urine from within the cover. Not that his mother would be cross under these circumstances. How could he control himself if he couldn't even feel his lower limbs? The cover would be burned, presumably, when his body was found.

How long had the woman and the girl been upstairs? Not long, he thought. How many days? Was it weeks already? Time was dancing inside his head, and it wouldn't stay still.

He coughed, spat up a mouthful of blood, and two more teeth landed on the carpet. Whether they were casualties of his illness or the blows from the staircase didn't matter any more. His stomach clenched tight, leaving him gasping for breath. Still some pain, then. Just enough to guide him home. Without

117

pain, how could you ever let go of life? The pressure in his neck was building, and he could feel his eyes bulging. The photos on the wall were too hard to see now. He let himself roll onto his back. Who needed photographs when he could join his mother in person.

He felt her kiss on his brow, her breath on his cheek. His heart slowed so that its beat was no more than an occasional speed bump. His pulse, that slave ship drum beat to the endless misery of his life, had lost its potency. His eyes slipped shut, and behind them there was light and warmth. His jaw fell open, relaxing, as his head fell to the side. There was a hand outstretched for him to take. His mother was there, at the bottom of the slide of his life.

Fergus Ariss waited to see if this time, at last, he would stay dead.

Chapter Fourteen

The house in Prestonfield Road where Angela Fernycroft had lived so happily then died so brutally had soaked sadness into its bricks and mortar. The crime scene had long since been cleared of the paraphernalia of investigation and the detritus of death, but Angela's family had declined to move back in. The house would have to sit unoccupied for a couple of years before public memory was erased. It wasn't going to sell until then. Angela's husband, Cal, had agreed to meet Connie there and let her in.

'Anything,' he'd told her on the phone. 'If it'll help, you know . . .'

'Catch him,' were the words he hadn't been able to say.

She introduced herself and the two of them sat at opposite sides of the kitchen table. Cal Fernycroft wept a while before he could speak. Connie said nothing. When he'd been crying for some minutes, she slid her hand across the table, palm up, to see if he was ready to reach out and be comforted. At first he just looked at the hand, then he took it gently and began to cry harder.

Connie studied the kitchen. Someone had been growing

pots of herbs on the windowsill. Connie guessed that was Angela's handiwork and felt a rush of affection for her. People who liked growing things cared for their environment. Tending a plant required commitment and love. Connie was no good at it.

Next to the back door, a photo of the family was mounted on the wall. In it, each parent had a child on their back, and the four of them were grinning into the camera as if they'd all just been told the funniest joke.

'Last year,' Cal Fernycroft croaked. 'On holiday in Wales. We'd just raced along the beach. I don't think I've ever laughed so hard.'

Connie relaxed her hand and pulled it gently away. Cal was done crying.

'Do you have photo albums? I'd like to get to know Angela better and sometimes that helps.'

'They're in the roof,' he said.

'Are you able to get them? If it's a problem then just say.'

'No, no, I can do that,' he said. 'It's just that I haven't been upstairs . . .'

'I'll have the police fetch them. You don't even have to stay while I'm looking around. I can get the key back to you later.'

He frowned. 'No. That's not . . . I should be able to be in my own house. I need to feel close to her again. Before, I could feel her in the house. If I came in unexpectedly from work, I could tell just by walking through the door that she was here. I didn't think about it until she was gone, that she was on my mind every second. Like a magnet that guided me home. Could you help me?'

Connie nodded. He wasn't talking about retrieving the photos.

'Do you want me to go first?'

'Please,' he said.

They walked from the kitchen to the bottom of the staircase. Cal gripped the bannisters. Connie let him take each step in his own time. The weight he was dragging kept threatening to pull him to the bottom again, but he forced his feet upwards. It took three minutes to cover the fourteen steps. Cal was panting by the time he reached the top.

'Your choice, postpone this or get that door open and face it.'

He shuddered.

'Do it,' he said.

Connie slid her hand around the doorknob. It turned easily and that felt wrong. For some reason she'd expected the door to be harder to open. Cal stepped into the room with his eyes closed.

'I don't want to see it,' he said, then opened his eyes anyway.

Connie took his hand as he surveyed the damage to his life. It was a negative, a stripping away of what had been. The mattress and bedding had been taken for testing, as had the curtains. The carpets, blood-spattered, had been removed too. No items of clothing were in sight. Those that had been left out when Angela had died, also taken to the forensics lab. The book Angela had been in the middle of reading at her death, gone. She would never find out how it ended.

Cal gave a wavering smile. 'It's like when we moved in. Before the children. No curtains, just a couple of bits of furniture. We saved up for everything over time. We . . .' His first attempt at the sentence was drowned with tears. 'We wanted a boy and a girl, and that's what we got. This house, the kids, a park just down the road. It all worked out, and I don't know . . .' He fell to his knees. 'I don't know how she could be taken and not me. I can't understand what we did to deserve this. I want her back.' He looked up at Connie, his hands outstretched. 'Please, you have to bring her back.'

Sitting on the floor behind him, Connie put her arms around Cal, her chest against his back as he rocked backwards and forwards, raging and keening. She leaned her head against his shoulder and kept him pinned to her, grounded in the world between his dead wife and the living children who needed their dad.

Connie looked at the window space that had held floor-length curtains. Angela's murderer had hidden there, statue-still, and watched her. She'd bathed just before getting into bed that night, and he'd waited for the duration. Before that she'd cleaned the kitchen and put overnight washing in. It had churned away unaware in the utility room below as she'd fought for her final breaths.

'What is it?' Cal asked.

Connie hadn't even been aware that the man in her arms had stopped crying. He was staring at her over his shoulder.

'You should go. The police will fetch the photos for me. You're going to be exhausted for a couple of days. Sleep is essential. Lots of it,' she told him.

Cal nodded. She released him and he stood up, offering a hand to pull her off the floor, too.

'Thank you,' he said. 'I won't ever come in here again.'

'I get it,' she said. 'People who haven't lost a loved one think you only say goodbye once at the funeral. But you don't, you say goodbye in a thousand places. A favourite coffee shop, a road junction, while you're eating a curry, wearing a special jacket. The goodbyes keep on coming. It'll seem endless. You should know that it isn't, but the process is long and sometimes it's a roundabout not a straight road. Your children will get you through.'

He gave a sharp nod. 'I'll leave the keys in the door, if you could have the police return them to me.'

'Sure,' she told his already departing back.

Waiting until she heard his footsteps in the kitchen below, Connie went to stand where the murderer had. She put her back against the wall.

'Why this room?' she asked the empty space. 'If you weren't planning on raping her, it would have been easier to have taken her from the kitchen, avoiding the stairs. Maybe when she was putting the washing in. Anywhere downstairs.'

But she'd answered her own question, and she'd known it while she was still holding Angela's widowed husband. This was the version of Angela that he'd wanted to steal. In that moment, and in the place where she was all wife and mother. This was how he'd wanted her. He'd watched her preparations, seen her most private rituals and routines. The practicality of lifting an unconscious body down the stairs hadn't even been a factor.

Connie didn't wait for a police officer to retrieve the photos from the loft. There were plastic boxes in a row, carefully labelled. Angela's handwriting, she guessed by its curvy slant and small precision. The middle drawer gave her what she wanted. Pulling out three bulky albums, she climbed back down the ladder and sat with her back against the hallway wall.

There was nothing unusual about what was contained in the albums. Photos from when Angela and Cal had met then married. Holiday photos, their parents and siblings, Christmases and birthdays. Then the children had come along, and page after page of snaps had been lovingly printed out in spite of the digital tendency simply to drop photos into desktop folders.

Connie touched a close-up photo of Angela sitting on a park bench, both children on her lap, largest to smallest, like Russian dolls. A picnic was laid out beside them, complete with coloured plastic cups, tiny sandwiches and miniature cupcakes. They'd taken a series of images that day. These were the most recent photographs in the album. They'd had no idea what was coming.

She stood up, taking the photo albums with her. It required more time than she felt was reasonable in Angela's house to go through every photo carefully, and that was what she needed to do. To immerse herself in Angela's life and persona. To find the common link, if there was one, between her and Elspeth Dunwoody.

Sighing, she checked her watch then her mobile. The day had ended, and there was still no sign of Elspeth, or update on Meggy. No corpses either, which was the only good news. Hoping Baarda would be free soon, she decided to text him. It occurred to her that she hadn't eaten for twelve hours, and breakfast had been fruit and coffee.

'Meet me at my hotel bar,' she messaged. '10 p.m. Debrief and plan for tomorrow over dinner and alcohol.'

The yoga studio on East Broughton Place in Edinburgh's city centre – iYoga – was midway through one of its evening sessions when Connie arrived. The police had already retraced Elspeth's steps on the evening of her abduction, taking statements from everyone in her class. Who'd last spoken to her. Who'd seen her leave. What CCTV was available. All the normal stuff. Connie wanted something more personal.

She roamed the hallways between studios, drank orange-and-cucumber water, and checked out the changing rooms as she waited for the classes to finish. It was a hypermodern space, dressed down to feel falsely cosy, in a period building on a street struggling to attract commercial tenants. The shiny hardwood floors and full-length mirrors were at odds with the grand facade and sense of history the place should have conveyed, and Connie liked that. Nothing had to be on the inside what you assumed it was from the outside. People certainly weren't.

The yoga teacher who'd taken the class the night Elspeth had been abducted was Darpana Chawla. Engaged in a final relaxation and meditation with her students, she was willowy and solemn-looking. Connie wished, in a rare moment of regret, that she could see the colours in the room. Darpana was wearing an eye-catching combination of sports Lycra with flowing scarves. Metallic fibres in the material glinted in the light as she waved her arms slowly in the air, hands wafting up and down. Inhale for three, exhale for three, Connie read her lips. Then the eyes of the class participants opened slowly, like some sprawling beast waking up and contemplating its existence. They stretched on their mats and brought themselves back into the moment. Some would be going home, others out to socialise, a few on to night shifts. For all of them, their slice of escapist exercise was over for the night.

Darpana was the last to leave, bidding farewell to each student in turn and by name. She was good at her job, Connie thought. People wanted an acknowledgement from her, or a kind word, an encouragement to attend the next class. A man called out before Connie could approach the teacher and explain herself. Darpana's mouth opened fractionally, and her jaw flickered instantaneously sideways. She knew him by voice, and was stressed by his presence. Better to wait until she'd dealt with him before making a further demand on her time, Connie decided.

'I asked you to meet me at home,' Darpana told him as she rolled up her own mat and put a water bottle and wrist weights into a training bag.

He gave a lazy smile in response. 'I thought we could get takeaway together,' he said. 'That vegan place you like around the corner is still open. I'm buying.'

She continued jamming items into her bag.

'You sure it's your stomach you were thinking about?' Darpana sniped.

Connie had only seconds to decide to step up or step back.

Darpana was in the middle of something private, and if she revealed herself it would be clear she'd overheard the conversation. Connie decided to remain in the space between overgrown yucca plants and a water dispenser. The yoga teacher had given a statement detailing the number of years she'd been Elspeth's teacher. They'd become close acquaintances over the years – Darpana's words – although that seemed more formal than was necessary for someone who saw you contort your body twice a week.

'Don't start,' he groaned. 'We agreed to put it behind us. That's not why I'm here.' He moved closer to her as she exited the studio. 'You have to start trusting me again for this to work, otherwise we're both wasting our time.'

'I have to? Really? What if I can't?'

'Then this is over,' he shrugged. 'I can leave tonight if that's what you want.'

He sidled away, chin aloft and shoulders back to reveal a wide, taut chest and enhance the slimness of his waist in the tailored shirt. He was peacocking. Darpana tried looking at him, and lowered her gaze quickly back to the floor.

'You know that's not what I want,' she said. 'It would just be simpler, easier to forget, if we could separate this place from our life. You coming here just makes me think about it.'

'Hey,' he said, softening, giving her the reward for backing down. 'It was a one-off. I'm not stupid enough to risk losing you twice, am I?' He cupped a hand under Darpana's chin and kissed her softly.

It didn't take a psychologist to know he was lying about both parts of his assertion. Whatever it was, presumably an infidelity, he'd done it before – and given the opportunity, Connie decided it was entirely possible that he'd do it again. Only a woman in love would be incapable of hearing the silken deception and failing to notice his too-earnest frown

126

and too-concentrated a gaze. He wasn't a good liar, but with his body and looks he'd probably never needed to perfect the art.

Darpana melted, sickeningly, in his arms, allowing him to wrap her jacket around her, throwing her bag over his shoulder like any well-trained twenty-first-century knight and leading her to the door. Connie cursed and went to the front desk, picking up a leaflet and checking the schedule for Darpana's next class. Tomorrow morning at 9 a.m. If she could get here early, she might be able to catch the instructor while she was still in the right frame of mind to talk about Elspeth.

Connie's stomach rumbled. Even vegan food was inviting right now. Enough for one day, she decided. Baarda had returned her text to confirm he would meet her at the hotel. It was a short walk back and the evening was balmy. Trying to piece together her day, from Dr Ailsa Lambert to Melanie Chao, then the grieving Cal Fernycroft and the badly deluded Darpana Chawla, there was a clamouring inside her head for assessment and unravelling. Also for vodka. Maybe with tonic, maybe without. More likely, she decided, without.

Chapter Fifteen

Bar Prince in The Balmoral was refined and hushed. Connie wasn't sure the ambience was exactly what she needed, but the alcohol definitely was. She'd beaten Baarda there, and given that she was already running a few minutes late, it didn't bode well for the sort of day he was having. There'd been progress, though, as she'd walked Edinburgh's streets back to her hotel. Elspeth Dunwoody's husband had provided a vast digital trove of photos to MIT, and a secure link had been sent to her inbox. Retrieving her laptop from her hotel room, Connie downloaded the files.

Elspeth had a lot of media dedicated to her courtesy of her husband's family. There were photos of her at galas, charity balls, cutting a ribbon somewhere. But those images, that public facade, wasn't the version of Elspeth she was interested in. That wasn't the link to Angela. She found what she was looking for after just a few minutes. It began with the baby photos.

'Good evening,' Baarda said quietly. 'Can I get you another of whatever that was?'

'Hey, I saved you a stool. Do you mind sitting at the bar,

only I always feel like I'm with my parents if I sit at a table? I'll take a frozen Grey Goose, as you're offering.'

'The bar is fine,' he smiled, ordering a Château de Laubade Armagnac.

Baarda had changed his usual white shirt for a navy blue version and rolled up the sleeves.

'Did you spill something?' Connie asked.

'It seemed impolite to turn up in the same shirt I'd been wearing for the previous fourteen hours.'

'I hadn't figured you for the turned-up-sleeves thing. Letting your hair down?' she smiled.

'Are we back at *Downton Abbey* again?' He raised his glass to hers, and they touched the edges of the crystal together lightly.

'My timeline got messed up.' She tipped her head to one side. 'I think maybe I jumped ahead a century or two. Who's the guy who comes out of the lake in that Jane Austen movie? The one who either doesn't speak, or when he does he's just devastatingly polite?'

'For the love of God, it really has been a long day. "The guy who comes out of the lake"? You're referring to Fitzwilliam Darcy.'

'Give me a break. I studied psychology, not literature from the dawn of time. And yeah, you're a dead ringer for the Darcy guy.' Connie raised her glass and rewarded herself with a drink.

'Coming from anyone else that would be a compliment. How do you manage to be the opposite of everyone?'

'Practice. The thing about Darcy in that book . . .'

'*Pride and Prejudice.*'

'Uh-huh, the thing is, he was closed off emotionally.'

'I'm aware,' Baarda said.

'The reader has to assume all the passion. It happens out of

129

view. His anger, the retribution, his feelings. You even have the Darcy curly hair and serious eyes. What colour are yours?'

'Brown,' Baarda sighed.

'No, won't do,' Connie said. 'How many shades of green do you think there are?'

'I have no—'

'Neither do I, but lots, right. Green is a category of colours, not a colour. You have to be more creative. Look, I have an app on my cell that lists colour shades.' She flicked the screen. 'Here you go, colour names with shades and little samples. Choose the right one.'

'Fine,' he said. 'I'm going with burnt umber. Does this really help?'

'Frame of reference,' she said. 'Facial expressions give me mental overload sometimes. Other things become less vivid, like items of clothing. But without colour, the minutiae of people's faces become a movement of lines. Those lines form recognisable patterns. Trying to fake an emotion forms a pattern, too.'

'So you can tell when people are lying?' Baarda asked.

'That kind of misses the subtleties of it. Sometimes people tell half the truth but conceal a detail. Emotions are considered absolute, which is how we teach children. Draw a happy face, a sad face, or an angry mouth. The best example is grief mingling with relief at the passing of a loved one who's been ill. The eyes, forehead, and upper part of the cheeks shows the pain whereas the lower half – the mouth in particular – registers relief.'

'Sounds like a useful skill,' Baarda said, sipping the Armagnac and flexing his shoulders.

'You'd hate it,' Connie said. 'It's like being permanently wired. Sometimes I find it easier to talk to people by phone just so that I can't see their faces. My brain needs downtime.'

'Are you single?' Baarda asked.

Connie laughed. 'Yes, and thank you for leaping ahead in that minefield of a conversation. It's hard trying not to read the expressions of the people I'm close to. Like a tap you can't turn off.'

'Which when you're emotionally invested would be complex,' he noted.

'You, on the other hand, are remarkably refreshing to be around because of your natural control and understated behaviour. I spent some time with Angela Fernycroft's husband today. It was his first time back in the house. Have you ever drunk frozen vodka? It thickens, which should be gross, but the harsh edge of the flavour disappears so you can taste it properly. Here.' She slid her glass a foot down the bar into his hand.

Baarda took a sip. 'It's good. Are you okay?'

'Nope, but I'm processing. It's tough seeing people in that much pain, even when you're trained to be objective. Tell me the deal with the missing girl.'

'I helped as much as I could, but my job is to find Elspeth Dunwoody. I can't get distracted. There are protocols, and Police Scotland officers are exceptionally well trained. It was important to get the jump-start. Thanks for speaking with the witness. The description she gave will be helpful.'

'Yeah, a Jack Skellington lookalike. That's messed up. That guy's got to stick out a mile, right?'

'I didn't know the reference, although I've looked it up since then. Just images,' Baarda said.

'You have kids and you haven't seen that movie? It's amazing. The thing about Jack Skellington is that he's actually a good guy. He just makes errors of judgement.'

'Like shoving a girl in his boot and driving off with her?' Baarda asked, motioning for the barman to pour them fresh drinks.

'That would be where the similarities stop. Where did you get to with Meggy's mother?'

'Living in Guernsey, airtight alibi. Carmen – Meggy's step-mother – claims her car was tampered with so she couldn't drive to the school to pick up Meggy. We have no idea if that's true, a coincidence, or an excuse and she's involved.'

'Poor kid,' Connie said. 'I need to go back to Elspeth's yoga studio in the morning to speak with her instructor. They've known each other for years. If Elspeth was being stalked or felt concerned about walking from yoga to her car, her teacher might have noticed something.'

'There was nothing in her statement,' Baarda said.

'I know. Might be that the police officer taking the statement didn't see any value, but it bears chasing up. It really hit me when I was reading through the evidence folder.'

'After that we should go and see her family. They're desperate for an update and without any further leads, it feels as if we need to go back and see if there's anything we missed,' Baarda said.

'Agreed,' Connie said. 'Although I hate the sense that we're chasing our tails, hence the downtime now. I've immersed myself as much as I can. The only link I can find between the victims is that both Angela and Elspeth regularly took their kids to parks.'

'Them and several million other parents,' Baarda said.

'I'm aware,' Connie agreed. 'But it's all I have. What I really need is to think about something else for a few hours.'

'Like vodka?' Baarda smiled.

'Like vodka indeed. Tell me about your name. Where's Baarda from?' Connie asked.

'My father was the Dutch ambassador to the United Kingdom. He met my mother when he was posted here. They married and he never left. My mother was a socialite. They made the perfect couple. I had older sisters – twins – three years my senior. When I was thirteen, they went to a party, the house they were in caught fire, and they both died. I'd just started at Eton then, and I didn't go home for a long time. I was sent to relatives during holidays. My mother never recovered, and my father worked increasingly long days. Eventually, he took a posting in Eastern Europe, and my mother became a shadow of herself. If I went home, which was rare, I was looked after by housekeepers and staff.'

Connie stared at him.

'You said you wanted to take your mind off the case.' He tossed back the remains of his drink.

'I can't imagine losing a sibling at that age. I absolutely adore my big brother. He was the only . . . wait, did you just tell me that to prove a point?'

'You know a lot about me, I have very little facade. Frankly, I don't see the point. Intrigue bores me. What's interesting is how few facts you give people about yourself. I know you're American, that you can't see colour, and that you're good at reading faces, but nothing personal.'

'What is it you want to know?'

'Why you do your job the way you do.'

'I'm a psychologist. We don't follow an operating manual. It's not like police procedure.' Connie grabbed a small dish of dried wasabi peas from a passing waiter and tossed a few into her mouth.

'I've worked with a few psychologists. None of them have ever been caught in the mortuary cuddling a corpse before.' He swivelled his stool round 90 degrees to watch her profile.

Connie put her head in her hand, elbow resting on the bar, and met his gaze.

'Dr Lambert told you.'

'She had to report it to someone in case there was ever a query about it. For what it's worth, I got the impression that she rather admires you.'

133

'I can only tell you what I told her. It's about perspectives. The murderer's, the victim's. This only works if I allow myself to see and feel what they saw and felt. Broad-brush profiling is like using a baseball bat to pick a lock. The killer's Caucasian and unlikely to step outside his own racial group. He's between twenty-five and fifty-five, because that's what statistical likelihood tells us, plus he needs a house, a car, money. He's got a home in the Edinburgh area somewhere. That's too much stalking to have done for someone out of the area. His intellect is within average ranges because he didn't give himself away and has the ability to adapt and persuade. All of which is a good baseline profile, but where is he? What's he doing right now? Has he killed Elspeth? If not, what's he saying to her? What's he asking her for?'

'You've done it again,' Baarda said, getting up from the stool and slipping his jacket over his shoulders.

'What?'

'You answered a question about you by talking about the case. I'm not sure if you've practised until it's a flawless skill, or if you don't even realise you're doing it.' He deposited a pile of notes on the bar. 'I think I'll skip dinner in favour of sleep. See you at the yoga studio.'

Connie watched him go then raced after him, catching him just as he exited onto the street.

'Baarda, wait.'

He stopped.

'I'm sorry. You're right. I spend a lot of time soaking up the details of other lives, and I counter that by burying mine.' She shoved her hands deep in her pockets. 'For nearly a year of my life, I couldn't talk. Couldn't communicate at all, in fact. So now it's all I do. I find ways to enable people to communicate with me. Even when they're dead, I guess.'

'Okay,' he said softly.

'Goodnight, then.' She shrugged and took a step backwards. 'Goodnight.'

He walked away, Edinburgh's streets taking a welcome rain washing after the unusual spell of hot weather. The city lights reflecting on the wet streets reminded her of Boston. Connie went back into the bar. There was at least one more measure of Grey Goose with her name on. There were memories best left alone and questions she didn't have the answer to yet. Neither was going to allow her to sleep for at least another hour. She could just as well spend her insomnia at the bar as staring at the ceiling from her bed.

Chapter Sixteen

The lights hadn't come on all day; nor had Fergus appeared. Meggy and Elspeth had huddled in bed, sleeping only fitfully, that first night. In the morning – they knew it was morning only courtesy of Elspeth's watch – they both finally fell fast asleep, waking in sweaty panic, imagining themselves somewhere terrible and unknown, only for the nightmare to continue.

Meggy was the first to force herself out of bed.

'We have to pick the lock on the door,' she said. 'It's no good waiting here then trying to fight him. If we can get out into the main house, we stand a much better chance. There'll be things we can use to hurt him there, hit him with or spray in his eyes or something.'

Elspeth sat up in bed. The dim lamplight did nothing to reduce the appearance of the overloaded bags beneath her eyes and was unflattering to the sickly white of her skin. Still Meggy thought Elspeth was beautiful. Sweet and kind, and beautiful. It would have been better, of course, to have landed in this situation with a female survival expert like Megan Hine, an Olympic martial arts gold medallist like Kayla Harrison, or world champion powerlifter Manon Bradley. Meggy liked reading about powerful women. There weren't enough of them in her own life.

But Elspeth had held her all night, and not minded when she'd cried. When Meggy had woken up screaming, terrified, the sheet wet and reeking beneath their bodies, Elspeth had stroked her hair, and moved her gently to change the sheet. Elspeth, it turned out, had children of her own – a boy and a girl. She was the sort of mother who would never decide that she needed to pursue her own 'mindfulness needs and soul development', whatever the hell that was, and dump her kids with a bitchy step-mother and emotionally stunted father.

'Meggy,' Elspeth said softly. 'Have you ever picked a lock before? Not that I'm saying you can't do it, but I just don't know how we'd even go about trying something like that.'

'Well, no, but we'd need something thin and tough. On TV it's usually a credit card. Do you have one with you?'

'I'm sorry,' Elspeth shrugged. 'I have no idea what he did with my bag. I don't have any of my things here.'

'That's okay, I've got another idea.'

She opened the wardrobe, grabbed a pair of leggings and a top, grateful for a fleeting moment about the lack of light that enabled her to ignore the hideous pinkness, and threw the clothes on. 'Kitchen.'

Elspeth followed her with less energy but more curiosity, obliging by plugging in the lamp where needed, as Meggy opened every drawer and cupboard. Nothing useful there.

'Back to the bedroom,' Meggy ordered, once there ripping open every board game until she held a square aloft. 'Here,' she said. 'It's been laminated.'

'What is it?' Elspeth asked.

'Some magic spell card from a fantasy game. Come on, this has to work.'

137

They went to the apartment door and positioned the light so they could both see, crowding either side of the door lock as Meggy pushed the card into the slim space and began wiggling it.

'It's not hard enough. The plastic's getting all scrunched up at the edges.' She pulled the card back out and held it to the light.

'It's a Chubb lock; there's no way we'll be able to pick it,' Elspeth said.

'We just need to try something stronger,' Meggy declared. 'It'll have to be metal. What is there that's metal?'

'Breakfast first,' Elspeth declared. 'I need a drink.'

'That's it, we can take the microwave apart, get to the workings.'

'You can't take it apart, it's set into a cabinet that's all sealed up. I tried getting the door off, but there are no tools or metal cutlery in here. Every screw is turned so tight you can't shift it. I broke all of my nails and snapped every plastic knife trying. Even if we did get the microwave apart, we'd never put it back together, and he'd know what we'd done as soon as he came into the kitchen. Plus, we need the microwave. There's not much here we can use to look after ourselves. If we don't get out, then losing the microwave will be a disaster.'

'We can heat up some water until it's boiling hot, hide when he comes in, then throw it in his face. If it burns his eyes, we'll easily be able to get away. Seriously, it'll work, we can hold a pan each, wait for him—'

'That's what the two peepholes in the front door are for,' Elspeth said quietly. 'He has rules so you can't duck down and wait for him. He can see everything. He knocks to announce that he's coming in. He makes me stand in the bedroom at the far end of the corridor with my back against the wall and my hands on my head before he enters. We attack him and I doubt we'd survive.'

'Whatever,' Meggy huffed. 'You get breakfast. I'm not hungry. We might not have much time left, so I'm going to carry on.'

'But we both need the light. You have to come into the kitchen.'

'Nope,' Meggy grinned. 'I just realised there's one in the microwave. Leave the door open when you're not using it.'

'Clever girl.'

Meggy grinned. Those words weren't much. But they were everything.

She left Elspeth making coffee and made her way into the sitting room. The light coming from the microwave was minimal but it cast the slightest bloom on the hallway walls. Lamp plugged in, she gave the furniture a further inspection. Old and stuffed, with heavy wooden frames.

She dug her hands into the back of the cushion. A cloud of dust erupted, but the cushion itself didn't budge, and the rough stitchwork scratched her fingertips. Everything was sewn together. She tried the back of the sofa, then the sides, up and down each edge of the wood frame and the base. Nothing shifted. It was sewn, glued and screwed together so hard it would take a bomb to get it apart. Same with the armchair.

Throwing herself down onto the sofa, Meggy glared at the ceiling. They needed tools to make weapons. Every bed was firmly fixed to the wall, and the cupboards had been stripped of any wood that might have been movable. Her dad would have known what to do. Not that he was a giant in the DIY world, but there had never been a need to pay anyone to do jobs in the house, whether it was basic plumbing, maintenance, or electrics. She wished the lights were on. Half the problem was that she just couldn't see enough. Above her, two lamps hung from the ceiling, one at each end of the room. Flowery paper lampshades would cast patterned light onto the ceiling when they were lit – when he decided that they'd earned the right to light.

Meggy hated him. It had occurred to her to wonder if she were capable of killing him or not as she was falling asleep the night before. The question took only half a second to answer. She didn't want to die here. She didn't want to die anywhere aged twelve, but especially not here, in the dark with the stupid pink clothes and the stupid board games, and the stupid painted windows. If it meant securing her escape, what Meggy Russell knew with absolute certainty was that if she needed to, she wouldn't have a problem with killing Fergus. Maybe even if she didn't absolutely have to.

Meggy stood up, staring at the light fitting. The ceiling was uneven. She couldn't be sure, but it looked as if the mounting plate was casting a shadow onto the ceiling. Turning her head left then right, she tried to get a better view.

Dragging the armchair inch by inch across the unhelpful carpet, she stood first on the seat, then on the arm. She was still nowhere near the ceiling. Shifting the chair across even further, she fetched the lamp and moved it as far as she could to the centre of the room. There was only one possible option for reaching the ceiling. Taking a deep breath, Meggy climbed onto the back of the chair, arms out straight either side like a tightrope walker.

'Meggy!' Elspeth shouted.

The noise made her turn her head, her upper body following suit. One foot slipped down the chair back and the other ankle collapsed outwards. Torso hitting the chair back as she fell, the air gusting from her lungs, she managed to slow her descent to the floor, Elspeth running to catch her too late.

'Oh my God, are you okay? Did you bang your head?'

'I'm okay,' she panted.

'Can you breathe?'

Meggy nodded rather than trying to speak again. Her lungs felt like someone had punched her from both the front and the back at once. Elspeth slipped an arm around her shoulders and helped her to sit up.

'Why didn't you wait for me?'

'No time. Sooner or later, he's coming back.'

'But what were you trying to do? That's really dangerous. What if you'd been electrocuted?'

Meggy dusted herself off and stood up, rejecting the offered help.

'I'd rather get electrocuted than wait here for him, wouldn't you?'

Elspeth looked at the floor. 'I just want to survive. I need to make sure I see my children again. I don't want to make him angry.'

'If he comes in, we'll say I did this when you were asleep,' Meggy said. 'Then he won't get mad at you.'

'He's not logical like other adults. You can't take this on yourself. We have to be careful.'

'We have to be fast,' Meggy corrected, staring at the chair. 'If you stand there and hold me, I'm less likely to slip.'

'One last try,' Elspeth conceded. 'Then we should put the chair back where he had it, or he'll know we were up to something.'

'We'll hear his footsteps on the stairs first though, won't we? I mean, we'll have a bit of time.'

'Sometimes. Other times he creeps up here, then shouts at me to stand at the end of the hallway, as if he thinks he'll catch me doing something I shouldn't. I don't know what.' She shrugged and looked vacant.

Meggy didn't like that look She'd seen it at school from a few kids who got bullied all the time. They knew reporting the bullies only made it worse. Their parents either couldn't or wouldn't step in. It was . . . there was a good word for it. She screwed her face up in concentration.

'Resignation,' she said.

Elspeth's face didn't register the semi-insult. Meggy climbed up again.

'Right, hold my leg and my back.'

Elspeth stood to the rear of her. Balancing was much easier just with someone else's touch to give her some boundaries. Making sure she was properly steady before fully extending her body upwards, this time Meggy could see the base plate clearly. One corner of it wasn't fitted flush against the ceiling. She reached, slid a fingernail under it and tugged, putting her weight through her hand and yanking hard on the plastic fitting above the light bulb.

Plaster exploded into the air, dust and debris raining down onto them both as the lamp gave way. Meggy wheeled her arms in the air, landing on top of Elspeth, who managed to stay upright by pushing Meggy forward to land in the armchair. The lamp swung dramatically, holding on by its bare wires like a loose tooth on a thread of gum.

'No!' Elspeth cried, standing up and holding her hands uselessly up towards the light as if she could push it back into the ceiling through sheer force of will. 'No, no, no. We have to put it back, Meggy. He'll go crazy. This is bad. It's really bad.'

She started to climb onto the chair, when Meggy grabbed the leg of her trousers.

'Wait,' she said. 'Let me see what's there.'

Pretending not to feel terrified would have to do as a substitute for actually remaining calm, Meggy decided. It was a mess. The screws that had been holding the plate in the plasterboard had fallen away, and there was no chance of tucking it all back up neatly again. All they could do now was attempt to get out of the flat before he came in.

Scrambling for the light fitting with Elspeth holding her again, Meggy felt for anything she could remove. She came away with two screws and a thin sheet of metal that acted as a base for the fitting against the ceiling.

'Yes!' she shouted. 'I knew it. Come on.' She grabbed Elspeth's hand. 'You bring the lamp.' Jumping off the armchair, she ran for the front door.

Pausing, waiting for Elspeth to catch up with her, she forced herself to take a calming breath. Her pulse was so loud in her ears that the sound was warped, a special effect in a sci-fi movie. Rushing would be useless. Calm and careful. Last chance, she reminded herself. They had to be out of time now. Soon, Fergus would be there to role play or fantasise, or however his delusions worked. She wasn't planning on being there, waiting.

Stepping forward, she cleaned the sliver of metal on her leggings and willed her hands to stop shaking. Then Elspeth was there, her arms around Meggy's shoulders. Neither of them dared breathe.

Inserting the metal adjacent to the lock, Meggy pushed to the right, bending the inserted part between the door and the latch bolt, applying gentle but firm pressure. There was a noise like an envelope sliding through a letter box followed by a miniature but satisfying clunk.

Elspeth gasped and Meggy cried out. It had been a dream. A stupid thing to occupy herself with. It was never going to work out. Reality wasn't so kind. She whirled round and threw herself into Meggy's arms, both of them crying already.

'Ready to go?' Elspeth whispered. 'We'll have to be careful. He could be anywhere out there.'

'I'm ready,' Meggy said. 'But if we see him, we have to fight. Agreed?'

'Agreed.' She squeezed Meggy's hands. 'Come on. Nearly there.'

Meggy put her hand on the door handle, Elspeth put hers over the top. Together they pulled.

Nothing happened. They pulled again, pushing down harder. Meggy grabbed the metal plate and shoved it back into the gap between door and frame, sliding it up and down. It met with no resistance.

'Why won't it open?' Meggy screeched, thumping the door.

Elspeth took the plate from her fingers and ran it upwards. It hit metal with a delicate clunk. She ran it downwards and the same happened. Took it out and ran it all the way down to the bottom of the door. Repeated the manoeuvre at the very top. Same. Then she tried pushing the plate into the other locks.

Letting her head fall against the door, eyes closed, hands hanging at her sides, she sighed.

'I'm sorry, sweetheart. It's a five-bolt door. It must be on a central system that doesn't work when you move one catch individually. We can't get out.'

'No,' Meggy growled. 'I don't believe you. I think you're scared and you want to stay in here so you don't have to fight him. Give me the metal.'

Elspeth did as Meggy asked, taking a step back and letting her work it out for herself. Rushing her would do no good. She looked into the sitting room at the broken, dangling lamp and knew they were just filling in time. Fergus wasn't going to appreciate the redecoration. No amount of pushing would get the lamp to stay on the ceiling, and they sure as hell weren't going out through the front door.

'We have to get out,' Elspeth whispered. 'We have to get out of here right now. We can't survive this.'

She stared at the hole in the ceiling, at the grime around the edge of the ancient plasterboard, at the crumbling fixture.

'Do you think we could get out through the ceiling and the roof?' Meggy asked.

Elspeth considered it. 'It's too high. We barely reached the light fitting, so doing any serious damage to the ceiling without ladders and tools will be impossible. Gravity's going to work against us, and in the roof there'll be thick joists, brickwork, and tiles outside.' She crossed her arms and looked around the room. 'How long do you think he's lived here? I think it's a long time. The internal fittings are old.'

Not trusting her legs — they'd been through too great a disappointment to act reliably — Elspeth crawled to the corner behind the couch and dug her fingers behind the carpet, pulling on strands where it wasn't completely tacked down. It took an effort, but the carpet was becoming threadbare and hadn't been renewed in years. The tacks had little body left to hold on to. Her fingernails screamed at her, but she would not relinquish her grip. Her heart was thumping like a drum. Only that wasn't right. It was Meggy, hitting and kicking the door. The girl had finally lost it. She was bound to sooner or later. Elspeth realised she'd been much too calm. Now the dam was bursting.

'Hey,' she said, releasing the edge of the carpet. She walked over and pulled the screeching girl away from the door. 'Hey, honey, we have to try something else, that's all. It's not over. But you can't carry on making that much noise, all right? He'll hear you.'

She cradled Meggy's head against her chest and rocked her for a minute. When the girl looked up, Elspeth smoothed down her hair and kissed her forehead.

'Do you know what a plenum is, Meggy?'

The girl shook her head.

'Neither do I, not really, but we were having some work done to our house, and they had to leave a space a certain depth between the floors. It has wooden joists, the long beams, and some smaller cross-beams, maybe insulation, something to attach the plasterboard to, that makes up the ceilings we see. But there are some weak points. Some gaps. So when too much water spills from your bath, and the ceiling collapses, it's because the water has found the gaps and run through. We need to find the weak points, okay? Look at the state of that ceiling.' She pointed at the dislodged lamp. 'If we can't go out through the door, and there are no windows, then we have to find another exit, even if that means making one. I need you to help me, Meggy. Can you do that?'

The girl nodded and wiped her cheeks. 'Sure,' she sniffed. 'I can help.'

'Okay, just one minute.' Elspeth disappeared into the kitchen and returned carrying a packet of biscuits and a glass of milk. 'He left some supplies. You haven't eaten anything since you got up. That won't help us. You'll start feeling ill and panicky. Here.'

Meggy did as she was told, chewing biscuits that felt like building rubble in her mouth. She couldn't taste anything but disappointment. She'd been so sure she'd done it. She'd wanted to rescue Elspeth, to be the heroine. And to beat him. That more than anything else.

Elspeth took the empty glass from Meggy's hand and set it down, leading Meggy to the spot in the corner behind the sofa.

'Here,' she said. 'We just have to get a big enough section of the carpet up, then we'll see if there are any loose boards we can get to.'

They began pulling. It was slow work. Fingernails snapped, and their skin rubbed down to raw. Inch by inch it came. Some of the carpet tacks popped out with the carpet, or they stayed in the boards and the carpet gave way around them. Every few minutes they would look up, become still and direct their ears towards the door. The lights hadn't flickered. No noise had come from the staircase. Not a sound passed beyond the outer walls to disturb them in their prison.

'What's the time?' Meggy asked.

Elspeth checked her watch. 'Ten.'

'Has he normally come by now?'

'He normally comes in the evening, then again briefly in the morning. Last night was weird, but then he'd just dropped you off, so maybe he was letting you settle in.' Elspeth stopped pulling the carpet a moment and reached a hand out to take Meggy's. 'The police will be looking for you. For me, too. By now, they'll be combing the city. Someone will have seen something. You can't just take two people from their lives without anyone noticing anything at all. I kicked my shoe into the bush so the police would know I hadn't just decided to leave, or had some sort of breakdown. Your parents will be frantic. It'll be all over the TV, I bet. We just have to hang on in there.'

She smiled and gave a strong tug on the carpet. A strip of it pulled back, exposing a large section of floorboard. Meggy sneezed and covered her eyes as the dust flew up. Elspeth covered her mouth and nose with the loose end of her shirt.

'There,' Elspeth said. 'This is what we were looking for.'

She began knocking along the board. A hollow sound echoed back.

'What do we do now?'

'We keep pulling the carpet back until we find the right board. Somewhere there'll be one with a gap big enough to put our fingers in, or the saucepan handle or something. We'll either knock the board in from this side or pull it up if we can.'

'Can you tell me about your children?' Meggy asked.

Elspeth closed her eyes, her brows darting upwards momentarily. She gritted her teeth and puffed out hard.

'Yes, of course. It's hard to think about what they're going through right now, that's all. They don't even know if I'm alive or—'

'Don't say it,' Meggy said. 'Let's not say it. We're not . . . so we don't need to think about that. Do they go to a really nice school? I bet they do.'

'They do,' Elspeth confirmed. 'They're very lucky. And I love them more than the world. But, Meggy, you didn't need the posh school. Look at you. Tougher than me, clever, resourceful. Your school is lucky to have you. I hope they know that.'

Meggy rubbed her eyes with the back of her hand, feigning dust interference.

'We should get on,' she said.

'Yes,' Elspeth agreed. 'Yes, we should.'

Chapter Seventeen

There was little mistaking the stress on Darpana Chawla's face as she unlocked the yoga studio ready for the day's classes to begin. Connie and Baarda had been waiting for her, clutching steaming cups of takeaway coffee and sheltering in an opposite doorway. Shoulders hunched against the rain and wind, Darpana looked older than her years and less serene than someone who worked at an establishment called iYoga ever should. They waited for her to get inside and shed her wet coat before entering.

'Sorry, we're not open for another—'

Baarda held up his badge. 'Terribly sorry to be here so early. I'm DI Baarda and this is Dr Woolwine. We have a few more questions for you about Elspeth Dunwoody, if you wouldn't mind.'

Darpana turned away and fiddled with the class schedules on the reception desk.

'I gave a statement. I don't think I can really add anything else, and I have a class soon.'

'We can talk while you set up, if that's more convenient,' Baarda suggested. 'We promise not to take up too much of your time.'

She shrugged and pointed in the direction of Studio 3. They followed her in.

'I understand you knew Mrs Dunwoody for some time. This must be upsetting for you,' Baarda began.

'Of course,' Darpana said, switching on heating and clearing a few stray water bottles from the edge of the room. 'But, I mean, we weren't that close. Not as friends. She was in my classes for quite a while.'

'But she followed you here from another studio when you moved employer, is that correct?'

'Sure. That's not uncommon.' She unrolled her mat and began stretching.

'Mrs Dunwoody's husband mentioned that he thought the two of you were rather close. He said you socialised occasionally and went through a period where you would text each other regularly.' Baarda let the information hang in the air without attaching a question.

It was clever. When you asked people a question, they had a safe space to limit their answer. Put a statement to them, and the information they chose to respond with could be telling. Connie stayed in the background and let him work.

'I message a lot of people,' Darpana said. 'We had coffee sometimes, the odd lunch. I liked her. I hope she's going to be all right. I saw something on the news about it. Was there a ransom?'

'Actually, no,' Baarda said. 'That was a false lead. Mrs Dunwoody is still missing. We're trying to find out as much as we can about her, who she was friends with, where she went that might have exposed her to the wrong sort of attention. Sometimes it's the smallest pieces of information that turn out to be the most useful.'

'Are you speaking to everyone again, or just me?' Darpana asked.

Baarda glanced over his shoulder and met Connie's eyes fleetingly.

'As you were the last person known to have spoken to Mrs Dunwoody, we thought we'd begin with you and work backwards from there. Is there someone else you think we should be talking to?'

'No,' she snapped. 'It's just that all I did was teach the class she was in then say goodnight to her. I really do need to get ready now.'

Baarda ignored the dismissal. 'So, when did the two of you last meet up socially, rather than just in a class?'

She let out a small huff of air. 'Three, perhaps four months ago. We went to the Timberyard on Lady Lawson Street for dinner.'

'And how was that?' Baarda asked.

'I'm sorry?' She stopped stretching and stood up.

'How was your evening with Mrs Dunwoody?' Baarda clarified.

The muscles under Darpana's eyes seized momentarily, and she shifted her lower jaw to one side as she prepared to answer.

'It was fine, thank you. It's a good restaurant.'

'I'll remember that. So, what did you talk about?' Baarda gave her a half-smile.

'The same stuff we always talked about.' She turned her back on them, reaching for her water bottle and unscrewing the cap. 'Her kids, what she was up to, my classes, who we'd seen, I honestly can't remember the details. Any reason?'

'So there was nothing troubling her? She hadn't noticed anyone acting strangely around her. Maybe internet trolls, old friends suddenly popping up unexpectedly on social media, any conflicts in her life.'

'No, nothing.'

'Ms Chawla,' Baarda said quietly. 'It seems to me that

151

there's something worrying you. That's not an accusation, and you're not in trouble. But Mrs Dunwoody is. We don't know if or when we're going to find her, or what state she'll be in when we do. What I do know is that when people withhold even the tiniest detail in circumstances like these, it can lead to serious regret later on. Perhaps I'm misreading your answers, but you seem a little upset. Now would be the time to tell us why, if it has anything to do with Mrs Dunwoody at all.'

Tears arrived in her eyes before she could open her mouth to continue lying.

The studio door opened and the first of that day's students entered, complete with breezy greeting.

'Is there somewhere quieter?' Baarda asked.

'Staff room,' Darpana said, leading the way.

It was cramped and smelled of old sweat and body spray. They each took a seat.

'I don't want to get in trouble,' Darpana said. 'He's not worth it.'

'Who's not worth it?' Baarda asked. His tone was warm and kind.

'My boyfriend.' She seemed to notice Connie for the first time. 'Am I allowed to ask who you are?'

'I'm a forensic psychologist. My role is to assimilate the evidence and help build a profile of the man who's abducted your friend Elspeth.'

'My friend?' she laughed. 'Do you have many friends who sleep with your partner?'

Connie gave the disclosure a few seconds of silence, in recognition of its enormity in the context of Darpana's life.

'Is that what Elspeth did to you?' she asked.

'Yes, it is. Just once, or at least that's what Nick told me. I found a photo on my boyfriend's phone.'

'Sorry to have to ask such an indelicate question, but what was the content of the photo?' Baarda said.

'Elspeth, naked, in our shower. Afterwards, apparently. She obviously didn't know he'd taken the photo.'

'Yet Elspeth was still attending your classes, and you're still referring to him as your boyfriend. How was that resolved?' Connie asked.

Darpana rubbed her forehead. 'We'd been going through a hard time. My fault as well as his. I'd been away at a training weekend, and I got too close to another trainer. Combination of alcohol and stress. I admitted to Nick that I'd been unfaithful, and he said he understood. Then he met Elspeth at a social here a couple of months later. They connected on social media, which was fine because I'd known her for years. It was six months ago now. I was visiting family, and they met for dinner. He said none of it was planned, and you know the rest. I could hardly complain. I'd done it to him first.'

'Must have made things difficult with Elspeth, though,' Connie said.

'I invited her out to dinner. I guess I wanted her to confess it to me. We'd been friends. I suppose I was expecting too much. We went out, like I said, and it was as if none of it had ever happened. She was perfectly normal. Halfway through the evening, Nick phoned. I told him where I was, and he went crazy. Said she'd know he'd taken the photo without her consent, and that he'd end up in a lot of trouble. She'd got young kids and a husband. So I didn't say anything. I think she realised there was something wrong, but she kept coming to my classes. Maybe she felt that if she left, I'd know something was wrong. I just tried to avoid her and be polite when she spoke to me. Now I don't know if she's alive or dead, and I don't know how I feel about that. She betrayed me. I can't forgive her, but I never wanted this.'

'Life has a way of making things complicated,' Connie said. 'Does anyone else know about this?'

Darpana shook her head.

'Your boyfriend's full name? We'll need to speak with him, I'm afraid,' Baarda said.

'Nick Bowlzer. We live together. I'd rather you spoke to him away from our flat. Is there any way you could talk to him without telling him I spoke to you?'

'We can't lie, but that doesn't mean we have to reveal our source. You should be aware that it might come out later in legal proceedings. I'm going to have to ask you to make another statement setting out everything you've told us today. I'll have an officer contact you to sort that out.'

'Okay,' she said. 'Am I in trouble for not telling you earlier?'

'No, you're not,' Baarda said. 'I understand why you'd have kept that information to yourself. Could I ask what Nick's reaction was to the news that Mrs Dunwoody had been kidnapped?'

'He didn't have anything to do with it,' Darpana said.

'These are standard questions,' Baarda said. 'Your boyfriend isn't on our radar as a suspect.'

'Sorry, I'm a bit sensitive. It was weird that she suddenly disappeared in the middle of everything, you know, and I suppose I wondered if he'd been in touch with her. He said he hadn't. That they hadn't been in contact at all since that night. He didn't want me talking to the police about it, though. Said he'd end up in the middle of the investigation.'

'Where does Nick work?' Baarda asked.

'At Edinburgh Castle. He does ticket sales, guided tours, organises events.'

'And he's there now?'

She checked her watch and nodded.

They said their goodbyes, Baarda put in the call for officers to attend and take the written statement, and they walked to the car. It was gale-force winds outside. Connie dragged her fleece over her head and shivered.

'How do people who live here know what to wear? Yesterday there was bright sunshine. Today it feels like I'm on a fishing trawler in the middle of the Atlantic.'

'That's Scotland for you. It would be boring if the weather was predictable. As I recall, Massachusetts isn't all sunshine.'

'You've been there?' Connie asked.

'A few times.' Baarda unlocked the car. 'Beautiful place. We holidayed in Nantucket once or twice, and I always enjoyed Boston when we were flying in and out. My father had friends there.'

'Nantucket isn't real. It's all old money and competitive yacht purchases. Martha's Vineyard is different. People live there all year. It's a proper island community. We off to the castle?'

'We are. You need breakfast before we do this?' Baarda asked.

'No, if I don't eat until lunchtime, I can persuade myself that I'm fasting. Do you think Elspeth's husband has any idea that she had an affair?'

'I doubt it. If I were in his shoes, it would have been one of the first details I'd have given the police. Nick would have been an obvious suspect initially, and then there's the option that she'd run off with him rather than having been abducted. I'm hardly a good advert for husbands having their fingers on the pulse of a marriage. It never occurred to me that my wife would ever be unfaithful. Perhaps superficially everything seemed absolutely fine.'

Connie stared out of the window as Baarda negotiated a section of roadworks where the traffic lights were down.

'You're going to have to tell Elspeth's husband,' she said.

'That had occurred to me,' Baarda said. 'But perhaps not yet.'

They crossed North Bridge and took a couple of turns before Baarda pulled into a hotel car park.

'I saw Nick last night at the yoga studio,' Connie said.

'Your assessment?'

'If I had to summarise, I'd say he came across as a manipulative dick.'

'That's colourful,' Baarda said, pulling on a coat.

'Not a word that really applies to me, I'm afraid.' Connie got out of the car, pulling an elastic hairband from her pocket and tidying her hair against the wind's endeavours.

'Apologies,' Baarda said.

'I'm kidding. And you're right, it was colourful language, but it's as good a description as any psycho-blurb I could give you. Which makes me wonder why a woman as intelligent and high society as Elspeth decided to risk so much for so little.'

They walked in the direction of the castle, passing the restaurants, kilt shops and tourist traps lining the road. It was early enough not to be busy, but as they neared the castle, a crowd of visitors catching the first entry of the day greeted them. Baarda dispensed with the queues by showing his badge and asking to see whoever was in charge. They were escorted to an administration building and from there, Nick Bowlzer was radioed to attend.

'What's up?' Nick said, dropping into one of the low, comfy coffee-room chairs, legs spread wide.

'Mr Bowlzer,' Baarda began. 'We're here to ask you a few questions about Elspeth Dunwoody. I understand you knew her.'

'Is that right? Who told you that?'

'This is a police investigation and as such, we often can't reveal sources of information. We're only speaking to you as a potential witness. You're not obliged to speak with us, but it's important that we get a full picture of Mrs Dunwoody's life and her movements in the months before she was abducted. Is there anything you can help us with?' Baarda asked.

'Not really. I'm not entirely sure how it is you think I can help you.' Bowlzer was cocky and self-assured, but not stupid.

'All right,' Baarda said. 'Did you have an intimate relationship with Mrs Dunwoody?'

Bowlzer gave a broad grin and scratched his stubble. 'Do I need a lawyer?'

'I don't know. Do you?' Baarda asked, his tone tightening. 'I'm sure I can arrange one if there's something you need to confess.'

'My private life's none of your business.' The grin was gone.

'It is in so far as your private life intersected with that of a missing woman, so you can be helpful voluntarily, or you can be helpful in a police station under caution. Your choice,' Baarda said.

'Fine. What do you want to know?' Nick rolled up his sleeves.

'When were you last in contact with Mrs Dunwoody?'

'We met for coffee about a week before she was taken.'

'And how would you describe the state of your relationship at that point?' Baarda asked.

'The state of my relationship? Are you asking if we were shagging?'

'I suppose I am.'

Baarda sounded irritated. Connie felt the same.

'Not then. We had been. I met her through Darpana, then we saw each other again at a charity event here. She looked bored, and I was going out for a cigarette so she came with. After that we saw each other a few times.'

'So it wasn't just a one-off event, then?' Baarda clarified.

'There were some hotel rooms, couple of times at my place. Couldn't go to hers for obvious reasons.'

'Who paid for the hotels?' Baarda asked.

'She did. Cash. Didn't want her husband finding out, I guess.'

'Did she ever express any concern to you that she was in trouble or being followed?' Baarda said.

'The only thing she ever told me was that if her husband found out, he'd kill her. He's one of those public-school rugby-player types who don't appreciate anyone else touching their stuff, like she were his new car or his yacht. I've got to be honest, when I first heard she was missing, I was a bit worried it might have something to do with her old man. To be fair, I wouldn't want my wife messing around behind my back.'

'Are you married, then?' Connie asked.

Nick swung round and lifted his chin a fraction higher. 'Why, you interested?'

'You don't seem very upset or concerned about Mrs Dunwoody. Were you affected by her abduction?' Connie said.

'She'd already broken up with me by then. Did you expect me to be sitting around crying?'

'Were you angry with her for that?' Connie continued.

'You trying to set me up for this, is that what's happening?'

'No, Mr Bowlzer, we're not. Did you tell anyone else about the affair, anyone who could have used it to their advantage to catch Mrs Dunwoody off guard and insist that she meet them to talk, for example?'

'No one knows.' He crossed his arms.

'Not one single other person is aware of it?' Connie checked.

'Well, someone must be, as you lot found me. Now who would that have been?'

'We can't reveal that information, I'm afraid, but obviously if the disclosure didn't come from you, it's possible that it came from Mrs Dunwoody herself,' Baarda said.

'Hmm,' he said. 'She wasn't happy, I know that much. She had the money, the big house, the family, but she always felt like something was missing. Maybe she just ran off and doesn't want to be found.'

'All right, Mr Bowlzer. We might need to speak with you again. I'd like you to try to remember the dates and times when you were with Mrs Dunwoody and any phone records that might be relevant. I'll be sending officers round to take a statement from you.'

'Yeah, you know, could I come into the station to do that?' Nick leaned forward, legs together now. 'I mean, that would just be easier. I'm in a relationship.'

'Lucky girl,' Connie said.

'Of course,' Baarda said, handing over a card. 'Call me to arrange it. I'll expect to hear from you in the next day, though, otherwise your home address will have to do.'

Nick didn't bother with goodbyes, letting the door slam shut as he walked out.

'So it wasn't just a one-off,' Connie said. 'Poor Darpana.'

'Indeed. But other than that, it looks like another dead end. Even if Elspeth's husband had found out about it, his alibi for the period when she was kidnapped was watertight, and his distress seems genuine. He works abroad regularly, so I suppose it wasn't difficult to cover up the affair. They have a nanny for the children. Elspeth would have had a fair amount of freedom.'

'Everything about Angela's murder revolved around her being the perfect wife and mother. Superficially, Elspeth seems the same. Roughly the same age, two kids, happy marriage. If we're formulating a profile of a man who either wants that woman for himself, or alternatively who wants to desecrate a woman with those attributes, then he can't possibly know about Nick Bowlzer.'

Baarda stood up. 'I need to decide how much of this I reveal to Elspeth's husband.'

'None,' Connie said. 'Not one word.'

'Do you not think he has a right to know? It might be relevant.'

'It might be, but I seriously doubt it. Nick Bowlzer is an idiot, and the female race deserves better than men like that, but he didn't hurt Elspeth. He's too lazy. If you tell Elspeth's husband, there's every chance he'll tell his parents, or a friend, or his lawyer, the list is endless. And if it leaks, if the press gets hold of it, the only thing keeping Elspeth alive – this idealistic opinion her kidnapper has of her – is dead in the water. I suspect that's how we'd find her, too.'

Chapter Eighteen

Blood dripped into the carpet, not that Meggy and Elspeth cared about the state of the furnishings. Their fingers, however, were raw. They'd taken a break and made an attempt to push the dangling light back into the ceiling cavity, wrapping the loose wires around a wooden spoon from the kitchen to take up the slack, and slotting that into the plasterboard hole. The result was messy and wouldn't stand even the most cursory of inspections, but it was better than it had been.

Having cleared up the pile of plasterboard dust, and eaten some cheese and softening crackers, they went back to ripping up the carpet. No loose boards so far, and they had to shift the furniture again to give them more to play with. But now there was hope. A cracked board missing a sliver of wood along its side was wide enough for Elspeth to slip her fingers into and pull. Not in their current state, though. They were damaged enough already. One large splinter followed by an infection with no access to first aid or antibiotics and there would be more than just Fergus to worry about.

Using two clean tea towels from the kitchen, Meggy wrapped

one each, tenderly, around Elspeth's hands, tucking in the end above her wrists.

'I don't want you to get your hopes up,' Elspeth said. 'Whatever is down there, there'll be beams. Maybe steel, insulation, and all sorts of hardware. Chances are this is just another dead end.'

'We're already at a dead end,' Meggy said.

'True. Now, stay back in case any splinters start flying. And don't forget. It's his flat below us. If we disturb him and he comes up here in a rage, you just go and get into bed. Pretend you've been asleep this whole time.'

'How much do you think he can hear?' Meggy asked, whispering suddenly. 'When I ran up here there were two flights of stairs. We're at the top of the house. Would the noise go all the way to the ground floor?'

'It might. I guess we'll find out pretty fast. He usually comes up to me in the evenings, so maybe he's out during the day. You willing to take that chance?'

'It's better than doing nothing,' Meggy said.

'I agree, but let's be as quiet as we can anyway. If we make a loud noise, we'll stop to see if we can hear him coming up, okay?'

'Okay,' Meggy said.

'Right, well, I'm ready.'

Elspeth knelt to the side of the damaged floorboard and carefully slid her fingers in deep enough that she could bend them, knuckles still showing above the cavity. Bracing herself, knees pushed hard into the floor, she tugged. The floorboard creaked and allowed itself to be bent fractionally in its centre, but did not give. Elspeth tried again. More creaking, some splinters coming away from the edges of the gap. But nothing more.

'Here, let me help,' Meggy said, kneeling behind Elspeth and wrapping her arms around the woman's chest.

'On three. One, two, three!'

Meggy pulled, wrenching Elspeth's shoulders. The board gave a bonfire-style crackle, and Meggy flew backwards, tumbling over her own feet. Elspeth landed hard on her backside, holding a small piece of floorboard in her hand. She waved it at Meggy.

'Got a piece! We did it. Come on. It'll be easier to work on now.'

They threw themselves into it, pulling away a section of the board that was beginning to rot but still holding on to its strength. At last it was gone, a four foot by five inch black hole in its place. Grasping the next boards to either side, they tried to increase the hole, pulling, bashing, finding themselves fighting proper carpentry and more solid wood.

'It can't just have been one rotten board,' Elspeth said. 'There must be others. We have to lift more of the carpet.'

'Wait,' Meggy said. 'I can get my leg down into the space and kick upwards. I should be able to shift the board at the end.'

She raced away, reappearing seconds later clutching pink-and-white striped trainers.

'He bought me shoes. What a bloody idiot,' Meggy declared.

Lying down across the top of the opening they'd already made, lengthways with her trainers fastened, she wiggled her right leg to get her foot and ankle beneath the floorboard at the far end.

'There's enough space for me to bend my knee. Come up by my head and hold on to me.'

Elspeth gave her some support to lean back against, and Meggy began to kick. No point after that in pretending they wouldn't be overheard if Fergus was in the house. In the room below it must have sounded as if the ceiling was about to fall in. The board protested, fought, took its time, then flew into the air, flipped and landed the other side of the room. Meggy and Elspeth hugged one another then stared at the chaos before them.

'Wasn't much point fixing the light,' Meggy said.

'It'll be okay. All we'd have to do is hide the floorboards, roll the carpet back over and hope he doesn't tread in the gap. How near can we get the lamp?'

The answer was not very. The removed boards were mid-room, and the tiny lamp's cord extended no more than two feet from the power points at the edge.

'Have you seen an extension cable anywhere?' Meggy asked.

'No. He'd be too worried about us wrapping it around his neck. And now we've got floorboards as a weapon too, not that these are good for much more than a single hit. They must be decades old.'

'He must be a coward if he's scared of a woman and a girl beating him up. It's been nearly twenty-four hours. Maybe he's left us. Or perhaps he got caught by the police, but they don't know where to look for us.'

'Or it could just be part of whatever sick game he's playing. I don't know. Do you ever think you end up with what you deserve in life? That there really is such a thing as just deserts? I don't know what scares me more – the thought that him taking me was completely random and that nothing I did contributed to his choosing me, or the idea that maybe this happened to me because of something I did wrong. That there's some giant invisible scale in the sky for each of us and that when you screw up enough you tip it over, and that's when bad things happen.'

Meggy stared at her. 'I'm twelve,' she said, shaking off the heavy conversation. 'We need to find out what's down there. Come on.' She lay on her stomach, head flat on the floor turned to the side, then reached her hand in, grimacing. 'I can feel some wires. There's a big beam running crossways, and it has

164

some metal bits on it.' She shifted over to get more of her arm in the cavity. 'It's disgusting in here, loads of dust and spiderwebs. Hold on. I've got something. It's loose. Maybe we can use it to get the other boards up. It feels quite long, but it's stuck on something else.' She rolled over, pushing her shoulder into the gap to give herself room to manoeuvre. 'Hold on . . . it's moving. I've got it,' she cried, shifting her body backwards again and turning her wrist to allow her to pull the object from the hole.

She brought it out into the half-light and threw it in Elspeth's direction. It hit the bare floorboards with a dull thump. Elspeth put her head to one side, frowned, drew nearer to get a better look, then clambered backwards, her hands and feet dragging awkwardly along the floor as she went.

'What—'

'Don't look at it,' Elspeth said.

The girl picked it up again.

'Meggy, put that down right now. Just throw it back in there.'

'Is that . . . ?' She dropped it and stood up, brushing her hands on her leggings. 'It's not real. Why would it be down there?'

'I think it is real,' Elspeth said. 'We should just block this hole back up, right now. Come on, help me clear up.' She grabbed the far edge of the rolled-back carpet and began pulling it towards the first corner they'd uncovered.

'Is it from a human? It's long. What bone is it? How come it's there? Do you think someone had an accident and died in there?'

'You really are twelve,' Elspeth muttered. 'Oh, God, I'm sorry. Meggy, listen to me right now. This was a mistake. We were never supposed to see in here. Help me put it all back.'

'No. I need to know. I want to see.' She threw herself back onto her stomach and let her upper body down into the hole. 'There's something there. It's just a bit too far back. Hold on.'

There was a moment of silence, Meggy puffing hard, then

a dragging sound, something heavy moving closer to the edge of the hole. 'I don't understand what this . . .'

Meggy screamed and the room echoed with the violence of the noise.

'Quiet!' Elspeth shouted, throwing herself to the ground beside the girl and wrapping a strong hand over Meggy's mouth.

Meggy pulled her head from the hole and thrust her face into Elspeth's shoulder, sobbing, shaking her head to and fro.

'I'm sorry,' she said. 'I'm sorry. You were right. I shouldn't have looked.'

Elspeth pushed Meggy away from the hole and took a deep breath. Genie, bottle, too late were the phrases that occurred to her as she bent forward. The scrap of material that was catching the light came as no surprise. Pale pink cotton. The end of a pink ribbon a little further into the cavity. She didn't want to look but did anyway.

The last person to have worn the dress had auburn hair. It was matted, looked infested in the half-light. The face, or whatever remained of it − small mercies − was turned away from the light. One arm was clearly visible, though. Not that you could really call it an arm any more. Whatever fleshy padding it had once possessed had dried out, leaving only leathery skin clinging to the outline of bone. There was no way of knowing how old the woman had been, nor how she'd died. But the fabric of the dress was more than just dirty. Patches of it were filthy with mud.

Elspeth sat up again, contemplating the death of the woman below the floorboards. Multiple bones of different sizes, and a fresh body. Fergus had killed before, definitely more than once, possibly many times. No doubt he'd kill again. Another woman, same dress, she thought. It wasn't her previous life that flashed before her eyes as she'd expected, but the life she'd carelessly assumed she had left to live. Her children's graduations. Weddings. Grandchildren. Holidays, Christmases, birthdays . . .

'Did he do this?' Meggy asked, weeping. 'Hurt these people and hide their bones down here? You think he did. You think he's going to do the same to us.'

'Put the bones back under the floor,' Elspeth instructed her softly. 'We should never have seen any of this.'

'No,' Meggy said. 'Whoever ended up down there, we should get them out. I don't want to die here and be put under the floor. Why should they stay there, in the dark?'

'Meggy, be sensible. If he comes back now and finds all this, we're going to end up under that floor much sooner than we need to. Now put it back!'

'I won't, and you can't tell me what to do. When I came in you were under the bed covered in shit, and I had to look after you, so you don't get to be the grown-up now.'

Meggy thrust her hand back into the cavity again, circling her arm wildly, reaching in every direction. When she finally surfaced, it was with a handful of tiny bones clutched in her hand.

'Is that . . . is that fingers, do you think?'

Elspeth sat looking away, shaking her head.

'It's bones from a hand, I reckon. Only they're tiny, really tiny. Like . . .' Meggy said.

'Don't say it,' Elspeth whispered.

'Like a child's,' Meggy finished anyway. 'There's lots more down there I couldn't reach. There's definitely another skull – I touched the round bit. And loads of—'

'Would you stop?' Elspeth screeched. 'Just stop talking. I don't want to hear this. This can't happen to us.' She punctuated each word with a stamp of her foot. 'Do you hear me, Meggy? Whatever happened to these poor people, it can't happen to us. It can't.'

Meggy started to sway, arms wrapped around her knees on the floor, staring blankly through the fake window on the wall.

'Got to clear up now,' Elspeth chanted to herself as she swept the bones back into the hole. 'Got to clear up.'

She replaced the single floorboard that was in one piece, pulled Meggy up and deposited her in the armchair at the end of the room, then began pulling the carpet to cover the bare boards.

'Better,' she whispered to herself. 'Come on, Elspeth, you can do this.'

She pushed and heaved the sofa so that it pinned the loose carpet to the floor. Picking up the scattered shards of wood and carpet tacks, she surveyed the sitting room. The same but entirely different.

'Meggy.' She pulled the girl up to a standing position. 'Honey, we have to wash our hands and faces, and get clean clothes on.'

'No point. We're going to die here. Like those other people. Do you think their ghosts are in here with us?'

'No,' Elspeth said. 'There's no such thing as ghosts. Those people are dead. They can't hurt us now, but he can, Meggy, and I don't want that. So we're going to sort ourselves out, okay? You can get into bed after that if you like. It might be best, anyway. You've had a shock.'

Meggy nodded, holding out a hand for Elspeth to take. In the bathroom they washed off the dust, and the smell of disintegrating bones.

'Elspeth,' Meggy whispered, and they went to settle down for the night. 'I'm so scared.'

'I know, sweetheart,' Elspeth said, stroking Meggy's hair and kissing her forehead. 'I'm scared too. But we've got each other, okay? We're going to take care of each other now.'

'Okay,' Meggy said. 'We'll take care of each other. And there are no ghosts. Promise?'

'No ghosts at all. I swear it.'

But in her imagination, a dead woman was slowly turning

her head towards the light, wanting to be seen. Elspeth squeezed her eyes shut tight. It wasn't her face on that corpse, she told herself. It wouldn't ever be her face. Same dress didn't mean the same fate. They would be smarter and more determined. They didn't have to die like the others before them.

'No ghosts,' she said one more time. It wasn't for Meggy's benefit.

'Can you see me?' Fergus croaked from the doorway.

They screamed.

Chapter Nineteen

He'd been dead. It was no illusion. The moment of death had been marked with a blinding flash. There had been a sense of lifting out of his corporeal body and travelling instead with his spirit. Burdens behind him, Fergus Ariss had risen up to take his place in the afterlife.

He'd steadied himself before opening his eyes. It would undoubtedly be more colourful, more vivid than the earthly world. His mother would be waiting for him. Perhaps there would be a celebration, and an explanation as to how it all worked. He'd felt fleeting concern, but then remembered he was dead. What was the worst thing that could happen now?

Letting his mind float free, he focused on his breathing. Gone was the tight throat that had made his voice ugly and small when he was scared. There was no discomfort or grief. No restriction in his stomach or bowels. Bodily concerns were washed away. There was only warmth and an anticipation of the love to come.

Fergus had opened his eyes.

'What the fuck?'

He'd run his hands over his body. It was intact, his soul still contained within. He'd slid his fingertips over his wrist and felt no pulse. The room around him was the same one he'd died in. The photos were still on the wall, the bed still out of reach. Sitting up, his limbs had strobed through the light, leaving little past images of his movements in the air. Everything was the same and yet a world apart. His heart was still in his chest. The lack of sensation in his body had left him floating, in spite of the fact that he could see his body making contact with the floor.

'What went wrong?'

He'd walked slowly to the dusty mirror, hardly daring to look. Approaching the image by sliding sideways into view, he'd found he could still see himself. There was a representation of himself still in the world. It moved its eyes when he moved his, yet he saw no breath on the glass when he blew. There was blood on the floor and on his clothes from his fall, but no pain in his body. Fergus had pinched himself, hard. The result was the faintest buzz through his skin, as if someone were shouting to him from a great distance.

Ripping open a cupboard, he shoved aside box after box until he found what he was after. The sewing box was a biscuit tin from decades ago, paint peeling and faded. Inside were needles that hadn't seen the light of day in more years than he could recall. He'd plucked one from its pin cushion, wiped it on his sleeve and stuck it firmly into his thigh before letting go, glaring at it, daring it not to hurt him.

'Nothing,' he whispered. 'Why am I still here?'

He'd grabbed the sewing tin and launched it across the room. 'Why? Where's my mother?'

Fergus kicked the wardrobe door, his foot smashing through the cheap pine. He'd punched and hit until the upper section was in pieces on the floor before turning his attention to the bed, ripping the covers off and flinging them impotently around.

They'd watched him from the floor, nothing more than crumpled bedding waiting to be picked up again.

'What am I?' he'd demanded of the photos on the wall. 'If I'm not dead and I'm not alive, how can I still walk and talk and move things?'

He'd given a cry that turned into a bark, caught between the tides of fury and fear, slapping his own face, one cheek then the other, screwing his eyes tightly shut then opening them again, finally realising the needle was still stuck in his thigh. Wrenching it out, he then dropped it where he stood.

'Did I not do enough yet?' Fergus had demanded of the woman immortalised on his wall. 'I got a wife and a daughter. They're in my house, living with me. I should be allowed to come to you now. This isn't fair.' He'd fallen to his knees. 'You're not being fair.'

Crumpling into a ball, his forehead touching the floor, he'd cried. When he'd sat back up, nothing had changed. The sky had been completely dark, the house silent. There'd been a new feeling inside his body, a liquid softness, as if the tension that had tethered his organs in place while alive had allowed everything to blend. He'd been able to smell his own breath, and it was more animal than human.

'I'm rotting,' he'd said. 'I have to make things better before I decompose. How much time do I have? Shit, I'm going to fall apart.'

In the kitchen, he'd taken a laptop from an old satchel hanging on the back of the door, booting it up with shaking hands. He hated using technology. Being on the grid meant being visible. But he'd needed information fast. A little circle turned round and round as Fergus had stood chewing his nails.

When the search engine had finally bothered springing into life, he'd typed in 'stages of decomposition' and hit return, sitting down at the table to read the pearls of wisdom the ether had to offer.

'Internal organs decompose twenty-four to seventy-two hours after death,' he'd read. 'Bloating and bloody foam leakage from facial cavities, three to five days after death. Bloating from decomposition gases will happen after eight to ten days. After a month, body starts to liquefy.' He'd slammed the lid.

'How long have I been dead?' Fergus asked himself. The last time he'd come into the house, he'd brought Meggy with him. It was her fault he'd fallen down the stairs. His plans had gone wrong, and she'd behaved badly. He'd been distracted, unwell.

They were upstairs, he'd realised. He didn't know how long he'd left them alone, but Elspeth and Meggy could give him the information he needed.

All had been quiet behind the door. Or perhaps his hearing had been altered as well as his sense of his own existence. He'd placed both palms on the door, trying to get some feeling for what lay beyond. Could he pass directly through the door if he concentrated hard enough? Maybe his whole atomic structure was different now. He'd taken a deep breath and pressed his body into the wood. Nothing shifted. He was firmly tied to his body until either the flesh slipped from his bones, leaving his soul nowhere to call home, presumably damning him to a lifetime of echoing uselessly around the house, or until he found a way to pass into the next world. More hoops to jump through first. Weren't there always, just as there had been in life? Even his death was a fuck-up.

He'd had a security procedure before, he'd realised, only suddenly it didn't seem important. He just needed someone to talk to. The key, miraculously, was still in the door where he'd left it. He turned it in the lock and entered.

Feet making little impact on the carpet beneath him, he'd shut the door to the world silently behind him and walked into the lounge. There they'd been, on the sofa, curled up together. The screaming had begun as soon as he'd spoken.

'Can you see me?' he asked again.

Meggy cried and Elspeth buried her face in the girl's hair.

'I said, can you see me?' He strode forward.

'Yes,' Elspeth shouted. 'Yes, we can see you. We can!'

'And what am I?'

Meggy stopped crying and stared at him. Elspeth frowned.

'I . . . I don't understand,' Elspeth stammered.

He stepped forward, arms held out. 'What am I? What do you see when you look at me? Come here and touch me. I need to know if I'm real.'

'Don't,' Meggy said, clutching Elspeth and trying to hold her down.

'Shh,' Elspeth said. 'It's all right.'

She stood up, stepping forward slowly, gingerly, as if approaching an injured beast, a single hand held out, fingers bent softly.

Close enough, she put her hand on his and squeezed it lightly.

'I see you. You're here with us. Can you feel me touching you?'

Fergus shrugged.

'You're real,' Elspeth said.

'No.' He shook his head. 'You're just telling me what I want to hear. I died! That makes me a ghost. I'm trapped in this body, but I know I'm dead. Everything inside me is jelly. It sloshes and floats, and the whole world smells like death. Don't you smell that?'

Elspeth gave Meggy a sharp look and a single shake of her head.

'I smell nothing,' Elspeth told him. 'Why don't I make you a warm drink. Perhaps that would help.'

'Why do I need to drink? I just told you I'm dead. Corpses don't need food or liquid. What would be the point? It'll run straight through me. This . . .' He pushed his own stomach.

Elspeth took a step away.

'This isn't mine any more. I'm just inhabiting it before I move on.'

'Okay,' Elspeth murmured.

'I fell down the stairs because of her.' He pointed at Meggy. 'I brought her here for you, then I got hurt and I died too soon. No one was ready for me.'

He peeled his lips back from his teeth and took a step towards the sofa, where Meggy was trying to disappear into the far corner. Elspeth stepped into his path.

'She heard you fall. We were both worried about you. In fact, we stayed by the door for hours calling, wishing we could get out to help you. What happened was terrible, but we still care about you. We want to help you, don't we, Meggy?'

The girl sobbed.

'Were you really worried?' he asked.

'Of course we were,' Elspeth confirmed. 'We're your family now.'

'It's not finished,' he said. 'There's still an empty bed. I have to fill it. That must be it.'

Elspeth froze. 'What do you mean?'

'It's not done yet. I'm not finished. How long ago did I die?'

'I don't know . . .' Elspeth said.

Taking her by the shoulders, Fergus shook her.

'Tell me.'

Her head flew backwards then forwards again.

'When did I die? How long ago?'

'It was only one day!' Meggy shouted. 'Leave her alone. Let go. You only died yesterday.'

Releasing Elspeth, Fergus collapsed backwards against the wall.

'Thank God. I still have time before the foam starts leaking out of me. I'm going to bloat like a balloon, did you know that?'

His eyes were holes in his face.

'I'm going to liquefy. I'll have to finish everything before that, or I'll be useless. You have to help me.'

'What do you need?' Elspeth asked.

'Tidy up, for a start. You're going to have someone else to look after. You'll like that. Mothers like looking after people.'

'Sure,' Elspeth said. 'Whatever you want. Meggy and I will help, won't we, sweetheart?'

'Sure,' the girl said as she moved to stand in the pool of light where the lamp was plugged in.

Fergus gave a gaping open-mouthed grin, and Elspeth turned from the stench of his breath. He leaned forward, planting a wet kiss on her cheek.

'I'll be back soon. Try not to miss me.'

Meggy ran and ripped the lamp from the wall and blackness fell. In two footsteps, she was at Fergus' back, throwing the electrical cord over his neck, crossing the ends over and pulling them tight.

'Help me!' she screeched at Elspeth.

Elspeth let out a strangled cry as Fergus let his body fall backwards, toppling onto Meggy, who went down beneath him. He grappled with the cord uselessly then went for Meggy's face instead, behind his back. Elspeth was feeling in the dark for his hands, attempting in the chaos to disable him so Meggy would have the time to cut off his air supply.

There was a soft whoop as Fergus brought up his knee and smashed it into Elspeth's stomach. She cried out and flew off him, clutching her body and retching.

176

'Elspeth?' Meggy called out, terror and exhaustion slackening her grip on the cord.

Fergus seized the moment to lean to the side, the electrical wire tightening for a moment as he hammered a fist back to where the girl was, connecting with her face in a satisfying series of crunches and thuds. Fist – face – head – floor.

Elspeth was still crying a few feet away, her breath whistling as she gasped for air. Meggy was crawling towards her, when he caught her ankle and dragged her backwards.

Death, apparently, had made him stronger.

'Teach you a lesson,' he muttered, pulling his penknife from his pocket. 'So you don't forget.'

'No!' Elspeth found air and a voice from somewhere. 'Don't you hurt her!'

'You're going to stop me?' he asked.

'Please, I'm begging you,' Elspeth cried.

'You or her. One of you has to learn. Which?'

Meggy was crying and clawing at the floor in vain to get away.

'Me,' Elspeth said. 'Teach me the lesson. That way we'll both remember.'

The chink of light from the miniature bulb in the microwave, crossing the hallway and entering the lounge, shone off the edge of the blade.

'Hand,' he told Elspeth, letting go of Meggy's foot.

Elspeth began to cry. Meggy cried with her, climbing into her lap. The woman reached her hand out in the dark. There was no fight left in her.

As he pressed the tip of the knife into her little finger above the central knuckle, she called out for her own mother and Meggy howled. The blade pressed home, through the skin and tendons, cracking the bone and severing the digit.

As Elspeth thumped to the floor, Meggy cradled her head

177

and called her name. Fergus grabbed a thick handful of the girl's hair.

'Don't be naughty,' he said, spittle flying through the dark into her eyes. 'See what you made me do to your mum.'

Fergus stood up, reaching for the wall then fumbling his way to the exit, cursing as he went. Turned out that being dead was just as shitty as being alive. He left the woman and the girl in the dark.

Chapter Twenty

They sat in Connie's hotel room, Baarda at the desk, her on the floor, and stared at photographs. On one wall, Connie had printed out a list of all the places Angela went regularly – supermarket, doctor, dentist, school, friends and family, bank. On the opposite wall the same had been done for Elspeth. There was no crossover. These were women at different ends of the financial, educational and social spectra.

Yet, the photos of the two of them were remarkably similar. Not their faces or their clothing styles, just the types of photos. With the kids on a beach, at a playground, a horse ride, a play centre. First day of school. Family Christmas, Easter egg hunt, Halloween. They both kept themselves trim, ate healthy food. They each valued friendship highly and were careful not to drink too much. Neither smoked or took drugs. Each appeared to be the perfect wife.

'What did you call this?' Baarda asked.

'A frantic information grab,' Connie said. 'We've hit a dead end, so we go back to all the information at once. We have certain links already. The key is that the same man was at the scene of both Angela's murder and Elspeth's abduction. No other crime scene similarities. But there's something we're missing. Like they both love ballet, or have the same favourite soccer team.'

'Football,' Baarda corrected.

'If you knew what I meant, you didn't need to correct me. The point is that he found them, stalked them, chose them. So there's a link. It's in here somewhere.' She rearranged a pile of emails from the previous twelve months sent by each woman. 'What keywords did the technical team search for when they were comparing the emails and messages?'

'They went through everything including dates, place names, people, products, even online purchases. There was no crossover between the two women that we can find. If they were in the same place on the same day, it was a one-off and a coincidence. We can't place them anywhere together. No mutual friends.'

'Phone records?' Connie asked.

'Both landline and mobile. None of the same numbers were called by both women.'

'That's it, I'm calling down for room service,' Connie sighed. 'What'll you take?'

'Anything with salmon,' Baarda said, pinning a map to the wall with a solid and a dotted line on it. Solid for Angela's known movements on the day of her death, dotted for Elspeth's the day she disappeared.

Connie ordered and put down the phone. 'Tell me about your first love. I'm guessing . . . university. Am I right?'

'I thought we were here to work,' he said.

'Diversion helps shift my thought pattern on and off large amounts of data. Frantic information grabs work like those weird dot sequences where you can't see them when you're looking straight at them.'

'So tell me about the time you spent unable to communicate. No reason we have to dwell on my private life, is there?'

180

Connie sighed. 'I'm not sure that's very gentlemanly of you. Isn't there some sort of British code that says you're supposed to do whatever a lady asks of you?'

'Given how well that's worked out for me over the past year, I've decided to try a different tack, which was your advice to me.'

'Yeah, shot myself in the foot there. What do you want to know?' Connie threw herself on her bed and arranged the pillows beneath her head.

'Comfortable?'

'Just getting on the couch ready to talk to my shrink. Want to play?'

'Is it a game?' Baarda asked, turning round in his chair to watch her.

'Actually no, now that you ask. It's not a game at all.'

'How did it happen?'

'Playing lacrosse,' she said. 'So often the moments that define your life are the ones you're ignorant about at the time. Until you learn to deal, you spend countless hours rewriting history in your head. If I'd turned left at the roundabout instead of right, if I'd remembered to turn the gas off. In my case, it was if I hadn't run quite so hard to take a shot at goal.'

Freshman year, already accepted into a great college, aiming to study astronomy. The future had been nothing but a gleaming sunlit day. The lacrosse game had ended prematurely for her. She'd been tackled fairly, but her head had clashed with another girl's, and they'd both ended up on their backs on the pitch. Her opponent had got up first with an egg growing from her forehead. Connie had sat up, staggered slightly, felt the world lurch beneath her and swallowed down the vomit that threatened to rise and embarrass her in front of the whole team plus spectators.

All the signs had been there, and the aspect of it that haunted her more than anything was that she'd known better. Truly. Concussion wasn't an unusual side effect of a blow to the head. She'd seen enough members of the local high school's American football team carted off the pitch to realise how seriously it should have been taken. But the nausea passed, then the dizziness wore off. The ice helped to reduce the bump, and the fact that the bruising was coming out not staying internal was a good sign – she'd read that somewhere, too. There was a party that evening. She had a few hours to sleep off the blow, get rid of the headache. Her mother was away, and her father would be in his study working. No one would notice. And they hadn't.

The school year had ended. Connie had graduated with an impressive grade point average. Her mother, father, brother and grandmother had celebrated with her. There'd been a party at their Martha's Vineyard home and a long, hot summer to look forward to. The President had a daughter vacationing with him who her brother had a massive crush on and, as happened every June and July, normal social structure and restraints became meaningless. There was no snobbery on the Vineyard. You could and would rub shoulders with film stars, world leaders, fishermen and waitresses, and no one pointed or whispered. It was a typical summer.

'Only by then I'd met Ruben. He lived in Edgartown, I lived on the outskirts of Oak Bluffs. I had a job in an ice-cream parlour during the day, and he'd come over to meet friends. God, I never reacted to anyone like I did when he walked in. I dropped the cone I was making him, my hands shaking, and I must have sounded like a complete idiot. He was nice about it. He could afford to be. I'm pretty sure every girl on the island had him at the top of their wish list.'

'Was he everything you thought he was going to be, or an illusion?' Baarda asked.

'I never got the chance to find out.' Connie closed her eyes. 'He asked for my number, which I gave him, pretending it wasn't a big deal. It was. I hadn't really had a boyfriend. I went to an all-girls school on the mainland, and because so many girls got in trouble during the summer with tourists and parties, my parents were strict. Curfews, chaperones, endless rules. But I'd turned eighteen and I was going off to college anyway, so I guess they realised it was too late to keep me locked up. Ruben called me after a week. We agreed to meet on Squibnocket Beach at eight p.m. It would have been dark by then. We were going to take a couple of beers – his idea – I didn't drink. You could light a fire in the sand on Squibnocket if you took your own wood and were careful about it. The track to the beach is hard to find at night and there aren't that many passersby. You can swim in the dark and the water around you will light up with comb jellies if you bump them.'

She'd spent the entire day getting ready. Waxing, washing, choosing clothes, making them more revealing than less. Messing her hair up so she didn't look like a try-hard. It was more than halfway through the summer vacation, but if things went well with Ruben, they'd still have August.

Taking the jeep, she'd thrown a picnic rug in the trunk, some wood for the fire, matches and a couple of blankets. Stopped before reversing out of the driveway to apply a final layer of lip gloss. It was called naked honey. Funny the things that lodged in your brain. The note she'd left for her parents was that she'd be spending the evening with her best friend Gemma. Gemma, primed for the deception, was ready to make excuses if a phone call came. Every tiny detail was perfect.

'It was a clear night. Really starry. They often are in the Vineyard during the summer, but this was particularly beautiful. We were going to watch the sun go down. The sunsets there are like Turner paintings. More a work of art than an event.

God, I was excited. You know that feeling low in your stomach? I don't mean just the sexual thrill of being in contact with someone you want. It's the anticipation of breaching boundaries, the thrill of making yourself vulnerable to another human being. It was supposed to be a revelatory evening. I guess I got that bit right.'

The knock at the door signalled the arrival of room service.

'Don't move, I'll get it,' Baarda said, bringing in the food and setting it down on the bed. Neither of them began eating. 'So what happened?'

'I don't remember. I woke up in hospital. My car was found in the woods on the lane out to Squibnocket. They assumed I'd become disoriented in the dark, taken a wrong turn and hit a tree. I have no idea if Ruben was waiting for me or not. I hope he was, but then he'd have spent the evening waiting for a girl who never turned up. My parents phoned Gemma when I wasn't home by midnight. She admitted everything, and they sent out a search party. The problem was . . .' Connie sat up on the bed and took the cover off the food, picking up a fork and shifting morsels around the plate. 'When I regained consciousness I couldn't speak or write. Couldn't make myself understood at all. Trying to talk made my brain spin. Focusing on individual words was impossible. I could walk, eat, dress myself – do everything except communicate.'

'But inside you were processing thoughts normally?'

'Yeah. That was almost worse. It was terrifying. Frustrating, painful, isolating. I was locked inside my own brain.'

Baarda stood up and walked to the window, looking down at the street and frowning.

'I can't even begin to imagine how terrible that must have been.'

'The story gets worse before it gets better. Over the years, my grandparents had contributed substantial amounts to a hospital in Boston. They were great friends with a psychiatrist – Dr Webster – one of their own generation, not known for his empathy, although that was something I only learned later. My grandmother called him immediately. He assessed me, I had all the usual scans, and upon finding nothing physically wrong with me, he decided that having lied to my parents, intent on having my first sexual experience, I was suffering from teenage hysteria. His version of events was that I had crashed my car deliberately to avoid the sexual confrontation and to avoid becoming fully adult. He also decided that my decision not to communicate was wilful. He wanted me in intense therapy, open to treatments, and guaranteed that he would have snapped me out of it within three months. You're not going to touch your food?'

'I'm not hungry,' Baarda said. 'Your parents didn't get a second opinion?'

'He was one of the most respected psychiatrists in Boston and an authority on teenage disorders. They had no reason to doubt him. That's how I was admitted to a psychiatric ward, age eighteen years four months, when I should have been packing my bags for college. It was . . .' She threw the fork to the end of the bed, lying back down. 'It was like dying. I wasn't a part of anyone's life any more.'

The unit was in Boston, her family were on Martha's Vineyard. Dr Webster had instructed them not to visit too often, to avoid feeding her hysteria. Soon, he declared, without an audience to play to, Connie would conform.

The hospital was a coin. There were two sides to it. In front of family and friends, doctors would issue concerned nods, studiously read charts. Nurses would be jolly and sweet, never in a rush. There was a sense of calm and of community.

The flip side, when the doors were locked and the staff went unseen by those beyond their number, was of a curious form of discipline. Didn't want to take your medication? Privileges were withdrawn, such as your choice of food, clean clothes, and privacy while using the bathroom. Get frustrated and show your temper? That was more serious. There were ways of giving sedative injections that were relatively painless, and alternative means designed to let you know you were having inches of surgical steel shoved into you. Decide not to comply with therapy? You'd be held down and stripped.

'I learned fast. I watched. That's all I could do, after all. Everything my brain did was input while it couldn't output.' She sighed and stretched her arms above her head. 'My recovery wasn't going as fast as Dr Webster had promised my grandmother, and he was concerned that I was making him look foolish, so he chose shock tactics. One day, he had a male nurse come in and shave off all my hair. It was the only time I saw my mother really lose it when she visited. She was furious. They told her I'd stolen a razor and done it myself.'

Her hospital suite had comprised an uncomfortably thin mattress, a bedside table with no lock, a wardrobe with an open front, and a bathroom with a door that anyone could open any time. For her own safety, of course. Nothing sharp. Nothing heavy and blunt. Nothing she could ingest other than water. No media that might be upsetting. Decor in pastel colours that reminded her of old ladies' hair. Food designed to be soft and slip down easily. She still couldn't look at Jell-O. But what haunted her, and what had kept her alive, was her fellow patients. Studying them, knowing what would set them off and what would soothe them. Night-time in the teenage psychiatric ward was never a quiet event. It was as if the darkening was a trigger.

'What struck me most was the people in my unit who shouldn't have been there. Teenagers suffering from depression who simply needed a better form of care. Not that I was qualified then, but when you watch day and night, it becomes possible to identify the sad versus the mad and the bad. The issue was the few genuinely dangerous kids there whose parents had been able to divert them out of the criminal justice system, probably by making the sort of generous donations to the hospital my grandmother had. Kids who couldn't be treated and who posed a lifelong risk to society.'

It had been a rude awakening, feeling the bouncing of her mattress as a fellow patient had sneaked into her room to stand on her bed. He'd found or fashioned a blade that flashed in the dim glow of the light from the corridor, and he was attempting to cut a section from her ceiling.

'They're coming,' he'd told her. 'They want me to give you to them. As a sample.'

Connie had attempted a scream. He'd dropped to his knees on her bed and shoved a sweaty palm over her mouth.

'Don't do that. Not that anyone will come. Someone brought in cakes for the night shift, and they're all stuffing their faces in the staff room. My friends up there,' he pointed at the space beyond the ceiling, 'saw you. They chose you. They think you'll taste nice.'

With that, he'd removed his hand and extended his tongue, licking her face from cheek to cheek, pushing into her mouth and out again. She tried to shove him off, but he was stronger – far stronger, almost an impossible force – and he knew it.

'Mmm, they're right. You do,' he'd panted. 'You do taste good. Maybe just a little bite for myself before they come. There's plenty of you to share.'

He'd bitten into her earlobe before she'd had time to consider whether or not the threat was serious. That time the scream wouldn't be stopped. Her pillow was a bloody mess in the seconds between him biting, sitting up and beginning to chew. Three or four minutes later, the nurses had become sufficiently cross that they'd decided to see what was happening, syringe in its neat little kidney tray, ready to enter her thigh. It was their faces in her doorway that had reinforced her horror. The fact that they'd backed away rather than enter, calling for backup from the male nurses before tackling the monster sitting astride her who was taking his time, rolling the morsel of flesh around in his mouth to properly savour the flavour before swallowing.

It was resolved in a fight, after he'd lurched for her other ear and been tackled off her bed, smashing his head on the radiator and spraying a further dose of blood up her wall. Connie had sat shaking in her bed while they'd wrestled him first into submission, then medicated unconsciousness.

She'd heard him whispering to the strange beings he saw above her ceiling for weeks before the attack. He'd had an odd habit of licking his lips when he passed her in the corridor. Sometimes he could be seen standing in corners of rooms, staring intently into the walls, muttering then listening for a reply. Connie had been determined never to leave herself vulnerable to attack again.

'What happened to you?' Baarda asked.

She shook free of the memory, giving a small fierce smile and lifting her hair away from her left ear. Baarda walked to the bed and sat gently on the edge, pushing the hair back further with his fingertips to inspect what was left of the lobe. The ragged edge was still clear. He ran his thumb over the rough scar tissue.

'It's helpful,' Connie said. 'Every mirror is a reminder of why I do this job.'

'They allowed male and female patients on the same ward?' Baarda sounded horrified, rightly so.

'The door between the wards was supposed to be locked at night, only it was a shortcut to the outside for staff to take breaks, so it was often left unlocked. Safety came second. There were a lot of attacks and abuse, but the staff didn't report it up the chain for fear of reprimand.'

'Is that why you decided to become a forensic psychologist?'

'At that point I was thinking of something more active and interventionist. I wanted to join the FBI. Get trained, get tough, if I ever learned to communicate again, which by then had become a matter of survival.'

Baarda's mobile rang. He dropped Connie's hair and stood up, walking across the room before answering. He gave a variety of commands while Connie wandered into the bathroom, splashing cold water on her face, flushing the recollections down the sink with the drips.

Baarda ended the call before knocking softly on the bathroom door.

'Connie, are you all right?'

'All good,' she declared, opening the door. 'Anything new on Elspeth?'

'I'm afraid not. Just an update on the missing schoolgirl. Uniformed officers have canvassed the school area and the streets surrounding Meggy's home address and got nothing, save for one of Meggy's friends, who said she'd talked about seeing someone in the park who'd made her feel unsettled. Makes sense that he'd been following her. If it had been an opportunistic snatch from a school, he'd have been there at the normal end of the school day. He was obviously aware that Meggy was always picked up later.'

'Sure,' Connie said, the word faint in her own ears. She was staring at her laptop across the room, reconstructing the masses of images contained in the files but seeing those on the walls at Angela's house. 'Parks are good places to watch people. You can be jogging, walking, birdwatching, almost anything. Public spaces where it's normal to be going slowly or just sitting around. Chances are, no one would notice you.'

'Is there something . . . ?'

'Can't be. Doesn't make sense.'

'Connie,' Baarda said. 'What's going on?'

'Pull up all the photos you have of Elspeth where she's in a park. Go through everything, whether it's her, her husband, their children. They have dogs, right?'

'Correct.'

'Them too. And get someone to double-check with her family which parks those photographs were taken in. We're only interested in those in or around Edinburgh.' She grabbed her laptop and began clicking and scrolling.

'But everyone with children or dogs has taken photographs in parks. It has to be one of the most common threads in family images.'

'Exactly,' Connie said. 'Look. Angela has these photos on her walls.' She pointed at images from the Fernycrofts' house. The park was a focal point.

'That still doesn't link it to Meggy's disappearance. I may not be a profiler, but even I'm aware that offenders shifting victim type to such a vast degree is highly unusual.'

'Yup.'

'You don't think we should talk about that before we alert Police Scotland to the fact that a predator might be lurking in their green spaces? Because that's not so much a profile as an invitation to every would-be vigilante to start beating up any single male seen on parkland within a hundred-mile radius.'

'Okay,' she said, putting her laptop aside. 'You're a predator looking for a particular type of woman. Someone with youngish children. Where do you go to find her?'

'School playground?'

'Now limit the parameters. You don't just want a mom who drops off and picks up the kids, you want that extra-special mother. You want to witness parental engagement. You probably want to be able to do more than just imagine what she's saying to her kids. That requires being able to get close enough without standing out.'

'Could be done in a number of different places. Shops, restaurants, even on the street.'

'That's generic. The conversations will all be the same. What shall we put in the shopping cart for dinner? Are we running late? You're looking for somewhere where the mother can let her guard down, where she has the chance to showcase her parenting skills.'

'You mean . . . is she actively playing with her children, or sitting on a park bench checking her social media?'

'Exactly,' Connie said. 'A park is an underrated arena for assessing relationships. Teenagers go there either for headspace or to cause trouble. Elderly people who live alone might go there hoping for a chat with a passerby. Parents go there because it provides exercise and a chance for play, but playing with kids is hard work. It requires imaginative and physical effort. Swimming pools are the other place where the same is true.'

'Except at a pool there would be a higher likelihood of cameras,' Baarda said. 'But Meggy's twelve years old. Angela and Elspeth are both in their thirties. You said yourself there had to be some sort of psychosexual motivation to those crimes. Meggy wouldn't fit his type.'

'This is Edinburgh, not Lagos or Caracas. One dead woman, another kidnapped, now a kidnapped child. That's a substantial crime spree. What's the probability of those events being unrelated?'

'Have you seen a photo of Meggy?' Baarda asked.

Connie shook her head.

'I'll show you.'

He opened his laptop and brought up an image of a girl who, if anything, looked younger than her twelve years.

'This is recent?' Connie asked.

'From a few weeks ago. A classmate took it at school as part of a science project. No makeup, nothing precocious in her clothing or hairstyle. If she looked or was attempting to act older than her years, then I could see how a mistake about her age might have been possible, but until now we've been working on the basis that the link between Angela and Elspeth was the fact that he was attracted to this concept of the perfect mother. The fact that Meggy had noticed a strange man in a park isn't enough to establish a link for me.'

'What exactly did the friend say about Meggy noticing the man in the park?' Connie asked.

'Meggy's home address is Durward Grove in the Inch area, south-west of the city centre. At the northern end of that road is Inch Park, which has a play area. The friend who also lives locally says Meggy saw a man there who she felt was watching her. He initiated a conversation, following which there was some incident where he bled. The friend wasn't clear on the details of that. Meggy has haemophobia, so she was badly affected by that, and she told her friend the man was . . . I think freaky was the word, but she didn't elaborate on that. It's a large park with plenty of benches. Meggy made some comment about how most grown-ups know they should keep away from girls on their own, not choose the nearest bench to them. Bright kid.'

'Really bright kid. Was that a one-off event – her trip to the park?'

'No, we established from her father that her routine was to go to the park after school whenever it wasn't raining, sometimes even when it was. She'd take a book and read there,' Baarda said.

'Take a book and read there? How many twelve-year-olds read a book in preference to plugging into social media these days?'

'This is still a reach,' Baarda said. 'The shift in victim type alone makes the link between these offences tenuous.'

'Meggy said the man looked freaky,' Connie reminded him.

'Plenty of adults look freaky to children. That could be anything from the way he was dressed to what he was doing, to the fact that he might have been humming or had a twitch.'

Connie pulled up a map of the area on her laptop.

'Think about this,' she said. 'Meggy's address at Durward Grove is in Inch, south of Inch Park. Angela's address is in Prestonfield, which is north of the top boundary of Inch Park, but still just about within walking distance.'

Baarda typed into his mobile. 'Inch Park itself covers sixty-one acres,' he read aloud. 'So while their addresses look relatively distant, the parkland is the common ground between their homes.'

'We need to gather the relevant information. Photos, maps of the park, information about how often Angela and Meggy each went to that park,' she said.

'Connie, you're still talking about the same man shifting from adult females to a girl who isn't even a teenager yet. I just don't want to leap to any conclusions and get sidetracked. We were supposed to be looking for links between Angela and Elspeth.'

'I'm not asking you to assume you have a single predator out there. I just need to see if there's a chance Meggy and Angela frequented the same area,' Connie said.

'Okay, but Elspeth's home is in the city centre, nowhere near Inch Park.'

Connie shrugged. 'You got anything better than this at the moment?'

'Fine,' Baarda conceded. 'You concentrate on Angela, I'll follow up with Elspeth's family, and I'll ask one of the officers from MIT to do the same for Meggy. Given what her friend said about the man in the park, it's an exercise they'll be under-taking in any event.'

Nodding her agreement, Connie was already entering search terms into a database of psychiatric profiles. The photographs could wait. She already knew what those would show her.

'Profile: Adult female victim + child female victim + violence + abduction + organised.'

She hit the search key and waited for the results.

Chapter Twenty-One

Wheelchair access to the sports centre wasn't through the front door, and that suited Xavier fine. He had a priority parking space at the rear. When it was raining and holding an umbrella wasn't practical, taking the shallow ramp down to the alleyway was just fine. There had been times in his life when he'd resented being made to feel different. An alternative doorway avoiding steps that also kept him out of queues and therefore out of sight — he'd had that with night clubs before. Seating at the edge of venues, purportedly with easier access but that actually just kept less able bodies out of view.

The sports centre wasn't guilty of that. Twice a week he met up with friends and played wheelchair basketball. The benefits were social as much as they were fitness. He got out of the house whenever he could, but that was getting increasingly difficult as muscular degeneration caught up in the race they'd been having for several years. Sometimes he felt strong enough to believe that it would never get the better of him. Then there were days when just lifting his arms to pick up the kettle and make a cup of tea was the effort equivalent of a boxing match.

Today was about medium on the scale of useless to

extraordinary. The basketball team was diverse in terms of how each had arrived at wheelchair status. From army veterans to car-crash victims, those who'd been born lacking a functioning pair of legs to one who'd attempted suicide from a high building only to smash both legs beyond repair but with a renewed appreciation of the value of life. They all carried a label.

Sport had always been a part of his life. He'd played football, rugby, hockey, jogged whenever he could and never felt it was a chore. Then, as if in slow motion, his body had begun to fail. The misdiagnoses in the early stages had veered from the ridiculous to the just plain negligent. Glandular fever. Food poisoning. Excessive growth spurt. Gluten intolerance. Hypochondria. And excessive masturbation: if only.

He still loved getting outside. These days things just happened a little slower. He'd be on the sidelines watching his local team playing football rather than scoring goals himself, and offer encouraging words to those doing their utmost to shift from the sofa to completing their first park run. Sidelined pretty much summed up how he defined life in a wheelchair. That wasn't self-pity – just his reality.

The girls who'd giggled when he'd spoken to them in his past life – a tall, well-muscled eighteen-year-old – now slid their gazes towards his able-bodied friends. Potential employers saw him as either a diversity tick box or as requiring additional investment. Not everyone, not everywhere. Life still had its moments of hilarity, warmth, and fulfilment. But had the edge been taken off? You fucking bet it had.

It was only a couple of minutes to the car park. He had his sports kit on his lap, keys in one hand and was self-propelling with the other. It was dark, raining and the lighting wasn't as good as it should have been. He checked the upper guttering of the sports centre, below which movement-triggered lighting usually made the access more useable. Two of the four lights weren't working. The cause of that wasn't immediately obvious until he reached a spot directly beneath one of them and found splinters of plastic and half a brick. Kids. Not that he didn't understand the desire to break things during those testosterone-fuelled fury days when the world was a constantly rolling ball of hate and hilarity. The destruction of physical things served a purpose to teenagers, offering much-needed relief from societal structure. He just wished they didn't have to practise it down already dim alleyways.

To his left was a dead end filled with the usual detritus of big cities. Skips for rubbish, recycling bins, a stack of wooden pallets, and darkened doorways into industrial buildings that were never used. He headed to the right, where in about fifty yards a left-hand turn would get him to his vehicle in a matter of seconds. The footsteps behind him were nothing unusual. It wasn't only wheelchair users who took the back access, although the only parking spaces out here were reserved for disabled badge holders. Sometimes the odd staff member could be found sneaking out for an illicit cigarette, or to make a call they didn't want overheard, which was why he didn't turn round. Even when the footsteps got louder, he didn't look to see who was coming. It had never occurred to him that he was at risk.

Xavier heard a rustling, no more suspicious than a hand rifling through a bag for keys. By the time he decided to look round to see if the nearby pedestrian was anyone he recognised, there was already a pair of hands and a vague black shape heading towards his face. He had time only to issue a garbled 'whayygg' combination of question and outcry before his head whipped backwards, his chair performed a sharp 180-degree turn, and everything went dark.

Engine oil assaulted his nose as he sped backwards, pulled along by the pressure of the material against his neck, and he fought to remove the bag that was blinding him. The thickness of the material made shouting futile, and he needed all the oxygen he could get to fuel his muscles. Two hours of exercise though, and he was all but done. His super-lightweight wheelchair, designed to make his movement around the basketball court speedy and fluid, offered no resistance to whatever lunatic had decided he was fair game.

The bag tightened around his neck as he grappled with it. Words flew like bullets through his brain as he thrashed, but none would come out of his mouth with his windpipe cut off.

Pranksters? he thought.

One wheel of his chair hit an obstacle along the alleyway and he tipped perilously to the side. Abandoning his efforts with the bag, he clung on.

Neo-Nazis?

There had been an upsurge in the far right's outspokenness. Only two weeks earlier someone had shoved a leaflet under his door, disconcertingly professionally designed and printed, that suggested ancient Ugly Laws should be resurrected. Not so ancient in the USA, where the last of those laws had only been repealed officially in the 1970s. Unbidden, the wording came back to him as his chair righted itself and banged, hard, back onto solid ground.

'Any person who is diseased, maimed, mutilated or deformed in any way as to be an unsightly or disgusting object . . .' was forbidden to expose themselves to public view. When he'd picked up the brochure, he'd assumed it had been broadly distributed and only ended up in his possession by chance. Now, it seemed more likely that he was the subject of a deliberate targeting, and that the pamphlet had been the precursor to the treatment he was currently receiving.

Mistaken identity?

He clung to that. Perhaps it was all a mistake. He wasn't the only one on the wheelchair basketball team, and at least three of them were former military. Those men had enemies in several quarters. What would they do to him if he couldn't convince his attacker that he had the wrong man? Kneecapping? Beheading? Immolation?

'You fucker!' Xavier recognised his teammate Danny's Geordie accent.

The bag around his neck flapped loose and he wrenched it off, gulping air and spinning round.

Danny wheeled his chair towards them at speed and threw a hammer fist punch at the chest of a man who was still grappling to take control of Xavier's wheelchair. The blow landed, but its force was softened as the man took a half step back. Xavier took his sports bag by the handles, whirled it over his head and into the man's face, buying Danny time to wheel in closer and line up a further punch.

His attacker was unmoved. The sports bag fell to the floor.

Xavier did his best to scream for help, but all that came was a hoarse rumble.

'Get the fuck out of here, X,' Danny said. 'I'll deal with this bastard.'

Xavier didn't need to be told twice. Heading for the door he'd exited through, he knew that there were times to fight and times to send for help. If Danny – ex-marines, weightlifter, and all-round powerhouse – couldn't fight off the lunatic, then he didn't know who could. He looked around for signs of anyone else coming to help as he headed for the ramp. Danny was making plenty of noise, but there was a main road nearby, drowning the sounds of the fight, and it was night-time in an industrial area. Typically, the gym was well soundproofed to keep the noise in. It hadn't occurred to Xavier until then that the soundproofing would work both ways.

'Come on then, you mother . . .' Danny growled.

The man didn't make a sound, instead sidestepping around

Danny's chair and neatly avoiding contact. Not attempting to engage in a fight. It wasn't a general attack then, Xavier realised, and it certainly hadn't been a prank. Whoever the man was, he had come for him and him alone.

He pushed forward, his right wheel grating and catching. Xavier leaned down to rectify the problem. There was damage, presumably from when he'd landed too hard after tipping. He reached into his pocket for his mobile, knowing as he did so that he'd left it in his sports bag and not yet retrieved it. The bag lay in the alleyway the other side of the man, who was staring blankly at Danny, entirely unconcerned.

Danny rushed in, fist smashing into the man's abdomen and issuing a battle cry worthy of the fiercest Highlander. The attacker folded slightly but didn't crumble. Danny's mouth opened, and Xavier could see his friend trying to process what had happened. His fist was an unstoppable force. Their team told jokes about it. It had become something of a legend. And the man was little more than a reed. Even in the dark and with a jacket on, his build was insubstantial.

The man looked Xavier in the eyes as if Danny weren't there at all and walked towards him again. Steady but unrushed. Passing under one of the remaining pools of light, his face became clearer and Xavier finally recognised him for what he was. The skeletal body, sunken eyes and stark cheekbones. The sense that nothing earthly could touch him.

Death had arrived. He might be wearing jeans and a denim jacket, but there was no mistaking the lack of humanity in that gaze.

He stopped trying to mend the wheel to free his chair and stared at the oncoming ghoul. Danny moved in again, ramming from behind. The man went down, and Danny leaned over him, delivering blow after blow to the man's head and shoulders. He didn't even raise his arms to protect himself, just got to his feet again. Grabbing for the back of his jacket, Danny yanked him backwards, and Xavier saw the glint of Danny's ring flashing in the light as his friend went for the genitals.

Xavier saw the blade before Danny. There was no drama to it. The movement of the knife through the air lasted only half a second, from drawing it out of his pocket to depositing it in Danny's chest. There was no sound at all. Danny's head fell to his chest, eyes still open, looking in his final seconds at the weapon that had felled him where gunfire, bombs and a terror network had failed. His hand dropped from its crushing grip on the man's balls, which should have been enough to deter even the most determined attacker.

When Danny tumbled from his chair, Xavier's surrender was complete. There were some forces you couldn't withstand. Danny was a born warrior, had never given in for a second of his glorious trail-blazing life. Xavier wasn't the same. Somehow, letting fate take its course seemed a less terrifying prospect than engaging in conflict.

Danny was dead before he hit the ground. It was no place to die, the back of a sports centre on a bed of asphalt and a pillow of cigarette butts. Not fit for the hero his friend had been, his legs gone in an explosion, his passion for life only enhanced by having so nearly perished.

In the few steps it took the man to reach him, Xavier mourned. Death hadn't wanted Danny that night. The appearance of the knife had been a cursory means of dispatching a nuisance, no more. He wished his friend had stayed in the bar for one more pint before exiting and attempting the rescue. He wished he'd skipped basketball that night rather than persuade himself that the exercise and company would be good for him in spite of his tiredness. He wished he could cheat death for one more day, write letters to the people he loved, and put his affairs in order.

Then the black bag was in front of his face — no surprise this time. Xavier bowed his head and allowed it to be slipped on. He neither wanted to see what was coming, nor what he was leaving behind. A car boot opened. He was lifted out of his chair and deposited, quite gently, into the space. Then the rumble of an engine, the rolling movement of the vehicle, and the end of a life he had not loved a fraction as well as he should have. Xavier mourned.

Chapter Twenty-Two

Edinburgh city's architecture was picture-postcard perfect through Connie's monochromatic gaze. The arched windows above doorways, bold brickwork, floor upon floor of precisely measured glazing lining the broad streets and imbuing the most casual stroll with grandiosity. It seemed to her to be a place in conflict with itself. The same visitors who were its lifeblood were damming the thoroughfares, overworking the centuries-old streets and disturbing the peace night and day. In black and white, facing the right direction, avoiding shops, billboards and buses, Connie might have stepped through time.

Gazing across the city in the direction of the castle, the hustle and commerce of Princes Street at her back, she wondered what she was missing. Her frantic information grab had yielded nothing more. Angela had regularly taken her children to various green spaces, Inch Park included. It had been Meggy's regular haunt too, but the land area covered was vast, and the psychology involved in shifting one's focus from adult females to a prepubescent female was immense. Sexual predators had fixed fantasies. They could change the place, the name, the finer points of a face, but rarely the race or age band of their victim.

In spite of that, Connie's every instinct was screaming that the same person who had taken Elspeth was also holding Meggy somewhere, dead or alive. Alive, she believed, or at least hoped. Baarda was off evidence gathering and organising officers to scope out Inch Park and the surrounding neighbourhoods. He was cynical about her theory but willing to act on it in the absence of anything more concrete to follow up.

The police had waited too long already. They'd waited for Angela's killer to reveal himself, and that pause had resulted in Elspeth's abduction. Then they'd waited again for the forensics, for door-to-door enquiries to bear fruit. And Meggy, too, had been taken. It was time to stop drumming their fingers and make something happen.

She dialled Baarda.

'We have to appeal to the kidnapper directly,' Connie said. 'I know the team's been worried about stirring up another false ransom request, but we can ask him to contact us with information only Elspeth will know. It'd be easy to avoid copycats or fake claims.'

'Why is it you think he'll respond?' Baarda asked.

His voice was low and slow. Not a challenge. An exploration of her thought process.

'The classic psychopathic profile often lends itself to communicating. He might be waiting for us to reach out to him.'

'Connie, I know you suspect the same offender in both Elspeth's and Meggy's abductions, but we can't jump into a press conference because of that,' Baarda said gently. 'Meggy's parents would have to be approached first, and that would be an extremely sensitive reveal given Angela Fernycroft's death.'

'I get that,' Connie said. 'But in all three cases, the guy has acted as if he's invincible. Maybe normal psychosexual parameters don't apply. It could be that he's not playing out a single fantasy, it's more complex than that. If Meggy is the third victim then the ramping up is exponential. We've gone from stalking and an indoor, carefully controlled crime scene, to a public approach and a kidnapping on a driveway, this time at a school.'

'You think he feels bulletproof,' Baarda said.

'Bulletproof's not exactly right. He's still taking some precautions. He doesn't want to get caught. He has purpose, even if we haven't figured out what that is yet, whether it's sexual, retributive or whatever. There's planning. The choices he's making can't be entirely random. But removing people from public places is unique. It's like he feels unseen.'

'Which is why you want to tell him that he isn't?'

'Exactly,' she said.

'What if that's a trigger for him? Say he feels safe while he's invisible, as if he's off our radar. When we start trying to communicate with him directly, is there not a risk that his behaviour will deteriorate? He's holding one captive who we hope is still alive, possibly two if your instincts about Meggy are correct. He could easily decide that it's less risky for him to kill them before he's discovered.'

'You got a better idea?' Connie asked.

'Failure to have a better idea doesn't justify taking a leap into the unknown. If the risk is unquantifiable then I'm not sure I'll be able to, or should, convince my superiors to reach out publicly to this man. Could you put a profile report together, as far as you've got, with hypotheses that link into the hard evidence? As little speculation or supposition as possible. The detective superintendent here – Overbeck – is asking to see results. If we want her to back us, we'll need to reassure MIT that we're travelling forward rather than in circles. If you can get that to me before midnight, I'll set up a meeting and see if the media liaison team will assist.'

'I have a couple of things to do first. We've been ignoring our possible first victim. I'd like to assess how and if she fits in.'

'Connie, if you're thinking about going to Advocate's Close alone—'

'I'm losing reception,' Connie lied. 'Keep your cell on. I'll be in touch.'

Connie stared from High Street through the tunnelled entrance into Advocate's Close, believed to have come into existence in 1544. Edinburgh would have been a hub of crude trade and brutal human suffering. Doctors causing more harm than good, although she was living proof that some of them hadn't changed all that much. The monied classes would have controlled everything, from the courts to the military. Education would have been a gift exclusively for men. She'd have been nothing more than a chattel.

Opposite St Giles' Cathedral, and nestled between a cigar shop and a tourist goods emporium, the entrance to Advocate's Close sat beneath a crushing five floors of offices and residences. She entered.

The narrow alleyway, in spite of the life in the surrounding buildings, was as quiet as the grave. The view across the city from the steps within the close was spectacular, yet the paving flags reeked of stubborn urine, and the natural timeless beauty was marred by a pool of vomit. Footsteps echoed behind her. Stopped. Retreated. Connie continued.

Light came and went in pools of safety. The alley would have seemed like a haven, offering substantial respite from the biting winds. There were few windows overlooking the thin path through. Safety was an elusive concept. Here, the homeless could escape public harassment and passing police cars. They could erect their temporary accommodations against solid walls and find a little peace. Those who walked past were familiar with the city. No one could accidentally take such a passageway, save for the very drunk seeing an after-hours outdoor restroom. Or those looking for trouble.

Part way down, the alleyway steps restricted the view back up to the High Street. Connie stopped, putting her back to the wall, imagining what it must be like to have your whole world wrapped in plastic bags, with only the money you'd begged that day to feed you, and no more than a sleeping bag to keep you warm at night.

Footsteps again, heavy and slow. Sound could be intimidating. Her heartbeat matched the left–right, left–right of the beat, and she realised it was impossible to know for sure if she was being approached from High Street above, or from the pathway below. The noise echoed slyly off the bricks above, bearing false witness.

Reaching into her pocket for her rape alarm, Connie realised she'd changed jackets and failed to take her usual precautions. Careless. She considered calling out, then felt foolish, then resented both the idea of shouting for help, and the fact that she was embarrassed to do so. No threat had been issued, yet the hairs on her arms were bristling.

The figure of a man appeared at the top of the steps above her. Hood up. Tall. Shadow concealing his face. In her imagination he was holding a twenty-pound note that would flutter to the ground when she rebuffed him. He stopped still and watched her.

Connie considered continuing her journey down the steps, but that would require her to turn her back on him.

'You got a problem?' she called to him.

He was silent. A worm of fear slithered in her guts, and it made her furious.

'Do not fuck with me tonight,' she shouted. 'You will totally regret it.'

A growl issued from the back of his throat.

Too many thoughts at once. Psychosexual killers' propensity towards revisiting the scene of their crimes. Stupid of her for not checking if she was being followed before entering the passageway. Expertly trained in self-defence or not, a man twice her build approaching from a height advantage was likely unbeatable. She didn't want to die without seeing Martha's Vineyard one more time. And lastly, dying wasn't an acceptable option. She had too much left to do.

'Screw you,' she said, shoving her fear down deep and sprinting up the steps towards him, fists hard, relying on agility and surprise.

He jumped down towards her, taking the steps two at a time and lighter on his feet than his size had suggested he would be. Connie regretted her decision instantly, wishing she'd run for it.

'Excuse me,' a voice called from above them.

The man was only fifteen feet from her now. Her would-be assailant looked back. Connie took the opportunity to retreat instead, racing off in the opposite direction.

There was a shout from above, the thud of a body hitting the ground, followed by the tumble-yelp-tumble of ongoing pain. She got well clear before pausing and turning back.

Above her, Brodie Baarda was standing over a body, holding one wrist behind the man's back. They were talking too quietly for her to hear against the ragged gasps of her breath. Shaking her head, Connie reversed direction a final time, walking slowly back up to Baarda. Her legs were shaking. Fear turned to fury.

'Get up,' Baarda told the man, hauling him to his feet and yanking down his hood.

The face revealed was fleshy and pockmarked, the red marbling at the end of his nose the sure sign of a long-term heavy drinker.

'He says he was looking for a prostitute. A local pimp regularly leaves him a girl here late at night,' Baarda explained.

'You looked like you were waiting for me,' the man directed at Connie.

'On account of my having a vagina and being in an alleyway late at night?' Connie asked.

'I've got fifty quid here with your name on it,' the man smirked.

Baarda smashed a fist into one side of the man's ribcage and he revisited the floor with a high-pitched gurgle.

'Come on,' Baarda said. 'Whatever you were looking for here, he isn't it.'

He took Connie by the elbow and began guiding her back up the steps. She didn't fight him.

'You hit him,' Connie said. 'Really goddamn hard. Is that normal police procedure in the land of tea and biscuits?'

'And you came out late at night with no backup plan, looking – for all your blasé toughness – as if you'd break like a twig in the wrong hands.'

'Okay, hold on there, are you saying this is my fault? That women walking around looking vulnerable somehow attract trouble?'

Baarda indicated his car. 'Fine,' he said. 'How exactly did you plan to deal with that particular situation?'

'I normally carry a rape alarm,' she said.

'Oh, forgive me, then. Obviously, the fact that you normally carry a rape alarm would have kept you completely safe in this instance. I clearly shouldn't have intervened. Now, we have another crime scene to get to, so perhaps we could argue inside the vehicle.'

'I just wanted—'

'I understand precisely what you wanted to do,' Baarda said. 'I'd have come with you if you'd asked.'

Connie sighed as she climbed into the car. 'I don't need babysitting. Women, in fact, don't need men to protect them. Men need to stop attacking us. That's what'll keep us safe.'

'I'd never figured out that particular social equation before.

Thank you for explaining it to me. Did you get what you wanted from the experience?' he asked.

'Maybe not what I wanted, but probably what I needed. Advocate's Close seems like a safe place, but actually the second a woman goes in there, she's vulnerable. It's narrow and dark, no overlooking windows, the proximity to pubs meaning there would be a fair amount of screaming and noise at night, so passersby wouldn't know what to take seriously. If you wanted to hold a knife to someone's throat, it'd be a simple manoeuvre.'

'A good place to locate an easy target then,' Baarda said.

'Yeah.' She ran her hands through her hair and let herself relax. 'Hey, thank you. Sometimes I try so hard to be unafraid that I step right into the eye of the tornado. I didn't mean to be a bitch. I'm grateful you came to find me tonight.'

'My pleasure,' he said.

'It was pretty hot watching you punch that bastard. Not a move I was expecting you to pull.'

'If anyone expected me to pull a move like that, it wouldn't be terribly effective, would it?' Baarda smiled.

Connie turned in her seat to look at him. His curly hair was tousled, but otherwise Baarda was completely unaffected by the incident, and entirely in control.

'You're incredibly attractive, Detective Inspector Baarda. Do you know that?'

'I know we have another crime scene to get to,' he said. 'Could we talk about that instead?'

'Sure,' Connie agreed. 'But I saw what I saw. You're a dark horse, Brodie. Women just know.'

Chapter Twenty-Three

Baarda dropped her as close as he could get to the crime scene, then drove off to park the car where it wouldn't disrupt traffic. The area at the back of the sports centre had been sealed off, as had the car park at one end and the road that met the pathway at a junction the other end.

A uniformed officer barred her entry as she stepped over the crime scene tape.

'Detective Superintendent Overbeck asked me to attend,' she announced before the constable could speak. 'I'm the forensic psychologist profiling the Dunwoody and Fernycroft cases.' She flashed her ID.

'I think it's still an essential police-personnel-only situation, ma'am. I can go and ask—'

'I gather there's an eyewitness,' Connie said.

'Um, yes, but he's a bit drunk from what we can gather, that or drugs. If you'd just wait here.'

'My orders came from the superintendent directly,' Connie lied.

'I'll vouch for her, Sam. Let the lady in,' a reedy voice came from behind.

'Of course, Dr Lambert.' The young constable spoke deferentially to the forensic pathologist.

'Why do I not have your gravitas?' Connie asked, following her in.

'You're too young, too pretty, and around here you're also too American. If it makes you feel any better, I spent the first twenty years of my career being referred to as the wee lassie with the glasses who never smiles. Now, suit up. I assume there's a reason for you being in attendance.'

'Too many deaths and disappearances, too few answers, and I don't believe in coincidences,' Connie said, grabbing a white suit and shoe covers, pulling her hair into a band and pushing it into the hood.

'We have that in common. This, however, is a far cry from your Angela Fernycroft murder scene. If it's linked, it'll be hard to see how.'

They walked together to the overturned wheelchair. The corpse was on its side, face to the ground, one arm splayed. Even in the dark on the asphalt, the pool of blood beneath the victim was unmistakable. Connie didn't need to see in colour. She could smell it.

'Knife wound,' Ailsa said, kneeling next to the body. 'Single entry as far as I can see. Straight into the heart. There wouldn't have been this much blood normally, but the knife dislodged when the victim fell from his chair, and the blade's exit wound allowed a substantial amount of blood to spill as the heart was stopping.' She picked up the blade. 'Approximately a seven-inch blade, metal handle, sharp tip. Resembles a butcher's knife. Delivered with substantial force to get through into the heart.'

'He has other injuries, too,' Connie said. 'There was a fight first. If the assailant had the knife, why not use it straight away?'

'I can identify three clear contusions plus cuts and grazes to the face. There's swelling and some bleeding in patches, indicating that those injuries occurred before death. Perhaps the use of the weapon was a last resort. This gentleman's been dead no more than an hour.' She picked up each of his hands in turn. 'Judging by the damage to his knuckles, I'd say he put up a remarkable defence.'

Pulling bags from her pocket, the pathologist slipped a trace evidence preservation cover over each hand and secured each around the wrist.

'Ge' the fu' off me,' a slurred voice projected from the far end of the alleyway.

'Excuse me, Ailsa,' Connie said, checking the lighting as she walked past the rear exit to the sports centre, noting the large bins and the darkened doorways on the other side of the street. Plenty of places for a man or woman to have stood waiting, unseen.

'Would you calm down, sir? You're not under arrest, but we need to get you to the station so we can take a full statement,' a woman replied.

'Nae going to no fuckin' polis station, sod yous.'

'We'll get you a hot meal and as many cups of tea as you like, but it's freezing out here now and this'll take some time,' the woman kept trying.

Connie could see him now, wrapped in layer upon layer of coats, blankets and a tatty sleeping bag, his face mottled from dirt, the cold and substance abuse.

'I'm gettin' going, me. That fuckin' monster'll be back, you bet on it.' He leaned in close to the female officer. 'He didn't say a friggin' word! Not a one. Just kept taking punches until he pulled out that knife and then slam. It was like he was doing no more than carvin' a turkey. Didn't even look at the poor bastard as he fell to the floor. You think I'm making a fuckin' statement? I may be drunk, love, but I'm nae stupid. I dinnae want that demon after me. His fuckin' face!'

'What about his face?' Connie interjected.

'Ach, it was like a moon wi' holes for eyes.' He began picking up a collection of bags and rucksacks from around his feet.

'How did the man not notice you?' the officer asked.

'Under cardboard. Can I get some money?'

'You know I can't give you money,' the officer said gently. 'But I can get you food. You just need to help us with—'

'I'll give you some money if you'll look at a photo for me,' Connie told him, typing into her phone.

'Ma'am that's not permissible,' the officer told her.

'I'm a contracted civilian, not police. The rules don't apply to me.' She took a twenty-pound note from her pocket. 'One photo, but I want your honest reaction. No bullshit, okay?'

Connie held up her phone.

The man's eyes widened. He took a step closer to the screen and peered at the image there. Stepping away, he raised a hand, swiping the mobile from Connie's hand and sending it flying.

Grabbing him by the collar, Connie pulled him towards her. 'Was that him?' she asked.

He shrugged and muttered.

'You want the money, you look at me and tell me if that picture looks like the man.'

'Is he real? I thought maybe I'd imagined him, then I saw the blood,' the man whispered.

'He's real,' Connie said, thrusting the money at him. 'Now, give the nice officer a statement and you can go.'

'Ma'am, I need to see the photo so we know who we're looking for,' the officer said.

Connie held up her mobile.

'What is *that*?' the officer asked.

'That . . .' Connie sighed, '. . . is a character from a kid's movie. Apparently, we're looking for a goddamn cartoon.'

'Better find him before he kills that other one, too,' the man mumbled as he hid the twenty away inside his shoe.

Connie and the police officer turned in unison.

'What did you say?' Connie asked.

'Other one. The one he took. Poor bastard. Dragged him backwards in his wheelchair.'

The officer was on her radio in a heartbeat. 'All units, we have an active kidnapping situation . . .'

Connie waited for the uniformed police to gather the remaining details about the victim, then got Baarda on the mobile.

'He's done it again, and now I'm certain he took Meggy. I need you to get me some TV coverage straight away.'

'Sightings of his car?' Baarda asked.

'Nothing. Small car park, no CCTV – he must have checked it out. It's pretty dark around here and industrial, so no dwellings overlooking the car park. Probably why he kidnapped this victim from here rather than at his home, which is an assisted housing unit, so there'd be people there around the clock.'

'Clever bastard,' Baarda said. 'One moment.'

Baarda began speaking on a radio. Connie listened in.

'All units, be aware. There is a kidnapping in progress. The kidnapper is a single white male, who may be driving erratically. Sounds may be heard in the boot of a vehicle. Inform other agencies – include accessible undercover officers, paramedics, fire service. I want a stop-and-search on every major route out of the area. All cars with single male occupants to be stopped and searched over the next four hours.'

'That's a huge task,' Connie said when he was back on the line with her.

'What are our chances of success?' Baarda asked.

'Doesn't help if I'm negative.'

'I prefer honesty. Say what you're thinking,' Baarda said.

'I think he's very familiar with this city. He's stalked his victims, so he'll have staked out the places he planned to abduct them from. He'll be taking a route he's already checked out. Side roads, residential areas, even if it takes four or five times as long. We shouldn't mistake desperation for stupidity.'

'So what can I do? If he's a step ahead of us every time, how do we catch him?'

'Look for him in the places he'll have to go when he's not committing crimes. We have a photofit from Meggy's kidnapping. Can you get it out to supermarkets – have it put up in staffrooms? Job centres and pharmacies as maybe he's living on benefits – I doubt he's working at the moment and the description of him sure makes him sound unwell.'

'Good work,' Baarda said. 'I'm heading out to speak with Elspeth Dunwoody's husband. He confirmed that in spite of their home address, he plays rugby out at the Liberton Club. Elspeth and the kids regularly went to watch him play at weekends.'

'Relevance?' Connie asked.

'It's a short walk from Inch Park. Just over Gilmerton Road, in fact. I may owe you an apology. Can you get a ride back to the station?'

'I sure can, and fuck the apology,' Connie said. 'Go speak with Elspeth's husband.'

Chapter Twenty-Four

Fergus had changed vehicles in a small private car park where he paid a monthly fee. There was no one on the gate in the city suburbs. He knew the combination to the lock and let himself in and out as needed. Cash payments up front. No formal paperwork. Having two cars gave him some flexibilty. Shopping centre car parks were his other great love. They offered access to large areas where he could get from one major road to another, breaking the CCTV chain. Internet road maps were amazing these days. You could complete whole journeys without leaving home, refining your route, finding shortcuts, avoiding major junctions. Traffic lights were the bane of his existence. Far too many cameras these days.

He'd heard the sirens this time. Local radio stations were reporting long delays on certain roads. The roadblocks had gone up faster than he'd liked, but he hadn't had to be so careful this time. Xavier was, after all, the last piece of the puzzle.

Fergus checked the hallway through the peepholes, upper then lower. Neither woman nor girl was anywhere to be seen. He banged the door hard and waited for them to appear as he'd taught Elspeth, far enough away that they couldn't be planning anything nasty. They appeared slowly, heads hanging low, went to the far end of the flat, facing the wall, and put their hands on their heads. He unlocked and kicked open the door.

Xavier was a dead weight over his shoulder, but it didn't bother him. He ate only for pleasure now. His body didn't need the calories. The concerns over allergies and food poisoning that had plagued him for years were allayed. He couldn't get sick. Nature had no more nasty surprises for him. Every morsel of food that passed his tongue was a new experience. He'd forgotten what it was to be carefree. He consumed what he wanted, threw it away after just a bite if it didn't please him. His body clock might be ticking down towards a level of decomposition that would render it useless, but he had discovered an extraordinary truth beyond the inevitability of his rotting corpse. Death came with zero consequences.

He staggered into the sitting room, dumping the latest addition to his new family on the couch.

'Get in here and meet Xavier,' Fergus called to Elspeth and Meggy.

No response.

'I said come here!' he yelled. 'You're being rude. I did this for all of us.'

He stormed into the corridor. Elspeth and Meggy were stood, arms clutched around each other, red-eyed and whimpering. The woman had a strip of material wrapped around her hand. He stared at it a moment then shook his head. Her injury wasn't his problem right now.

'Move!' he commanded.

Meggy turned her face into Elspeth's shoulder and began to sob.

'Boring.'

Reaching forward, he grabbed Elspeth's wrist and began

dragging her. Scrabbling with her feet, she protested, with Meggy pulling her other hand and screeching.

'Please, no . . .' Elspeth cried.

Something had changed. They hadn't been like that before. Quiet, yes, but compliant. Perhaps they were hungry. He tried to remember when he'd last fed them, but time had become an eel in his brain, and he couldn't get it in a straight line.

'Do . . .' he dragged her along, 'what . . .' another heave, 'you're . . .' by then she was through the hallway into the lounge, '. . . told.'

Elspeth scrambled into the corner, quaking. Meggy stood in the hallway watching, shifting from one foot to the other, ready to bolt even if her options for where to go were limited. Fergus raised a slow arm and pointed to the male on the sofa.

'That's Xavier,' Fergus said. 'You have to look after him.'

Xavier pushed himself over to face them, his right eye a swollen mass.

'Where is this?' He rubbed the back of his head. 'Who's she?'

'That's my wife,' Fergus said. 'Pretty, isn't she?'

'What did you do to him?' Meggy asked, appearing from the hallway and standing open-mouthed. She stepped closer to Xavier. 'Why isn't he getting up?'

'Meggy, honey, calm down and come to me,' Elspeth said.

The girl walked towards the sofa, one shaking hand outstretched.

'Don't make a fuss. You two should look after him. He's my brother now.'

Fergus had chosen Xavier especially. There'd been an article about him and his wheelchair basketball team in a local paper, and Fergus had felt a surge of pride in Xavier's determination and fighting spirit. He knew Xavier would be the sort of brother he could be proud of. There had been practical considerations as well as emotional ones. It didn't work to have a brother who could play the hero. Fergus had made that mistake before, and it had almost ended in disaster. Xavier wasn't going to be breaking down the flat door any time soon, especially without his wheelchair. Choosing a sibling with a physically limiting disease ticked every single box. That was why Xavier had been on Fergus' radar for a long time now, longer even than Angela.

'What happened to Angela?' Fergus asked, staring at the wall with the painted window. In his mind, the curtains were blowing and birds were singing outside.

'Who's Angela?' Elspeth asked.

'You were supposed to be Angela,' he told her. 'She was perfect.'

'Elspeth's perfect,' Meggy said. 'Why isn't that man getting up?'

'His legs don't work; don't be rude about it. Xavier is very important to Daddy.'

Meggy glared at him. 'You're not my dad,' she growled.

Elspeth was on her feet, striding between Fergus and the girl.

'I don't want to do this any more. I want to leave. He's not my dad and he can't make me say he is!'

'Don't get mad,' Elspeth cooed at Fergus. 'Meggy's just upset. I'll talk to her. I think that bringing someone else in just threw her off balance . . .'

Fergus took a single pace forward and shoved Elspeth sideways. She flew into the wall, smashing her head against the painting of the window. Its glass panes cracked in his mind.

'You killed my friend, Danny,' Xavier said. 'Why did you do that?'

'Forget about it,' Fergus declared. 'There is no Danny any more. I carried you up all those stairs, didn't I? I brought you into my home. You were alone before. There was no one to look after you. Now you'll have company all the time. My wife and my daughter will look after you, and I'll visit. I wish you'd been at the wedding. You'd have been my best man. Imagine the speech you'd have made. Elspeth looked beautiful. But there's still time. We'll . . .'

Fergus shook his head. Everything was fuzzy inside his brain. Suddenly he couldn't remember why they were all there.

'You look tired,' Elspeth said. 'It must have been exhausting carrying Xavier up the stairs. Why don't you go for a rest? You've earned it.'

'I am tired,' Fergus said.

He smiled at her tenderly, taking her in his arms and leaning against her. Elspeth put her arms around him and rubbed his back softly. That was nice. It was something his mother might have done. 'You're just as good as Angela. Better, even. Do you like remembering our wedding day? I wish our families could have been there.'

'I do,' Elspeth smiled. 'I think about it all the time. It was . . .' She paused, swallowing hard.

It was wonderful to see her so emotional, he thought. It was so good that she felt the same way he did.

'. . . magical.'

'I should bring you more food. I hadn't even thought about that!' He slammed the palm of his hand into his forehead and Elspeth took a half step away. 'Stupid, stupid, stupid me.'

'You've had a lot on your mind, and we still have plenty of biscuits, cheese and tinned fruit from the last supplies you brought. Worry about that tomorrow. How about I make Xavier comfortable, and you bring us supplies in the morning. We'll have the flat all tidied up by then, won't we, Meggy?'

The girl folded her arms and glared at the floor.

'Someone's hormonal. You do what your mother tells you, young lady,' Fergus chided.

'What the fuck is going on here?' Xavier panted.

221

Elspeth put her arms around Fergus' shoulder again and gave him a brief tight hug. 'I think everyone's overtired. Bedtime for us.'

'Thank you,' Fergus said. 'You're doing a good job.'

'Thank you,' she replied.

'He killed Danny,' Xavier repeated. 'He's insane!'

'Nonsense,' Elspeth said. 'Fergus was just doing what needed to be done, isn't that right?'

'It is,' Fergus said. 'I was just keeping my family together. Everyone needs a family.'

'Absolutely,' Elspeth said, pulling him gently towards the front door of the flat then standing back to let him exit. 'We'll see you tomorrow. Fresh milk would be good. I expect Xavier'll be wanting a cup of tea by then.'

'Fresh milk,' Fergus said, locking the door behind himself.

It was all working out fine. He remembered what he was doing now. He had a wife who loved him. A daughter who might need to be taught a lesson if she didn't buck up her ideas, but wasn't that the way with children? Now his brother was home too, and he'd be grateful to have been saved from his lonely existence.

He plodded down the stairs towards his bedroom. Sleep was, apparently, the only thing his corpse required to the same extent that his living body had.

'Soon, we can all leave together. One big happy family, forever.'

Chapter Twenty-Five

'Normal profile categories don't apply,' Connie told the audience of stony faces. 'That's because he doesn't have a standard motivation for killing or kidnapping. With each offence, our offender has grown bolder and less afraid. His appearances are increasingly public. We now know that the dead man found at the rear of the sports centre had intervened only once the abduction attempt had begun. Xavier Coghill is missing. That leaves us attempting to profile a man who has killed one adult female and is currently holding a woman, a female child, and an adult male hostage.'

Connie looked around the incident room. Every police officer not out on active duty was gathered. They were tense, frustrated, and reaching boiling point. Law enforcement professionals gathered with a single aim became a pack. Their mentality changed. They became less rational and reasonable. They also disliked listening, craving action and resolution. She felt the same, only traditional police work – knocking doors and watching CCTV – wasn't working.

'Our perpetrator has gone from failing, to organised, to chaotic again in just a couple of weeks, yet he's proving more successful than ever at obtaining his targets,' she continued.

'So what's he after? There must be a pattern,' someone called out.

'I don't think it's a pattern as much as a collection,' Connie replied. 'He must be fulfilling some sort of fantasy, but not the sort we're experienced with. Maybe he's not playing a single fantasy over and over in his head, like most predators do. It seems more likely that his particular fantasy is story-driven and still developing.'

'You want to talk in English?'

Connie didn't bother looking up to see where that came from.

'Look at it this way. A standard serial rapist replays the same fantasy. They have a victim established in their mind, and in most cases they'll be pretty repetitive with the things they do. It's a movie on repeat in their brain, and while there might be variations such as clothing or location, the basic scenario remains stable. We learn more about them because replaying the same scenario makes them predictable,' she explained.

'Are you trying to be helpful, or explaining why you're no further forward?' A woman stepped from the back wall, arms crossed, killer heels on full display.

Unfamiliar as Connie was with the finer aspects of the Scots accent, Connie had no doubt that she was hearing the upper-class end of it. Stick-thin and sporting nails that wouldn't have looked out of place on a high-class dominatrix, both the suit and the attitude screamed senior officer.

'Sorry, we haven't been properly introduced. I'm Detective Superintendent Overbeck. Do carry on.'

Connie gave Baarda a quick sideways glance. He'd warned her about Overbeck, and had failed to do the woman justice. She was unlike any police officer Connie had seen before.

'Thanks, I will.' Connie gave Overbeck a flash of an unperturbed smile. 'As I was saying, most offenders play out the same scenario. We're struggling to get ahead of this man because he's moving his story forward. Each abduction – and we know now it's the abductions that are relevant to profiling him, not the murders – is the next chapter in his story. It's unfolding as he goes. We won't know when it's reached an end. I doubt even he knows when it'll end. It's not a completely unknown scenario in criminal offending, but it is rare to the point that no past cases will assist us.'

'Still not hearing anything useful,' Overbeck interjected.

'You are, actually, it's just that you haven't had time to process the information and decode it yet,' Connie said.

There was a moment where no one breathed, all eyes on Overbeck.

'Go on,' Overbeck said, not the least bit bothered by the attention or by the challenge.

Overbeck was her own woman. Probably a complete bitch and quite possibly a sociopath. The sort you could girl crush on in the right circumstances, Connie thought.

'I'm not convinced he's psychopathic, in spite of the two murders. Angela's death was unintentional. He wanted her, for whatever reason, and the forensic evidence points to an accidental killing in the course of a kidnapping. He replaced her with Elspeth – no corpse – we assume she's still alive. Meggy was a clean kidnapping, cleverly and carefully planned, and we know he made contact with her in Inch Park. The same park Angela has visited, that's also in close proximity to Elspeth's husband's rugby club.' Connie took a breath. 'The risk-taking involved here is increasing exponentially. I've never seen anything like it. What we know of the last victim – Danny's death – is that his killer was completely unbothered about being seen.'

'If that's true, then why wait in a dark alleyway at night? There's evidence that some of the street lighting was smashed.

That could have been our kidnapper preparing in advance,' one of the MIT officers said.

'Good point, but that conflicts with him going to Meggy's school in daylight. I think there's a difference between those actions he takes to ensure he fulfils each mission successfully, and the need to conceal his identity. He was in the alleyway at night because that's the exit Xavier uses regularly. Less lighting meant a reduced prospect of anyone else intervening, plus it made it easier for him to conceal himself from Xavier until he was ready to attack. Danny's part in it was unforeseen, but he'd planned for the eventuality, hence the knife.'

Baarda stood up and walked to the laptop that was controlling the images on the screen.

'We're currently working on the basis of a character from an animated film. I'm not sure how well that's going to translate into enabling a real-world capture. We have descriptions from the girl at Meggy's school and an inebriated homeless man. Is there anything in particular we should be looking out for?' he asked.

'What's interesting is that, in spite of the fact that we only have evidence from a child and someone who was drunk, they vary remarkably little in detail. The man you're looking for is thin to an extreme. This is making his head appear larger and his eyes look sunken and dark. He's wearing clothes that are tight enough to show how emaciated he is. The description of the denim jacket is interesting. It sounds like something from the 1970s.'

'So we're looking for a skeleton who hasn't updated his wardrobe for forty years,' someone laughed.

'Essentially yes. This skeleton, if giving him a name helps fix him in your heads, is delusional. He's gathering jigsaw puzzle pieces from his fantasy to take somewhere and fix together. He's willing to be seen and willing to kill to bring his imagined scenario to life. The emaciation of his body that both witnesses describe might be part of a physical illness that's contributing to his delusions, or it might be a symptom arising from the delusions. Either way, he's making no effort to hide his physical condition, which gives us the benefit of using it to try to identify him.'

'So we should be approaching healthcare workers, clinics, local mental health services to see if they recognise anyone of this description?' Baarda asked.

'That'd be a great start,' Connie said. 'Focus on referrals for eating disorders or physical conditions that involve wasting. What I'm more concerned about is the link between his physical appearance and his psychological condition. If he's collecting people, he has an end goal. Given how reckless he's becoming and how coldly he killed Danny tonight, I'd say he's getting close to the end. Too reckless too early and he'd be jeopardising his big ending.'

'And what might that so-called big ending look like?' Overbeck asked.

'No idea,' Connie said. 'But you'd have to assume all options are open. What we should avoid, at all costs, is interrupting his fantasy. That's his no-go zone. Anything or anyone who gets in his way will be disposable or replaceable. He's chosen each person for a reason. They're playing a role. Particularly Elspeth. To suggest he has a mother fixation is kind of trite when it comes to men offending against women, but I believe she's the lynchpin. He's either reproducing a mother or wife figure, or he's trying to create one he never had. Either way, I'd put money on his own mother no longer being alive, and on him being single. Critically, his fantasy has to remain intact.'

'All right. We've heard the psychology, but there are more important practical considerations. How much time do we have, and how do we find him?' Overbeck asked.

'In terms of time, you should assume not much. Angela

Fernycroft was murdered nine weeks ago. Elspeth was kidnapped five weeks ago. As to how we find him, we have to change a crucial element of his offending pattern. He's unconcerned about being seen, acting with impunity. I need to know more about him to tell you how to find him. That means opening a dialogue. I'd like to do that tonight.'

Overbeck ignored the crowd and walked between bodies until she was just inches from Connie.

'But you said we shouldn't interrupt the fantasy. You don't think that announcing to him that he's being hunted will burst his twisted little psycho-bubble?'

'Not if we play along with it,' Connie said. 'No threats, nothing that changes his sense that he's in control and that this will all play out exactly the way he wants it to.'

'All right, Dr Woolwine,' Overbeck said. 'Hold your press conference. We'll organise the cameras and get you a platform. If he's that deluded, though, there's no guarantee that he'll be watching or listening.'

'He's still linked to the real world somehow,' Connie said. 'He's been going out, researching, stalking, checking his facts and interacting. If Elspeth, Meggy and Xavier are all still alive, he's also feeding them and caring for them. That's a commitment. If we can get my message on enough screens, fill the headlines with it and bombard the press, then he'll see or hear it somewhere.'

'You said, "If Elspeth, Meggy and Xavier are still alive",' Overbeck said. 'You should know that I don't like the word "if", Dr Woolwine, but I just don't have your natural optimistic personality. Angela Fernycroft was brutally murdered in her own bed.'

'Yes, but you have to remember—'

'While I talk, your lips need to remain firmly sealed, dear,' Overbeck said.

Connie shrugged and perched on the edge of a desk.

'Don't tell me again that her death was accidental. Accidental death is discovering an adder in your car footwell when you're driving down the motorway, getting bitten, passing out and helplessly ploughing into another car. Angela Fernycroft was suffocated and left in the marital bed for her children and husband to find. Her killer had stalked her and broken into her home, likely watching and waiting while she took a bath and read a book. In my eyes, and forgive me if I use the wrong terminology, that makes him a complete fucking psycho.'

There was a murmur of agreement from around the room. Connie bided her time.

'I'm also aware of the little factoid that our man's DNA has been linked to another case where an unidentified woman possibly disappeared in Edinburgh no fewer than five years ago. Five years, Dr Woolwine. Let that sink in for a moment. It means that this maniac might have been roaming our streets, selecting his victims, sharpening his senses, and building up a head of steam for half a fucking decade. That's the equivalent of him taking both an undergraduate degree and a master's in stalking and slaughtering, assuming he hasn't been at it for even longer than that.'

'Agreed,' Connie said.

'What that makes him is dangerously criminally insane as far as I'm concerned. So why on earth should I believe for a single second that Elspeth, Meggy and Xavier aren't already dead?'

Connie stood up again, giving the room a moment to settle before speaking. Overbeck was a compelling orator in front of an audience predisposed to agree with her. They would take some persuading.

'Fair question,' she said. 'We know this man kills when a scenario goes wrong for him. He leaves the body where it is.

No fuss, no attempt to conceal it. We don't have Elspeth's, Meggy's or Xavier's body, so your starting point is that you have to assume kidnap rather than murder. As yet we've established no motive for him to have killed them. Ergo, they are alive until proven otherwise. More than that, he wants them for something. They're precious to him. The stalking, his knowledge of their lives – which yoga class, which park and school, which sports centre at a specific practice time – means he's invested in them. He's doing something with them. God only knows what, but this is purposeful, not impulsive. Could they be dead? Absolutely. Have they been tortured or abused? The statistics tell us that it's almost inevitable. Will he kill them at some point in time?'

Complete silence from the crowd.

'Yes,' Connie said. 'Yes, he will. He's unstable. He's dangerous. Whatever fantasy is in his head will prove unfulfilling one way or another. When that day comes, his emotional dam will burst. Has that already happened? Maybe, maybe not. Which is why we assume alive, so we proceed as speedily as possible before he does kill again. At the moment, calling him out via the press seems an option worth pursuing.'

'So be it,' Overbeck said. 'But a word of warning. This tactic requires us to reveal to the families of all our missing persons that their loved ones are part of a larger scheme that is at best terrifying and at worst shows that their precious abductees are in the hands of a ruthless killer. So I'm going to need results.'

'I understand—'

'Let me qualify that. I'm going to need fuck-up-free results. No one dies because of the decision I've just taken. This man has kidnapped the daughter-in-law of an extremely prominent philanthropist, a little girl and a physically vulnerable adult. For this to end well, each one of them needs to survive unharmed.

I'm assuming also that you'd like your career to continue with your reputation intact hereafter.'

Connie folded her arms and stepped even closer into Overbeck's face.

'I suspect that sort of professional intimidation is more effective on people with a different history than mine. I'm going to do my best to make this work because lives hang in the balance. Not for any other reason. But nice try.'

'Whatever the fuck it takes,' Overbeck said. 'Press conference in one hour. Make me proud.'

'That was better. Has no one ever told you, you're much more effective when you're motivational rather than threatening,' Connie said.

'Has anyone ever told you not to shit where you eat?' Overbeck replied, walking away.

Baarda gave it a few seconds before taking her place.

'Everything all right?' he asked.

'She likes me,' Connie said. 'Which is what I need from our skeleton man, too. Let's get to work.'

Wearing the skinniest jeans she could find and a t-shirt so tight it might as well have been sprayed on, Connie sat on a chair on the small stage in the press room, alone. It was a far cry from normal police press conferences. A representative from the media liaison team had gone into meltdown while Connie was explaining how she needed the press call to go. There wasn't to be a uniform in sight. No panel. No desk, nor formal microphones. Just informal clothes and a lapel mic. She wasn't going to wear any makeup, and there would be no questions taken when she'd finished speaking.

'You're still representing Police Scotland,' the liaison officer had groaned. 'We have protocols. The families of the missing persons will be watching too, and they'll expect a level of respect.'

Connie kept her voice low. 'If it's a choice between respect and getting their loved ones back, I'm pretty certain they'll choose the latter. People respond to reflections of themselves. I need to present myself as physically and emotionally close to the murderer as I can so he can relate to me. Every image means something different to him than it does to you.

'Here, the uniforms represent safety and structure. To him, they're a threat and a brand for a world he's rejecting. If I look like him, I might be able to appeal to something in his subconscious that tells him I can empathise. Thin like him, unadorned, functional. So no desk, no formality, and you're going to need to inform the families that I'll be saying a few things they might not appreciate hearing. I'm aiming to have a conversation with the kidnapper. It'll sound one way to you, but if I get this right, it'll sound very different inside his head.'

'It's not the established method for press conferences,' the liaison officer said.

'Amen to that.' Connie clipped on her lapel mic and took her seat.

Chapter Twenty-Six

Elspeth fetched water and a cloth and cleaned Xavier's cuts. She and Meggy had helped to get him into an upright position on the couch, much as he'd protested when they first went to touch him. Elspeth understood. She must have sounded just as maniacal as Fergus, but if inhabiting their captor's world was the only way to keep them all safe, then that was what she intended to do.

'I saw your photo in the paper,' Xavier said between sips of tea and applying a wet cloth to his bruises. 'It didn't occur to me that the same man was kidnapping me.'

'You're in the wrong place if you're expecting an explanation. I have no idea why he took me, even less how he chose Meggy. Are you hungry?'

Xavier shook his head before checking that Meggy wasn't within earshot, but Elspeth had sent her to the unoccupied bedroom to get the bed ready.

'I just watched him kill my friend,' he whispered. 'He stuck a knife in him like it was nothing at all, as if he didn't even register that he was killing someone. I was so certain I was next.'

Elspeth sank onto the sofa and closed her eyes. 'Please don't give Meggy the details.'

'Of course.' He reduced his voice to an almost inaudible whisper and leaned forward to Elspeth. 'How long have you been here?'

'I don't know. There's no natural light, and he turns our lighting on and off randomly. I lost track with my watch between night and day.' She looked up suddenly. 'What's today's date?'

'October 7th.'

'I've been gone that long? My children will think I'm dead, they'll stop looking for me. My God . . . what did the papers say? Does anyone know what happened to me? Please tell me they don't just think I ran off.'

'At first they thought it was a ransom situation. There was some copycat attempt asking for money. The police caught them and realised it was a scam. There was a lot of coverage about your disappearance at first. It's quieter now,' he explained.

'And Meggy? Was she in the papers, too?'

'Yes. There was a police raid, something to do with her mother, and after that there were general appeals for information. But they'll find Danny's body and they'll be looking for me. He left my wheelchair in the middle of a car park. They'll be looking for us all now. If we can just stay alive . . .'

'You haven't told him what we found under the floorboards, then,' Meggy said from the doorway, sounding petulant.

Elspeth wanted to hug her and tell her everything would be all right, but the girl was too old for lies, and she was too tired to tell them.

'He already knows what Fergus is capable of. I think we need to focus on keeping each other safe. There are three of us now, and that'll make it much harder . . .'

'A kid, a woman who's never been in a fight in her life, and a man who can't walk. That's just fucking great,' Meggy said.

'Meggy!' Elspeth cried, stung by the honesty.

'She's right,' Xavier said. 'He had a knife on him when he took me. If he feels threatened, we won't be able to defend ourselves against him.'

'We'll barricade the door. You said yourself the police will be looking for you now. It's just a matter of time until they track him down. All we have to do is wait it out.' Elspeth stood up, wringing her hands in spite of the attempted injection of conviction in her voice.

'He controls this whole place, right? He can turn off the heating, the electricity, even the water. We'll have no food. Nothing. We'll all be dead within a week, and that's if he doesn't decide to smoke us out or take the door off its hinges and finish us even faster,' Xavier said. 'We need to create an escape route, not block them up.'

'He's going to kill us all anyway,' Meggy said. 'There are bones under the floor. And . . .' she pressed a hand against her stomach, '. . . and a body. I mean, there's not much, you know, left on it, but it's not just bones.'

'A body?' Xavier looked at Elspeth.

'Tell him about the clothes,' Meggy persisted.

Elspeth sighed. 'The body – the woman – is wearing the same dress he left for me when he brought me here. This pink thing.' She tugged at what she was wearing, her mouth a grimace of distaste that had nothing to do with the cut of the cloth. 'We don't know whose bones they are. They might not be anything to do with him. They could even just be members of his family who he didn't want cremated . . .' Elspeth said.

'Who keeps members of their family turning to dust under their floorboards, dressed in these same clothes as people they kidnapped?' Meggy shouted. 'Why do you say such stupid things? I don't want to pretend any more. He cut off your finger, and he's going to kill us. Say it!'

'He cut off your finger? Jesus . . .' Xavier said faintly.

'Please, stop,' Elspeth said.

'No. I won't stop. Say it, Elspeth. He's going to kill us, and you need to say it!'

'I don't need to say it!' She waved the bandaged stump of her finger in the air. 'This hurts like hell. I can barely think about anything else. Except this . . .' she pointed at the bloodied, crusted bandage with her other hand, '. . . is the least of our problems right now. How dare you think I need reminding of just how much shit we're in!'

Elspeth pushed past her and stormed into her bedroom, slamming the door as she went. Meggy stared at Xavier, who was studying the illustrations of windows and the bookcase on the walls.

'Sometimes he forgets us for a day,' Meggy said. 'He doesn't turn on the lights or bring food. Then he comes and it's like he didn't even realise the time had gone. He asks weird questions. One time he kept asking if we could see him. I reckon he had other people up here and forgot them. I bet they died waiting for him to bring food, so he shoved their bodies under the floorboards and just got himself new people instead.'

'How did he cut Elspeth's finger off, Meggy?'

She shook her head. 'I don't want to talk about it, but he keeps a knife in his pocket. He'll use it if we make him angry.'

'I won't let anything bad happen to you,' Xavier said. 'But I need you to be kinder to Elspeth. She's been here weeks, and it must feel like a year.'

Meggy reddened and looked at the closed bedroom door, just visible across the corridor.

'I hate it when she plays along with him,' she muttered. 'Calling me his daughter, and agreeing that she's his wife. He made her marry him. Got her a dress and everything. She even has to wear a ring he got her.'

Xavier breathed out heavily and shook his head. 'But when you got here, she was here to help you figure out what was going on. If the two of you hadn't been here when I arrived, then I'd be going crazy right now. She was alone when he brought her here. No one to talk to. Just Fergus and some batshit fake wedding. Can you imagine how she must have felt?'

Meggy took a seat next to Xavier.

'I think . . . I think he did other bad things to her,' she said quietly.

Xavier reached out and put one hand over the top of Meggy's. 'There are three of us now. Perhaps we can stop him from doing that to her again if we all work together.'

'Your cheekbone's swelling up,' Meggy said. 'You should put the cloth on it.' She didn't pull her hand away from beneath his.

'I'll be fine,' Xavier said. 'How did you find the body under the floorboards?'

'We were trying to escape,' Elspeth said, reappearing.

Meggy ran to her and threw her arms around her. 'I'm sorry I was a bitch. My step-mum's a bitch. I told myself I'd never be like her, and I was, and I know you're only trying to protect me, but I got so cross and I—'

'Shh,' Elspeth soothed, stroking her hair and kissing the top of her head. 'It's okay. You didn't upset me. I was cross with myself. Don't cry, Meggy.' She continued to hold her.

'Look, if he's taken that many people, that many victims, then the police are bound to be on to him. He must have slipped up by now. There'll be a trail of some sort. No one can kill that often and get away with it.'

'They're all at different stages of . . .' Elspeth shrugged. 'It looks to me as if they were taken at different times. Some of the bones are dusty and literally snapping in half, then there's the body that can't be all that old. What if he's taken these people over years? Various ages, genders, from different places.'

'So there's no pattern. Nothing to link the disappearances.'

'Yeah,' Elspeth sighed.

'Can you show me everything you found?' Xavier asked.

Elspeth nodded. 'All the bones we've found are scattered under the floorboards in here. We haven't checked any of the other rooms. This was the only place where we managed to take the carpet up. After that we were too scared of him coming back and figuring out what we'd done, so we put the boards back and replaced the carpet. There's some damage. One of the floorboards is badly broken, so we shifted the sofa over the top of it.'

'You've been really brave,' Xavier said. 'Do you believe he's gone for the night?'

Meggy looked up at Elspeth, who thought about it then nodded.

'How long would it take for you to open up the floor again?' he asked.

'Not long. The carpet's already loose. We just need to move the furniture again. Half an hour, no more, but it won't help us. They're definitely human. We could tell by the skulls. There's no way of telling how old they are though.'

'It's not the bones I want to see,' he said. 'You nearly got through to the floor below. I understand why you stopped, but it's the closest you've come to finding a way out. It seems like a waste to give up on it now.'

'He owns the whole house,' Elspeth said. 'To start with, I was on the ground floor then he moved me up here. I saw the kitchen, other bedrooms below. If we start banging around again, he'll hear us, and then whatever he did to the poor people who're already buried in here . . .' She let the sentence hang.

'Whatever he did to them, he could do to us anyway, at any time. He's not rational. You can't reason with him. What I saw him do tonight . . .' He looked at Meggy and broke off. 'And your finger. How is it?'

'Infected, I think. I did my best cleaning it with hot water, but it's oozing and starting to itch.'

'We need to get you to a doctor,' he said. 'You're right that his bedroom might be below, but if we don't investigate, we'll never know if we missed an opportunity to get out.'

Elspeth sat in the armchair and pulled Meggy onto her lap.

'It's too quiet now. Wherever he is in the house, he'll hear. If we're going to do this, it needs to be in the daytime when we've some hope of traffic noises or pedestrians or even just birds singing.'

'All right,' Xavier said. 'We'll get some sleep. He took my mobile but not my watch. It's midnight now. I say we start at eight a.m. I'm not sure exactly where we are, but I was in his car, and we didn't drive for more than twenty minutes. We can't be far outside the city, so if there's going to be traffic or any other noise, that's our best bet.'

'Fine,' Elspeth said.

Meggy kissed her cheek and laid a tired head on Elspeth's shoulder.

'Maybe, by some miracle, we'll have been found by then anyway.' Elspeth attempted a smile.

Xavier couldn't find the words to respond.

Chapter Twenty-Seven

Fergus stood in the supermarket and stared at the front-page spread of the newspapers. Almost all of them featured a series of photographs. Angela, Elspeth, Meggy, Xavier, and the other man he'd dispatched who was getting in his way. The name was irrelevant.

All of them together, with one final image of a woman. He looked closer. She was about his age. Pretty. Wearing a T-shirt, her hair long and loose over her shoulders. No jewellery. No makeup. Looking directly into the camera.

So there had been a press conference. It didn't matter. He could be tracked but neither stopped nor contained. He was free from the burden of the breakable mortal body. Pain was meaningless, and sooner or later his cells would turn to no more than biological soup and seep back into the earth. Fergus was unafraid.

He walked on towards the fruit section, intending to buy apples and oranges for his family. Their bodies needed sustaining even if his did not. Selecting decent fruit from the largely bruised pile, he glanced back at aisle number 4. He couldn't see the headlines, but he could still picture the woman's face, cheekbones prominent in the black–and–white picture, her eyes large and sad. He wanted to go back and look again.

That was what they wanted, of course. Instead, he wandered off to find rice and noodles. Clean carbohydrates that were long–life and simple to cook. Placing several packs in his basket, he wondered what her name was. Why not just circulate his description if they were trying to catch him? The woman had been saying something to the camera when her photo was taken. Fergus wanted to know what that was. He made it as far from the newspapers as the freezer section before turning back. Dropping his half–full basket, he grabbed a copy of *The Scotsman* and walked out into the car park.

In a well–sheltered parking spot between a giant clothes recycling bin and a billboard advertising the latest must–have toy, Fergus pulled his mobile from the glovebox. He rarely touched it. It wasn't as if he had anyone to call, but it was handy to keep charged for emergencies. Now, he typed in the words 'Constance Woolwine' and 'Edinburgh', keeping his eyes on her face in the paper as he waited for the results of his search.

The video had been uploaded the night before by a local news outlet. Fergus leaned the driver's seat back and got comfortable, volume on max, and pressed Play.

She was sitting on a stool, one foot resting on the floor, the other leg bent to allow her heel to rest on the edge of a crossbar between the stool legs. Black jeans hugged limbs made for running, a copper–buckled leather belt cinched her waist, and her pale skin glowed in the harsh lights required for the cameras. She kept her hands folded loosely in her lap as she looked into camera and began to speak.

'Hi,' she said. 'My name's Constance Woolwine. Connie to my family.' She gave a small smile.

Fergus pulled the screen a little closer. She reminded him of someone.

'I'm here because I want to get in touch with someone.' Connie lifted her chin a little higher, shifted on the stool and leaned into the nearest lens. 'I don't know your name but I know a little bit about you. I'd like to know more, though. I think there are things we have in common.'

'I doubt that,' Fergus told her.

'I know what happened to Angela was a mistake. I think that must have affected you very badly. I believe she was very special to you.'

Air snagged in Fergus' throat and he was back in Angela's bedroom, lying on top of her, smelling her, touching her soft skin. It was a trick. He knew that. The American woman on his screen was working for the police. He was dead, not stupid.

'I also think you're keeping Elspeth safe. I'm certain you haven't hurt her. She's such a precious person to her family, and I believe the reason you took her is because she's precious to you, too.'

Fergus gave a small nod. He hadn't done anything bad to Elspeth. The police knew he wasn't some sick fuck randomly killing women. Not that it mattered what anyone thought of him now, but it was still good to hear. He liked Connie's voice, her accent. Her vowels were soft, and her voice had a husky edge that made him think of country-and-western singers.

'Is Meggy there with you, too? She's a great kid. Everyone says so. Maybe she wasn't fully appreciated by her own family.' Connie paused and shrugged. 'Not everyone is really cut out for parenting. But if Meggy's with you, and if she's with Elspeth, then I bet she's being really loved.'

'Of course she is,' Fergus said.

'Elspeth had two children before,' Connie said. 'She was a loving wife and an amazing mother. Dedicated, kind, and loyal. I'm sure you're finding the same. She and Meggy must be wonderful company.'

'Being a father is hard,' Fergus replied. 'You're right about Elspeth, though. She's my angel.'

'I guess I'm a bit worried about Xavier,' Connie continued. 'I don't think that went according to plan. Not your fault. Are you tired? I get tired. Having people to care for is tiring, isn't it?' She put one elbow to her knee, cupping her chin with the palm of her hand.

Fergus leaned in towards the screen.

'The world takes its toll on us. Certainly it does me. So, Xavier's okay, right? I don't often talk about this, but I have a problem with my vision. Not my eyes, they're okay. It's the way my brain translates the signals from my eyes and turns them into pictures inside my head.'

Fergus held the mobile with both hands and brought it close to his face. His breath frosted the glass, and he wiped it with his sleeve.

'I should have said. Xavier has a muscle-wasting condition that requires regular medication. Because I know you care about the girls, I think you care about him, too, so I just wanted to let you know that he might need some extra help.'

Fergus thought about that. He wasn't sure how long he'd need Xavier. There was only one step left in creating his ideal life, but that might take a few days more. It really depended how vital the medication was. It seemed unlikely that anything would happen if someone missed a few days of tablets, but then he didn't want to have to replace Xavier as he had Angela.

'Sorry, I got distracted,' Connie was saying. 'About my eyesight. I'm an achromat, which means I only see in black and white. It's a strange thing, because while I exist in the same world as everyone else, it looks very different from my perspective, and I feel . . .' she gave a shrug, 'I guess I feel cut off from everyone else a lot of the time. As if they're all sharing some great secret I'm not allowed to know.' Connie gave a vague smile. 'I don't think I'm explaining myself very well. I suppose a lot of the time I just feel invisible.'

Fergus held his breath. He touched her face through his screen with his fingertips.

'I wonder if you do, too. Sometimes people like us see the beauty in the world but it seems like we can't really connect with it. I'm not here to judge you, and I'm not a police officer, by the way, in spite of how this looks. I'm a psychologist – although that's a fancy title for someone who tries to figure out how other people think and feel. I'm reaching out to you, to say I get it. Not all of it – I haven't walked a mile in your shoes.'

'No one has,' Fergus whispered.

'Is that the right phrase?' Connie continued. 'Anyway, I hope that makes sense. I was hoping you'd let me know that Elspeth and Meggy are okay, and so that I can give you the information you need about how to get medication for Xavier. I can arrange it all and just leave it somewhere. But also so you know someone can see you. You're not invisible, even if it feels like it. There'll be a number on the screen when I'm finished. You'll be put through to me. I won't ask your name, number, where you are. Nothing.'

Seeing the world in black and white. He paused the video stream and stared out of the window. The tarmac was grey, but even that was marked with yellow lines, and it sparkled with glass broken over the years, sending thousands of minute arcs of coloured light upwards. The recycling bins were green but mottled from weather and scratches, giving them a more interesting worn look that revealed layers of older paint in different colours. In comparison, the billboard above him was a riot of tones, each designed to grab a child's attention and subject the parents to demands to be bought whatever crap was being advertised. How flat her world must be, Fergus thought. Like his. A black veil between each of them and everyone else. He touched the screen and Connie came back to life.

'Or I'll meet you. Name the place. I'll guarantee to be alone. I know that seems unlikely and you'll be thinking it's a trap, but I wouldn't do that. I'm staying at The Balmoral hotel.'

There was an audible gasp from the background. He stopped the video, rewound a couple of seconds and played it again. The gaspers were out of sight, but the sound was loud, a mixture of men's and women's voices. She wasn't supposed to have told him where she was staying. He couldn't keep the smile off his face. There was no script, and if there was, she'd just gone off it spectacularly. He wished he could have been there. Connie Woolwine played by her own rules. Like him. Conventions didn't apply to some people. Certainly not to either of them. He hit Play.

'You can find me there. No one needs to know where or when. I'm giving you this information because I trust you. I think you have a reason for everything you've done. I know the things you've done aren't random or gratuitous. We understand each other.'

Connie sat back on the stool and wrapped her arms around her waist. Fergus wondered if she had children, but there was no ring on her left hand, and her stomach was so flat it was impossible to think her body had ever been stretched by a baby.

'But call me soon,' she said. 'Xavier will get ill, and I need to know that Elspeth and Meggy are still alive. I think we have a lot to say to one another. Thank you.'

She gave a final gentle smile, then the picture faded to black, and an information screen with a telephone number came up. Fergus paused it, grabbing a pen from the glove compartment and writing the number on the back of his hand. Not that he was seriously contemplating calling. He had things to achieve to ensure his passage into the next life. No point jeopardising it.

Rewinding the footage one last time, he paused on a still frame of Connie. So slight and vulnerable. So haunted. Of course she'd reminded him of someone, he thought, staring in the rearview mirror. It was him.

Fergus left the car park at 8.30 a.m.

Chapter Twenty-Eight

Once they'd helped Xavier in and out of the bathroom, and settled him back on the sofa, Meggy and Elspeth began rolling the carpet back once more. At least Fergus was leaving the lights on for them now – they were learning to be grateful for small mercies.

'What time is it now?' Elspeth asked.

'Eight forty a.m. We'd better get on with it,' Xavier said.

The single broken floorboard revealed nothing but a dark hole. As they pulled up the second that had been loosened during their first excavation, there was a hint of a grey mass in the cavity.

'Show me,' Xavier said.

Elspeth covered her hand with a tea towel and pulled out a long, dry bone.

'It's a femur.'

'Are you a doctor?' Meggy asked.

'No,' he replied gently, 'but when your legs stop working properly, you suddenly learn a lot about anatomy in a very short time. Pull out the bones and anything else that's in the way, but keep them in one pile right next to the opening so we can shove it all back if we hear him coming.'

'I'm holding someone's leg bone,' Elspeth said. 'Why don't you seem bothered by it?'

'I am bothered by it. Don't think I'm not, but I don't want it to be my leg bone,' Xavier said. 'And not yours or Meggy's, either. That bone and the others in there mean we're on borrowed time, so we sit around and lament our fate, or we find a way out. Which would you prefer?'

Meggy looked from Elspeth's face to Xavier's, shoved her arm as far into the cavity as she could and began joining in, dragging out bone after bone.

'Where's the complete body?' he asked.

'Further in. We saw it but couldn't reach it.'

'Good. I don't want it to be in the way. We'll need to get another floorboard up,' Xavier said. 'Can you get me down onto the floor next to the hole? My legs might be useless, but my arms might just make up for it.'

They helped him to the floor, and he worked on loosening the next board while bones came out of the hole fast.

'There are so many bones,' Elspeth said.

'Two hundred and six in an adult,' Meggy said. 'We just studied it in biology. Maybe they're all from one person?'

'Only if that person had five legs,' Xavier said, looking at the bone pile. 'Keep going. This floorboard is nearly out. Then we'll need something strong and heavy.'

Ten minutes later, and nails screeched against wood. The floorboard flew upwards. The three of them sat back and looked at the much larger hole. As one, they bent their heads to see inside.

A door slammed, and they jerked backwards, Xavier cracking his head against Elspeth's. Meggy raced into the hallway and pressed her ear to the front door.

No one breathed.

'Is he coming?' Elspeth panted.

'Shh,' Meggy said.

Sweat trickled down Xavier's forehead. Elspeth shook. Meggy gritted her teeth and made fists of her hands as she focused on what lay beyond their prison.

Another slammed door, then silence again. No footsteps on the stairs.

'I don't think he's coming up,' Meggy said.

'We should clear up anyway. Put all this away. It's too risky,' Elspeth said.

'I think it's too risky not to carry on,' Xavier said. 'We should keep going.'

They looked at Meggy. 'I'm twelve,' she shrugged. 'I can't decide.'

'Look, we're nearly through. Meggy can get down in the gap now. She's small enough to get between the rafters. Is there anything here we can use to bash in the ceiling below? It needs to be strong enough to smash through the plasterboard.'

'If we had something like that, we'd have hit Fergus over the head with it,' Meggy said. 'Everything useful in here is fixed to the floor or the wall.'

'She's right,' Elspeth said. 'We don't have anything that's substantial enough to do any real damage. He's been careful. But then I guess he's done this before.' She picked up a small bone and snapped it in two. 'Nothing wrong with his learning curve.'

'Then we'll have to do it manually. Meggy, you ready?' Xavier asked.

She looked at Elspeth, who held her arms open. Meggy walked across the room and accepted the hug.

'You sure you want to do this? No one will blame you if you're too freaked out,' Elspeth said.

'I'm sure,' Meggy said. 'What is it you need me to do?'

'Okay. These floorboards are resting on top of rafters, thick, strong wooden beams that go between the floors of a building. Inside, there's insulation – that yellow stuff you can see – and usually some space. With the bones out of the way, you should be able to shove your feet between the rafters and kick away the insulation between this pair of beams . . .' He pointed downwards. 'Attached to the underside of those beams from below is the ceiling you'd see if you looked up from below. The plasterboard might have been decorated, but basically, it's just a thick piece of board. You'll need to make sure you don't put all of your weight on it at once, and that we're holding you, because I need you to stamp your way through that board, okay? We have to make a hole in it, and that hole will have to be big enough for us all to get through.'

'What then?' Elspeth asked.

'Then we'll have to tie some sheets together for us to get down, or one of us will have to get out and get help. He might even have a phone in the rooms below.'

'That won't help if we can't give the police an address to come to. How long do you think he'll be out? And what are we supposed to do about you? We can't just drop you through. Shit, I'm sorry, that came out much worse . . .' Elspeth's face reddened.

'Forget it. Now isn't the time for political correctness. You're right. It's not going to be easy getting me out, which is why one of you two needs to get through and escape. Time is limited. If we're going to do this, we need to get on with it.'

Meggy sat on the edge of the hole and pushed her feet inside. Elspeth wrapped an arm around her waist, and Xavier took hold of her right hand. She scuffled her feet inside the space, kicking insulation aside. A cloud of dust rose up into the room. They turned their heads aside and covered their mouths.

'It stinks,' Meggy complained.

'Never mind. Can you feel the plasterboard?' Xavier asked. Meggy nodded.

'Good. Now kick. The fewer kicks and the harder they are, the better. The longer we're doing this, the more chance that we'll draw his attention. Okay? Now make them count.'

Elspeth tightened her grip around the girl's body.

'Go!' Xavier said.

Meggy raised her right knee, closed her eyes and slammed her foot down as hard as she could. There was a fierce crack, and Meggy's body slipped to one side. She cried out, reaching down into the space.

'My ankle,' she said. 'My foot hit something.'

'Here, let me see,' Elspeth said, lying on her stomach and reaching into the void, rummaging around through the remnants of the insulation where Meggy's foot had gone down. When she pulled her hand back out, it held a tiny, round white ball.

A crack ran through the skull, and a section had come away, but the features were still clear.

'It's a baby,' Meggy said.

'It was a baby,' Elspeth corrected.

Xavier put his hand over the sphere of bone and took it gently away, putting it delicately on the floor.

'Now it's one more reason for us to get out of here as quickly as possible,' he said. He put one arm around Elspeth and the other around Meggy. 'We can do this. But only if we don't get distracted by our fear. When we get out, we'll make sure everyone who died here is taken away and buried. We won't let them be forgotten. I promise. I need you to be brave. Nothing's changed. Meggy, ready to try again?'

'I guess,' she said. 'Not with my right foot, though. I really hurt my ankle.'

'Left foot this time,' he said. 'Clear more of the insulation before you try again. We can't have any more injuries.'

They returned to their original positions.

Meggy made a space so she could see before she stamped again. She brought her foot up and smashed it downwards. No impact. They peered into the hole. The plasterboard hadn't even registered the blow. Again, Meggy raised her leg and slammed her heel into the board. There was an echo that seemed to hit the ceiling above them and come back down towards their heads, but no result.

'We've got to keep trying,' Xavier said. 'If he was in, he'd have heard that by now. Give it a few more goes, then Elspeth will have to take over. I know it'll be harder to get your feet in, but we're out of options.'

'How do you think he killed those other people?' Meggy asked.

'I have no intention of finding out,' Xavier said, gripping her chin and making her look straight into his eyes. 'Because it's not going to happen to any of us.'

'I have an idea,' Elspeth said. 'Meggy can't harness enough force to damage the plasterboard. But if I stood on it long enough, put all my weight through a single small area, then sooner or later it would weaken, right?'

'The rafters are pretty close together. Meggy can't hold you, I'm not mobile enough to guarantee I can stop you from falling, and you might get yourself injured either by the rafters or if you fall too far, too fast. There's your left hand to think of, too.'

'You can't do that. It's dangerous.' Meggy shook her head. 'I won't let you.'

'Nonsense. If it's that or be killed by some lunatic in this bloody flat, then I know which I'd choose. At least we'll have tried to escape. Come on, Meggy, out of the way. We might as well go for it,' Elspeth said.

'We only get one chance at this,' Xavier said. 'If he walks in while you're dangling from the ceiling, you'd better be prepared to fight.'

'You look after Meggy,' Elspeth said. 'I can take care of myself.'

Chapter Twenty-Nine

'You shouldn't have given him the name of your hotel. That was too risky. One of the most basic rules of police work is that you never make it personal,' Baarda told her.

Connie raised a hand at The Balmoral's barman and motioned towards her empty glass.

'Not personal? I'm not sure how that works. I suppose you can classify some crimes as not personal. Corporate banking frauds, illegal benefits claims, car ringing. But murder? Kidnapping? There's nothing more personal than that, and if we don't approach it the same way as the perpetrator does, then how do we understand his mindset?'

'That wasn't an invitation to play psychologist with me. There has to be a bottom line, and it should be not making an already dangerous situation more perilous. Now, the Major Investigation Team is not only stretched to its limits looking for Meggy, Elspeth and Xavier, but we also need a detail watching you and this hotel around the clock.'

'He needed me to prove that I was willing to cross a line for him. Empathy isn't as straightforward as being able to understand how someone feels. It's communicated subtly.

Dressing like him, sharing with him, trusting him. We can't find him, Baarda. I don't think that's because he's clever. I think it relates to the extent of his risk-taking. He's not working on a level with other offenders. His agenda's completely unique. It has elements of omnipotence and out-of-body delusions.'

Baarda drained his drink. 'Yet here we are, sitting in your hotel bar, waiting for him to call. How is that any different from where we were before? We're not even chasing our tails. Now, we're just sitting around staring at our tails. Only if you misread the situation, at any moment a man could run in with a knife and decide to finish the person he saw on the television who's helping the police identify him.'

'He doesn't want me,' Connie said.

'You're much surer of your position than is warranted, given that we still know nothing about this killer.'

'I'm a profiler. You don't profile with a perpetrator sitting in front of you giving you information. And it's a science, thank you. This is as certain as profiling gets. I have all the different strands. I just don't have a single psychological diagnosis that pulls it all together yet.'

'Is there one?' Baarda asked.

'Actually, yes. You hungry?' she asked.

'Not hungry, but curious about how things got resolved for you.'

'The psychiatrist who diagnosed me as suffering from teenage hysteria – not a real thing, by the way, just a convenient phrase – was involved in a car crash. Coincidence is occasionally kind. A replacement consultant was sent to the ward, younger and more up to date than the great Dr Webster. He insisted on reviewing all the cases from scratch and was willing to spend time with me. I did my best to communicate with a sort of sign language, but it got muddled every time I started to send signals. He understood that my tears were of frustration rather than a fit of pique.'

'So what happened?' Baarda asked.

'He ordered another brain scan, looked more carefully than Webster had and drew the conclusion that there was a small blood clot sitting in the part of my brain that controlled communication. They operated, and – thank God – he was right.'

Baarda drew in a long, slow breath. 'That's when you lost your colour vision?'

'Same moment I got my life back. You win some, you lose some. Cheers.' She raised her glass and clinked the edge of Baarda's.

He left it untouched. 'What happened to Dr Webster? He had you locked up for no reason at all. It was clear malpractice – in fact, nothing less than cruelty.'

'Webster never fully recovered from the car crash. I know enough now to recognise him as a sociopath. Intelligent, incapable of empathy, manipulative, utterly self-centred. Hated women, especially women who didn't pay him what he regarded as his due respect. My grandmother was furious, mostly I suspect for her own blind belief in Webster. A conversation was had with Webster's lawyers and insurers. The money they paid put me through college and grad school, and there's still plenty left over. This is a vocation. I don't actually need the cash. I suspect you're in the same position.'

'Not exactly. School fees and a wife who likes our second home in Tuscany are expensive.'

'Divorce her,' Connie said.

'It's not that simple.'

'Yes it fucking well is. Take back control.'

'You know, you're a very angry psychologist,' Baarda smiled.

'I'm a very practical psychologist. Sometimes there's

unequivocal right and wrong. It's okay to acknowledge that. Anger is important. It's cathartic and paves the way for resolution. I'm prescribing a daily dose of fury for you. Get mad, Brodie Baarda. You're owed it.' Her mobile rang and she picked up. 'Connie Woolwine.'

'But it's really Dr Woolwine, right?'

Connie pointed at the mobile, and Baarda grabbed his own phone to send a text.

'That's right. Who's this?'

'You sent me a message. I assumed you'd be expecting my call.'

'I was, and I'm glad you've reached out. I'm just not sure what you want me to call you.'

'Nothing. You don't need to call me anything. That works. You said you wanted to know that Elspeth and Meggy are all right. They are. That's all I called to say. I'm looking after them the way I'm supposed to. Do you have children?'

'I don't,' Connie said.

'That's too bad. You'd be a good mother. I can tell.'

'I'm not sure about that,' she laughed gently. 'Sometimes I worry that I'm too set in my own ways to become a mother now.'

'That's not what's important. It's about being able to make a commitment and stick with it. Being a parent is about staying the course.'

'I agree,' Connie said. 'Listen, it's a formality, but I need to check you really are . . .'

'Elspeth lost a shoe somewhere. I didn't notice until I got her home. It wasn't mentioned in the papers. Is that good enough?'

'It's perfect,' Connie said. 'Speaking of which, does Meggy need any more clothes, or maybe her schoolbooks? I'm sure we could find a drop-off point that wouldn't require you to come into contact with us.'

'No. She'll be fine. I thought of everything before . . .'

'And Xavier, he'll need his medication soon.'

'How long can he go without?'

Connie paused. Questions about time were difficult. Pretend there was no urgency and she'd lose the chance to make contact. Make it sound too desperate and there was a chance he'd decide Xavier was a liability.

'He's good for another couple of days, but after that, Xavier will struggle with muscle control, and his general functioning will start to become more impaired. Activities like feeding and washing himself will become difficult.'

'That's what Elspeth's for. She's already agreed to help. You don't need to worry. How do you see people in black and white? Do they all look more alike? Is it harder to recognise faces?'

Connie scribbled notes as she thought about it.

'It's more of a challenge with younger people. I'm from the East Coast of America. On any one of our beaches in the summer, you could see literally hundreds of sixteen-year-old girls, all fairly skinny, wearing cut-off jeans and skimpy tees, long, straight hair, clear skin. Then it's hard. Among older people, it's easier. We have more facial anomalies as we age.'

'Not everyone ages,' he said.

'That's true. Do you mind if I ask why you took Xavier?'

'The world you inhabit is not the same as everyone else's. Mine is even less so. Xavier's necessary. I wouldn't do anything unless I really needed to. I have to pass this time. I thought you got it.'

'I think I do. Certainly I understood that Angela was a mistake. What do you mean pass? Are you facing some sort of test?'

Lots of background noise, she wrote for Baarda. *He's somewhere busy.*

258

'I grieve for Angela,' he said. 'She was angelic. Everything a mother should be. I never once saw her . . .' He broke off.

'Hello?' Connie asked. 'Is everything okay?'

No response.

Line still open, Connie wrote.

Baarda was busy demanding answers on his own phone from MIT's technical team, who were listening in.

'You were saying you never saw Angela do something. What was that?'

'Lying bitch!' he yelled.

'Can you tell me what's going on? Maybe I can help—'

'He's got a photo of Elspeth naked in the shower!'

Connie flipped open her laptop and thrust it at Baarda. *Someone talking about Elspeth. TV/online?* she scribbled.

Baarda began tapping away furiously at the keys.

'Photos can be manipulated. It's impossible to know if what you're seeing these days is real. Please don't—'

'Shut up!' he ordered. 'He's speaking.'

Connie could hear a different voice in the background, familiar, but she couldn't place it immediately. A second later, it was joined by her own laptop streaming a feed of a video that had obviously gone viral given the way the numbers beneath the video were hopping up by hundreds every few seconds.

'I knew Elspeth for quite a while,' Nick Bowlzer was saying into his laptop camera. 'The real her. Not the fake version you see in all the photos or at those posh dinners. Bethy – that's what she liked me to call her – wasn't really like that. I really thought we were . . .' He paused for dramatic effect and wiped a sleeve over his eyes, 'Soul mates. I know she was married, and I'm making this video partly to say how sorry I am to her husband.'

Fuck! Connie scribbled on her notepad.

'But also so the world gets to know Bethy better. It's important to me that everyone can see how human and fragile she was. Flawed like every one of us. The truth is, we both fought it, but I guess the heart wants what the heart wants.'

'She was supposed to be pure!' Elspeth's captor howled. 'I knew she could never be as perfect as Angela, but this . . . she's a whore! Did you know about this?' His panting into the phone was furious.

'The man talking just wants his five minutes of fame. He might not even know Elspeth . . .'

'She has a birthmark! I've seen it. It's in the photo. And I saw her with him once, after her yoga class. Are you lying to me now as well?'

'Whether he knows her or not, it doesn't mean Elspeth did the things he's saying,' Connie soothed. She paused the video then rewound to the start where Nick Bowlzer had split his screen and was displaying a photo of Elspeth in the shower – a few body parts blurred with a crude editing tool, but enough on show to prove his point.

'I think she knows him really bloody well,' he growled. 'She misled me. Elspeth's my wife! You don't think she ought to have told me about this? You think I'd have chosen her if I'd known?'

'People make mistakes . . .'

'Fucking right,' he said. 'Elspeth just made one she'll regret forever.'

The line went dead.

'He's going to kill her,' Connie said. 'Get that fucking attention-seeking prick off the air right now. Do whatever you have to do to get that video off every server.'

'Impossible. It'll have been downloaded by now.'

'Shit!' Connie shouted. She scrolled forward to the end of

the video, where Nick Bowlzer had his name, email address and social media tags displayed across the bottom of the screen. 'That little son of a bitch is doing this to get media likes, not to mention the money he'll be demanding to give a kiss-and-tell story to the gutter press.'

'We have to focus on what we've got. Did he say anything that might help? A name? An idea of what he's doing with his hostages?' Baarda asked.

'Nothing. Did MIT manage to trace the call?'

'No, the number was from a burner mobile, and the call wasn't long enough to triangulate. He's in Edinburgh city limits somewhere. That's the best they could do. At least we have his voice now. If we pick him up, we'll be able to confirm his identity immediately.'

'No voice changer,' Connie said. 'No speech impediment. I'd put him in his thirties, which fits the previous descriptions of him.'

'He was angry this time, though. At the sports centre, when he killed Danny, the witness said it was as if he was on autopilot, like he felt nothing at all when he used the knife. This is his trigger. So what do we know?'

'He wouldn't have made that call from his home address,' Connie said. 'He's delusional but still functioning. We need officers on the street looking for someone driving badly. He's lost control, and he'll be trying to make his way back to Elspeth as fast as possible. If he's on foot or on public transport, he'll be visibly agitated, possibly confrontational. In this state, he poses an immediate threat to anyone who approaches him. We need an all-agencies alert, contain but do not approach. Assume he's armed.'

'I'm putting the alert out now. Anything else?' Baarda asked.

'I need to review that call somewhere quiet so I can really

listen to his voice and see what I can get from his language. Let's go up to my room, and don't waste any more units here. Get them out on patrol. We're safe, but thanks to Nick fucking Bowlzer, Elspeth is most definitely not.'

Chapter Thirty

'We have to barricade the door first,' Xavier said. 'If he walks in on us when you're dangling from the ceiling, Elspeth, we're all dead.'

'There's no time,' Elspeth complained.

'We'll make time. It's too dangerous any other way. I'll be tied to you and unable to protect Meggy. Just run that scenario through your head for a moment.'

'That's fine, but what do you suggest we use? Almost everything in the flat is bolted to walls or to the floor. The sofa's too big for us to get through the doorway – it must have been put together in here – and we have no tools.'

'There are three mattresses – that's a start. Use mine and Meggy's first as they're singles, then you'll have to bend yours as much as you can. Lean them against the door. Add all the other items from cupboards you can. Toys, clothes, pots and pans. Anything not pinned down. It may not hold him for long, but it'll make it hard to get in quickly.'

Meggy and Elspeth got to work, with Xavier issuing directions from the lounge. The double mattress was hardest to move, bulky with old-fashioned springs that complained as they shifted it. Shoving it as hard as they could against the door, they flung everything else into a pile.

'Well, now we have to escape,' Meggy said. 'We can't put that lot back.'

'I like it better like this,' Elspeth said. 'It feels more homely.'

At the base of the hole in the floor, the plasterboard was proving strong and unyielding, the close-set rafters added to its strength. By the time Xavier had concluded that Elspeth would need to jump up and down to break through, he'd also had time to think about the height of the ceiling in their own flat. If that was matched in the room beneath, then Elspeth was looking at a drop of perhaps fifteen feet. Without a means of controlling that fall, she'd be lucky to escape with just a broken ankle or two, and that was if she went straight down. More likely, she would slam her head into one of the rafters on the way, risking damage to her head and neck.

Fifteen minutes later of time they could barely afford, and they'd tied three sheets together and wrapped them around Elspeth's chest beneath her arms, securing the loose end with the armchair as an anchor.

'Ready?' Xavier asked.

'As I'll ever be,' Elspeth said.

She jumped as high as she could given the constraints of the hole in the floor and gripped her arms tight by her sides over the sheet-rope.

A soft crunch followed, the equivalent of biting into crisps when the packet has been left unsealed for a week. Still an identifiable crackle, but the sound was soft around the edges. Elspeth's head flew upwards as her feet passed through the plasterboard. Xavier grabbed for the sheet, to add his own weight to the counterbalance of the chair. Meggy reached out as Elspeth tipped to one side, the plasterboard choosing that moment to break unevenly, the area beneath Elspeth's right foot giving way before the left, leaving her lurching into the edge of the cavity as she plummeted.

Meggy got her hand between Elspeth's head and the jagged edge of a broken floorboard, and howled as Elspeth's head bounced off the back of her hand, forcing her palm into the splintered wood. Too late, Elspeth reached one arm upwards to try to grab on to the remaining floorboards to prevent the fall. One arm down, one arm in the air, the sheet pulled, noose-like, around her left breast and the outside of her upturned shoulder.

The armchair spun in place, knocking Xavier from his position and pushing him into Meggy, crushing her hand further into the ragged protrusions of ageing wood. The girl cried out. Xavier did his best to clutch the slippery sheet, but the knot wouldn't hold. Elspeth slipped away into the room below, with barely time to scream.

'Elspeth!' Xavier shouted.

The last of the sheet had slipped silkily through his hands and landed in a spiral on top of her unmoving body like a gymnast's ribbon.

'Don't let her be dead,' Meggy was chanting. 'Please, please, please, don't let her be dead.'

'She's not dead,' Xavier told her. 'It's not a big enough drop for that. We just need to give her a moment. She's had a shock, and she may have bumped her head. Try to stay calm.'

'You stay calm!' Meggy shouted. 'You only just got here. I can't do this without her.'

'Meggy, stop!' Xavier commanded. 'That won't help us now.'

There was a low groan from the floor below. Xavier and Meggy shoved their heads as low into the hole as was safe.

'Elspeth!' Meggy shouted. 'Wake up. You have to get up.'

Face down, her right arm above her head and across the back of her head at an alarming angle, Elspeth's feet twitched, then her left leg jerked.

When she began to scream, it was as if the entire house was echoing her pain. The noise bounced off the walls around her and the fractured ceiling above. She tried to roll over and ended up flopping back onto her belly, kicking her feet into the floor. Her right arm floated horribly, uselessly, above her head, her fingers frantically grabbing thin air.

'Elspeth,' Xavier shouted. 'Listen to me. You've dislocated your shoulder. You're going to have to get it back in.'

She was crying, helpless with the pain.

'Meggy, you're going to have to get down there. I'm too heavy for you to lower me, but I should be able to get you down. I need you to fetch all the bedding.'

Meggy was sprinting to help before he'd finished speaking. She dumped a pile of sheets and pillows in Xavier's lap.

'Come on, then,' she said.

Xavier shoved three pillows through the hole and onto the floor below to give Meggy a chance at a softer landing, then tied a blanket and a sheet together, one end around her waist.

'Same as with Elspeth, only she had three sheets. You'll have to drop the last bit. It's important to remember to keep your ankles and knees soft, drop to your side, let yourself collapse and roll. Don't try to fight it. Say it back to me.'

'I'm not a baby,' she groaned.

'Say it back,' he insisted.

'Land soft, let myself roll, knees and ankles, blah-blah-blah.'

'That'll have to do. When you're down, I'll talk you through how to help Elspeth. Did he give you any medicine for emergencies, paracetamol maybe?'

'Don't think so. Elspeth didn't say.' She looked over the edge of the hole to where Elspeth was now lying on her back and groaning, eyes still shut.

'Okay. That'll be the priority when we get downstairs. I'm going to tie the other end onto my waist, and I'll hang on to the chair. When you're as low as I can get you, I'll warn you and you'll have to brace to drop. Got it?'

'Hurry up, then,' she said.

'Just hold on to the sheet above your head, so if the knot slips—'

'Ugh,' Meggy sighed, putting her feet into the cavity and taking a firm hold of the bedding rope before pushing away from the edge.

Xavier gripped the chair with one arm and held tight to the knot around his waist with his free hand, wishing harder than he ever had before that his legs still worked, unable to brace and hold the girl's weight with his whole body. More importantly, unable to fight their captor.

It was hard work with the clumsy makeshift rope and the limitations of his movement, but he found he could cut himself some slack with his left hand, rebalance, then allow the rope to feed through his other hand and run a decent rhythm. It was slow going, but the would-be rope was holding.

'You okay?'

'Yes, go faster!' Meggy shouted back.

'Got to take it steady,' he said. 'Be patient. How high above the floor do you think you are?'

'I don't know . . . maybe, like, three of me. It doesn't make any difference anyway, just let the sheet thingy out. Her arm looks all funny, and her breathing's weird, like she's sucking through a straw.'

'Shit,' Xavier muttered under his breath.

He tried to let out another half a foot of sheet and heard a ripping.

'Meggy, look up. Can you see where the sheet is going through the cavity?'

'Too dark,' she said.

The tiny scream was a knife in his heart. The sheet suddenly

gave a few inches then stopped dramatically. He felt the movement of Meggy swinging in mid-air at the end of the length
of material and grabbed frantically at the fabric that was still
intact in his grasp.

'Stay still!' he ordered. 'It must be snagged somewhere on
the rafter.'

'Like I've got a choice,' the girl muttered. 'Oh, gross, the
ceiling is covered in brown stains and it stinks in here.'

'Don't worry about that now,' Xavier told her, tying off the
end he'd been holding around his waist, hoping the chair was
heavy enough to balance the girl's weight, then using his hands
to pull himself across the floor to the cavity. He knew perfectly
well what the stains on the ceiling were. Their cause was the
same as the smell Meggy was complaining about. Decomposing
bodies leaked fluid, and the plasterboard would have soaked it
up like a sponge.

At the opening, he lowered himself to lie on his chest,
jamming one arm across the other side to hold on tight, then
leaning in to unhook the sheet.

Meggy's problem was apparent straight away. A careless
carpenter sometime in the previous hundred years had been
sloppy with a nail, which had been left sticking from a section
of wooden beam. The sheet's tension had helped the nail to
pierce the weave of the cotton, and the puncture had become
a rip. Now, with every inch that he allowed Meggy to drop,
the material was splitting further, and that meant it was
weakening.

'Holy shit,' Meggy said.

'It's okay. I'm going to reach in and unhook the sheet, just—'

'No,' she said. 'Not that. Look at the walls.'

He glanced down into the room. In spite of the limited view
and the lack of natural light, he could see enough to catch the
psychedelic patterning of the walls.

'What the hell is that? Wallpaper?'

'Photos,' she said. Her voice cracked. 'So many that it looks like wallpaper. Only creepy. Really creepy bloody wallpaper.'

There was a sudden cough and the sound of a wet wheezing from the floor below.

'Right, I'm reaching in to free up the cloth. Don't be scared if it slips a bit.'

'This isn't normal,' Meggy continued. 'Some of these photos are really old. And I think he's scribbled on some of them. Crossed the faces out. There are layers of them. New photos stuck over old ones.'

'We can't do this now, Meggy. Elspeth needs you. We have to concentrate.'

'But it's the whole room. And I think . . . I see photos of me. Lots of them. Like maybe hundreds. How long has he been watching us?'

Ice flushed through Xavier's veins. His fingers were suddenly giant sausages working against his will, and the old pain was back in his legs where he'd had no sensation for years. Nausea coated his tongue and threatened to overwhelm him. He tried to block out Meggy's words as he worked on the sheet.

'They're in sections. I'm only on one wall, but there are photos of other girls there, too.'

The end of the sheet in his hand suddenly twisted dramatically.

'Meggy, whatever you're doing, stop. You have to stay still. This won't hold your weight if you move around.'

'No, I need to see another wall,' she insisted.

'You'll fall!'

'I see that other woman. The one who got killed in her bed. Oh my God. Oh shit, shit, shit. He killed her, too.'

The door opened.

'You're right, I did,' Fergus said. 'Not deliberately. Angela

269

didn't deserve to die.' He walked into the room and stood over Elspeth. 'This bitch does, though. She owes it to me, for the lying, the deceit. Fucking around behind my back.'

'She's not your wife!' Meggy yelled, swaying on the thinning threads. 'Elspeth hates you.'

'Meggy, stop,' Xavier said.

'Oh, don't stop now. We're just about to have a very honest conversation. Why don't you come down?'

Chapter Thirty-One

'Nick Bowlzer has been taken into custody, but it's on pretty spurious grounds. I'm not expecting him to be charged with any offences,' Baarda told Connie.

'Shame. The world would be a much better place if being a complete dick was made illegal.'

'The problem might be finding a judge to pass sentence who wouldn't be guilty of gross hypocrisy.'

'Did Bowlzer offer any stunning insights as to why he chose to put Elspeth's life in even more danger?' Connie asked.

'Apparently, his girlfriend finally wised up and decided to break off their relationship, so he figured he had nothing left to lose. The lure of his fifteen minutes of fame and the cash from selling his story were too much of an enticement. Says it didn't occur to him that it would hurt Elspeth, although he was concerned that her husband might come after him, but he calculated that the video was so public he'd made himself untouchable.'

'Do me a favour and plant a huge stash of class A drugs in his apartment shortly before executing a search warrant, would you?' Connie asked.

'I'm afraid I left all my cocaine at home today.' He smiled softly. 'It's been an hour since our kidnapper hung up. Do you think Elspeth Dunwoody's still alive?'

'It's not just Elspeth I'm worried about,' Connie said. She scribbled notes on a board then stood back to consider what she'd written against the backdrop of the wall of images, notes and maps that now covered a large section of her hotel room. 'What became obvious during that call is that our man has undertaken a substantial world-building exercise. He's given his delusion not just scaffolding, but also interior decoration. I'm not sure it's possible to burst just one section of that balloon without the whole thing exploding.'

'Meggy and Xavier?'

'Might be secondary casualties. He may feel his entire world is tainted and decide to wipe the slate clean. If they try to intervene, they might end up wounded as a result of his rage with Elspeth. The important thing is that we've spoken to him now. Every word he said is additional information. It's a blueprint to his brain.'

'What does he want?' Baarda asked.

'He's taken a woman we now know he idolised, fantasised about, as his wife. That was his primary motivation. She won't be able to maintain that illusion for him, so how's that going to resolve?'

'He either ignores the fact that she doesn't feel the same and carries on regardless, or he disposes of her and develops a new obsession,' Baarda said.

Connie stared at the collage of photos of Elspeth. 'This man feels passionately about Elspeth. His feelings aren't a delusion, they're real in terms of the chemical reaction they fire in his brain. He's studied her and sees aspects of her personality that perfectly match what he wants. She ticks all his boxes. Elspeth Dunwoody sets him on fire. Does your wife still do that for you?'

'Not going there,' Baarda said.

'This isn't gratuitous prying, Baarda, it's a comparable study. Work with me. Somewhere deep inside, you must fantasise about you and your wife being reconciled. For that to happen, the affair would have to end. You've imagined it. What goes through your head in those small, dark hours when people screw and cry and imagine killing their abusive partner, or suddenly decide to embezzle money from their company?'

Baarda was silent. He sat down on the edge of Connie's bed and leaned back on his elbows.

'It's about time,' he said. 'Enough months go by that the affair becomes dull. It's not exciting any more. They grow bored of one another. Their relationship becomes as much a routine as our marriage, and she sees that she's just swapped one thing for another.'

Connie pressed a hand against her stomach.

'Brodie,' she said softly. 'I knew you had the answer. That's what he doesn't have. He's out of time. It explains the decreasing periods between each offence. He's taking more risks because he has less opportunity to reorganise. There's no scope for repairing the relationship he's imagined with Elspeth. He's under pressure, unlike you. You feel no urgency because giving your wife time allows you to ignore the reality of the situation.'

'Which is?'

'That your relationship is dead. You don't feel anything for her any more.'

'Bullshit,' he said.

'Really? When did you last imagine your wife naked and get hard in the middle of the day?'

'Are you saying that's what happens to our murderer when he thinks about Elspeth?'

'I'm saying he's running out of time, and we need to figure out why. That's the key.'

Connie closed her eyes and saw the image of the man every police officer in a hundred-mile radius was hunting right now, so gaunt he was almost the physical embodiment of the ghoul the public believed him to be. She stopped breathing. Her heart hammered wildly out of rhythm in her chest. She gasped.

'What's wrong?' Baarda asked, crossing the room in two short strides and taking hold of her upper arms. 'Connie?'

'He's not just physically ill,' she said. 'If that was why he's so thin, he'd still be conscious of consequences. He could still be arrested and imprisoned. Maybe he's not dead enough for our liking, but he might not agree. If he was more than just unwell – in his own mind at least – it would explain the risk-taking, the urgency . . . everything.'

'What are you talking about?'

She lurched for her desk and grabbed her laptop.

'There's a syndrome . . . I can't remember what it's called. He's not acting the way a rational person would. This isn't just accelerated behaviour, it's beyond all normal parameters. So maybe he's acting as if he's invisible because he genuinely believes he is. He feels no fear, has no sense of consequences. There's little attempt to cover his identity. When he was asking me about my achromatopsia, he said . . .' She flicked hurriedly through her notebook. 'Here it is, "The world you inhabit is not the same as everyone else's. Mine is even less so."'

'Sounds like science fiction.' Baarda joined her in front of her laptop.

Connie typed the terms 'mental disorder, belief in death' into the search engine and waited for results to come back. The top few results were either true crime reports, studies in faith in life after death, or zombie movie references, followed by a reference-book-style definition.

'Cotard's delusion,' she read aloud. 'See also Cotard's syndrome or walking corpse syndrome. It's extremely rare, but there are documented cases. The affected subject mistakenly believes that they do not exist, that they're dead or in the process of dying, sometimes that their organs are in the process of putrefying, or that their body is decaying. Sometimes sufferers believe they are immortal. Named for the nineteenth-century neurologist Jules Cotard, who first diagnosed it as a syndrome. I read about it when I was studying, but cases are too rare to expect to find one in the course of normal practice.'

'Apart from the risk-taking, why is it you think this syndrome fits our case?'

'He's so thin we have witnesses describing him as almost skeletal. It's a regular feature in Cotard's. Sufferers believe they no longer need to eat. Look,' she pointed to a footnote on the screen, 'there are documented cases where the sufferers ended up dying of starvation. The evolution of his offending hasn't matched any other known profile. That's because he was reacting to his perception of his illness. Believing that he was dying but not yet dead allowed him the time to be careful and studious with Angela Fernycroft. When that went wrong, there was a downward spiral. His own perception of his demise would have increased. He became desperate, taking hostages faster. And he used a really weird phrase that I misunderstood.' She flicked through her notes again. 'Here we go. He said, "I have to pass this time."'

'So he believes he's running out of time on this earth?' Baarda asked.

'Maybe. Imagine what you might be capable of if you genuinely believed you were dead.'

'Consequences would become irrelevant. The police, the courts, prison. None of it would matter. He's capable of absolutely anything.' Baarda stuck his hands in his pockets and wandered to the window. 'So what's the relevance of Elspeth, Meggy and Xavier?'

'We can't be sure of that yet. He was so enraged when he realised Elspeth wasn't the pure and untainted specimen of a wife he'd envisaged that he became irrational. If he wanted Elspeth as a wife, then maybe he also wanted Meggy as a daughter.'

'Why does a dead man need a family?' Baarda asked.

'Maybe he's scared of the sense of invisibility he feels. Don't we all just want to be remembered, to be missed by the people who loved us most, when we die? Perhaps that would make the end of his life more bearable,' Connie offered. 'That could be why his victim type has varied so greatly. They're playing individual roles. It's part of a larger scheme.'

'If Cotard's syndrome covers anything from believing you might be dying to deciding you must be immortal, how do we know what stage his symptoms are at?' Baarda asked.

Connie referred back to the text on the screen. 'This says the syndrome has three stages. Germination, where symptoms of hypochondria and psychotic depression become apparent, although depression may pre-date all symptoms, of course. Then there's the blooming of the delusion of negation, where the sufferer becomes more aware of the change in their body, the loss of a part of themselves or their whole existence. Finally, there's the chronic stage, where the delusions are at their peak. You're looking at schizophrenia mixed with psychotic depression. Chronic sufferers will be unable to distinguish reality from delusion, may not recognise the world around them and will be unable to maintain normal relationships. Physical health, hygiene, the simplest of interactions will become impossible to maintain.'

'All right,' Baarda said. 'Practically speaking, if you're right about this, how does it help us find him?'

'I need broad access to health-system workers in the wide geographic area. Is there a system for putting out an alert?'

'I can organise that,' Baarda said. 'What are you going to do?'

'I doubt he's been diagnosed if he's still in the community, but there will have been physical symptoms, and some indicators of a patient struggling with their physical and probably mental health. Give me half an hour? I'll put together a list of likely symptoms, which we can combine with the broad physical description we have. I'd like to see if there are any mental health workers, primary carers, hospital staff, or community support specialists with whom this rings any bells. This didn't come on overnight. If he suffered from a high level of hypochondria and depression in the early stage, there's every chance he sought help.'

'What might have caused it?'

'Could have been anything from a brain atrophy to a tumour or an accident causing damage. Most cases come from frontal lobe injury, such as resulting from seizures,' Connie said.

'And how dangerous is he right now, in his current condition? I need to formulate a plan to apprehend him securely.'

'Armed police, shoot as necessary. He doesn't believe he has any limitations. You should be thinking the same way.'

Baarda walked to the door. 'But he's not immortal, and he's not dead. What happens when he figures that out? Does that make him more dangerous, or less?'

Connie crossed her arms and thought about it. 'Well, he'll no longer have a use for Elspeth, Meggy and Xavier, so my advice would be to find him before that happens. Long before.'

Chapter Thirty-Two

Meggy swung from the ceiling. Her body was beginning to ache, and she could hear Xavier's increasingly laboured breathing from the floor above. The droplets of sweat that were soaking into the sheet rope were making it hard to grasp. Fergus stood below her, grinning. He was insane. It was a word she'd read and heard, but so far in her twelve years she'd never actually met anyone who matched the description. His eyes looked like they might extend from his head at any moment on wild tentacles, reaching up to inspect her more closely. Hands twitching at his sides, body coated in oily perspiration, he appeared to Meggy as if he'd just emerged from a coffin. There was so little of him, and yet she knew that his strength would be formidable.

It was a playground assessment, but no less accurate for it. At school there were the physically large kids who nevertheless posed no threat. They lumbered and were slow, and the majority had a gentleness about them that they could not hide from the slighter, slipperier bullies. They were fast and mean, and their viciousness was an emerald flash in the eyes, side-glancing to their mates. Watch this, that swipe of vision said. Watch this and play your part. Titter at my cruelty, taunt my prey, and worship me, or it'll be you next. Still the bullies weren't the scariest. They were a known quantity. Their showmanship hid a vulnerability. Get anyone else to laugh at them, just for a single second, and you might as well have thrown that iconic bucket of water over the Wicked Witch of the West.

The playground hustle and bickering was camouflage for a genuine monster. Those who had no fear of consequences. Whose older siblings had shown them just how brutal a beating could really be. Silent and deadly, a misused phrase, but that was how she'd always thought of them. Mitch McConnaught had once got wind of the fact that another boy had been telling his friends how much he fancied Mitch. That boy had been held down in an alleyway after school and a lighter applied to his hair, necessitating skin grafts for the burns. Tricia Leigh, another quiet one everyone knew to avoid, had decided that being called weird was sufficient cause for smashing a bottle and shoving it into another girl's forehead. No amount of surgery was going to remove the scarring. It was the ones who could watch and wait, with whom no amount of pleading made a difference. They didn't want an audience or adulation. They wanted a quiet place, relative dark, and the time to enjoy the whimpering of their victim. Meggy stared down at Fergus and let her terror inform her decision.

'I'm not coming down,' she told him, 'and you can't reach me.'

'Fine,' he said. 'You'll keep. It's not as if you're going anywhere, after all. How's it going, Xavier?' he yelled gleefully.

There was silence from the floor above.

'Getting tired yet, or have you just tied off the sheet? She'll slip, sooner or later, and when she does, she could break a limb. Maybe fracture a hip. Perhaps little Meggy will even damage her spinal cord so badly that she'll end up just like you.'

'Don't listen to him,' Meggy told Xavier.

'Come back up,' Xavier whispered. 'I can't pull you. You're going to have to climb.'

Meggy looked up at the ceiling.

'You don't have the strength left in your arms, do you?' Fergus hissed. 'How long have you been there? Not as long as Elspeth has been on this cold floor waiting for help.' He raised a foot and allowed his toes to rest on the unnaturally bent shoulder joint. 'Perhaps I can persuade you to join us.'

Elspeth's shriek as he applied pressure with his foot was subhuman. Meggy was reminded of a trip to a safari park where she'd heard wolves howling as they'd fought over food.

The bedding rope jolted upwards as Xavier tried to yank her skywards.

'That's right, up you go,' Fergus said. 'You two run and hide. I'll be up shortly.'

'You're a fuckhead!' Meggy screeched. 'A fucking bloody fuckhead!'

'Meggy, get up here. The door's blocked. You'll be safe,' Xavier shouted.

Meggy looked up and down.

Fergus giggled and wagged his finger at her. 'You're a bad girl.'

Elspeth growled as she turned her head to where Fergus' foot was still pressed on the back of her dislocated shoulder. Dropping her jaw, she latched on to his ankle and bit.

'Bitch!' Fergus screamed. 'Oh my God, you evil bitch, let go!'

Her damaged arm flopping uselessly to one side, she grabbed his free leg with her good hand, keeping him still.

Fergus bent to beat her across the head and face, fists flying as he tried to pull his leg away.

'Let me go,' Meggy yelled at Xavier.

'No way!' he replied.

'He'll kill her,' the girl said, working her fingers into the knots she had tied around her waist.

'He'll kill you, too.' Xavier gripped harder than ever. 'Get up here, Meggy, please!'

'I want to,' she sobbed. 'I want to come back, but he cut off her finger because of me. It was all my fault. She stopped him from hurting me. I'm sorry.' She gulped deep breaths, then released her grip on the sheet and dropped through thin air out of the loop.

In the moment, her courage failed her. She'd seen herself flying towards Fergus, aiming for his head, feet outstretched to do maximum damage, but her hands got the better of her bravado, flailing, reaching out for anything to reduce the speed of her descent. The pendant light was the only object between her and the floor, an Eighties-style uplighter lamp on a single cord that swung low in the room. Meggy's hand slid down the cable, smacking onto the light bulb and dragging the fitting from its electrics as she went.

Glass shattering in her hand, the room turned black. The final feet of her fall were through blackness into the unknown. She could feel the multitude splinters of glass in her hand and had time to regret her decision as her up-tucked knees struck the back of Fergus' shoulders. He crumpled beneath her, yelling as he fell, then her forehead was hitting the back of his skull, and they were both flying forward together. Another scream, this time Elspeth's, as they bundled onto her fragile body. The light fitting landed on them all – more glass, a long snake of wire, and a metal frame.

Elspeth began choking again, and Meggy scrabbled to get off so she could breathe, avoiding Fergus' fists as he hit out at whatever flesh he could find.

'You're dead,' he slurred, and his voice was different, his words mushy.

She'd hurt him. The knowledge was a sliver of light in the darkness.

Skittering away, Meggy kept low on the floor so she didn't fall. One of her knees felt like it was on fire, and there was a sticky liquid on her head she didn't want to think about. Trying to control her breathing, she huddled into a corner. There was no light at all. Whatever he'd done with the windows in their upstairs flat, he'd repeated on the lower floors as well.

Elspeth was crying now, sobbing with her exhale then groaning on the inhale. Fergus was muttering to himself and throwing items around in the dark. Meggy kept her head down and reached out her hands. She needed a weapon. One good hit would do it. If she could just get him in the head, she could run for the door and get help.

'Oh, Meggy, what have you done?' Fergus snarled.

She shoved a hand across her mouth, forcing herself not to give away her position as she shifted on her knees to locate anything that might help her.

'Do you want to know what I'm going to use to kill Elspeth with?' Fergus said.

His tongue sounded too thick in his mouth, like he'd just been to the dentist and the anaesthetic was still in full force.

Ignore him, Meggy told herself. Keep going. He's bluffing. He's obsessed with Elspeth. He'll pretend to hurt her, but he wouldn't really dare.

The whiplash through the air changed her mind. The cable caught the outside of Meggy's left elbow, and she gave a small cry.

'Hurts, right? I'd never have thought of it if you hadn't brought the light down with you, but now it only seems fitting. Do you want to listen as I strangle her with it, Meggy? I've got to warn you, it'll be upsetting. Takes longer than you'd think. Minutes sometimes, as a person fights the loss of air. It's painful, too, Nothing peaceful. She won't pass out until the very end. Probably will scratch her own neck to pieces trying to get the cable off.'

He dragged his body across the room, and Meggy could hear him heaving himself into position. Elspeth let out a whomp of breath, and she could imagine Fergus astride her in the dark, winding the cable round and round.

'Don't,' her tiny voice whined in the blackness. 'Please don't.'

'Too late now. You hurt me. I'll hurt her.'

'I'm sorry,' Meggy cried. 'I didn't mean the things I said. You can beat me or . . . whatever. Don't kill Elspeth. I need her. Please?'

There was a gasping noise, the slither of cable, a satisfied hiss from Fergus.

Then the drumming of feet on the floor.

'Please, what?' Fergus growled.

'Please, God, please. I'll do anything. I'm sorry. I'm so, so sorry.'

Pathetic slaps rang in the air. Elspeth's hands, Meggy realised, grabbing uselessly at the cord around her neck.

'Please . . . Daddy,' Fergus said.

'Okay, okay, please, Daddy,' Meggy cried.

'Please, Daddy, even though I don't deserve it.'

Meggy let out a howl. 'Please, Daddy, even though I don't deserve it!' she screamed.

There was silence, a whisper of plastic on plastic, then the whoosh of air and a gasping, choking gobble of oxygen.

'Elspeth,' Meggy sobbed, rushing forward, hands reaching out to the source of the sound, throwing herself to the floor at the woman's side and burying her head into her chest. 'Please don't die, please don't.'

'Say, thank you, Daddy,' Fergus hissed into her ear.

Meggy paused. She was beaten. They all were.

'Thank you, Daddy,' she whispered in return.

Elspeth was gasping air into her lungs, her hands clutching her throat for support. Fergus gently took each of Meggy's hands and drew them behind her back, finding another use for the cable, connecting wrists and ankles as he looped and knotted.

'I haven't forgotten you, Xavier,' he called up. 'I think it's nearly time. This body won't last much longer, and we still have things to do. I'll be up in a few minutes. Let me see to my girls first. I can forgive Elspeth. She's suffered enough, or she's going to. Families make sacrifices for one another. It'll all be worthwhile in the end.'

Chapter Thirty-Three

'What do you mean, they won't accept my profile?' Connie demanded.

Baarda sat on the edge of a desk in the incident room and glared at the few other police officers until they decided it would be politic to leave.

'The superintendent had to run the profile past some other people. One of them is a psychiatrist who regularly works with the police. He apparently did some research of his own and found that Cotard's syndrome is something of a fallacy, because it doesn't appear in the International Classification of Diseases register as maintained by the World Health Organization.'

'That doesn't mean it's not documented elsewhere.'

'It's also not mentioned in the *Diagnostic and Statistical Manual of Mental Disorders*, which is the reference point for many pharmaceutical companies and legislature. The feeling was that if a court wouldn't accept the existence of such a disorder, then it was a waste of time to base a profile on it when resources are so short.'

'So they think this is some sort of Wild West quackery from the crazy American?'

'No one doubts your experience or your qualifications, Connie, but we're trying to present them with a disorder that goes by the alternative name walking corpse syndrome. They're struggling with the science, not you,' Baarda said.

'That's bullcrap, of course this is about me. I've been brought in from the outside, and I'm advocating for psychological profiling when half of them are still stuck in the 1970s. Would they rather have nothing to go on at all?'

'It's not a complete dead end. They're continuing to attempt to track the murderer by traditional means. They'll be filming a reconstruction of the attack on Xavier, which will air as soon as the edit is complete, working around the clock, and they've drafted in every spare officer from other Police Scotland areas to provide backup. In the meantime, we've been invited to present the Cotard's syndrome theory to MIT as a whole and to the powers that be.'

'By then, we'll have lost valuable hours, when we could have had every medical professional in the area checking their files and compiling a list of possible subject matches. That's great.'

'The superintendent's view was that asking medical professionals to report any male from his twenties to his forties with a history of hypochondria and weight loss might be such a broad outline that we'd receive too much information to process.'

'It's not just that. We have a rough image of him, height, weight, he's Caucasian, Scots accent. We even have some information about his car to cross-reference possible suspects. Cotard's syndrome is very psychologically specific. Any decent medical practitioner would have picked up the uniqueness of his presentation.'

'Maybe, if he weren't being dealt with by an overstretched National Health Service, but the reality is that he may rarely have seen the same doctor, nurse or psychiatrist twice, and he could well have described different symptoms on each occasion.'

Baarda sighed. 'Connie, I'm on your side, but these people need persuading and not without cause. We're asking them to put all their eggs in one basket. This is more than just a generic profile. It's a diagnosis based on a practitioner's instinct when she hasn't even come face to face with her patient. It's no good just stamping your feet and telling me they're all idiots. They were hoping for a profession, an address, a social group, a list of his likely hobbies. Instead, they got something that sounds like it came out of a movie.'

'For fuck's sake,' Connie muttered, glaring at the ceiling. 'Fine. If they want persuading, then that's what I'll have to do. But we're going to need help. How long do we have?'

'Two hours,' Baarda said.

'So let's use it. We need your car, my laptop, and some private information about a government employee. Can you get that?'

'Do I have a choice?'

'No,' Connie told him. 'Let's go.'

It was dark by the time they knocked on the door of the Edwardian town house. Connie had rung the doorbell three times before there was any sign of life at the property. It had taken several phone calls, and a trip to the city mortuary, followed by a lengthy pleading session with the on-duty assistant before they got Ailsa Lambert's home address, and only then with some extremely creative definitions of an emergency.

'An emergency here usually comes with a body attached,' the assistant pathologist had said. 'This sounds like something that can wait until morning.'

'If Dr Lambert doesn't help us, there's a real possibility that people will die,' Connie had countered.

'Well at that point the chief pathologist might come in handy, but until then, I'm not convinced.'

Baarda had stepped in. 'Dr Lambert would want to help.

She's familiar with the case, so she has a stake in ensuring that this killer is brought to justice. If it could wait until morning, I promise you we wouldn't be here.'

He'd kept his voice low and intimate, letting the concern show in his face. Connie decided the way the assistant pathologist was looking at him probably didn't do them any harm, either. Baarda had rediscovered himself.

'She's been on call for twenty-four hours now. Dr Lambert needs some sleep. It doesn't seem fair . . .' the assistant's voice had dwindled.

'I wouldn't ask if it weren't vital and from what I've seen of Dr Lambert, I'm guessing if she feels I'm wasting her time, she'll send me off pretty quickly with a flea in my ear.'

Baarda had given a gentle smile, in response to which the assistant's skin darkened a fraction of a shade. She'd been blushing. Connie watched Baarda grow in stature at the reaction.

'All right, I'll give you the address, but please be respectful. Dr Lambert isn't as young as she used to be. For God's sake don't tell her I said that.'

'I won't,' Baarda had said, taking the slip of paper from the assistant pathologist's hands. 'And thank you. Dr Lambert is lucky to have you.'

The door opened wide, no hesitation. Dr Lambert had been expecting them.

'In you come, both of you,' the pathologist instructed. 'I find the kitchen the best place for late-night business. I take it neither of you is injured?'

'Um, no,' Connie said.

'I have to ask. It's happened before. Usually someone has something to hide. Sit yourselves down, and I'll put the kettle on.'

Connie looked around. The house was grand in an

understated way. Old money. It reminded her of her grand-mother's place – perfect taste, sparse but immaculate pieces of art, lush rugs, and cream wallpaper. Ailsa Lambert would fit right in with the Boston elite.

'Sorry to disturb you,' Baarda began.

'Nonsense, I sleep very little. When you're staring down the barrel of old age, the last thing you crave is to lie alone in the silence and darkness for hours. So, what do you need? You didn't come here at this time for tea and biscuits.'

'Validation,' Connie said. 'You'll need time for research. Sadly, that's now limited to . . .' She checked her watch. 'Forty-five minutes.'

Ailsa raised her eyebrows and dumped several spoonfuls of loose-leaf tea into the pot.

'That sounds more fun than sleeping. Detective Inspector, would you mind making the tea, please? I believe your colleague requires my full attention.'

The briefing room should have been full of people rubbing their eyes. The small hours was far from the ideal period to be imparting information and attempting to engage minds, but Connie had spent enough time with police forces to know that lethargy was best countered with an endless supply of strong, hot coffee, and as many sugary baked goods as could be consumed.

Detective Superintendent Overbeck was sat within a circle of unimpressed faces in the centre of the room.

'Dr Woolwine,' Overbeck began, bringing the room to a tense hush. 'You have fifteen minutes to persuade us that your theory holds water. After that, the team will need to continue pursuing other avenues.'

Ailsa Lambert walked through the door, familiar black bag in hand, raincoat still on, as if she had been called in to give her opinion on a corpse. This, Connie had not asked her to do, but it was a subliminal stroke of genius. Present herself as the known element, the trusted, the authority. Much harder for her words to be ignored against such a backdrop.

The pathologist deposited her bag on a desk, shed her coat and began talking immediately.

'In 1880, a 43-year-old woman presented to her doctor, describing herself as without a brain, a chest, or nerves. She claimed to be made entirely of skin and bones, and immortal. Since that time, cases of Cotard's syndrome have been well-documented . . .'

'One moment, please,' Overbeck said, standing up. 'Dr Lambert, while I'm sure we all appreciate your time and assistance, I wasn't aware that this was your area of expertise. We certainly wouldn't want to be keeping you from your other valuable services to our community.'

'You're not, Superintendent. And I'm very well qualified in reading medical journals and applying the expertise gained therein to current cases. As both Angela Fernycroft and Danny Taylor are currently open cases in my district, I judge myself to have a compelling reason for being here tonight.'

Overbeck gave the sort of smile that Connie thought was usually reserved for a prison yard shortly before a nasty fight but sat down again, crossing her long legs in a gesture that was pure female dominance. Ailsa smiled with victorious warmth.

'Cotard's syndrome is hard to classify unambiguously owing to the crossover with depression, suicidal thoughts, and psychosis. Often, the aspects of the disorder that delineate Cotard's are secondary to the more obvious disorders. It is, however, not difficult to diagnose, given its entirely unique presentation. My research from established and respected medical journals has shown that sufficient cases have been studied over the past century to be clear about the primary delusion. The belief that one is dying or dead. In the most comprehensive studies, sufferers were fairly evenly split between males and females. Most cases were in adults. The vast majority were found to have had an underlying brain injury, disease or pathology that could explain the delusion.'

'With all due respect,' Overbeck interjected, this time without troubling herself to stand first. 'We're not dealing with someone who is simply deluded about their own existence. This is a dangerous predator who has killed twice to our knowledge, and who is holding other victims hostage who might be dead or alive. This man is not depressed. He's clearly a psychopath.'

'I'm not a psychiatrist, Superintendent, so I can't answer to that. I can tell you, however, that I've researched cases of Cotard's syndrome, and I find myself compelled to believe that it is a properly documented, real disorder that offers a credible explanation for the murders and kidnappings in this case.'

'Could you give us another example of a case of Cotard's syndrome, Dr Lambert?' an officer called.

'Certainly, there are plenty to choose from.' Ailsa opened a filed and scanned the page. 'Here we are, a female – twenty-four years of age – in Perth, not far away at all, suffered what appeared to be nothing more than a concussion in a car crash. Soon thereafter, she began experiencing episodes of depression. Her self-care suffered. Her hygiene was found to be lacking by her mother, who tried to care for her daughter and finally took her to the doctor. She reported a sense that there were parts of herself missing. The doctor prescribed antidepressants. The girl had to cease work. Six months later, she was dramatically losing weight. Wrongly diagnosed with post-traumatic stress disorder, she was sent for counselling. Her therapist became concerned when the young woman began to express the idea that her organs were failing and that her death was imminent. She was referred to a psychiatrist who ordered scans, and a lesion was found in her brain. Various attempts at treatment were made, but the young woman eventually died from heart failure having lost so much weight that her body could no longer tolerate the stress it was under.'

'So, can you point us towards any cases where someone suffering from Cotard syndrome ended up killing or seriously harming another person?' Overbeck asked.

Ailsa glanced sideways at Connie. 'I cannot,' she said. 'That does not mean it has never happened; nor does it mean that this must be the first case of its kind.'

Connie got to her feet. 'That's all right, Dr Lambert,' she said. 'I'll take it from here.' She waited for Ailsa to sit, then took centre stage. 'We know more about our killer than we realise. We have a good physical description. But we also know that he's single.'

'We haven't established that,' someone shouted.

'Actually, we have. He was obsessed with Angela, who was the model wife. He didn't want to kill her. That wasn't part of his plan. When he found out that Elspeth had been unfaithful, he was distraught. He talked about Elspeth as if she were his wife. As if she'd been unfaithful to him person-ally. If our killer had a wife, or was in a successful relationship, he wouldn't need to abduct a woman to play that role. He might be physically off-putting to women, which fits with being emaciated and perhaps having poor hygiene, or he might make them instinctively feel ill at ease. Either way, it fits with Cotard's syndrome. Furthermore, a close-knit family might well have reported their concerns by now to a doctor, or even to the police. So we can also assume he lives alone, has accommodation that he doesn't share, has access to a vehicle that he doesn't share, and has an income that doesn't require him to work.'

'Disability benefit?' Baarda suggested.

'That would fit. The weight loss alone would be enough to concern a doctor, and he would likely be suffering additional symptoms, such as regular migraines from the failure to eat, low blood pressure, anaemia, bowel and stomach problems. Regular work would be unsustainable.'

'He killed Danny Taylor in cold blood. The witness reported that he hardly seemed to notice what he was doing. If he's not a psychopath, how can you explain that?' Overbeck demanded.

'I didn't say he's not a psychopath,' Connie corrected. 'It's possible that he is. Statistically speaking, enough cases of Cotard's syndrome have now been reported that sooner or later, a sufferer is also going to have other mental health conditions, and then all bets are off. But I think Danny's death indicates something else. At its most developed, Cotard's syndrome is an absolute delusion. It's world-destroying. This is perhaps the only time when it's helpful to refer to it by the name walking corpse syndrome. Imagine believing you're dead. I mean, truly being immersed in that belief. What stops you from killing at that point?'

'My humanity,' someone offered.

'Good starting point, but is a dead person still human? Do they still feel or exercise humanity?' Connie held her hands up in a gesture of submission. 'Before you all start groaning, this isn't *Psychology 101*, but the point's valid. When you believe you're dead, are you still constrained by the human idea of conscience, or rules? If there are no consequences, the brain is free to deal only on the basis of need, desire, or reaction.' There was silence from the crowd. 'Consider the sense of grief, of loneliness at being a walking corpse, unable to find a single person who can comprehend what you're experiencing.'

'Why take Xavier?' Overbeck asked.

Connie shrugged. 'We don't know yet. The details of that are probably bound up in his delusion, and they may never become clear to us, even after he's apprehended. What we need to do now is issue the description to all medical practitioners.'

'Dr Woolwine,' Overbeck said. 'We cannot ask medics across the whole of Scotland to check their files. The amount of information we'll get back is—'

'Another woman's been abducted!'

The female officer who'd burst through the door was panting and sweating. Every eye turned on her and she shrank backwards towards the doorframe.

'In, Biddlecombe,' Overbeck ordered her.

'Ma'am,' she replied, running a sleeve over her forehead.

'Details, and make it concise.'

'A man called saying his daughter had been taking their bins out when he heard screaming. He ran down the pathway to help, but by the time he got there, all he saw was tail lights heading out of the road, one of the bins on its side, and his daughter's phone thrown onto the pavement.'

'Name, description and address,' Overbeck prompted, waving officers up from their seats to ready themselves for action.

'Right,' Biddlecombe un-scrunched the scrap of paper that was clutched in her hand. 'Farzana Wakim, nineteen years old, five foot five, slim build, wearing long trousers and a pale blue hoodie. Black hair, brown eyes, very dark skin tone. Lives in Moat Place, Slateford. Uniformed officers are en route.'

'Time of incident and description of the vehicle?' Baarda asked.

Everyone in the room was slipping coats over their shoulders and grabbing notebooks.

'Fifteen minutes ago, sir. He wasn't able to describe the car. Said it was too dark,' Biddlecombe said.

'Right, this could be our man. I want the major routes west of the city blocked with checks on any single male drivers. Close down the whole Slateford area while we get this contained.

No one talks to the press. CCTV from every source we can get,' Overbeck said. 'Baarda, liaise with the family en route. I want every house in the locality canvassed tonight, I don't care how antisocial the hour.'

'Superintendent.' Connie stopped her at the door. 'I need permission to send out an alert to medical practitioners.'

'Dr Woolwine, we have an active lead. That seems to me to be the more likely means of tracing the offender.'

'But you have no idea if it's the same man . . .'

'We don't have multiple adult females killed or kidnapped in Edinburgh each year. The statistical likelihood of this being a coincidence is extremely low, as I believe you yourself argued earlier in the investigation.'

'I just need to put out the alert. I'll process the responses myself. Your team won't have to deal with it.'

'Fine,' Overbeck snapped. 'You stay here and field responses to the alert. Baarda, I need you with my squad.'

'Sure,' Connie said, pulling a draft of the alert from her pocket.

Ailsa Lambert walked past, patting Connie on the shoulder and offering a sympathetic smile.

'Well done,' the chief pathologist said. 'It's progress.'

'Too little, too late, given that another woman's been taken,' Connie said. 'If he needs another woman, it can only be because Elspeth is dead.'

'You don't know that yet. Don't lose hope,' Ailsa said.

'I'm more pragmatist than optimist, I'm afraid.'

'Then channel the pragmatism into getting results. People's lives still need saving.'

Connie looked at her watch. 'It's two a.m. Who the hell takes out their trash at this time?'

Chapter Thirty-Four

Elspeth didn't sound good, like a living bike tyre with a puncture. Her arm was a mess too, and while he could probably have fixed that for her, why bother? In pain and unable to use one of her arms, she was much easier to control. Meggy, too, consequentially. Right now, they were bound to one another on the floor of his bedroom. He was resting in the kitchen. The fight had worn him out, and he was trying to capture a memory that had stuck its tongue into his brain as he'd been choking Elspeth. He'd felt it there, squirming and elusive, as he'd pulled the light cord tighter. It wasn't a sensation of enjoyment exactly, more a familiarity. A sense of prior knowledge, expertise even. The way he'd wrapped the cable around her neck three times to provide enough width to crush the windpipe rather than simply cutting straight through the flesh. The understanding that she would inevitably waste her energy on trying to release the cord rather than attacking him. It was a reliving of sorts, yet he really couldn't figure out how he'd come by the knowledge. It had felt like an ending, though. Closure, the Americans would say. Connie Woolwine would know what it meant.

He heard her voice in his head, husky and exotic. He wished he could have seen America while he was still alive. Now, his body was in an advanced stage of decomposition. Perhaps that was why he'd become so thirsty during the fight. His corpse was shedding liquid from its cells and beginning to succumb to the bacteria that would reduce him to nothing but bones and hair eventually. He was beginning to bloat and his body reeked. There was mossy green growth between his toes, and the fingernails on his hands were blackening. Last night, two of his teeth had fallen from their sockets. He'd helped them along with some insistent tugging – the thought of swallowing them in his sleep had been disgusting – but they'd exited his gums with no blood loss. Naturally, how could he bleed while his heart wasn't pumping?

The girl had been a handful. Little viper. It wasn't just Elspeth who'd proved a disappointment. He thought he'd chosen so well. A child who wasn't happy at home should be pleased to be given a new loving family. Still, she'd done nothing but whine and complain since she'd arrived. Fucking Emily. How could a ten-year-old be so much more trouble than an adult? He'd had to punish her on multiple occasions already, showing her who was boss with the sole of his shoe on her behind.

Only that wasn't right. Emily had been blonde. She'd been sweet and giggly, hiding in the woods from her brother. He remembered throwing the girl's pink running shoes into Linlithgow Loch after he'd put her in the boot of his car. Emily had been his only act of spontaneity. His first and last.

He tried to recall the hair colour of the girl tied up in his bedroom, only her features and colouring kept shifting in his mind.

'The girl's a monster,' he told himself. 'She's been tricking me. She changed her face.'

And there was something else he'd forgotten. He'd left

297

something somewhere. Not in his car. He was careful about keeping that free from anything that might make anyone suspicious.

Fergus looked around the kitchen for a clue. Nothing there. He would ask Elspeth and Emily. They'd know.

Climbing the stairs slowly, his legs cramping and head thumping, he tried to figure out what the date was. He only had a little time left now. Not sufficient to achieve all he'd wanted to, but the world around him was disintegrating. Soon, his legs would be unable to support him. He had to finish preparations for the end while he could still drive. His eyesight was fading, too. There were pixelated edges to his peripheral vision, and he was having to turn his head left and right to see around him.

Stumbling into the bedroom, Fergus pulled the gag from the girl's mouth and leaned down to see her clearly.

'Emily,' he whispered. 'I can't find something. What is it?'

The girl squeezed her eyes shut and shook her head.

'No, Emily, you have to help me.' He shook her shoulders. 'Open your eyes now.'

'I'm not Emily,' she said. 'You're insane.'

He sat up.

'Then who are you?'

The girl opened her eyes. They were a different colour than he'd been expecting.

'I'm Meggy,' she said. 'I'm Meggy, and you took me away from my dad. I want to go home now.'

'What happened to Emily?' he asked.

Meggy sobbed and shut her eyes again.

'Did Emily run away?' Fergus asked.

The girl screamed. She screamed in his face, then turned her head and screamed into the floor. The woman next to her groaned and dribbled blood from the corner of her mouth. Fergus looked up at the hole in the ceiling. That's where they'd come from. The flat above. Perhaps that was where he'd left . . . the thing he'd forgotten.

'Be quiet now, Emily,' he said, slipping the gag back over the girl's mouth.

She simply continued screaming into the wad of material. He decided to let her. Negotiating was exhausting.

He took the final flight of stairs one by one. Muscle memory kicked in and he stepped towards the upper peephole. The view inside was a bleary grey. The right-hand side of the corridor was completely obscured. Fergus took the key from the ring on his belt and opened up. The door budged three inches then jammed. He put his shoulder against it and shoved harder. There was another inch of movement, but the door rebelled, springing back to hit him in the face. He recoiled angrily and kicked it.

'Let me in!' Fergus yelled. 'You can't shut me out. This is my place, d'you hear me?'

He stood, head cocked to one side. Giving a final kick, he stormed off down the stairs to the ground floor, out of the kitchen door and into the tumbledown garden shed. Minutes later, he was on the stairs again.

He swung the axe high over his shoulder, bringing it down into the upper panel of the door with crushing force. The wood groaned and splintered but refused to break. Changing his grip, Fergus gritted his teeth and went again. This time the blade made some headway into the surface.

He moved to the left and swung again and again. The sound of splitting wood was music each time he pulled out the axe. Finally, he was able to damage enough of the upper panel that he could chop vertically downwards into the lower panel. He muttered encouragement to himself as he swung, each blow a monumental effort, but the pain was clean, refreshing, and real.

Ten minutes and there was enough of a hole in the door

that he could step through, crawling on his hands and knees between two mattresses lying on the floor of the hallway and another bent in two, tense against the walls.

His brain was pulsating, and red lights were flickering on the inside of his eyes. Breathing through a wave of nausea, he entered the lounge.

The view from the window was magnificent. Walking to the wall, he looked out at the blue sky and across the green fields, relaxing in the warmth of the sun on his face as it filtered through the glass. Fergus felt joy. It had been so long since he had been peaceful. He gave a contented sigh and studied the furniture. It was a little frayed but designed for comfort. The only thing ruining the perfect room was an overturned rug and a pile of floorboards – two whole, one splintered in the corner. None of it made sense. He'd built this sanctuary, this idyll, and someone had ruined it with mess and disorder.

Fergus frowned. He was feeling anxious again. All he wanted to do was go back to the window and stare out into the countryside beyond, but now he had to clear up. He walked towards the hole in the floor, and the boards beneath his feet crackled and squeaked. Whoever had done this had weakened the entire area. He sat at the edge of the opening and looked down. The area below was dark, the only light spilling in from the hallway beyond. The light bulb must have blown. And there below him were a woman and a girl tied up.

'You're not Emily,' he said to Meggy. 'Emily went away. Where did she go? There's still Angela, though. I love Angela. She's my wife.' He stroked the wedding ring on his left hand and grinned at the memory of the ceremony. 'Maybe Emily made this hole.'

Leaning over, he stared into the pitch-black between the two floors. From deep inside the cavity there came a scrabbling, scraping, rustling. Fergus reached inside to find the cause.

'Do I have mice?' he asked. 'Come on, little mouse. I won't hurt you.' His fingers felt a long, thin limb. Fergus yanked. 'Got you!'

The fleshless femur appeared from the cavity and landed on Fergus' lap. He stroked its length.

'Who were you?' he asked the bone. 'Were you kind to me?' He held it next to his mouth. 'I'm dead, too,' he whispered. 'Don't be scared. You're not alone any more.' Standing up, he took the bone in both hands and held it up to show the sun that streamed through the window. 'This is it. This is what I forgot. We should go. All of us together.'

He moved towards the flat door, but the mess behind him wouldn't let him leave. The flat wasn't secure any more. The home he'd made for himself and his family was ruined. And the bone from the cavity wasn't the only one. He should be honest with himself about it. There were ghosts beneath the floorboards, and now they were free to roam as they pleased.

He couldn't put a figure on how many past loves had disappeared beneath the newly disturbed floorboards, but it was enough. There were faces jostling in his mind, fleetingly in focus then fading again. He didn't want those memories. They were white-hot needles of loss and disappointment in his brain.

Someone coughed. A short bark of a cough from below his feet. A male tone cut short.

'Who's there?' Fergus shouted.

As if he didn't know. His brother had died in that house alongside their mother. He stamped violently on the floor and was rewarded with a cry in response.

'Come out!' he demanded.

Nothing.

'Why did she choose you?'

There was no reply. His mother had chosen his brother for the same reason everyone else in his life had chosen someone else. Because Fergus wasn't good enough for them. He never had been. He lay down on the floor, his mouth to the floor-boards.

'Come out, come out, wherever you are,' he sang.

No response. The ghosts had gone quiet. They always did when he needed them most.

Fergus crawled to the cavity, lying on his stomach and letting his head dangle into the hole, peering into the darkness. He looked around, his eyes adjusting to the gloom, breathing in the scents of time and decay.

'I see you,' he hissed. 'Did you think you could hide?'

Hair, dirty, bedraggled.

A pink dress.

He recognised her, although she was different now.

'You've lost weight,' he said. 'I wondered where you'd gone.'

An earwig of a memory squirmed in his brain. A man called Finlay from Wester Hailes − a nasty piece of work − delivering the woman to him, a baby in her arms. He'd exchanged money for them, and at the time that had seemed easier than kidnapping a woman himself. But the woman wasn't right for him, spoke barely any English, and the baby had screamed and screamed. He was better suited to be a father to older children, he'd realised then.

Soon after that, Finlay's face had been plastered over every newspaper in Scotland, identified only by his tattoos after his headless body had been found. Better for Fergus that way. No chance of anyone finding out about his purchase. From then on, he'd begun selecting his own loved ones through careful research. He couldn't remember how many there'd been. Or why none of them had stayed with him. Those facts were slipperier than oil in his conscious mind. No one stayed with him for long.

He was tempted to crawl into the cavity himself, to hide in

the darkness and wait for the end, but that would take too long. He was done with waiting. If he didn't end things himself, they might never end.

He stood up. The thumping of his heart was the painful beating of an animal trying to escape a cage. How could he come back to this house now? The memories needed eradicating. He no longer needed bricks and mortar, after all. The bones, the ghosts, the grief – they should all become dust with him. Perhaps this house had been the problem all along. It had been an anchor for his body to return to. A reason to keep living. Without a connection to his past, perhaps his soul could finally be free.

There was a solution in the kitchen, he realised. Stacks of newspaper. A can of fuel kept for the lawnmower. Matches in the cupboard. It would be as if none of his past lives had ever happened. No past, no present, no future. Just peace. All he had to do was pack up the girl and the woman first – he paused and frowned – their names would come back to him soon. Then he would be able to move on at last.

'Goodbye,' Fergus muttered as he crawled through the debris in the hallway then stepped over the shards of wood that had been the door to the flat.

Silence.

Chapter Thirty-Five

Connie sat alone in the incident room and stared at the phone while randomly clicking the refresh button on the secure email address she'd been given for responses to the alert. It had gone out four hours earlier.

In that time, a media alert had been circulated for the car that had been seen at Farzana's house, a vague image of their suspect had been released to the press, and an all-ports warning had been sent out across the UK. In addition, there was a whole room of people doing nothing but checking CCTV footage across the city between 1 a.m. and 6 a.m. There were few stones left unturned, and a palpable sense of desperation. Every ringing phone was grabbed. Every possible new detail immediately added to the evidence boards, but nothing was helping. Baarda had called a couple of times to check in, and Connie had gone back over the information already gathered. Nothing new. She could have screamed.

She rechecked her watch for the hundredth time in as many minutes. Scotland's medical practitioners would be getting up, making their kids' lunch boxes and beginning to think about their day. Many would not yet have even seen the alert, let alone have addressed their minds to going through their files to identify matches. Yet, she had sat at her desk all night waiting for something. Anything. Overbeck had made it clear she wasn't welcome at the Farzana abduction crime scene. Hers was to be paperwork profiling only from now on. Connie got it. The scepticism that greeted her profession was a known quantity. For every cop who valued her input, there was another who consigned her to the realms of hocus-pocus before she'd even opened her mouth.

To kill time, she'd conducted a little research on Farzana's address in Slateford. Moat Place had a few small shops, a church, some hairdressing salons and takeouts. That morning was indeed bin collection day for that area. The council website had been remarkably helpful, but a local-issues forum had informed her that the bins weren't likely to be collected until 11 a.m. at the earliest. So what had Farzana been doing at 2 a.m.?

The realistic chance of Elspeth's killer stepping beyond his established racial group was so low that she'd dismissed it as soon as she'd heard the victim's description. Their killer had murdered one Caucasian woman and abducted another. After that, he'd taken a white girl, presumably to play the role of his child. Another white male for purposes unknown. The fact that a young woman had been walking to the end of her garden at 2 a.m. to perform a task that didn't need to be done until the following morning was simply confirmation of what Connie already felt in her gut. Farzana Wakim had undoubtedly disappeared, but not as part of some delusional fantasy inside the head of a man who believed he was one of the walking dead.

The first email in response to the medical alert came in while she was flicking through Farzana's social media presence. It was from a community mental health team leader in Paisley who'd had a male matching the physical description three years earlier suffering bulimia and depression, but missing the other indicators for Cotard's syndrome. Connie marked the email negative and carried on scrolling through Farzana's selfies. She could only afford the time to chase up responses with both a positive indicator for Cotard's and a match for the patient's description, or she'd end up flooded.

Connie turned her attention back to Farzana Wakim, who had two styles of selfie online. One was proper and traditional, when she would wear a headscarf and appear makeup-free. On others the scarf was slipped so far back as to be virtually invisible – and when Connie enlarged those images, there were traces of mascara and lipstick, even a little glitter. Connie went back to the start of the photographs, wishing young people would learn to keep their profiles private but equally glad that she was able to access so much of Farzana's life.

There were family members in most of Farzana's formal photos, and a few people listed as friends – but those, without exception, were female. Connie texted Baarda.

'Not to stereotype but please check. Evidence around home of religious devotion/strictness? Check Farzana's room for hidden clothing, makeup. Recent deletions from mobile.'

A second medical alert response came in as she hit Send.

It was from a clinic in Glasgow, written up by a nurse who had discharged a patient from her care four years earlier, who had repeatedly attended with different ailments relating to his internal organs. On no occasion did any testing reveal a cause, and thereafter, the complaints would shift to a different organ to start again. He resembled the physical description, but with more hair and less emaciated. After that, the emails started flooding in. Connie knew she should have anticipated it, but as the minutes passed, the enormity of the task she'd created for herself became apparent.

Her mobile pinged.

'Affirmative. No social media/calls/texts visible for the last week. Thoughts?' Baarda replied by text.

'Either Farzana erased everything to cover her tracks, or someone else deleted information to cover motive for harming her. Do not believe this is Elspeth's abductor. Starting to get . . .' Connie stopped typing.

An email had come in from a doctor's surgery in Niddrie Mains asking to speak by telephone and leaving a number. Connie dialled.

'This is Dr Ross,' a woman answered.

'Good morning, Dr Ross,' Connie said. 'I'm Dr Constance Woolwine. You were kind enough to respond to the medical information alert issued through MIT.'

'Yes, hello. I don't have long, I'm afraid; my clinic opens in a few minutes.'

'Hold on,' Connie said, turning down the police radio that had been playing in the incident room next to her so she could keep up to date with what was happening at Farzana's house. 'That's better. Sorry to have interrupted. You have some information that might match the alert?'

'I do, although it might prove to be a bit vague. I've been working at this practice for more than a decade now, and I'm used to patients going through phases, coming in and out. There's one particular male who I referred for a brain scan last year, as well as a psychiatric consultation. He didn't attend either. He explained that he'd been traumatised in his youth. Having suffered severe depression, which hadn't been managed effectively through medication, he was sent for electroconvulsive therapy. Since then, he hasn't been able to tolerate any sort of treatment relating to his head.'

'I see,' Connie said. 'What was it about his symptoms that made you think of him today?'

'He's come to us over three discrete periods in the last five years, on each occasion attending regularly for a few months then disappearing for around six months each time. The symptomology follows a similar pattern each time. He starts off by reporting a general sense of unwellness. Generic stomach pains, aching limbs, headaches, reports of mild fever but nothing that ever shows on a thermometer. No discernible physical presentations when we begin investigations. Urine and stool samples come back clear. Same with bloods. The first time we ordered both an endoscopy and a gastroscopy.'

'Both clear?' Connie asked.

'Both clear. But by then he was presenting with new symptoms that bore no clear link to the original ones. At the end of the first period of presentation, he told me he could no longer feel his heart beating. I put his fingers on his wrist, let him listen through my stethoscope, and he told me I'd completely validated his complaint. He heard and felt nothing. After that I asked him to allow me to refer him to psychiatric services. While he was with me, he agreed. I said he'd get a date through. He didn't appear to be any threat to himself at that stage, hadn't self-harmed or threatened suicide, so when the hospital notified me that he hadn't attended his psych appointment, there was no further action I could take.'

'And then?' Connie asked.

'He didn't come to the clinic for . . .' there was the whisper of turning pages, 'seven months. The next time he came back he asked to see a different doctor, which was fine. In fact, at that stage he was presenting with a stomach complaint, saying he couldn't keep food down. It was diagnosed as a virus, advice was given. The notes say he was rational and not expressing any of the previous symptoms that had given rise to the psychiatric referral, so we treated him normally.'

'Did his symptoms worsen?'

'They did. At one point he believed his lungs were disin-tegrating. He lost a massive amount of weight and with that, many of his symptoms became real, but in a self-fulfilling circular way. His blood pressure became so low that he would regularly pass out, then suffer injuries as a result. You can imagine. Anyway, on that occasion, my colleague also recom-mended a psychiatric referral. He disappeared from view very quickly that time. Thereafter, we heard nothing from him for eight months.'

'And then?'

'Then a young man registered with the clinic. As part of the context, you should know that we have over 5,000 patients registered with us and twelve doctors. We're busy, we perform both clinic and home visit practices, with a high turnover of administrative support staff.'

'Okay,' Connie murmured.

'So, earlier this year, one of my colleagues came to me for advice. We do this whenever necessary, as well as conducting formal weekly reviews. The more junior doctors in the prac-tice have an opportunity to discuss their complex cases with the team, get a second opinion and see if the right approach is being taken. The doctor in question reported that he was treating a young man who was presenting with a series of increasingly serious but unconfirmed complaints. He'd ordered all the right tests, so I recommended continuing to treat as and when he presented.'

'It was the same patient?'

'Yes, and alarm bells should have rung then, but we were in the middle of an inspection, and when I read the file, it didn't occur to me that it was the same man.'

'But why . . .'

'Because he'd given a different name. Presented new docu-mentation. Re-registered. And had specifically asked for a male doctor when previously he'd been treated by women, so he was guaranteed not to see either myself or the other doctor who'd treated him before.'

'Active avoidance facilitated by fraud,' Connie said. 'Clever, organised behaviour.'

'Indeed. Had the junior doctor not become concerned whilst the patient was still in his office and come to find me under the pretence of his stethoscope not working, we might never have figured it out. The patient had declared himself to be rotting internally. The details he gave were utterly convincing. He seemed to be completely immersed in the illusion. I went to see him myself and recognised him as soon as I entered the room. Of course, he recognised me, too, and left immediately.

'Again, there was no evidence he was a threat to himself or others – anything but, in fact, given that he'd been through the same process twice before and had never come to any harm from it. He didn't meet the criteria for involuntary committal, so there was nothing left for us to do. We wrote to him, of course, asking for him to contact us for assistance. We telephoned. Two of our nurses even visited the address we had on file for him. When we got no response, we had to leave the matter there. Until I got the police alert today.'

Connie breathed hard. There was a noise in her ears not dissimilar to nails being dragged along a chalkboard.

'I need his name,' she said.

'I can give you the names he gave us. What's interesting is that when I discovered his deception, I checked our computers. It turned out that there had been two other names registered from his stated address. Date of birth the same on each occasion. All male. He'd previously been treated by other doctors, one of whom had retired and another who'd passed away.'

'All right,' Connie said. 'Give me the list.'

'Randall MacGregor came first, as far as I can ascertain, then Rupert Brown. Third came Andrew Drummond – that was the name he used twice – and finally Fergus Ariss.'

Connie wrote them down in order on a piece of scrap paper. 'Date of birth?'

'Always given as 1st May 1985,' Dr Ross said.

'And the address?'

Connie's hands were shaking as she grasped the pen to write it down.

'Tamar House, Whitehill Road, Niddrie Mains,' Dr Ross said. 'I want to apologise. I feel as if I should have done something more . . . and sooner.'

'You did your job,' Connie said. 'That's all any of us can do. Thank you, Dr Ross.'

Connie hung up and stared at the address on the paper in front of her. Her phone buzzed. She'd forgotten to finish her text to Baarda, who was chasing a response. Clicking Send on her draft earlier response about the missing Farzana, she followed up with a second message: 'Interesting lead from a doctor. Checking out info. Off to Niddrie Mains. Call me.'

Running from room to room along the corridor, it became clear that the few officers left in the building were focused on the Farzana investigation and handling the other 999 calls that were coming in that evening. Grabbing the arm of a passing officer, she thrust the sheet of paper she'd written notes on into his hands.

'Check out all the names on this piece of paper,' she said. 'I need to know what contact any of them has had with police in the past, and any alternative addresses on file.'

'Very good, ma'am,' the officer replied.

'Call my cell as soon as you have anything; the number's on the bottom of that note. Also, what's Niddrie Mains like? High crime rate?'

'Niddrie Mains? Not much out there, really. Good access to the coast. Stays pretty quiet.'

'Of course it does,' Connie muttered to herself as she grabbed her coat. 'Quiet is exactly how he'd want it.'

She sprinted down the stairs, ran outside and hailed a cab to Niddrie Mains.

Chapter Thirty-Six

Xavier was stuck. Safe, for now, but he wasn't going anywhere in a hurry. As Fergus had been tying up Elspeth and Meggy, he'd made a decision. He wasn't going to sit on the lounge floor and wait for the maniac to come for him. The blockade in the hallway was going to last a while, but not forever. If he couldn't fight, at least he could make it as difficult as possible to be killed.

It hadn't been easy. The lack of light in the room below had helped to conceal his activity, but the success had been touch and go. Had his friends not pestered him every week to spend hours in the gym maintaining his upper body strength, and hounded him to play wheelchair basketball at every opportunity, he'd never had managed the feat.

Pulling himself to the opening above Elspeth and Meggy, Xavier had dragged his legs over the edge in the void. He'd moved as silently as possible while Fergus had come and gone, bringing in ropes and gags, talking to himself, cycling through a stream of different names. Trying to summon a strength he would never have thought possible and praying that his mental calculation was correct, Xavier had taken his whole weight on his arms and lowered himself by his hands into the void.

'Xavier,' Fergus had said suddenly, turning round as if expecting to see someone standing behind him.

Xavier was frozen, suspended, legs dangling through the hole in the ceiling.

'Who was that? Did he leave me, too?' He was talking to himself, clearly confused, going from one incoherent rant to the next.

Then Fergus had continued as before, checking the knots on the ropes before walking to the painted-in windows and pretending to close the painted-in curtains. Xavier had stared down at him, incredulous, through the tiny gap between his body and the edge of the hole.

Forcing himself to continue before his arms gave in, he'd looked inside the darkness of the cavity between the two floors for the most accessible rafter. His line of vision was too limited, and it mattered. He'd had to grab for the rafter in a single movement that could not be repeated. He had nothing to hold on to above the floorboards, and his body would have started to fall as soon as he'd shifted his body weight.

Lowering himself so that his forearms were flat along the floor, he'd given himself more manoeuvring space but made the required gymnastics that bit more awkward. The closest rafter was to his left, which was a shame given that he was right-handed, and that for some seconds he would be supporting the entirety of his dangling body through one hand. Not that he'd had any good choices. If his head, chest and hips didn't all fit into the cavity, he'd be stuck there waiting both to be rescued and also to be murdered by the same madman who was currently below having a multi-party conversation with himself.

Xavier had taken several deep breaths, sucking as much

oxygen into his muscles as he could manage. The memory of how this would have felt with a working set of lower limbs came back bittersweet, unbidden and unhelpful. He'd have been able to draw his legs up, or swing them to one side to get better movement and more purchase. He might even have been able to pull a single leg up to jam a knee into the gap. Of course, with working legs he'd also have had the option to have gone into the cavity feet first, using his legs to wrap around the joist and hold with his ankles.

No use crying over spilt milk, he told himself. He was what he was. He hadn't fought as hard as he should have at the sports centre. It was partly the shock of seeing his friend die, but some of it had also been fear. Easier to have let himself be taken in the hope that the hand of fate might intervene and save him. No one was coming though. He, Elspeth and Meggy were not going to be rescued. He knew that now. It was self-help, or an inevitable ending.

Xavier had taken the leap of faith and the dreaded drop, grabbing with his left hand as he'd begun to fall, scrabbling at nothing with his right. Several inches lower, his body had jolted to a halt. He'd felt two of his fingernails ping away into the void as he'd thrust his right hand in to join the left. His neck had caught the edge of the broken floorboard as his body spun, cutting jaggedly into his flesh. Xavier had bitten his lips to keep from crying out, but both hands were on the joist, and as much pain as his body was in, that was better than the sensation of falling and waiting to smash into the scene below.

If that had been hard, pulling himself up into the cavity had been almost impossible without his legs assisting. The next wooden beam was too far away simply to reach out and pull himself forward. Xavier had turned his head to the side to make entry easier and strained inch by inch to get into the gap. One elbow over the joist meant more stability, but he'd had to twist his upper body to achieve that. Then it had been even harder to get the rest of himself into the space.

Fergus had disappeared. There had been silence from below. Elspeth seemed to be unconscious, and Meggy was bound with her face away from him.

'Don't lose hope,' he'd whispered down to them. 'Not yet. If I can hide until he's gone again, then maybe I'll have a chance to get help. Stay strong Meggy, and look after Elspeth.'

She'd given a nod of acknowledgement, accompanied by a sob. Of course, why would she have believed him? There was no one to lower him to the floor to go for help, and no way out if he went back up. It was useless. He'd simply given the girl false hope.

Spreading his arms wide so he could keep his shoulders flat, he'd pulled himself further in. Once he was through as far as his waist, his body weight tipped the balance, and it had become easier. He'd hauled himself all the way into the cavity, hips scraping the top and bottom painfully, legs and feet catching on bones and skulls. Xavier didn't allow himself to think about the stench.

Echoing blows had reverberated through the floorboards above his head. Shouts, more blows, increasing in pace. The noise of wood splitting, then caving in. And finally, footsteps, right above his head. He'd moved, lizard-like, through the space, keeping his face turned from the little light, knowing that if anyone had looked inside, it would be his skin that reflected. His jeans were dark blue and his top was black. If he could just get into the far corner.

Xavier's face bumped something. Fabric. He shook it away, bile rising in his throat. He was out of time, and there was nowhere to hide.

He'd pulled the corpse past his face, alongside his body, and sheltered behind it. Wasn't that the ultimate act of cowardice? Hiding behind a dead woman.

The footsteps had paused near the edge of the hole. Xavier had risked a glance back as a hand had reached in, fingers patting the area until they'd found something, grasped it, pulled it back out. He hadn't breathed. The darkness had begun to swirl and create its own light before his eyes. Fergus muttering, walking away, stopping, shouting, stamping. Returning to shove his head inside the hole.

Discovery had seemed certain until Fergus had begun talking to the poor soul whose lifeless body was providing him with camouflage, then there had been the sweet relief of disappearing footsteps and blissful silence. The deep breath he'd finally been able to drag into his lungs, full of the cells of dusty bones or not, was nectar.

'Fuck,' he'd muttered to himself, letting his head drop onto a wooden beam and resting.

Somehow, bizarrely, in the gloom, regardless of the stress and adrenaline, he'd begun to fall asleep. That wouldn't do. He needed to get into position to exit when an opportunity came. For now, he'd avoided Fergus. Mission accomplished. But he hadn't thought further ahead. When your sole intent was to survive the next hour, consequential thinking wasn't the priority.

He managed to bend himself at the waist, then lifted his legs further away, pushing them towards the rear corner of the space. It wasn't until he began trying to crawl forward again that he found himself tethered from behind. Tugging at each leg in turn, he became frantic. Finally giving in and hauling his upper body back down to meet his ankles, the pitch-black in the corner behind him, he felt down his leg until his fingertips reached his right ankle. It was wedged firmly into an acute

317

angle formed by two joists and twisted horribly. He could neither reach it in the confined space, nor drag the leg out.

'Bollocks, bollocks, bollocks.' Xavier thumped the nearest rafter, achieving nothing more than adding a painful bruise to his knuckles to his list of problems.

From the floor below came Fergus' voice, issuing commands, complaining, swearing. Then the shush – halt – shush – halt of heavy objects being dragged for short periods. Elspeth cried out and Meggy's tears added to his misery. He was just feet away from the edge of the hole, with no hope of getting there to see what was happening. He wanted to call out to them, but that was only going to remind Fergus that he existed – a fact he seemed to have entirely forgotten for now.

Had he been able to do anything to help, he would have done. It was practicality. It was the need to keep one of them safe a little longer to get help. Not fear. Not fear for his own safety. No more than any other person would have felt, anyway. Warm water washed down over his cheeks and penetrated the edges of his lips. They were still alive. There was still hope. While they were crying, they were breathing. Meggy was tougher than she knew, and Elspeth . . . Elspeth needed medical help and Xavier knew it. But perhaps if Fergus was moving them, then something dramatic must have changed. He told himself they were much more likely to be found outside the house. Really, they were better off than him now. As long as they weren't simply being brought back up the stairs to the flat. Although at least then someone would be there to help pull him out.

Xavier focused on regulating his breathing and listened. He could hear the pipes in the walls delivering hot water for the morning and footsteps heavy on the stairs. Those were getting fainter. Going down to the ground floor, not up towards him. Banging, half a second behind each step. He was pulling their still-bound bodies down the stairs, Xavier realised. Elspeth wasn't up to that. Her arm was undoubtedly dislocated from her shoulder and the wet rasping sound as she breathed was almost inevitably an injury to her lungs or her throat, and either of those possibilities raised the spectre of internal bleeding.

A door closed downstairs, then another, much more distant.

What was he doing to them? If he were planning on killing them, why not just do it where they lay? Too messy, too much evidence. Perhaps he was moving them to a bath, where the blood could be flushed down the plug or onto plastic sheeting, which could be wrapped and put straight into the boot of his car.

Stop it, he yelled inside his head. You're as bad as him. You've killed them already.

More footsteps in the lower part of the house. A pause. The sound of furniture being dragged. Silence. Footsteps, much slower this time, walking away. A door shut, gently, carefully. He imagined he could almost hear the click of it in the latch.

There was a new sound below him now. Like waves rolling onto a beach on a stormy day. A soft, roaring whoosh. Then crackling and a sense that the air had come alive, of . . .

The smell hit him before he could fit the final puzzle piece into the image. It was just a memory in the air at first. Late evenings sat at his father's side in the summer, burning off the clippings from the garden. Lobbing sticks onto the bonfire from a safe distance. This aroma was neither woody nor so pleasant, though. It was man-made fibres and fabric, paper, and carpet. The noise was louder now, the sound of consumption, of the fire below flicking out its tongue to taste the room.

Ripping his top as he fought to pull it over his head in the fourteen inches of space, Xavier wrapped the material around his head. There was no heat yet, but the first tendrils of smoke were curling in through the hole, seeking him out. The smoke would kill him before the flames could get to him. The thought was both terrifying and comforting.

He pulled madly at his ankle to get free, knowing he was kidding himself. Suppose he could get to the hole, what then? Was he going to let himself drop to the floor below? By that stage, there was every chance another floor would simply give way and he'd drop into the heart of the fire on the ground floor. Going up into the flat left him behind a locked door, waiting for a slower death. Getting hotter now, and the crawl space seemed smaller and darker than before. His eyes were tearing up.

'Help!' Xavier screamed. 'Somebody help me!'

A window smashed somewhere below. There was still real glass on the ground floor, then. A loud bang, possibly furniture, maybe a door giving way. Not mains gas, please, he thought. If there was mains gas, he could be counting the time he had left in the world in seconds rather than minutes.

'Please,' he yelled, aware of the dryness of his throat and the chemicals entering his system. 'Please, I'm trapped. Help me!'

He began coughing. The air was thicker. Grey.

Xavier screamed and coughed and cried until he began to choke.

Chapter Thirty-Seven

Connie heard the sirens before she saw the fire engines. Two had overtaken them en route, and her taxi driver had pulled over to allow them to pass. As a result, the road they wanted to go down was closed off.

'No way I'm getting down there, love,' the cabbie told her. 'Doubt you will, either. Is there somewhere else I can take you? It's a few miles if I go round and approach from the other end of the road.'

'Just let me out.' She thrust cash into his hand and jumped out.

It was only a few miles out of the city but already rural. This was farming land, one side of the road lined with trees, the other nothing but fields with the odd farm building peeking above the flora in the distance. With a name rather than a number, Tamar House wasn't identified on her mobile phone maps. Grateful she was wearing trainers, Connie shifted gears, ducking under the first piece of tape fluttering across the road to stop traffic from turning into the junction. A police car appeared from behind her, an officer getting out to release the tape and allow the vehicle entry then remaining in place next to the tape to control vehicular flow.

Connie embraced a dawning nausea. A column of smoke was just visible above the treeline ahead, not that she needed the visual. The smell of burning formed a brilliant orange colour in her imagination. If that was the house, then maybe everyone was in there.

She raced towards the flashing emergency services lights.

Set back from the road up a gravel track was a disjointed-looking building, three storeys high, with an amateur-build porch starting to fall down at the front, and a garage with one door hanging half off its hinges at the side. No vehicles to be seen. No one hanging out of the windows, either, shouting for help. Smoke billowing from the ground-floor windows.

She knew better than to waste time on yet another argument with a police officer. Going to the farthest end of the driveway from the police guard, she slipped between vehicles, the temporary ID she'd been given by MIT held out in front like a cross in a horror movie, in case anyone should approach.

No chance of that. All eyes were on the house.

Clutching the arm of a firefighter, she didn't waste a moment.

'Is the property on fire called Tamar House?' she demanded.

He nodded.

'Listen, it belongs to a man in his mid-thirties, but I think there might be other people inside. I need you to make sure they're not locked up somewhere like a basement or an attic, possibly inside wardrobes or other large items of furniture. They'll probably be restrained in some way, unable to get out, maybe unable to even call out for help.'

'All right.' He beckoned to colleagues and they circled around. 'More information . . . how many people are we looking for?'

'Thirty-year-old man, might answer to Fergus. A girl aged

twelve, a woman also in her thirties called Elspeth, and a paraplegic male.'

'The people from the news reports?' one of the firefighters asked.

'Yes. I don't know what sort of shape they'll be in. They might not all be alive. If not . . . if not, it'll be important to the families to get the bodies out in good enough shape to know exactly what happened to them.'

'Step back, miss. We're making an entry with hoses. The area needs to be clear.'

Connie did as she was told. She retraced her steps to a distance behind the fire engines but stayed within the police cordon. Dr Ross' description of a man presenting himself with Cotard's delusion over the course of three years and matching the rough physical description of the man they were hunting was reason enough to have come here. The fact that the property was on fire, just a day after Elspeth had been outed as an adulterer, couldn't be a coincidence.

The blinding glow from the first-floor windows indicated either that the flames had penetrated the hallway and up the stairs, or that the ceiling had caved in. Probably both. She wondered how long the fire had been raging, but there was no one around to ask. She'd never been so close to a house fire before. The different odours were cloying and sickly. The chemicals that made the furniture, fittings and possessions combined to render the air hard to breathe.

If there were people still inside, how long would it take for them to perish from smoke inhalation? There was an ambulance on the scene already, not that paramedics would be able to assist if Fergus Ariss had decided to use a house fire as a mechanism for disposing of evidence and destroying the corpses. If Fergus Ariss was even the man they were looking for.

Water was being blasted into the ground floor now, and

clouds of thick grey smoke were hissing out in response. Connie turned her face away and put her sleeve over her mouth. A firefighter raced out of the property towards a vehicle and began to unload two lengths of rope, a large axe, a saw, and a flashlight. He was joined by a colleague, who took the tools and ran back inside.

'Did you see anyone?' she yelled, but they were gone already.

Connie knew when to stay out of the way and shut up. She wasn't going to see anything for a few minutes. In the meantime, all she could do was find out more about the property.

The front door, only partially obscured from the road, wasn't a safe enough bet for moving bodies from a car boot into the house. A passing tractor or dog walker could easily see too much. That meant there had to be another access to the property for a car to draw up. Connie skirted around the edge of the garden fence and made her way around to find the back door.

Tyre tracks in the long grass proved her right. It would be just a few short steps from the vehicle into the house, completely hidden from the road. Firefighters had bashed in the back door, and a kitchen table was just visible, as was the edge of an ageing cooker. The house was ideally positioned. Not far from the city as the crow flew. No close neighbours to get suspicious. The sort of thick farmhouse walls that lent themselves to natural soundproofing as long as the windows weren't accessible. Connie stepped further away from the house and looked up to check. There were no obvious signs of life behind the upper-floor windows. In fact, there was nothing visible in the upstairs windows. She shielded her eyes. No curtains, no wallpaper. Just darkness behind each pane of glass. As if . . .

'This is it,' she whispered to herself. 'Definitely fucking it.' She pulled her mobile from her pocket, getting voicemail in response to dialling Baarda's number. 'Baarda, you've got to get here right now. I'm at Tamar House, Whitehill Road, Niddrie Mains, and it's on fire. I have no idea who's inside.'

Firefighters began sprinting from the back door, waving at paramedics. Connie approached as near as she could without causing an obstruction, trying to catch the conversation. A stretcher was being taken inside, but there was much shaking of heads and shrugging. An oxygen face mask was carried through, and paramedics stood by tense, ready to act.

Connie could wait no longer. She had to know if this was the right house.

'Excuse me, they only took one stretcher in,' she said to the paramedic. 'Does that mean they only found one body?'

'You are?' the paramedic asked.

'With the police,' Connie replied.

The paramedic nodded, her eyes on the back door of the property. 'Just one, a male. They've done a full sweep now. It's proving difficult to get him out, and they're concerned about the level of smoke inhalation. The police certainly won't be able to speak with him tonight. We'll have blues and twos on getting him to hospital. If he survives, you can expect him to be there several days, and that's before we assess any burns.'

'So no one else at all in there?' Connie sighed.

The paramedic gave her a sharp look. 'Not that we know of, thank God. Just one victim in a fire like this is something to be pleased about.'

'Oh, I didn't mean . . .'

The paramedic strode away to talk to a firefighter. Connie stared up at the house. The flames had been extinguished, but a river of smoke ran from every window on the ground floor.

Perhaps she'd been wrong. If Fergus Ariss had been in there alone, there was no evidence that he was Elspeth's abductor and Angela's killer. Still, she thought, it was worth waiting and taking a look. She had a pretty accurate image in her head from Meggy's abduction. Almost skeletal had been the witness' description. If Fergus Ariss looked like that, Connie would know it was him when she saw him.

When the stretcher finally appeared from the rear door of the house, Connie could see virtually nothing of the man on it. Covered in a blanket, face obscured entirely with a mask and breathing apparatus, all she could tell was that he was Caucasian with brown hair. It wasn't as if she could ask to have the mask taken off for a better look. He was loaded into the ambulance.

Police officers were taking over now. The ambulance doors closed, and the cordon was lifted momentarily to allow it out. Connie stood feeling useless, staring into the house, where there may or may not be vital evidence remaining. Baarda would have the authority to take charge. Without him, she was merely a hired-gun psychologist with no licence to act.

'Excuse me, miss,' a firefighter called to her. 'Sorry, but we didn't find the girl or the lady you were looking for. Got the male out, though.'

'Fergus Arris, I heard. I don't suppose you could describe him to me. I mean, if he wasn't too badly burned or . . .'

'Luckily he was up on the top floor, or he wouldn't have made it. We nearly didn't hear him, given where he was stuck.'

'Is the property badly damaged inside?' she asked.

'The lower floor's gutted. That's where the fire started. There was evidence of the use of accelerants. The next floor up was beginning to burn as we arrived, but we saved some of it. The doorway into the upper flat was blocked, and one door had been broken down with an axe. The man you told us about was in the cavity between the second-floor ceiling and the upper-floor flat. His foot was wedged solid. We had to break through the floorboards above to get him out. Only heard him because he was hammering on the floor.'

'He's lucky you got to him in time,' Connie said.

'Especially given he doesn't have the use of his legs,' the firefighter said. 'No way he'd have survived if we hadn't got there as soon as we did.'

Connie's stomach clenched. She reached out and took the firefighter by the arm.

'I thought you said it was Fergus Ariss, the homeowner.'

'No, you said that. We didn't get a name. White male, approximately thirty years of age. He was barely conscious by the time we got him out. Carbon monoxide poisoning and probable thermal damage to his lungs from inhaling hot smoke.'

'Oh, shit,' Connie said. 'I didn't realise . . . sorry, I have to make a call.'

'Glad we could help.' The firefighter began to walk away.

'Wait,' Connie said. 'I need to see if there's anything else in the property that might give me a clue as to the location of the woman and girl we're looking for. Is there any chance I could go in, just for a few minutes?'

'None at all. The structure's considered unsafe until a full report is done. There's still a heat problem, poisonous gases, and a lack of oxygen, and that's before you consider the hazard created by all the water we just pumped in.'

'You don't understand,' Connie said. 'The man you just pulled out was abducted a couple of days ago. The woman and the girl have been missing longer, and we know they're in immediate danger. If Xavier's going to be unconscious a while, then the only evidence that might help us find them is going to be inside that building. I can't wait the amount of time it's going to take for it to cool down and be declared safe. I need a way of seeing inside, because if Elspeth and Meggy aren't already dead, then they're soon going to be.'

The firefighter frowned at her. 'What is it you're looking for?'

327

'I won't know until I see it. I know that's not helpful, but if you let me in . . .'

'That's not going to happen, but maybe we can find a compromise. Come with me.' He led her to a fire engine and tapped someone else on the shoulder. 'I need you to give this police officer access to the monitor. I'm going to hook up my headcam and go back in. I'll get shots in as many rooms as are safe, but it won't be clear. There's a lot of blackening from smoke damage, and all the electricity is out. Here, put this headset on. We'll be able to speak.'

Connie considered correcting him about the police officer status he'd given her, then decided not to get in her own way. There'd be time for complete honesty later.

'Right, I'm going in.'

Connie perched on the footstep of a fire engine and drew in close to the screen. There was a delay of a minute while he got himself suited up again, then the screen showed a hallway, which looked like any other entrance corridor in any other home. There was what must have been a mirror, only now it had shards of glass hanging from it, but everything else was a darkened wreck. The discoloration didn't bother Connie. Shades of grey were her specialty.

'The ground floor is pretty much destroyed,' the firefighter said. 'I'm going up.'

He avoided holding the bannister and took the wall side, taking the steps two or three at a time, carefully testing each with his weight before moving on up. Connie knew she had to phone Xavier's whereabouts through to Baarda. There were family members waiting for news, even if that meant waiting to see if Xavier survived the smoke inhalation or not. But this was the priority for the next five minutes. Somewhere inside the building might be the charred remains of other bodies. She needed answers.

At the top of the stairs, the firefighter put his head into another room. That was a bathroom. There was nothing other than the usual hygiene equipment and detritus. Nothing Connie could identify as specifically feminine.

'Carry on,' she instructed.

'There's a study ahead of us,' he said. 'I'll see what I can find.'

The study was less fire damaged, but the desk drawers were locked.

'Can you break into them?' Connie asked.

'I'm afraid not. That would be a police matter with a warrant. There's an old computer at the back here, but it's not switched on, and I can't do anything with it until power's restored.'

'All right,' Connie sighed. 'Carry on.'

Entering the largest room on that floor, he directed his head-beam to the ceiling. 'That's where we found the trapped male, between those plasterboards and the floor above.'

'I can't believe he survived,' Connie said. 'Did you make that hole in the ceiling?'

'No, that was already there. Must be how he got into the space in the first place. We broke through some other boards in the corner of the living room in the flat above.'

Connie peered closer into the screen. There was little to see except a greying ceiling and a black hole, but the idea that any human being could be so desperate as to crawl into the space between floorboards and the ceiling directly below, knowing they might never make it out alive, was beyond comprehension. The fact that such claustrophobic horror could have been preferable to whatever awaited him in the open space was devastating.

Pulling out her mobile, she began texting Baarda as she watched the progress of the camera around the room.

'Xavier unconscious & in ambulance. Fire out but building badly damaged. No sign of E or M. Call asap.'

There was a bed in one corner, with old blankets on it. No warm duvet or touches of comfort. A single bed, too. It was a big bedroom for a single bed. With it came the idea that the inhabitant had long since given up on the idea of sharing his house with anyone in the traditional sense.

'Could you open the drawers and wardrobe for me, please?' Connie asked.

The head-beam swung around towards the largest item of furniture, and distant faces flew in and out of view.

'Hold on. Go back.'

The firefighter retraced his line of vision.

'Oh, holy fucking shit,' Connie whispered.

The walls were alive. Frozen in time, but alive. Every inch was filled with faces staring out of Polaroids, photos, newspaper cut-outs, glossy magazine pictures. Black-and-white smiles, glances to camera, distant away gazes. Connie steeled herself against the desire simply to run inside and touch those photos, to drink in the information they contained.

'Move in,' she whispered.

'What is this?' the firefighter asked.

Connie watched the faces sharpen into focus in the monitor. 'It's obsession.'

Closer inspection revealed a theme. Of the thousands of faces staring out from the wall, each was female. Some might have been in their late twenties, the majority their thirties, the others in their forties but no older, each woman had a certain look. Difficult to reduce to a few words, but there was a kindness, a softness to them. Some shots had been taken in the home, others holding the hand of a child or two, maybe playing, plenty taken on beaches, or in gardens and parks.

'They're all mothers,' Connie said. 'I need you to walk along that wall. I'm looking for two specific faces. Go slowly and stay about a foot from the photos. I need a good view.'

Connie located Angela first. The shot had been taken while she was standing in a crowd of other adults, all lined up looking roughly the same way. Behind their heads, a climbing frame was just visible.

'That's a school playground,' Connie muttered. 'Look for other photos with that woman in, the one centre frame.'

The head-beam shifted left and right, then paused.

'These?' he asked, his fingertip in view as he pointed at a whole section.

There she was. Angela walking along the road ahead of her photographer, holding the hand of her daughter on the left and her son on the right. Angela shopping at some supermarket. Angela sleeping. Connie put one hand to her throat. Elspeth was there, too, somewhere.

'You want me to show you the other walls now?' he asked.

'Uh-huh,' she said.

Directly opposite the wall of mothers was one filled from top to bottom with girls. Connie estimated the age range to be from eight to fourteen, all happy, wholesome-looking kids, some studious, others playing sport. All picture-perfect children. The sort you could have with your loyal, sweet, faithful picture-perfect wife

Then Meggy. Coming out of school, getting into a car with her scowling step-mother. Meggy at the park, reading her book alone on a roundabout, looking wistful. Meggy's bedroom window.

'The other walls?' Connie asked.

He turned his direction left, where the bulk of the wall was taken up by a large wardrobe, but around its edges were photos of young men. They were largely in their twenties, varied in look and background, save for one section that was full of young men in wheelchairs. Xavier featured in several images, including a cutting from a newspaper. It made sense. Fergus had wanted a young man – for reasons best known to him – but not one who posed any physical challenge to him.

Her mobile rang. 'I need to take this call. Stay there,' she told the firefighter.

'Connie, what happened to Xavier?' Baarda asked.

'He was found trapped on an upper floor. Firefighters rescued him, but he's in a bad state. He wasn't talking when they got him out. The walls of one of the bedrooms in the house are literally lined with different images of people sorted into categories. It's like a shrine.'

'To what?' Baarda asked.

'To stereotypes. Mothers, daughters, and, I think, to . . .' She looked back at the screen. The photos of young men were diverse, but they shared a common theme. Men playing football together. Men at a bar together, or collaborating over a project, building a shed together. Smiling, laughing, hugging, back-slapping. 'Friendship? Or perhaps to an idea of himself that never became a reality. A better, healthy, socially integrated version of Fergus, maybe.'

'Was anyone else at the property?'

'It's empty now. Xavier had hidden himself. Neither Elspeth nor Meggy are here. I'm trying to find a clue as to where he might have taken them.'

'Okay, I'm on my way. I'll find out what vehicles are registered there and see if we can't trace any recent movement on CCTV.'

'Any luck finding Farzana?' Connie asked.

'Still none. The vehicle description vaguely matches the one seen at the school when Meggy was taken, but I know you don't believe—'

'I could have been wrong,' Connie said. 'Until I've had a chance to view absolutely all the images, we can't discount any potential victim.'

'All right. Do you have a name?'

'Fergus Ariss, but he's used other names in the past. He's lived in this house for years. If he's set fire to it now, he has no intention of coming back, and our chances of finding Elspeth and Meggy alive are diminishing by the minute.'

Chapter Thirty-Eight

Meggy kissed Elspeth on the cheek through the gag, wishing there was something more she could do to stop her pretend mother from groaning in agony. The car journey wasn't helping. Every time they braked or took a corner, Elspeth would roll and then scream. Fergus had carried them out of the house one by one and dumped them in the boot of his car. At least they were still together. She had no idea what had happened to Xavier. If he was safe, then good.

There had been a minute or two after they'd huddled together in the boot when Meggy had dared hope that Fergus was just going to leave them there and disappear. When the car engine hadn't started immediately, she'd imagined him falling over and hitting his head, or getting electrocuted in the kitchen. Sooner or later, someone would wonder why the car had been abandoned. She was listening for voices, ready to bang her bound feet on the boot. Then the engine had roared the end note of her hopefulness, and they'd pulled out of the driveway.

They'd stopped once since then, although he hadn't opened the boot. It had been terrifying. More than when he'd first taken her. Even more than when he'd discovered her mid-escape, hanging above Elspeth's broken body. Because now Meggy knew for sure he was intending to get rid of them. In the flat, they'd had a purpose. He'd wanted them to play house, acting all happy families. He hadn't packed any of their stuff as they'd left. No spare clothes, toothbrushes, food, or drink. It was a one-way trip. All he'd had with him were a few papers, some candles, matches. And a shovel.

She'd tried and failed to think of good uses a shovel could be put to. She might only be twelve, but all those horror movies and true crime stream on-demand programmes hadn't passed her by. Shovels meant a long trip into the countryside, where a hole would be dug and the end, she hoped, would be quick and painless. Meggy didn't want to watch Elspeth die first. That meant she would have to die alone, unseen, her cries unheard.

She wanted to cry now, but she'd run out of tears. She hadn't even known that was a thing. Meggy consoled herself with a daydream. Not of being safe in her mother's arms. If her mother had stayed at home, chances were she'd never have ended up in Fergus fucking Ariss' boot in the first place. Nor of her father, while she was sure he was terrified and beyond devastated right now. The fantasy that gave her the tiniest fragment of relief was more functional. In it, Fergus – exhausted from digging Elspeth's and her grave – sat down to rest a moment.

Elspeth might have been genuinely unconscious, but Meggy had been faking it. Until now.

She'd found a piece of flint on the ground and worked at the ropes binding her wrists until they'd frayed to shreds. Pulling her hands apart, she'd freed her legs too, then lay down again and waited for just the right moment. Fergus, looking into the pit he'd created, would be standing still. He wouldn't hear her coming as she approached across soft mud, rock in hand. He would turn at the last moment, though. She wanted the bastard to see what was coming to him, and to know it was her delivering it.

She would smash that rock into his skull. It wouldn't just knock him out, it would crash through his skull into his brains, and she'd be able to see the grey squish of his cells oozing out through his hair. Then she'd kick him down into that hole. He'd land on his back, dying slowly, as she used the shovel – his own shovel – to pile dirt on his face. Some would go into his mouth so she could hear him choking, then he'd try to scream, but his screams would be lost as the earth covered him. His eyes would still be open so he could see her as she shovelled more and more dirt . . .

The car stopped again. Meggy tried to stay in the moment of the fantasy. No point rejoining the real world now. But a car door slammed, and Fergus' footsteps were heading towards the boot. She shut her eyes, no desire to look him in the face again. What she saw there frightened her as much as it enraged her.

Reaching in, he grabbed hold of the shovel and an old, thick black jacket. Meggy opened her eyes just a crack. Past him, she could see trees. The ground was grassy, and the smell of rain floated on the air. Birds who had no idea what horrors were occurring beneath their perches were singing. There wasn't a sound otherwise. No traffic, no voices. Not so much as an aeroplane above them.

He whistled as he planted the shovel in the earth, untroubled by the rain. Earth flew, and the hole at his feet grew longer and deeper.

Meggy wanted to look away but couldn't. The rain pounded harder into the dirt and the sky darkened as he worked. Finally, he threw the shovel down at his feet and walked away into the shade of the thicker branches, then hauled something along the ground towards the car. Forgetting her previous attempt to play unconscious, Meggy couldn't help but lift her head. Out of the undergrowth, along the slippery grass, Fergus dragged it. Constructed from pale wood, unmarked but green and mossy, the long wooden box was the end of Meggy's rational thinking.

'Made for two,' Fergus called back to her. 'Recycled, so it's kinder to the environment. You and your mum can be together forever, and we can start our new life. This time, I'll be able to pass on. I did everything I was supposed to on this earth. It's time for my reward.'

He lifted the box into the hole in the ground. Brushing the dirt off a nearby gravestone, he muttered a few indistinct words to an invisible entity.

He lifted Elspeth from the boot of the car first, unconscious, lolling in his arms. Meggy heard the wooden thud of the woman's head hitting the base of the coffin. By the time he came back for Meggy, she was already screaming into her gag.

She screamed still as he closed the lid on the two of them.

She screamed as he pounded a handful of nails into the top of the coffin.

She screamed even louder as he began to shovel wet earth onto them in the deathly blackness.

No one heard.

Chapter Thirty-Nine

When Baarda joined her, Connie was sitting in the rear of a police car with a box on her lap. The look on her face was enough to stop him in his tracks, several paces away.

'Well, this place explains the mud–obscured number plate when he abducted Meggy Russell. It's pretty much a farm track. Either the car was naturally dirty, or it was an easy option for him to dirty his car to avoid detection. There's also not a neighbour in screaming distance. Couldn't have chosen this house better myself. What's in the box?' Baarda asked.

'Items retrieved from beneath the floorboards of the top apartment in Ariss' building. We underestimated him.'

Connie looked away from Baarda. The light caught in the watery rims of her eyes. He didn't comment.

'He's killed before. I don't know if he's even fully conscious of it. His delusions are convincing, but they're also recurring, meaning that he has periods when he resets, if you like. I think I'm most worried about how he gets to the reset point.'

'Connie, what's in the box?' Baarda asked.

She reached in a shaking hand a pulled out a tiny cracked

skull. It sat in the palm of her hand perfectly, as if there was still life hidden deep within.

'It's from a baby. The rest of the bones were there, too. Tiny ribs. Little legs. The firefighter found them when he went up to look for some evidence that might indicate where Fergus had taken Elspeth and Meggy. There are others, too. He wasn't able to estimate how many because they're scattered throughout the cavity, but lots.

'Fergus Ariss' doctor identified a pattern. He'd go through several months of increasingly serious and complex delusions, then at crisis point he'd disappear, only to reappear several months later back at the start of the cycle. There was also the unidentified corpse of a woman in the late stages of decomposition, clothed, no obvious wounds. We can't tell yet how she died. They had to pull up more floorboards to get her out. The dress she was wearing matches other dresses found in a top-floor bedroom with a double bed.'

'He's taking women, dressing each the same way, then killing them?'

'Which matches the concept of the pictures on the walls. He has a generic idea of a mother or a wife, how she should look, what she should wear, only something inevitably goes wrong, and then he needs to get rid of the . . . I don't know . . . the faulty model and get himself a new one.'

'He's a serial killer.' Baarda let that sink in for a moment. 'So, how come he doesn't conform to any established profiles?'

'Because he's unlike any serial killer ever profiled before. There's a lot to unravel, but here's the thing. Fergus knew he needed to change his name. He asked for a different doctor each time, producing fake documents to re-register. He just didn't have the means to change his address.'

'So as genuine and complex as the delusion is, he's still

functioning at some level that allows him to evade detection?' Baarda asked.

'Exactly. He may be delusional at times, but he's also devious and manipulative. I believe the Advocate's Close crime scene was the start of it. Abducting and killing the homeless, prostitutes or runaways was relatively low-risk. Anyone without a community to notice when they went missing. But those people didn't meet his needs – his standards, if you like.

'He kept starting the cycle over and over again, each time believing he was dying. Imagine how terrifying that must be for someone alone. Going through the trauma of believing that your body is rotting, and that no one can help or will even believe you. It's a recurring nightmare. When he found Angela, although the risk was much higher, he felt she was what he needed.'

'What for? I get that he wanted the family he never had, but how does that help him?'

Connie shrugged. 'Maybe it's as simple as wanting someone to mourn him after he's gone, then when he realises he isn't going to die, after all, he doesn't need his fake family any more. Safer to kill them than to allow them to return to their lives and reveal his identity to the police.'

Baarda folded his arms. 'What else was found in the crawl space?'

'Just bones and the body. No weapons. No personal items,' Connie said.

'So those people either weren't killed there, or he disposed of their clothes and personal effects later. He must have periods of time when he's aware of what he's doing. So let's start with what we do know. This property might be rural, but it has some real value on a plot out here. We should follow the money. You said he's changed his name previously. The first thing we need to know is who he really is.' Baarda began texting instructions into his phone.

Connie let him work as she stared at the fire-blackened lower floors of the building. It was 1 p.m. Fergus Ariss, or whatever his name was, had been gone a while. He was doing something, not hiding out. He had a purpose. The sky was boiling with fast-moving clouds, black underneath and blossoming with new shapes that hid a coming storm. It was getting cold. In moments like this she missed her colour vision. When the world was already grim, there was comfort in such green grass, the blues and browns of caring eyes, the pink of a sunset.

'Right, some progress,' Baarda said. 'The house is registered to a male named Harris Povey. That's helped us with the car, too. We have a match with that name and the vehicle description given at Meggy's school. Povey is thirty-six years old. I had the council go back through records of previous owners, and it looks as if the house was left to Harris by his grandmother, Delia Povey.'

'They have the same name,' Connie said. 'So I'm guessing his mother never married.'

'Got that, too. Harris' mother predeceased him. Records show that she died shortly after he was born. Looks to have been a suicide. Might have been post-natal depression, but that'll take a lot more digging into the original records.'

'So Harris Povey grew up with his grandmother, with no mother figure, no father. He told his doctor he'd had electro-convulsive therapy for medication-resistant depression. That fits.'

'That's not all. Harris Povey was one of twins. His brother, Arthur, died on the same day as his mother. Looks as if she killed him and then herself.'

'So Harris survived. That's a lot of emotional baggage. It's tough growing up without a mother under any circumstances, but those . . .' Connie's voice faded.

'But she let Harris live. He's the one who survived,' Baarda noted.

'Maybe all he can see is that she chose his brother to go with her and left him behind.'

'Is that what Xavier was, a replacement for his brother?' Baarda asked.

Connie gave him a half-smile. 'You could be right. Until Xavier regains consciousness, we can't be sure.'

'Was there nothing else inside that could give any clue as to where he might have gone?'

'Not really. The electrics blew during the fire. The computer won't switch on and apparently looks ancient. There are some drawers that won't open, but I'm not convinced we're going to find a map with an X on it that completes the puzzle for us.

'The upper floors had their windows bricked up, though. Not just in the apartment where he was keeping his prisoners. His bedroom, too. Freaked the firefighter out for a minute. There's a painted view where the windows used to be, crude, like a child painted it. Curtains and all. Makes me wonder if it wasn't Harris at all who bricked up his bedroom window, but actually his grandmother.'

'If his depression was that bad, maybe she didn't want the prospect of him jumping out of the window. It's a tall building,' Baarda suggested.

'Yeah. Can you imagine being that kid, though? He must have felt as if his very existence caused his mother's death. Dad never showed up, grandmother might not have been exactly thrilled with the way things turned out. What a shitshow his childhood must have been.'

'So he has therapy, it doesn't work, he begins to imagine he's dying. Where does that take him, ultimately, to try and rectify it?'

'Maybe he doesn't want it to be rectified,' Connie said. 'We spend so much of our lives in our own comfortable sphere, where we'd do anything at all to survive. We rely on medicine, the emergency services, luck, fate. Death is the worst thing we can imagine. Only for some people, that's not the case. I spent enough time locked up with people who felt death might be the less painful option to living that I can honestly say, we need to rethink our views on this.

'Perhaps he wants to pass on. It may be that his particular hell isn't constantly believing he's dying, but in repeatedly realising that he isn't. Someone that desperate is capable of doing absolutely anything to make it stop. To make their life, in this case their living death, end.'

'Why torch the house now if he's been in this cycle for so long? He still needs somewhere to live. All his photos are here. He's perfectly set up to house his replacement family.'

'Something must have changed, and dramatically enough that he's decided he's not coming back. There's a massive hole in the floorboards between the upper floor and the one below, so maybe his plans went badly wrong this time. If I had to guess, I'd say he's decided his life is about to end whether nature planned it that way or not. Maybe he just couldn't stand the pain any more.'

'Fuck,' Baarda muttered.

'Fuck would be a fair summary at this point,' Connie agreed.

'Sir, we've got a trace on the car,' a uniformed officer reported. 'Last seen exiting the Edinburgh bypass onto the Straiton Road and heading south.'

'Get vehicles down there, unmarked. Silent approach. Assume he has hostages in the vehicle. We don't want him spooked,' Baarda ordered.

'Yes, sir.' The officer disappeared, already talking into his radio.

Connie got a map of the area up on her mobile. 'Let's go. Harris Povey may not actually be dying, but other people almost certainly are.'

Chapter Forty

'What's down that way?' Baarda asked as they sped through the city.

'That road goes south, so it's possible he knows he's being pursued and he's fleeing. Although looking at the map, if I knew the area and that were me, I'd have gone another junction along the A720 and taken the A702 down to meet the motorway. Much faster route out of the area.'

'Assuming he has a reason for taking the Straiton Road then, he would be headed for a specific location.' He glanced across at her. 'Come on, Connie, your instincts have been good so far. He's been in that house his whole life. He's held hostages before, killed before, but he always went back there. Why set fire to the place this time?'

'Previously it seemed as if he didn't remember going through all the same symptoms before. He thought he was dying but didn't – went home, life carried on as normal for a while. Maybe . . . maybe this time he's had enough. Say there were some memories surfacing of the things he's done, of all those bones. If he knows there's a chance he might not be dying a natural death, maybe he's going to make sure of it this time.

'He doesn't want to go home. Who wants to spend their life looking out of painted windows? I spent nearly a year looking out through glass with bars the other side. Even I had days when death looked like a luxury vacation compared to what I was living through.'

'Talk me through the area on the map,' Baarda said.

The rain began. Huge droplets spattering lazily at first, followed by a more regular shower, then the wind hit them from the side and in seconds, the water was coming at them horizontally and obscuring the view.

'That's just great,' Connie said. 'So there's the Pentland Hills Regional Park, which looks like just a huge expanse of green with a few lakes. There's a university campus. Straiton itself isn't that big. It has the usual retail park, supermarkets, housing area. There's a nursery, a secret herb garden . . .'

'Poison?' Baarda suggested.

'Maybe,' she said. 'It's near a caravan park. That would be a good place to bolt to, but not easy to keep Elspeth and Meggy quiet and unseen there. There's a stables. The main road runs down to Rosslyn Chapel.'

'Of Dan Brown and *The Da Vinci Code* fame? You think maybe Harris has got himself caught up in hidden meanings and divine symbols?'

'It's a church. Maybe that's what he's drawn to. The natural venue for the end of life. We're christened there, we're married there in traditional ceremonies, and our bodies are blessed there before they begin their final journeys.'

'Busy place, though. Rosslyn Chapel must be packed out every day of the week. I don't see how—'

'Turn right,' Connie said.

'How soon?'

'Here . . . now!'

They turned into Pentland Road, Baarda leaning forward to peer through the rain-washed windscreen.

'This is pretty industrial. What are we looking for?' he asked.

Through traffic lights, past a supermarket on the right, a factory, furniture store.

'It's a long shot,' Connie said.

The road began to narrow and meander. She wiped the condensation from her window with a sleeve.

'It must be here somewhere. No, there's the Secret Herb Garden. We've missed it. Go back, slower this time.'

Baarda did a U-turn and they crawled along.

'There, on the left. Stop here!'

He pulled the car up on the verge, and Connie jumped out.

'Connie, there's nothing here. What are we looking for?'

'This,' she said, pointing at a wooden sign that bore the simple marker: Old Pentland Cemetery. 'There's a gate, come on.'

'Is there any guarantee he's here?'

'No, but you were right about Rosslyn Chapel. Only this is really a more final resting place. A church is a place of ritual. If you were looking for the dead, this is where you'd come. If he wants to pass over, this is where the veil is thinnest between this world and whatever afterlife you believe exists.'

'All right, we'll take a look. But we're going to keep low, stay quiet and at a distance. If he's here – and I don't see any sign of him yet – then I'll need to call backup units to handle this.'

'Fine,' she said. 'I'll follow orders.'

They climbed the gate and took the grassy lane between the trees that led to the cemetery. Even with the modern world just a mile down the road, it was eerily still save for the din of precipitation. Their conversation ceased. Passing traffic noise did not penetrate the treeline. Connie wished she could have visited there on another day, with less rain and without the potential for a murderer to be at the end of the lane. Not that there was any indication of human life. The torrential rain had removed any sign that the grass had been recently driven on.

When they came to the opening at the end of the lane, they could have wandered into a century before their own time. The graves were spaced out in the irregularly shaped plot, perhaps twenty of them that were immediately visible. Every side was surrounded by trees. The sky was dark above them, and there was no way of knowing who was watching from beyond the foliage.

The place was empty. No bird dared peck for worms in the wet earth. No rabbit, rodent or squirrel dashed for the cover of long grass.

'Nothing here,' Baarda said. 'We should—'

The shovel hit him a blow that sounded like a steak mallet bouncing off a butcher's block.

'Oh, holy fucking shit . . .' Connie shrieked.

The man who stepped forward from behind the place where Baarda had just been standing was no ghoul. He was as real and menacing as any psychopath Connie had ever met. Baarda's body lay face down in the grass, water beating onto the back of his head. Blood flowed in rivulets from his hair and down his neck. Connie wondered if he was still alive and – if he was – how long he had left to live.

'Hello there,' the man said. 'I'm Fergus.'

Connie dragged her eyes upwards from Baarda's body and forced her attention onto the man holding the shovel. The descriptions of him as skeletal were understandable but inaccurate. He was wire, bone, sinew, tendon – all stretched to their limits, absolutely taut – and clear through the skin, as if he

were an anatomical diagram of a human. His face was domi-
nated by cavernous eye sockets and painfully pointed cheekbones,
his dermis little more than cling film holding tissue tight within.
So many blood vessels had broken in the whites of his eyes
that the colour of them was demonic. There were more gaps
than remaining teeth, and as he breathed and spoke, there was
a fierce whistling from his mouth, as if he were a stove-top
kettle about to blow. Which in psychiatric terms was exactly
what he was, she thought.

'I'm Connie. It's nice to finally meet you.'

'How did you find me?'

He grinned and she saw blackened gums. The descriptions
of Cotard's syndrome hadn't done the condition justice. It wasn't
only the sufferer who believed he was dead. The man before
her was doing as good an impression of being a walking corpse
as she could have dredged from her imagination.

'Never mind. What matters is that you reached me. I thought
you might.'

'I was at your house before,' Connie said. 'There was a fire.
Did you know about that?'

'It's not my house any more. I don't live here.' He planted
the cutting edge of the shovel into the ground and stood with
one boot on its shoulder.

'Here . . . as in Edinburgh?'

Connie looked him up and down as he considered the
question. He was soaked through, deeply wet, not as if he'd
recently come out into the rain. The shovel was covered in
mud right up to its handle. Fergus/Harris was, too. His hands,
trousers and jacket, his face and hair. He'd been in the cemetery
a long time. And he'd been digging.

'Not just Edinburgh. This whole plane. This existence. I don't
live here any more.'

'Where are Meggy and Elspeth?' Connie asked.

In an ideal situation, she'd have spent a lot longer on the small talk, reassuring her patient, setting up the harder parts of the conversation. But she had the worst feeling.

'They're going to pass over with me. We're going to be a family together on the other side.'

'Harris—'

'I'm Fergus,' he said. 'Elspeth is Fergus' wife, and Meggy is Fergus' daughter. I had a brother too, but I lost him somewhere.' He glanced around as if expecting to see Xavier sitting waiting for him.

'All right. Fergus, then. I need you to show me where Elspeth and Meggy are. They don't need to die for you to complete your journey.'

'How would you know?' he yelled, stepping towards her and jabbing a finger angrily in her direction. 'Just how the fuck would you know what I need?'

'Do you remember Harris?' Connie asked standing her ground. 'I'm not saying you're him. You're Fergus, I accept that. But do you recall what happened to Harris?'

He frowned at her and shook his head.

'I know some things about Fergus' life. I think it might help you to hear them. I'm going to share a secret with you about that, then you have to share a secret with me.' She didn't wait for him to negotiate before continuing. Every second mattered. 'Harris' mother died a few weeks after he was born. He was one of twins, in fact. There was a brother. Their mother was suffering from post-natal depression. She couldn't help feeling sad, and she obviously didn't get the treatment and help she needed. The hormones in her body were messed up. It happens to lots of women, but if a doctor doesn't realise what's happening and intervene, it can become very serious.'

Fergus jabbed the shovel in the rivulets of muddy water at his feet.

'Harris' mother took her own life. It's hard to imagine how desperate she must have felt to have done that. In her confusion and bleakness, she also took the life of Harris' twin brother. There's no doubt at all that she wasn't in her right mind when she did it. Sometimes these tragedies just happen. I wish they didn't, but they do. It's an aspect of humanity we don't talk about often enough. Sometimes the machinery of our brain breaks.'

He attempted a shrug, but his hands were grenades of tension gripping the handle of the shovel.

'So?' he muttered.

'So, poor Harris,' Connie replied. 'That's a lot for a baby to grow up with in his past. He lost his mom and his twin brother. The only person left for him was his grandmother, who must have been devastated by her own grief. It would be too much for most people. Harris did nothing wrong, and there he was left without a mother, maybe feeling like it was all down to him. Harris needed an awful lot of love to get through that, and I don't believe he got it.'

'Okay,' he mumbled.

'Your turn,' she said before the conversation could continue. 'I want a secret in return, like we agreed. I need you to show me where Elspeth and Meggy are.'

'No,' he said.

'Yes, fair's fair. It's not as if I can do anything to change your decision. You've already proved how powerful you are. Look what you did to Baarda.' Connie glanced across at his prone body, hoping for the smallest sign of life, but Baarda was unmoving in the mud. 'I just want to see them so I can understand everything better. You deserve that.'

'You're tricking me,' he said, but he met her eyes.

'I'm a psychologist. If you want to think of this as me being selfish then you can. Yes, I'm here to learn. Yes, this is my job.

I'm curious about you. I'm also aware that you're the one holding the shovel, so tricking you is likely to prove futile at this stage, right?'

He jerked his head left and right. Connie was reminded of a bird, beady eyes, sharp beak, ready to swoop down and crack the shell of an unsuspecting snail.

'Then you'll tell me something else?' he asked.

'Absolutely,' she promised.

He turned and led her towards the treeline at the far edge of the cemetery, past an old brick building that looked long since deserted and more than a little haunted.

'It's the old watch house,' he told her.

'In a cemetery?'

'To guard against bodysnatchers,' he grinned. 'A long time ago. You don't need to be scared now.'

The irony of the statement made Connie shiver.

He led on into a deep corner of the plot and to his car, parked where the trees had provided shelter to cover it. She did her best to stop herself from shaking. Baarda needed emergency help, she was likely about to see two more dead bodies, and what would Fergus do with her when he got bored of their conversation? Letting her peacefully go on her way seemed unlikely.

'Here.' He pointed with the shovel at a recently dug grave.

Connie pressed the back of her right hand against her mouth and tried to swallow her nausea. The ground was awash – mud, ripped sod, footprints – a fresh mound of earth.

'Elspeth and Meggy are . . . they're down there? Underground?' Her voice was thin and raspy. It was proving hard to breathe, and harder to speak.

'They're waiting for me,' he explained. 'When I pass, which will be very soon now, I'll be with them again.'

'Fergus, did you hurt them? I mean, were they alive when . . .' She wanted to finish the sentence but couldn't.

'They're comfortable. It's a nice big coffin. And they're together, mother and child. Children should be with their mother.'

Connie dug her fingernails hard into the flesh of her thighs to keep from screaming.

'I don't think it works like that. Fergus, have you tried this before?' She kept her voice as light as the tension in her throat would manage, aiming for inquisitive rather than horrified.

'Why would I have tried it before? This just seemed the right thing to do.'

'Where did you get the coffin, then?' Connie asked.

'I . . . I think I found it. It was here. Waiting for me. Like I was meant to come here today.'

Connie looked at the weathered mossy gravestone, walking forward to brush off decades of dirt and read the writing, itching instead to reach the woman and girl beneath.

'There are several names on this grave. The last is Delia Povey. Before that is Arthur Povey, buried with Amanda Povey. It's a family grave plot. The coffins can be stacked on top of one another. I guess you knew that,' she said.

'I guess.' He turned his head away from her as he replied.

He was lying. Fergus Ariss might not remember everything, but his memory wasn't the complete blank he was pretending. Connie swallowed hard. He was neither just mentally ill nor entirely evil. Bad or mad was the question psychiatrists asked themselves when assessing offenders who had committed awful acts when either prison or a mental institution awaited. Connie had wanted Fergus/Harris to be one or the other. Madness was out of his hands. If he was entirely bad, incarceration was simple and clean. But he was a fusion of the two. He wasn't going to stop killing. She decided on a strategy among her limited choices.

'Harris' surname was Povey, too. I think Amanda was his

mother. Certainly Delia was his grandmother. She raised him after his mother died. Do you think Harris wants his wife and daughter to be near his mum so she can see that he had a proper family?'

'But that's my wife and daughter down there. That's Angela and Emily . . .'

She breathed deeply. 'Is it, though? I'm not sure now. I thought it was Elspeth and Meggy.'

'No, no, I chose others. Elspeth was bad. I remember her, and she was bad.'

'She was,' Connie said. 'I agree. Not right to be your wife at all. But is that who's down there? It could be someone entirely different.'

He pulled at his sparse tufts of hair and began shifting from foot to foot. Connie stared at the strands that had come away between his fingers.

'My mother wouldn't like Elspeth. She wasn't faithful. It has to be Angela down there. Otherwise . . .'

'Give me the shovel,' Connie said. 'You're tired. I'll dig. Let's see who it is, then we'll know if this is going to work out the way you wanted or not.'

'No!' he said, shaking his head violently. 'Not giving you the shovel; it's my special shovel. You might do something. You might take it, or—'

'Then you dig. Only quickly. If the wrong woman dies down there, Harris' mother might not be pleased. She might not let Harris be with her. She might just want to stay there with Harris' brother, Arthur. Maybe that's why she chose him in the first place.'

'She should have chosen me,' he muttered. 'I was a good boy. Good boy . . .'

He began to weep, tears rolling down his muddy cheeks. Frantic digging followed, with mud flying everywhere. It was all Connie could do to stop herself from leaping into the rapidly growing hole and scooping out earth with her bare hands.

It felt like hours, but the coffin wasn't as deep underground as she'd feared. The family plot must have been nearly full when Harris began his pattern of putting his victims in a coffin to see if their deaths would facilitate his. The shovel struck wood just a couple of feet down, and he looked triumphant.

'Found them,' he said, scraping mud off the coffin lid.

'We have to get the lid off, Fergus. Use the shovel. Come on.'

But the shovel wouldn't fit into the edge beneath the lid, where there was too much earth to allow leverage.

'Keep digging, free up the sides,' she demanded.

'You sound like my grandma,' he whined as he dug. 'She was bossy, too.'

Connie stared at him. Bringing Harris back to the surface of his psyche was a risk, but coming back he was.

'Let's try again . . . please,' she asked.

'That's nicer,' he said, stepping back and shoving the cutting edge of the shovel into the ill-fitting lid.

The coffin had been opened and resealed a number of times. That meant air could get in, but also water and earth.

The lid creaked open, the few poorly hammered nails popping out. Throwing herself to her knees, Connie helped to pull the lid off the coffin.

'Oh, God, no,' she panted.

The woman and the girl lay with their arms wrapped around one another, covered in stray dirt, their faces so pale their skin looked unreal. Reaching in, Connie grabbed for Meggy, dashing the dirt off her face and pulling her into a sitting position. The girl flopped in her arms, no more than a rag doll, and Connie could see the bloody stumps of the girl's fingers where her nails had scratched and torn at the wood.

'Meggy!' she shouted. 'Wake up. Wake up!'

She dragged the girl out onto the grass, laid her on her back, lifted her chin, checked her airways and knelt to her side, one hand on the child's wrist. There was a pulse, thready. But there. No rise and fall in her chest, though. She took the deepest breath she could and blew hard into her mouth, pinching the girl's nose shut.

'Which girl's that? I don't recognise her,' Fergus said.

Connie knew she should answer. Losing the progress she'd made with him was likely to put them all at the sharp end of the shovel, but she had to breathe, both for herself and for Meggy, and that made speech impossible.

She'd been at it for half a minute, maybe more. The pulse was weakening.

'Come on, sweetheart,' she muttered, sitting up to get a deeper breath. 'Come back to me.'

'Why is she your sweetheart?' he demanded. 'I'm no one's sweetheart. They all let me die.'

'Harris, your mother loved you,' Connie said, leaning back down to breathe into Meggy's mouth again. 'I promise you she did. That's why you're still alive.' Another breath into Meggy's mouth. 'You haven't died. Your brain is telling you lies.' A further breath. Connie was dizzy.

'That's not true. It's you who's lying to me. Stop doing that. Stop helping her. I need you.'

He pulled at Connie's shoulder, and she slapped his hand away.

'No! You hurt this girl, now you need to let me try to save her.' More breaths.

'I didn't hurt her! Say that's not true. I just wanted to take her with me. Why don't I deserve a family? Why not me?'

Meggy choked suddenly, the noise echoing from deep within her chest, a hollow rattle.

Connie jumped, then grabbed the girl and pulled her onto her side. She vomited watery mucus and black granules of earth in a grim stream.

'You're okay.' Connie stroked her hair. 'Meggy, you're okay. You're out now.'

The girl's eyes opened and rolled crazily in their sockets. She tried to scream, but only a hoarse whisper came out. Connie wanted to hold her, to protect her from seeing Fergus, the coffin, and the hole she'd just come out of, but she had more to do.

Rushing back to the grave, she took hold of Elspeth's shirt and hauled her upwards. So much harder with an adult, and Elspeth's right arm was bent back behind her, so it was difficult to get a good grip.

'That's not Angela,' Fergus said. 'You told me it would be Angela.'

'No, I told you we had to check it wasn't Elspeth. Your mother doesn't want Elspeth in there with her. Help me get her out.'

'I'm Harris,' he said. His speech was slurred, different. He yawned. 'Not Fergus. I don't care about Elspeth. She deserved to die.'

Harris Povey was awake.

'It doesn't matter who this woman is. If you help me, you'll have done a good deed, and then you can die in peace. Isn't that what you want? No more pain, no more heartache. Don't you long for sleep without nightmares?'

Connie gave one last monumental effort, heaving Elspeth upwards and into the open.

She collapsed onto the floor, Elspeth on top of her. Connie tried to get out from under the dead weight, and saw lights circling before her eyes. Catching her breath was becoming increasingly difficult. Freezing cold, exhausted, shock creeping in, she needed to calm down and maintain control of the situation.

'What's wrong with her?' Harris/Fergus asked.

'You suffocated her in a coffin. There's blood around her mouth.'

Connie managed to push Elspeth off, grabbing her wrist as she knelt next to her. No pulse. She dropped her head onto the woman's chest. No sound of a heartbeat, although the rain was doing a good impression of the pitter-patter Connie longed to hear.

She knew what she had to do, but exhaustion was threatening to overwhelm her. Pulling unconscious bodies from a grave and performing mouth to mouth while a deranged killer tried to hold a conversation with you was . . . she hadn't the hyperbole for it.

'Elspeth,' Meggy croaked, reaching for the woman. 'Her lung's hurt.'

'Oh, shit,' Connie muttered.

That explained the blood around the mouth. It also meant that resuscitating her was going to be even harder.

Connie shifted Elspeth so she was flat on her back, moved her arm into the best position she could manage and began chest compressions, thirty rapid pushes down on her central chest, head back, airway open, faster than one per second. Then two breaths. She would have to repeat that until either she collapsed, unable to do any more, or until Elspeth came back to life.

'Tell me about Harris' grandma?' he demanded.

Connie steeled herself. She was freezing cold, and her muscles were starting to seize. She needed to concentrate on compressions, and Meggy was dragging herself slowly across the ground to huddle against her back. Out-thinking Fergus was too complex for that particular moment.

'Delia Povey had Harris' bedroom window bricked up.' Chest compressions. Clear more mud from Elspeth's mouth. Breathe hard into her lips. 'Someone painted real windows over them, as if they could still see out. Who do you think did that?' Sit up. Try to catch her own breath before she passed out.

Fergus thought about it. 'Someone sad. Someone who didn't want to go back to the hospital. He probably didn't want the electric shock treatment any more.'

Connie put two more breaths into Elspeth's lungs and could taste the blood on the woman's teeth. Blood and dirt. If that wasn't death's own recipe, she didn't know what was.

'Did the electricity make Harris feel bad?' Connie asked.

Compressions again. Her arms felt weak, and there were tears in her eyes. She didn't know why she was bothering. Harris Povey could kill any of them at a moment's notice, and she had no strength left for either fight or flight.

'They said it wouldn't hurt. Should have been more anaes-thetic. But sometimes it wore off when the electricity got turned on. I . . . Harris was scared, and sometimes he fought and then they gave him even more.'

Struggling to breathe, to speak, Connie looked at the child in the man's body standing before her, and allowed her eyes to fill with tears for them all. For Meggy and the trauma from which she would never fully recover, for Elspeth who would likely not regain consciousness, for Baarda who might not be alive, for herself, survival seeming an unlikely conclusion. Even for Harris Povey, who had suffered depression, needed help, and instead got a negligent anaesthetist and treatment that had left him no less depressed but changed in other much worse ways, forever.

'Poor Harris,' she said. 'None of it's his fault.' She gave up chest compressions and prepared to give mouth to mouth again. 'It wasn't your fault.'

'Are you crying for me?' he asked, his voice childlike and high. 'Tears for me? Do you really care?'

'Of course I do,' she said, one breath down, one to go. 'You're owed some tears, Harris. These tears and thousands more. And hugs and love and tenderness. Whatever you did, you never felt you had a choice. I know that.'

'Tears for me,' he whispered. 'That's it. That's what I was waiting for. All these years. Tears for Harris. Now I can pass. It was you I was meant to be with, not them. You're all I ever needed. You really love me.'

He took a step towards her.

'Harris,' she said. 'You have to let me finish helping Elspeth. She'll die if I stop.'

'She's dead already,' he said. 'I need you now. It's my turn. We should get in the coffin together, you and me. We can hold each other. I like it when you cry. Other women look ugly when they cry. You're beautiful.'

He knelt in the dirt opposite her, the other side of Elspeth's unresponsive body, and framed her face with his hands. Behind her, Meggy gripped her harder than ever, crushing her face into Connie's back and trembling.

Connie's skin crawled at his touch, slimy and icy, his putrid breath was fiery decay.

'I need to help Elspeth . . .' she told him, pulling away.

'I just want to hold you forever,' he said. 'I want—'

'I'll give you anything you want,' she panted. 'Two minutes. You count the seconds, then I'm all yours.'

He gave her a wary look.

'On my life,' Connie said.

He sat back, letting her be, saying nothing.

Connie took a deep preparatory breath, ready to force air into Elspeth's lungs again, all sense of reality evaporating, fighting the sense that she had just made a deal with the devil.

Leaning forward, supporting the back of Elspeth's neck with her left hand as she pinched the unmoving woman's nose closed with her right, Connie tensed her diaphragm and transferred every atom of oxygen from her own body and into its recipient. Another breath, same again. Meggy was crying behind her. Fergus/Harris – even Connie was confused about his real name now, not that it mattered – was counting steadily in front of them.

Chest compressions, and every pump cost her a second of her life.

'Don't do what he says,' Meggy was muttering. 'Don't leave me.'

Fergus/Harris was on his hands and knees crawling towards the coffin. Connie put her fingertips on Elspeth's wrist. The tiny, weak skittering insect of a pulse made Connie's own heart stop a moment. She risked a glance in their captor's direction, but he was staring into the watery grave.

Connie whipped her head round to Meggy.

'She's alive,' she mouthed silently.

Meggy's mouth fell open, and the girl shifted to throw herself at Elspeth's side. Connie stopped her, raising a finger in warning.

No more than thirty seconds left before he insisted on being paid the debt Connie owed him. The competing emotions of joy and terror fought for dominance, and she pressed fresh air into Elspeth's lungs. She could stop compressions now Elspeth's heart was beating, but her lungs weren't rising and falling yet, and she needed Fergus/Harris to believe Elspeth was beyond saving.

Twenty seconds left, and he was staring at her now, cheeks red, his few remaining teeth gleaming in carnivorous contrast with the earth around his mouth. His transition from living being to the walking dead was complete.

Connie bent over again, taking gulps of air and blasting it

into Elspeth's lungs, keeping her grip on the woman's thready pulse, pleading internally for her to fight, to keep going, to know that there was hope.

Ten seconds – another breath. Six seconds – the world was not just grey but fading in Connie's peripheral vision – another breath. One second left. Breathe, Elspeth. Breathe without me, she thought. Give me a reason to stay strong. A final breath.

'Me now,' Fergus/Harris said.

'No!' Meggy howled, her fingers digging painfully into Connie's shoulders as she held tight.

'Honey, you have to let me go. I'm going to be fine.' She peeled the girl's arms away and sat her back on the ground.

'Don't go,' Meggy sobbed. 'I can't look after her . . .'

'She's dead,' Fergus/Harris said. 'But we need you now.'

Connie slapped a hand over her own mouth as Elspeth's dress shifted across her chest. She stared. It wasn't an illusion. She was breathing.

'Just do what he asks you, Meggy,' she said, shifting his attention away from Elspeth.

There was no knowing what he might do if he realised her resuscitation attempt had actually been successful.

'I won't.' Meggy shook her head.

Fergus was up on his feet again, and he stepped towards the girl, his face a contortion of fury.

'She'll help,' Connie said. 'Let me.' She pushed past him and went to hug Meggy, pushing her lips as close to the girl's ear as she could, beyond his hearing in the still-pouring rain.

'Elspeth's breathing. Do whatever he says then go for help,' she told her.

Meggy looked up at her with huge terrified eyes.

'I'm tired,' the girl said.

'That's okay. Not much longer now,' Connie told her, stroking her hair. 'Be brave. I'm going to be just fine.'

Fergus/Harris held out a hand like a groom at a wedding inviting his wife to the floor for their first dance as a married couple.

'Let's do this,' she said, placing her hand in his.

'You first,' he said, motioning towards the coffin.

Meggy sobbed.

Connie took a long look at Fergus' face. His eyes had taken on an evangelical glow, the sweat on his brow greasily distinguishable from the rain splashing there. He was on fire. His chest was puffed out, chin up. The pitiable broken figure – as dangerous as he had been when Connie had first laid eyes on him – had vanished. In his place was a maniac, glowing with the prize that lay within his perceived reach. She swallowed her fear. No time for that now.

Before stepping into the wooden box, already pooled with muddy water, she kicked off her trainers, emptied the pockets of her jeans and finally shed her coat. Two adults in the space meant no room for any additional bulk.

Meggy was huddled on the ground, rocking, crying.

'Please don't get in,' she whined.

'Do what you're told. Every word,' Connie snapped at her. 'Quickly.'

Meggy flashed a look at her that was venomous, her pain inflamed by Connie's cruelty, but the girl seemed to wake up.

Keeping her eyes on Elspeth as she climbed in, Connie saw the fractional rise and fall of her chest and knew she was doing the right thing to keep the woman and girl safe. She allowed Fergus/Harris to climb in next to her, his body pressed tight against hers, his rotten breath infiltrating her air space. She lay on her right-hand side, he on his left, their hair swirling in the half-inch of water, their faces awash with rain, their clothes – had she been able to note their colour – shades of brown, the earth already in the process of claiming them.

'Put the lid back on the coffin. I want to hear you jump on it, then kick the mud on top of it again. It has to be sealed tight, do you hear?' Fergus instructed.

Meggy remained where she was, glaring.

'If you don't, I'm coming back out to get you. It'll be you in here, drowning, suffocating. You'll die like she died. You want me to put you back in this coffin?' he growled.

Meggy glanced at Elspeth, looked to Connie, who gave a small silent nod. The girl crawled towards the open grave, hauling the coffin lid towards them, biting her trembling lip as she went.

Connie took a long last look at the furious sky, already crying for her. It was dark, but not as dark as things were about to get. She became aware of everything. The chill of the water beneath her, the grit of the earth seeping into her clothes, the closeness of Fergus' hands to her body, the small sounds of Meggy's exhausted breaths as she pulled the coffin lid in place. The disappearing light, pale grey, mid grey, dark grey, as wood scraped across wood.

And the world disappeared.

Chapter Forty-One

Connie's fists were curled at her sides. Panic had crawled into the box with her, and she had to fight that before she could even contemplate battling with Fergus. Feet landed heavily on the lid on the coffin. Connie felt a moment of joyous hope when she thought the girl might just come crashing through, splintering the lid beyond use and destroying Fergus' plans.

How much oxygen did they have? Not much for two adults, and Fergus wasn't just breathing heavily, he was panting hard.

'What's that word? When you're passing from one world to the next, like a holy experience . . . I can't think,' he said, his voice booming in the wooden walls.

The first thud of earth landing on the coffin lid came from above, and Connie's heart hammered in her chest with the volume and persistence of an MRI machine.

'Rapture,' Connie said. 'Is that how you feel?'

'It is,' he sighed, and his breath was maggoty meat in her mouth and nose. 'Is that how you feel, too?'

'I do,' she said. 'We don't have much time to talk, but I have a theory about why you and I seem so perfectly matched for one another. Would you like to hear it?'

'Yes, my love,' he said dreamily.

Earth thumped down, and Connie prayed the girl would do as she'd been told and keep up the noise and disturbance while Connie told her tale.

'I was in a hospital once, too. For a long time. I didn't belong there, either. No one could understand me, and so they decided I needed treatment. I was strapped into a bed. There was no privacy, no kindness. They made me take my clothes off when they decided I should wash, watched me as if I were nothing more than an animal, decided what I would eat and when. Told me when I should sleep and when I should wake up. Gave me pills without telling me what I was swallowing, and checked my mouth as if I were a disobedient child.'

'You too?' Fergus asked breathily. He pushed his forehead forward to press against hers as if their very brains could meld into one another.

'Me too,' she said.

More mud thumped onto the box, muffled now, the upper layers going on. Muddy water was seeping in through the sides of the box. Connie wondered what would get them first, the lack of oxygen or drowning.

'But that wasn't the worst of it,' Connie continued. 'The human suffering was . . . beyond anything I could have imagined. We were just kids, and we were locked up, competing for any little kindnesses we could get. Desperate for love. Willing to do almost anything to be treated kindly – the sane ones among us, anyway.'

'Doesn't matter now,' he said. 'No one can hurt us any more. We'll have each other forever.'

'What about the others? The ones before me?' Connie asked. 'The body beneath your floorboards. The bones. Their families.'

There was silence.

'That wasn't really me,' he said eventually.

She shifted her body the inch needed to release the buckle of her belt, making it easier to breathe.

'I understand that,' Connie said.

There was no noise from above them now. Either Meggy had stopped following instructions, or the mud was so compact above them that no more noise could get through. Either way, death was a calculable number of heartbeats away. The air was thinner, the water higher.

'When I was locked up, there were people like you. People who did bad things because they heard voices, because they felt compelled to act. Those people scared me the most. They can't be reasoned with.'

'I bet you were kind, though,' he said.

'I learned how to deal with them,' Connie said. 'It took me a long time, but I figured out what they really needed.'

'I felt it when I saw you on the video,' he said. 'I knew you understood me.'

'Those people, the ones who act compulsively, they can't be stopped. Can't be treated. Even hospitalisation isn't enough. They still hurt people.'

'What do you mean?'

'If we're going to die here together,' Connie said, 'let me put my arms around you. It's hard to breathe.'

There wasn't enough oxygen for them both.

'I'd like that,' he said.

Connie slid her right hand beneath his neck, bringing her left up to meet it above his body, then reversing course, praying he couldn't feel what she was doing, releasing her left hand again to reach down and take his right hand in hers, intertwining their fingers. She paused in the darkness. It didn't scare her. When you lived your life in black and white, you got used to darkness. Other things still did. Lack of privacy. Lack of control. Unwanted physical contact, prying eyes.

Above them, no more than a distant impact, was a rhythmic vibration.

Footsteps. More than one pair. Rapid. Her other senses had sharpened long ago to make up for her lack of colour vision. Whoever was coming was not above them yet, but they soon would be. Connie smiled in the darkness.

'What I learned was that truly dangerous people can never be released into the world, not into any environment. Not a prison, or a hospital, or even a psychiatric ward. Because sooner or later, someone screws up. Some well-intentioned doctor or probation officer decides they can be released into the community, or onto a general ward. And then they hurt other people.' Connie began pulling her right hand away from the back of his neck. 'They'll hurt anyone they can find. That's what mental illness does inside the wrong brain. It creates monsters.'

'What are you—'

She pulled sharply down, tensing for the inevitable smack against her own head, gripping his hand as tightly as she could bear. The belt she'd slipped off her waist and fed loosely around his neck whip-cracked against its buckle, the noose pulling tight only when his neck provided enough resistance. Pain exploded in her skull and she embraced him, pushing her body forward into his to ensure his left arm remained useless beneath him.

The struggle to free his right hand from her left began, but she was ready for that one. He screamed at her, and the noise was beyond human. Outrage, fury, defiance, hatred.

Above them now, voices reached through the mud and wood. The sound of shifting earth. Connie was out of time. She pulled harder on the belt loop, and the sound of his breath was the scrape of nails on a blackboard. He was fighting hard, still stronger than her. Still dangerous. Untreatable.

In the darkness, Connie saw a different face. A young man

convinced there were aliens giving him instructions through some special psychic link. Connie beneath him, fighting for her life.

Their hands slick with sweat, Fergus freed himself from her grasp, reaching up to Connie's face, searching for one of her eyes with his thumb. She scrunched her eyes shut tight, moving her head left and right in the confinement, his nail pushing its way through her eyelid and forcing its way to her eyeball. She grabbed his little finger, snapping it to the side, cracking the bone in half, then reached for the next finger in and repeated the exercise. Still his grip was iron on her face as she kept the pressure on the belt buckle, strangling him.

He couldn't face trial.

He couldn't live his life in a hospital.

Fergus/Harris couldn't be treated. He was far too damaged and dangerous for that.

This was the truth that Connie knew. It was the lesson she'd learned that no university course, no FBI training, no hands-on experience could teach her. This, you had to have seen from the inside.

Taking the deepest breath she could manage, sucking what tiny amounts of oxygen remained in the thin, stinking air, she released his hand. Let him try for her eyes.

With one last monumental effort, she slammed her left hand into the base of his throat, forcing it back against the side of the coffin and giving her the extra inches of space to pull the belt tighter. His thumb pressed into her left eye, and now she could hear the watery squelch of her eyeball, the pressure a pinless grenade inside her skull.

Shovelling above them. Shouts close by.

Seconds left to finish the job. To make sure the legal system didn't fuck up and release a demon back into the world. Keeping safe those people who might end up on a psychiatric ward with a man capable of using other human beings for his own ends regardless of the cost to them. A man too sick ever to be responsible for his own actions.

Too sick to be helped.

'I'm sorry,' she whispered to him. 'There's really no other way.'

She dropped the end of the belt, pushing both of her fists into his already partially collapsed windpipe, the belt having worked its preliminary magic.

Roaring, Connie thrust every last newton of force from her body into his.

Legs juddering, his body trembling against hers, he succumbed.

Connie imagined his expression as one of gratitude. Hadn't this been what he'd longed for? It wasn't vengeance. The protection of future potential victims was the worthiest cause there was. She took no joy from it.

As the light re-entered the box and fresh rain hit her face, Fergus/Harris surrendered to his first and last true death.

Connie gulped the blissful air of freedom. Her left eye throbbed, swollen shut, her arms burning with the acid of strain, body bruised.

They lifted her out to a waiting stretcher; Meggy, Elspeth and Baarda already gone.

'Might as well leave him where he is,' she muttered as police began the process of removing Fergus/Harris' corpse from the coffin.

'Dr Woolwine.' Ailsa Lambert appeared alongside the stretcher. 'Are you all right?'

'I am now,' Connie said.

The chief pathologist turned her glance to the body being lifted from the ground.

'Have you been practising more of that corpse whispering I witnessed previously?'

'It didn't start out that way,' Connie said. The world was greyer than usual, and the pathologist's face was veering in and out of focus. She lifted her hand, a length of leather still clutched in her fist. 'You'll be needing this as evidence.'

Chapter Forty-Two

Connie perched on the edge of Baarda's bed, reading a newspaper. She'd been allowing him to rest intermittently then reading him an article she found particularly amusing or outrageous. Mainly politics, some entertainment. No true crime stories. Enough of that. It had been three days. Visitors had come and gone – a steady stream of them – many travelling from London just to spend thirty minutes talking quietly to an unresponsive man. Baarda had no idea how popular he really was. Connie made a mental note to remind him of the fact when he was up to more lectures from her.

Even his wife had made a brief appearance. She'd managed to sit at his bedside for all of fifteen minutes before deciding the charade was too ridiculous to pull off.

'He's a good man,' Connie had told her. 'For reasons best known to himself, he still loves you.'

'I'm sorry, when did my marriage become your business?' his wife had hissed.

'When he and I put our lives in each other's hands. It's amazing how much you begin to care about someone in those circumstances,' Connie said. 'Listen, it's really not that difficult.

Just decide if you want him or not. If not, then do the decent thing and set him free.'

'How dare you comment on my personal life.'

'How dare you fuck my partner's colleague without any visible signs of remorse, or even an acknowledgement of the pain you're causing,' Connie said.

'I could make your professional life very uncomfortable indeed,' Mrs Baarda had hissed.

'You actually can't. I'm a free agent. More importantly, I'm not someone you want to threaten. Take it from me. I do whatever I deem necessary to protect innocent people. No limits.'

Anoushka Baarda took a long look into Connie's eyes, made the best choice she had in a long time by deciding that she wasn't going to challenge whatever she saw in them, gathered her bag and coat with nothing more retaliatory than a huff, and exited.

An hour later, there was a gentle knock at the door. Meggy entered, holding her father's hand. The girl was bruised and tired, but alive. That was all that mattered.

'They're letting me go home today,' Meggy said quietly. 'I wanted . . . I wanted to say . . .'

There were tears before the end of the sentence. Connie went across the room and held her until they stopped.

'You don't have to say anything. Meggy, you're amazing. You did what you had to. You saved my life, Baarda's and Elspeth's, too. Keep hold of that during the nightmares. You're going to beat him and survive every time, because that's what happened. There'll be people to help you through this, but the truth is that you are your best defence. The strength you have, your will to survive, your spirit, Meggy. You can beat him as many times as you need to in your imagination until you really understand that he's gone.'

She nodded, hugging Connie harder until her father pulled gently at her arm.

'We should go,' he said. 'Looks like your friend is waking up.'

Meggy reached up, sliding her arms around Connie's neck until her mouth was at Connie's ear.

'One day, when I'm a grown-up, will you tell me what really happened to him . . . in there?'

In the coffin, the girl meant. Sharper than all the adults involved, more able to stomach the truth as children always were.

'I will,' Connie whispered.

The girl released her grip.

Connie turned. Baarda's eyes were open a fraction. He smiled as Connie called the nurse, raised his hand an inch off the bed as a wave to Meggy, then went back to sleep.

When he woke again the following day, Connie was still at his side.

'Stop ranting,' he whispered.

'What are you talking—'

'You've been reading me political editorials. Could you not have read me a decent novel?'

Connie laughed, leaning over to kiss his cheek. 'Fergus, or Harris, is dead. Properly dead. Ailsa Lambert certified it herself.'

'How?' Baarda asked.

'There was an incident with a belt. The details can wait.'

'You look like hell,' he said.

'Fuck you very much. I'll call the nurse.' She stood up to leave.

'Not yet.' He managed to catch the tail of her shirt between his fingers. 'Tell me. Elspeth, Xavier?'

'Xavier is still here recovering from the smoke inhalation and some other minor injuries. He's going to be fine. Elspeth . . .

was very badly hurt. Her brain was without oxygen for a long time. They were lucky the coffin wasn't properly sealed and that there was still a little air in the cracks in the earth. Must have bought them half an hour.'

'Coffin?' he groaned.

'You know what? This isn't the right time . . .'

'Tell me.'

Connie sighed and sat back down on the edge of his bed. 'He buried them, together, in one coffin. I persuaded him to dig them up again. Meggy crawled on her hands and knees to the road while he was distracted. She's a tough one. By then other units had got concerned about us not responding. They'd found Farzana, knew that was a red herring and were wondering where we were. They tracked us using the GPS unit in the police car we drove to the cemetery.'

Baarda raised his eyebrows.

'Farzana was fine. Had a boyfriend she knew her father would hate, so she thought it would be easier to pretend to be kidnapped than just leave. Threw her phone out of the window so she couldn't be traced. Police caught up with them at Glasgow Airport.'

'Elspeth,' he insisted.

'Is alive. Not in great shape. It'll be a while before they know what brain damage she suffered. There's still a feasible level of function. She's being kept in a medical coma to allow her time to recover.'

'Well done,' he said, pulling her closer to him.

'Thank you. Also, I told your wife what I think of her. I hope you don't mind.'

'You what?'

'Hey, I stopped a serial killer and rescued two females who'd been buried alive, so could you give me a pass? Best intentions, isn't that what the British say?'

He frowned, then laughed.

'Forgiven,' he said. 'Fuck her.'

'Wow. When you talk like that, it's hard for me to think about leaving.'

Baarda stopped smiling.

'You're leaving?'

'Yup. I've been asked to present a series of seminars about Cotard's syndrome in Washington. The FBI are interested. I saw Harris Povey's old brain scans. Electroconvulsive therapy is supposed to induce small seizures. That's how it works. It closes down certain impulses. In his case, the treatment prescribed for depression created a larger lesion, possibly because not enough anaesthesia was given and he went into an uncontrollable fit. That lesion may have been the cause of the delusions. He went in as a teenager with some minor problems and came out a killer. Makes my experience of psychiatric treatment seem kind of tame.'

'Really? Even now you're making this about you?' A voice oozed disdain from the doorway. 'I would say don't stand up, but it's obvious neither of you are going to.'

Detective Superintendent Overbeck sashayed in, spike heels clacking loudly on the tiled floor.

'Ma'am,' Baarda managed.

'Don't "ma'am" me, Detective Inspector. I'm up to my ridiculously expensive breast implants in paperwork. A freelance profiler apparently climbed into a coffin with a serial killer who you let get the better of you. A woman and child barely made it out of the same coffin alive. I have a forensics team sifting through a pile of bones, not to mention the semi-decomposed body. By the time this is over, I'll have won an Oscar for the most impressive shitfest in policing history.'

'All three kidnap victims are still alive,' Baarda reminded her.

'Harris Povey is dead,' Connie shrugged. 'No messy trial, no psychiatric reports. I'd say that was a decent result.'

'Quite.' Overbeck's response was serpentine. 'That was an ending I hadn't anticipated. Tell me, Dr Woolwine, do you always wear that belt, or was it just blind luck on the day?'

Baarda stared from Connie to Overbeck, then back again. 'Is there a problem?' he asked.

'There had better not be,' Overbeck said. 'Very fortunate indeed that you had such a resourceful and strong-stomached partner, DI Baarda.' She stepped closer to look Connie directly in the eyes. 'Takes a while for an adult to die by strangulation. Not much oxygen, tight space. He must have been kicking wildly. And the noises he'd have been making, the horror. I can barely imagine it.'

'Really?' Connie smiled. 'It seems to me you're having no problem imagining it at all.'

'It pisses me off when I underestimate people,' Overbeck said. 'Leaves me feeling vulnerable.'

'You can get psychotherapy for that. I'd probably diagnose you with trust issues. I can recommend you a good psychologist, if you like?'

'I think I've had as much psychology as I can tolerate for a while,' Overbeck said. 'Baarda, get better quickly. There's paperwork to do, and if you're considering making a personal injury claim against Police Scotland, think again.'

'I actually wasn't going—' Baarda started.

'Other than that, officially, I've been sent here to say congratulations to you both, so we'll pretend that's what I did.' She spun on a heel to leave.

'Wait, what about the other victims?' Connie asked.

'We're working on identifying the bodies. There are at least twelve dead. The theory is that they were buried alive in the coffin then dug up each time Harris needed the coffin for his next attempt at creating a so-called family. He cleaned the bones and hid them beneath the floor. He either got sloppy with the woman only partially decomposed, or was in a hurry to move on. Her, we've identified.

'A particularly skilled scumbag called Finlay Wilson was involved in human trafficking until recently. He brought in hundreds of women over a few years, mostly from Eastern Europe. Fortunately, he was dispatched in suitably violent form last year. Ended up losing his head, I recall. The young woman was one of Wilson's victims, pregnant when she was trafficked. He let his clients indulge their fantasies, then sold her along with her baby.'

'Harris bought her?' Baarda asked.

'It appears so,' Overbeck confirmed. 'One of the many reasons why I'm not as concerned as I might otherwise have been about the circumstances of his death.' She glanced at Connie, who raised her eyebrows.

'And the other bones?' Baarda asked.

'We're checking missing persons records. Runaways, the homeless, prostitutes, not just from Edinburgh but across Scotland. It may also be that others were provided from trafficking. We've had two confirmed DNA matches. The first is a girl called Emily, a ten-year-old, believed to have drowned in a loch two years ago. Her shoes and a hairband were found floating in the water. We now believe that Fergus abducted her from the campsite. In addition, five years ago, a young woman was abducted from—'

'Advocate's Close,' Connie said quietly.

'Indeed,' Overbeck confirmed.

'He was still refining his methods at that point,' Connie said.

'God knows how many more he might have killed had he not been stopped,' Overbeck said. 'And there I was thinking that engaging a forensic profiler was a waste of money.' She crossed her arms. 'I should get back to work. You two have a lovely restful afternoon. I take it, Dr Woolwine, that you'll stay out of my way until everyone in the United Kingdom has forgotten the name Harris Povey?'

'Sounds like an order,' Connie said.

'Sodding right it's an order,' Overbeck said. 'Lovely chatting with you.'

She exited, and the warmth returned to the hospital room.

'I told you she likes me,' Connie grinned.

'I think there's a lot you haven't explained to me yet.'

'Nothing important. I probably just didn't explain what happened very coherently in my final report.'

'You killed him,' Baarda said. 'With your belt? Overbeck was right. That can't have been easy.'

'Self-defence,' Connie said. 'Easier than you think when it was his life or mine. There was limited oxygen in the coffin, and I didn't know how soon I'd be found. I want that belt back when the case is over. You'd better remember to send it to me. I've had it a long time.'

'Stop kidding around.'

'Oh, I'm not, that belt was handmade in Italy.'

'Connie, what you went through . . .'

'Let's not,' Connie said. 'I survived. You survived. It could have been much worse.'

Baarda lay unmoving, silent, watching her. Connie broke eye contact first.

'I wish you weren't going back to America,' he said.

'Really?' she grinned. 'As a matter of fact, I've been offered another consulting job in London when I'm done in Washington. I suppose I could consider it.'

'Don't get cocky,' Baarda said.

'Too late for that.' She stood up. 'I've got a plane to catch, Detective Inspector Baarda.' She kissed him briefly, gently, on the lips. 'But I expect a call every day. Just be aware of the time difference. I hate being woken up.'

'Noted,' he said.

'When I get back, then,' Connie said from the doorway. She gave a half salute, half wave.

'Hey, any chance you could show me Martha's Vineyard one day? Sounds like somewhere that might be good for the soul.'

'It is,' she said. 'And I will. There's no one I'd rather share it with.'

Baarda smiled and closed his eyes. When he opened them again, Dr Constance Woolwine was gone.

Acknowledgements

This book came into existence through a series of extraordinary coincidences that I would never have dared to write. When we moved to America from England one of the most painful moments was saying goodbye to my gorgeous friend Andrea Gibson who has been my beta reader and staunchest supporter since I began writing. To make our transition to the USA easier, Andrea had a friend – Matthew Sparks – from University who was living 'somewhere in California'. It turned out, as these things do, and because statistically in a country of 320 million it was inevitable, that Andrea's old friend lived less than a mile from our new home. In fact, I'd unknowingly met Matt's dog in the road long before I ever met him. Matt's wife, Marie Lewis, turned out to be a lawyer so we had a lot in common straight away (also a love of movies, cheese, dogs and cocktails which helped). Marie had a contact who had a friend working as a profiler. Emails were sent, calls were made, and THAT is how I ended up with a conference call to the FBI's Office of Public Affairs with SSA Jeffrey Heinze and the lovely SSA Molly Amman, to whom I am extraordinarily grateful.

You can research to a good level for books like these, but

you really can't pick up the language, the processes and insider knowledge, without first-hand contact. I sent my idea for the book off, and Molly came back with a detailed appraisal of how she would approach the case. It was absolutely invaluable. So to all the people named above, thank you. Not just for this, but for all the love and laughs and support. You all know how invaluable you've been in this last year.

Of course, back in England, there was still a whole team of people guiding me. My first port of call for the idea for *The Shadow Man* was my amazing literary agent, Caroline Hardman. She picked up the pieces of it, polished them and made them look presentable (none of this without her), and passed it along to my publisher. The Avon imprint of HarperCollins is full of dedicated, passionate hard-working book obsessives. There are a lot of people to name and I won't apologise for that. Books, in spite of their small size, are giant feats of creation. Thank you to Phoebe Morgan who has never once rolled her eyes at me, even though she would have been entitled to a thousand times. To Helen Huthwaite, Sabah Khan, Oliver Malcolm, Bethany Wickington, Ellie Pilcher, Caroline Bovey, Claire Ward, Holly MacDonald, Hannah O'Brien – know that I think you're all amazing, and that I appreciate every last one of you.

To everyone at Hardman & Swainson Literary Agency who got me here and who, to my amazement most days, are still putting up with me. I'm so grateful.

To David, who has not yet asked me to go and get a proper job, and Gabriel, Solomon and Evangeline who know my 'writing face' and don't ask me for food when I'm wearing it – you know how this sentence ends.

And finally to the readers, reviewers, bloggers, booksellers and librarians – thank goodness for you. Without you, these pages would have no purpose and no destination.

If you enjoyed *The Shadow Man* then you'll love Helen Fields' DI Callanach series.

Book 1

Available now in paperback, ebook and audiobook.

Welcome to Edinburgh.
Murder capital of Europe.

Book 2

Available now in paperback, ebook and audiobook.

**The worst dangers are
the ones we can't see . . .**

Book 3

Available now in paperback, ebook and audiobook.

**When silence falls,
who will hear their cries?**

Book 4

Available now in paperback, ebook and audiobook.

**Your darkest moment
is your most vulnerable . . .**

Book 5

Available now in paperback, ebook and audiobook.

He had never heard himself scream before.
It was terrifying . . .

Book 6

Available now in paperback, ebook and audiobook.